I0590856

The RISEN QUEEN

The Dragon Sword Histories

BOOK TWO

DUNCAN LAY

HARPER

Voyager

Harper*Voyager*

An imprint of HarperCollins*Publishers*

First published in Australia in 2010
by HarperCollins*Publishers* Australia Pty Limited
ABN 36 009 913 517
harpercollins.com.au

HarperCollins*Publishers*

Level 13, 201 Elizabeth Street, Sydney NSW 2000, Australia
Unit D, 63 Apollo Drive, Rosedale, Auckland 0632, New Zealand
A 53, Sector 57, Noida, UP, India
1 London Bridge Street, London SE1 9GF, United Kingdom
2 Bloor Street East, 20th floor, Toronto, Ontario M4W 1A8, Canada
195 Broadway NY, NY 10007, United States of America

National Library of Australia Cataloguing-in-Publication data:

Lay, Duncan.
    The risen queen / Duncan Lay.
    1st ed.
    ISBN: 9780732287696 (pbk.)
    Lay, Duncan. Dragon sword histories ; bk. 2.
A823.4

Cover design by Darren Holt, HarperCollins Design Studio
Cover artwork by Les Petersen
Typeset in 10/12pt Sabon by Letter Spaced

An interview with legendary US fantasy author Raymond E. Feist inspired Duncan Lay to begin writing fantasy, using the time spent on the train commuting between his Central Coast home, where he lives with his wife and two children, and his work at *The Sunday Telegraph*.

This is his second novel.

Talk to Duncan Lay at:
duncanlay.blogspot.com

Praise for *The Wounded Guardian*
The Dragon Sword Histories: Book One

'This is realist fantasy,
led by a believable cast of characters'
Daily Telegraph

'Martil is an enthralling character ...
The Wounded Guardian rolls along beautifully'
Adelaide Advertiser

'A tale of treachery, with a gentle hearted barbarian, a Queen with a passion for revenge, dark lords worshipping evil gods, politics, power and a young girl who could change everything. What more could you want from a fantasy book!'
Infinitas

BOOKS BY
DUNCAN LAY

THE DRAGON SWORD HISTORIES

The Wounded Guardian (1)
The Risen Queen (2)

The Radiant Child

THE DRAGON SWORD HISTORIES: BOOK THREE

will be available mid-2010

To Julia, Fiona
and
Christina

Acknowledgements:

Thanks to everyone who has read and supported both this book and The Dragon Sword Histories series, from friends and family to the fabulous people at HarperCollins and the wonderful booksellers.

A special thanks to agents Siobhan Hannan and Sophie Hamley, to copy editor Kylie Mason and especially to Stephanie Smith.

Character List:

Aroaril: The Sun God, God of Light

Argurium: A dragon

Alban: Priest of Aroaril who works with Derthals

Aviland: Fought in Ralloran Wars, defeated by the Rallorans

Albiona: The continent

Barrett: The Queen's Magician of Norstalos

Bayes: Officer of Duke Gello, who fights at Gerrin

Berellia: Fought in Ralloran Wars, defeated by the Rallorans

Bellic: Berellian town and scene of infamous massacre

Berry: Northern town; ruled by Baron Berry

Beq: One of Gello's War Captains

Borin: Martil's childhood friend; killed in Ralloran Wars

Byrez: Berellian Earl and opponent of the Fearpriests

Cessor: Count of Norstalos; he obeys Duke Gello

Cezar: Champion to King Markuz

Chanlon: Former priest of Aroaril and enemy to Rallorans

Chelten: Duke Gello's former bodyguard

Conal: Ex-bandit and friend of Martil

Croft: King of Norstalos; Merren's father

Cropper: Archer officer

Darry: Norstaline innkeeper on the Tetran border

Declan: Archbishop of Norstalos

Derthals: Primitive men who live north of Norstalos, cruelly
   called goblins

Dunner: Ralloran sergeant, friend of Kesbury and Nerrin

Edil: Father of Karia

Ezok: Berellian ambassador to Norstalos

Fearpriest: A priest of Zorva

Feld: One of Gello's War Captains

Forde: Militia officer from Gerrin

Gamelon: Bishop of eastern Norstalos

Garie: Ralloran officer; killed at Bellic

Gello: Duke of Western Norstalos; cousin to Merren

Nerrin: Ralloran sergeant who is inspired by Martil to join Queen Merren

Norstalos: Biggest country on the continent of Albiona

Nott: Priest of Aroaril and Karia's grandfather

Oscarl: Ralloran captain; a Butcher of Bellic

Onzalez: A Fearpriest

Prent: Archbishop of Norstalos, appointed by Gello

Quiller: Priest of Aroaril at Sendric

Rocus: Guardsman of Sendric and officer to Merren

Romon: A Norstaline bard who joins rebellion

Rowran: Ralloran captain; a Butcher of Bellic

Ryder: Ranger sergeant to Captain Kay

Saltek: Berellian priest of Aroaril who serves Earl Byrez

Sendric: Northern city of Norstalos; ruled by Count Sendric

Sacrax: The Derthal High Chief

Sillat: Owner of the Golden Gate brothel

Rath: A Derthal chief

Snithe: Ralloran captain; a Butcher of Bellic

Tarik: Chief Hunter of Count Sendric and a leader of rebellion

Tam: A soldier of Duke Gello

Tenoch: The Fearpriest homeland

Tiera: Servant girl who works for Prent

Tomon: Martil's childhood friend, killed in war; later the name of Martil's horse

Tolbert: King of Rallora

Turen: Militiaman of Chell who serves Hutter

Warnock: Berellian bard

Ward: A soldier of Duke Gello

Wilsen: Guardsman of Sendric who joins rebellion

Wime: Militiaman of Sendric and a leader of rebellion

Worick: Earl of Norstalos, who serves Duke Gello

Yertlaan: Tenoch war leader

Yvonne: Daughter of Count Cessor

Zorva: The Dark God

TENOCH

DRAGONARA ISLAND

ALBIONA

Gerrin • • Sendric
• Berry
*Three
Passes*

Worick
NORSTALOS
RIVER WORICK

• Cessor
RIVER BRACK
• Norstalos
City
• Wells
• Thest
• Wollin
TETRIL
*Kerez
Marshes*
• Byrez
• Chell
• Eraskar
*Dividing
Range*

BERELLIA
AVILAND

• Bellic
RIVER MEADS

RALLORA

RIVER BOURNE

N
W E
S

CONTINENT
Of
ALBIONA

1

'Captain! Wake up!'

Martil's eyes snapped open and he rolled out of bed, his heart pounding.

'What is it?' he demanded, unable to suppress a shiver. He could hear — and smell — rain in the dawn.

Only the day before, he had led his regiment up to the River Meads, to spend the next month protecting the Ralloran border. He'd spent most of last night writing out patrol orders and had left instructions not to be woken at risk of, if not death, then certainly a week's latrine duty. So what had happened?

He looked at the officer who had woken him, Lieutenant Garie, and toyed with the idea he was about to announce King Tolbert had demanded his presence back in the capital for a parade.

But Garie's face was grim. 'Scouts are back. And there's smoke in the dawn, sir.'

Martil scrubbed his face with his hand and ducked out of the tent. The sun was trying to appear over the horizon despite the dark clouds overhead, dropping a cold, fine drizzle. It was light enough to see the unmistakable sign of smoke on the horizon to the east, where the sky was brightest.

'Report!' Martil barked.

A pair of scouts hurried over.

'Berellians came across the river in the night and hit a village. We think between one hundred and one hundred and fifty of them,' the first scout announced. 'We've got men tracking them back across the border.'

Martil closed his eyes momentarily. After the devastating war, people were naturally reluctant to return to villages close to the Berellian border. So King Tolbert had offered them land with no taxes attached for the first three years, as well as constant patrols to ensure the border was safe. Martil had only taken over this section of river the day before but that still made this attack his responsibility.

'They must have known about our patrol schedules,' he snarled.

'It's the only explanation,' Garie agreed. 'I thought Captain Oscarl said he hadn't seen hide nor hair of a Berellian in the past month?'

Martil grunted. Although he heartily disliked Oscarl, he did not take up the invitation to criticise a fellow war captain.

'How bad was it — did the villagers hold them off?' he asked instead.

The scout hesitated. 'Sir, you really need to look yourself. It's — it's worse than anything I've ever seen before.'

Martil felt the anger roar through him and made no effort to fight it. 'I want to see.' He turned back to Garie. 'I want messages to Captain Rowran, on our right flank, to Captain Snithe on our left and to Captains Oscarl and Macord behind us. Tell them what happened and get them here. Then take our cavalry company. I want to see where those

Berellians are running to, so I can hunt them personally.'

The border patrols consisted of three regiments patrolling the River Meads, and a further two waiting ten miles behind, in relative comfort, in case of trouble. Their orders were to destroy any Berellians who came across the river — and they could pursue survivors into Berellia. The Berellians knew that, so why had they tried this? Martil could not see the sense in it but, then again, he had never seen much sense in the Berellians.

Orders were bellowed into the dawn and riders went off in all directions. Martil, along with the two scouts and a squad of men, rode east, towards where the smoke stained the sky.

Even if the smoke had not drawn them, the birds they saw circling overhead would have. The crows and ravens had become fat and plentiful over the years of war — they were perhaps the only creatures who were sad there were no more battles racking these southern lands.

Martil ignored them, dreading what he would find. He, along with every Ralloran soldier, had seen enough evidence of Berellian brutality over the years. This village was in a safe location — barely ten miles from his camp, the same distance from the river. No wonder their watchmen had been taken by surprise. He felt the anger bubbling away within him. He could tell himself that it wasn't his fault but the truth was undeniable — they had been under his protection, and he had failed them. Lured here by the chance of avoiding Tolbert's hefty taxes for a few years and soothed by the King's promises of a safe life, Martil had let them down.

The rain, which had stopped now, had slowed the fires doing their work. Most of the village still stood, although many of the roofs were gone and just about everything smouldered, sending the dull smoke spotted by Martil's men up towards the sky. Every animal in sight — from pigs and chickens to dogs and cats — was dead. But there were no human bodies.

'Spread out! See if there's anybody left hiding!' Martil ordered.

With only the scouts following him, Martil rode straight to the centre of the village where the small wooden church, alone of all the buildings, was untouched by smoke or flame.

'We only had a quick look, sir, but I think they're all inside,' one of the scouts said. 'If you don't mind, sir, I'd rather not go back in there.'

Martil dismounted and looked up at a handful of sleek crows perched on the church roof, plucking up the courage to enter. Just like him. The scent of blood was thick here, overpowering even the smells of charred wood and damp, singed thatch. He waited until the rest of his men had joined him after completing their sweep through the village.

'Not a soul, sir,' his sergeant reported. 'Most homes had some sort of hiding place — cellars, hollow walls and the like. Every one of them was torn open.'

Martil steeled himself for what he was about to see and pushed open the church door.

'Nobody else has to come in,' he told them.

Most of the squad glanced over at the two scouts, who were already backing away, but none wanted to look bad in front of the others, so they lined up to follow Martil inside.

The small church windows offered little light, but it was still more than enough.

'Out! Out!' Martil snarled, his voice harsh and strangled by rage and horror.

His men needed no second invitation and stumbled outside, where several took the opportunity to go around the side of the church to be sick. One solid-looking corporal, whose face was familiar but whose name escaped Martil, seemed to be crying.

Martil glared up at his scouts through the tears in his own eyes. 'I want all four war captains here to see this, then alert the regiments. We are going to Berellia and we are not going to stop until the bastards who did this are all dead! Move!'

The scouts raced away and Martil sank to the ground. He understood why the scouts had not wanted to go back inside. The scene was burned in his mind forever. The men had been impaled and left to die in twitching agony. The women raped, and their hands cut off, then left to bleed to death, while the children ... Dear Aroaril, the children! The older ones had their hearts cut out. The only ones who had been spared that were the babies — they'd had their brains dashed out on the stone altar. Terror and agony had been etched on every face. But one in particular seemed to accuse him. Somehow a dying woman had managed to crawl across to where the children lay and had gathered her baby into her handless arms, its mutilated head a horrifying counterpoint to her body. Martil's mind told him the expression of hatred and despair and anguish on her face was aimed at the Berellian murderers but his heart was certain it was aimed at him. What that woman had gone through, what her effort to reach her child must have cost her in blood and pain,

Martil did not want to think about. He had seen many terrible things in the war but this surpassed them all.

It was a shaky council of war that convened a few turns of the hourglass later outside the church. The other four war captains had been inside only to hurry back out.

'Why?' Macord asked simply.

'Terror. They want to scare every Ralloran away from their border. It's a message. Says nobody is safe and, if you want to live, you better run now,' Martil spat. 'They want word of this to spread, so the villages will empty.'

'We will hunt them down!' Snithe declared. 'No matter where they try to hide!'

'That is the one thing that does not make sense. They know we will come after them,' Oscarl mused.

'They must have a safe hiding place planned,' Macord pointed out.

'Nowhere is safe for them. We won't rest until they are all punished for this,' Martil stated.

Grim nods followed his words.

'Riders coming in,' Rowran announced shakily.

The five captains turned to see a pair of scouts gallop into the village and pull up in a spray of dirt beside them.

One shouted down at Martil, not even getting out of his saddle. 'We know where they went, sir! They've made for Bellic!'

'So that's their plan — they think we won't be able to get into a walled city before King Markuz sends a rescue force,' Martil snarled.

'And they're right. We don't have any siege equipment,' Macord said reasonably. 'And then there's the political angle. It's one thing to chase a bunch of raiders but quite another to attack the biggest town in southern Berellia. The King won't like this …'

'The King won't like that we let a pack of murdering bastards get away! I say we march on Bellic and demand they surrender the company of raiders. And if Markuz has a relief force close by, we'll smash those bastards as well!'

'But the King …' Macord again tried to inject some reasonableness into the debate.

'I'll send a message to him. Meanwhile, my regiment marches on Bellic! Who's with me?' Martil glared around at the other four, who could do nothing but nod. 'I'll bury those poor people in there and see you at Bellic!'

It had seemed so straightforward back at the murdered village. Martil had felt sure that Bellic would surrender as soon as they saw the instant Ralloran response. But it had not quite worked that way. His regiment had the shortest distance to travel, so had arrived first at Bellic, even after burying the murdered villagers.

Bellic, like all Berellian towns, had an impressive wall. Martil doubted its garrison was any more than five hundred soldiers but it seemed as though the entire town was packed onto the ramparts and crowded into its towers, brandishing crossbows, spears and other weapons. And it was not just men — women and even children could be seen on the battlements, shrieking defiance at the camp the Rallorans had set up.

Martil watched the crowd carefully before summoning his officers.

'They've been told to make a brave display, to make us think that any attack on Bellic would be impossible. Most of them aren't soldiers, they're shopkeepers, apprentices and labourers. They've even got their women on the walls, for Aroaril's sake!'

'But, sir, I hear that the Berellian women are more fearsome than the men!' Garie added, to general amusement, before a look from Martil stopped the laughter.

'I want our archer company to keep them awake all night. Aim for the men but if a woman or two collects an arrow, I won't complain. I want them tired and I want them frightened. Then, just before the dawn, march most of the men around to the north wall, to make it appear as if we are going to try an escalade. When their attention is diverted, I will take one company in and fire the main gates. With their gates gone, and the other regiments here by the morning, they will surrender.'

Martil looked around at his officers. He could see many thought this was not a good idea, that attacking the gatehouse was risky. But they all trusted him too much to say anything.

Martil knew the sensible thing would be to wait until the other regiments caught up, and then hope a show of force would impress the town. But he was in no mood to do something sensible.

The morning brought the other regiments, who were greeted by Martil and his men. The newly arrived Rallorans stared at the tired, mud-encrusted men who stank of smoke — and at the gates of Bellic, which were now in ruin. The top half of each one was still recognisable though charred, but the bottom halfs were gone. Martil had lost a dozen men in the attack but Bellic was now at their mercy.

'Magnificent work!' Rowran applauded, to the general agreement of the other captains.

'Who wants to take their surrender?' Snithe asked.

'It should be Martil,' Macord said firmly.

'Rubbish, man! We should all go!' Oscarl growled as Martil yawned. He did not have the energy for an argument over who was going to get the glory.

'Then we all go. Let's make sure we get some good Berellian wine in the surrender bargain. I could use a drink,' Snithe said.

The Lord of Bellic was a tall, muscular man with a face dominated by a hooked nose above a thick black beard. He strode out, wearing a fine suit of chain mail covered in his personal surcoat featuring a black lion on a golden background, and met them willingly enough outside the gate under a flag of truce — but that was where his co-operation ended. He did not even deign to introduce himself after the five captains had announced their names. Compared to the richness of his clothes, they looked like vagabonds. Martil, who had not been able to clean all the mud out of his armour and who still smelled of lamp oil, tried to stay at the back.

'We are here for the raiders who struck a Ralloran village across the border. Surrender them or suffer the consequences,' Oscarl told the Lord pompously.

'This is an extreme act of provocation! Men and women have been killed! Berellia will not surrender its subjects in the face of armed force!' the Lord snarled. 'Besides, King Markuz himself, with the entire Berellian army, will be here by the end of the day. I advise you to run now, while you still can.'

Martil's temper flared. 'You lying bastard! You probably sent those raiders out and you have the balls to stand here and complain about people being killed? Now give us the murderers who destroyed that village or we'll come in and take them ourselves.'

'You would not dare! We will fight you to our last breath! The glorious bravery of the Berellians will defeat the cowardice of you Ralloran dogs!'

Martil pointed to where an arrow was stuck in the ground, about a foot away from the shadow of the gatehouse. 'You have until the shadow reaches that arrow. Then we will be back to collect the killers. Don't make us come in after them.'

The Berellian spat on the ground in response, and then stalked away.

'That went well. What do we do now?' Macord said dryly.

The debate raged until the forgotten arrow was easily in shadow.

Oscarl and Snithe wanted to storm in now; Rowran and Macord wanted to starve the town into surrender. Martil was worried about the losses they might take in street fighting and suggested they take the gates and the walls and then demand a surrender.

'We have to be careful. There are women and children in there,' Macord stated.

'That didn't seem to bother the Berellians back over the border!' Oscarl snarled.

'We can't leave Bellic intact. Or the Berellians will think they can strike at us, then run back to Bellic and laugh at our response. No Ralloran within a day's march of the border is safe while this town still stands!' Martil declared.

But Macord and Rowran still wanted to wait for King Tolbert's orders, which arrived just before noon.

All waited while the messenger, dressed in mud-spattered royal livery, handed over an embroidered package. Macord took it and removed a scroll, then broke the thick royal wax seal and unrolled it. All leaned forwards to hear what he was about to say.

'King Tolbert has ordered us to catch and kill the raiders and to let nothing stand in our way.' He shrugged. 'He says the border must be protected. Nothing else.'

They thought about that.

'So he's not made any decision, he's left it to us?' Snithe growled.

Again the debate raged. Order the town to walk away, and destroy the empty buildings with fire? Sack the town and drag the survivors back to Rallora? Starve them out?

'Look, why don't we just demand their final answer?' Macord said in a frustrated effort to break the deadlock.

So a junior officer — Lieutenant Garie was the closest — was found and sent forwards with a squad of men under a flag of truce to deliver the final warning. The captains argued on, their dispute only broken when a howl of rage and anger that seemed to come from all around the Ralloran camp sounded.

'What in Aroaril's name is going on?' Rowran cried and they hurried outside, to see dead and wounded men being dragged back into the camp. Four men carried the writhing Lieutenant Garie.

Martil raced to his officer's side. The lieutenant had taken a crossbow bolt in the side and another in the chest. Martil knew from bitter experience that these would be barbed, and almost impossible to pull out. 'What happened?'

'We called for their lord to speak, and they just loosed a full volley at us, sir,' one of his men said. 'We were lucky we weren't all killed.'

'Sir!' Garie opened his eyes and coughed up a spray of blood that told Martil he had an arrow in his lung. 'I'm sorry, sir.'

Behind him the other four captains were still arguing but Martil could not be bothered to listen.

'You have nothing to be sorry for. It is my fault,' Martil told Garie, as he gasped and died.

Martil gently closed Garie's eyes. Another fine man dead — murdered by the bastard Berellians. Dead, like his friends Tomon and Borin. Like his family. Like that village over the border. Well, he had had enough. His rage was swamping everything now. The townsfolk wanted to stand against them, did they? Were happy to shelter murderers and break a sacred flag of truce? That made them as guilty as if they had each taken a Ralloran baby and smashed its head open on the stone altar.

'Martil, what is your decision?' Macord asked.

Martil wiped Garie's blood off his face and stood. 'What do you say?'

'We are locked at two apiece — two for destroying the city, two for starving them until they give us every nobleman and raider inside the walls. You have the deciding vote. Whatever it is, we will all support it,' Rowran said, his voice trembling with anger.

Martil looked over his shoulder but could not see the town of Bellic. Wherever he looked, all he could see were dead friends and villagers. 'Destroy them. We shall make every Berellian tremble to hear the name Bellic,' he vowed.

* * *

'Martil! Have some wine!'

Captain Macord shoved a goblet of wine into Martil's hand and he took a mouthful without thinking. His mouth told him it was a fine wine, perhaps one of the best he had ever tasted. Another time, he would have savoured it. But all he could do was stare out the window, at the carnage in the street outside. Bodies of Berellian men, women and children lay in heaps, with handfuls of Rallorans scattered among them.

Images flashed through his brain. A raging woman had flung herself at him, slashing at his face with a bloodied knife. One of his men was screaming nearby, because that long knife had cut out his eyes a moment before. Instinct had taken over and he'd cut her down. A cry of fury behind him had made him turn, his sword thrusting out — to impale a boy no more than twelve, her son, who had run forwards holding a rusty spear and now had Martil's sword deep in his lungs. His last act was to spit at Martil.

'How did this happen?' Martil asked softly.

Macord drained his goblet and poured himself another. Martil realised numbly that the other war captain was crying silently.

'Best not to think about it,' Macord advised.

But Martil could not help but think about it. The gate had fallen easily — with five companies of archers covering the gatehouse, the assault team had been able to throw down the barricade and open the way for the rest of the men to follow. But once inside the town, things had become confused. The Berellians had turned every house into a small fortress and every person in the city was armed. There had been no children under the age of ten — which seemed to indicate that the only ones who had stayed had been the ones who wanted to fight — but even the youngest children carried knives. Seeing friends stabbed in the back by those they sought to save was the final straw. Already angry because of what had happened to the Ralloran village and under the Ralloran flag of truce, the men lost control. They began treating anyone with a weapon as an enemy. Martil had felt it also. It became not a battle to take a town but to eradicate a pit of evil. By the time the Berellians wanted to give up, it was too late — the Rallorans were so filled with anger and hate that they would not accept surrender.

And now the town was dead.

'Is there anyone left alive? Did we even capture the bastard that started it all, the Lord of Bellic? Surely he wouldn't have fought to the death …' Martil trailed off as he realised, at the end, there had not been a choice in the matter.

'I don't think so,' Macord said softly. 'Here, have another drink.' Macord pushed the goblet into Martil's hand. 'We're going to need it.'

'Captain! Wake up!'

Martil's eyes snapped open and he rolled out of bed, his heart pounding.

'What is it?' he demanded, unable to suppress a shiver. He could hear — and smell — the rain in the dawn.

'You'd better come and see this, sir.' Lieutenant Nerrin's voice was grim.

Martil scrubbed his face with his hands. He had been dreaming — about Bellic again. It was a different sort of dream, although no less disturbing for that.

He knew he shouldn't have left Karia behind in Sendric. She had protested bitterly, bursting into tears and pleading not to be left. He had been tempted to give in, let her come along with him, although back in the caves, he had left her behind often enough while he was ambushing Havrick's forces. Now, he felt guilty, particularly when he remembered that small face peering over the battlement as he rode away. But it was only supposed to be for a couple of days. Just march his regiment of Rallorans to free the other two towns in the north: Gerrin and Berry. After Sendric, it was thought to be an easy enough task. The people would be frightened of the small garrisons Gello had imposed on them — and these garrisons would be terrified of the Rallorans. A quick march, demand their surrender, strip them of weapons and armour and then send them back to Gello. Then they could work on recruiting more men for the Norstaline part of the army.

It sounded so straightforward back in Sendric's keep, so logical. Only he was missing Karia badly — and dreaming about Bellic again.

To make things worse, it appeared something else had gone wrong. They had marched to Gerrin, arriving in the dead of night and setting up camp. Martil did not want to demand a surrender in the night; he wanted to impress the town and scare Gello's garrison with the size of his force. He had left Lieutenant Nerrin on guard duty while he tried to sleep.

'What is it?'

'You just have to see, sir,' Nerrin said grimly.

He dressed hurriedly then followed Nerrin until he could see the small town for himself. Gerrin was less than half the size of Sendric but, because it had been built in the north, back in the times when the so-called goblins had raided the area, it had an efficient wall and a strong gatehouse. In the first light of dawn it should have looked pretty.

Instead, it looked like a scene from his nightmare.

The battlements were packed. Men in the red of Gello, as well as men in ordinary clothes — and women also — all waving the closest thing to a weapon they had. Torches burned brightly along the embrasures as they yelled their defiance at the mystified Rallorans watching them.

'Aroaril's beard! It's like we're back at Bellic!' Martil breathed.

'That's what I thought you'd say,' Nerrin agreed miserably. 'Do you know what's going on, sir?'

Martil stared at the walls. This was so different from Sendric. There, they had been welcomed by the townsfolk, who had been terrified of Gello's men. Why were these townsfolk standing shoulder to shoulder with Gello's thugs, screaming at his Rallorans?

'What are your orders, sir?' Nerrin asked nervously. 'Do we assault?'

Martil glanced at the tough, solid soldier, hearing the worry in his voice. He glanced over his shoulder and saw many of his Rallorans were listening as well, something close to fear showing on their faces. He raised his voice for their benefit.

'We wait until full light, Lieutenant. There will be no assault. We will talk to them under a flag of truce.'

He could feel the ripple of relief go through the men. Looking again at the town, he said, 'I'm sure this will all make sense later.'

But while the rain stopped and the sun offered the promise of a warm day, things did not become any clearer to Martil when he marched forwards with a squad of men under the Queen's new banner, with the white flag of truce beside it. Since Bellic, he would not let anyone but himself go forwards under a white flag, instead ordering Nerrin to take command if anything happened to him. He did have Sergeant Kesbury with him, and the bulk of the powerful soldier was reassuring. He was conscious of the Dragon Sword at his side — and felt the familiar dread that it was doing nothing to help him win over these Norstalines.

He stopped his men half a bowshot short of the gate and waited. He did not call out, instead used the time to look up at the defenders on the wall. The men in red surcoats were clustered heavily at the gate but there were plenty of men and women in ordinary clothes beside them. They all seemed to be staring at Martil with a mixture of fear and hatred. He tried not to wonder why, just looked at the gates and waited for someone to come out.

Baron Gerrin, the eleventh of that title, had left behind his old name of Rhoden Salte but had been unable to shake the nervous habit of biting his nails. He chewed anxiously on his thumbnail as he peered out at the group of waiting Rallorans. He turned to his companion, a man dressed in Gello's red surcoat, with the crest of a first lieutenant on his shoulder.

'Do we go to them?' he asked. 'Won't they just cut us down?'

Lieutenant Bayes sighed. He was already worried about being the first man to test out Duke Gello's new strategy and this annoying fool with his disgusting habit was not helping. But he needed Baron Gerrin to pull this off, so he pasted a reassuring smile onto his face.

'We have to go to them. It is a flag of truce. They will respect it, no matter what that bard said. Remember, you need to start talking and provoke one or more of the Rallorans into threatening you — then the town council and that militia lieutenant will have no choice but to believe what the bard said was true.'

'But what if the town doesn't stand with us? After all, your presence here in Gerrin has not always been a happy one …'

Bayes ground his teeth together. 'I know that!' He took a deep breath. 'But the people are truly frightened of the Rallorans now. The bard did his work well. Otherwise we couldn't have got them on the walls last night. Now, we need to talk to the others, then go out there. They won't wait for much longer.'

He almost shoved, rather than showed, Baron Gerrin out of the office and into the next room, where half the town council were seated around a table. These were mostly rich, elderly merchants, picked for the position by Gerrin. With them was the local militia commander, a Lieutenant Forde, who had clashed repeatedly with Bayes over the behaviour of the soldiers in town. Nonetheless, he was the man the town respected — certainly more than the ineffectual Baron — and so the key to the plan.

'My friends, the Rallorans want to talk to us. We must go out there, convince them that honest Norstalines will not bow down before these brutal barbarians and that courage will keep our families safe …' Gerrin began nervously.

'Have no fear on that score, Baron,' Forde said immediately. 'We'll defend these walls to the last drop of our blood. There'll be no Bellic here.

Everyone knows what will happen if those Rallorans get inside these walls. We won't let them. Those Rallorans might be brave enough fighting women and children but we'll show them the true Norstaline spirit!'

His words were echoed by cheers and several of the councillors thumped the table in agreement.

Gerrin and Bayes exchanged smiles of relief.

'Then let us go out there and tell them that!' Bayes declared, and the group jumped to their feet.

Martil's patience was running dangerously low when, with a creak, the gates were hauled open and a strange party walked out to meet him. From his robes, the leader was obviously the local lord. With him was an officer in Gello's red, what looked like a militia officer and several elderly merchants, who were probably part of the town council.

The noble stopped several paces from Martil. 'You have no business here!' he called out, his voice thin and reedy.

'Baron Gerrin, I presume?' Martil asked, and when the man nodded hesitantly, Martil offered him a smile. He unrolled the scroll Merren had given him and began the speech she had insisted on writing for him — it sounded suspiciously like something from a saga to him but he had accepted it rather than start an argument where Barrett was sure to take her side. The closed gates and the men and women on the walls indicated their presence here was hardly welcome but he had to press ahead, regardless.

'People of Gerrin, you have nothing to fear. I am Captain Martil, the Queen's Champion and her envoy. She has claimed back her throne and wishes it known that she will be creating a new Norstalos, where all can live free and equal, without fear of war. We come to deliver you from the brutal oppressors of Duke Gello, the usurper, who has committed bloody crimes upon the innocent people of Norstalos. We are here to help you remove Gello's vicious forces from your town, and to bring peace back to these troubled lands.'

Martil finished reading and took a moment to compose himself before rolling up the scroll and seeing their reaction. He knew the speech had missed out a few things. Things that were better left unsaid if the town was to come onto their side.

First, these towns would make ideal supply bases for Gello, should he attack the north, so they had to be under the Queen's control. Second, by bringing them under the Queen's power, they were placing these people in danger from Gello and, finally, they needed as many of the townsfolk as possible to volunteer to fight, and possibly die. These were all good reasons for the town to be distrustful of them and he hoped they would not mention them.

Given what happened next, he would have preferred it if they had. Baron Gerrin, after a prod from the officer behind him, cleared his throat.

'Pretty words, but the Queen should know it is actions that speak louder! She sends a message of peace but who does she send to deliver it? A thousand murdering Rallorans, the Butchers of Bellic, led by the man who personally slew a hundred children that day! You want us to surrender to such as you? No sooner would you be inside the gates than you would be raping and pillaging again! It is all your kind knows, and all you live for!' he tried to roar, although it began more like a shriek.

Martil sensed, rather than saw, Kesbury start

forwards, but he simply raised his hand and the sergeant stopped in his tracks. He was having enough trouble holding in his own anger.

'I understand. Gello has obviously bought you off. Then I appeal to the militia, and to the town council with you. We are not here to fight. We are here to protect you from Gello. We saved the town of Sendric from Gello's men, who tried to sack it! I fought alongside men such as you to protect women and children from murderers who wore the red crest of Gello!'

But his appeal seemed to fall on deaf ears.

Gerrin, looking more confident, took a step forwards. 'We know the truth of the matter. The Queen wants her throne back, and she does not care how many have to die to put her there. Do you deny you are all Butchers of Bellic?'

'We are servants of the Queen and we are not here to harm you!' Martil had to grit his teeth to stop himself from exploding.

'Then why does she send men who have slain children? What is she paying you for this? Is your reward to be let loose on another innocent town?' Gerrin called, seeking to include everyone on the walls in the conversation.

Martil unclenched his fist only with a great effort. Behind him, he could feel Kesbury and his other men also struggling to control their rage, but any reaction would only prove these lies.

'You obviously do not know the real story of Bellic. Why do you believe that we are here to harm you …' Martil began carefully, only for the Baron to interrupt.

'You lie! On both accounts! A bard arrived here only days ago, telling us of what happened at

Sendric! How you and the Queen attacked the town, and killed hundreds of Norstaline soldiers who were trying to protect it! How scores of the townsfolk died as well, the rest made to work for you! He told us how the Queen has hired every Ralloran in the country to fight for her — and how every single one of you was kicked out of your own country because of what you did in Bellic. And he sang us the Real Saga of Bellic, the one Rallorans do not allow to be performed!'

'Lies!' Kesbury bellowed. 'That's a lie!'

'Keep that tame goblin of yours away from us …' cried Gerrin, and Martil had to grab Kesbury, hold him back from jumping at the nobleman.

'This is not helping us, Sergeant!' Martil hissed but he was barely in control himself. He turned back to the group with an effort of will. 'The Real Saga of Bellic?' he asked. Was there really such a thing? The one he had heard was hardly flattering to the Rallorans, telling how they slew an entire town in revenge for a dead village and a broken flag of truce. Could there be something worse than that?

'Aye! How the Rallorans themselves killed a village full of their own people, giving them an excuse to attack Bellic, and how they broke into the town under a flag of truce!'

Images of the tortured villagers swam into Martil's vision and he tasted bile in his mouth. Before he knew it, the Sword was in his hand and Gerrin was cowering away from him. The militiaman drew his own sword and stepped in front of the nobleman.

'Flag of truce, Ralloran!' he snarled, his broad face twisted in anger.

Martil came to his senses only with the greatest of

efforts and it took him two attempts to sheath the Sword. He pointed a shaking finger at Gerrin.

'You lie. The Berellians murdered a village, and the flag of truce was broken by the Berellians, not me. That is the truth,' he said thickly.

'And you expect us to believe that? What next, would you have us think that every bard in the land is in the pay of Duke Gello?' Baron Gerrin sneered.

Martil ignored him and looked instead at the militiaman, who had not sheathed his blade.

'And you all believe this, that we are here to trick our way inside this town and slaughter all who live here? That is why you fill the battlements with ordinary people, standing side by side with Gello's bastards?'

'Do you deny you are all Butchers of Bellic? Do you deny you drew a sword under a flag of truce? How can we trust such as you?' the militiaman asked harshly.

Martil looked at him and could not summon the words to convince him. They would never believe him. He clutched at the hilt of the Dragon Sword but it was cold and offered no comfort. He would give them a parting shot, then leave. He could do no more good. Besides, he had to get out of here — he felt sick.

'I speak the truth. You have been lied to, by Gello and his bards. I shall prove that I mean no harm. My men and I will march away this very day. The Queen herself, along with Count Sendric and her loyal Norstaline division, will come here instead, to prove that what the bard told you about the battle of Sendric was just one more lie!'

He grabbed Kesbury, turning the soldier around, and missing the look of fear that Bayes and Gerrin exchanged. Instead, he marched his men away, trying to ignore the insults that showered down from the walls; 'baby-killer' and 'murderer' were among the kinder ones.

'Sir, I'm sorry, sir, I don't know what came over me,' Kesbury said, and Martil was horrified to see tears running down the big man's face. He remembered then — Kesbury had been a corporal in the squad he had taken to the village. He had been moved to tears then, as well.

'You did better than I did, Sergeant,' Martil said. 'I was ready to turn the Dragon Sword on them when they claimed we killed the villagers …'

'What do we do now, sir?' Kesbury asked.

'What we told them. We are going to march away.'

Nerrin and the other officers, as well as the men, were surprised to receive orders to break camp and return to Sendric. They were horrified and furious when they found out why.

'This is an emergency, Lieutenant,' Martil told Nerrin. 'We have to get back to the Queen and warn her what Gello is doing. How many Norstalines are going to believe us after hearing those lies, when they're so obsessed with the bloody sagas? The Queen is the only one who can save this situation. Hopefully us marching away, keeping our word, will help her.'

'And if there's more of these bards spreading the tale of the Real Saga of Bellic? What then?'

'Just pray that there's not,' Martil said grimly.

He made it into his tent and closed his eyes for a moment. Where was Karia when he needed her? He searched desperately for happy memories of her, something to block out the looming darkness that threatened to overwhelm him; sought to find again the feeling he had when with her. Losing his family, his friends, his home and being surrounded only by death and pain for so many years had forced him to harden his heart, or go crazy. But then that little girl had worked her way inside. She had become the family that he had lost, the friends he had seen die, but, best of all, she could make him forget everything except what they did together. He smiled as he recalled sitting with her, reading one of those ridiculous sagas. She had been helping him out, making up silly voices. He had actually become lost in the story, lost in the moment. The peace he had felt then, the warmth between them — it had almost struck him like a blow. After years of being empty inside, to be given that ... It was something beyond price. But the strange thing was, feeling so good with her made him feel worse now, without her. He had to see her. And soon. Or he felt the darkness would overwhelm him.

2

Ezok nodded politely to the half-a-dozen nobles he knew and controlled the urge to smile triumphantly as he walked past them. It had only been a few weeks since he'd had his first private meeting with King Gello, yet his influence was such that he could call on Gello on a morning set down for the Royal Council. The Norstaline nobles, who had risked a treason charge to put Gello on the throne, were made to wait outside as Ezok, an ambassador from a traditional enemy, was ushered into the council chamber. It was heady stuff.

'My dear Ambassador — your bards are excellent! The effect they are having is extraordinary!' Gello's face was alight with triumph as Ezok entered.

'And this is but the start of Berellia's help, sire.' Ezok bowed deeply.

Ezok allowed himself to be shown to a comfortable chair next to Gello's own, and accepted a goblet of wine.

'And your own bards, they are performing the saga as we supplied it, sire?' Ezok asked.

Gello chuckled. 'Oh yes. Some of them are even doing it willingly!'

'Then I think it is time to move to our second

stage, sire. We have a special guest to accompany some of our bards — we'll be calling him the Lord of Bellic.' Ezok winked.

Gello laughed openly. This plan was working out better than he had dared hope. His people's love of sagas and blind trust in bards meant that instead of rebelling against him, they were actually now frightened of his cousin and her mongrel Rallorans! The unrest in the towns had dried up — people were starting to cheer him in the streets! He was even using the saga on the new regiments he had created, to ensure their loyalty.

'My dear Ambassador, why don't you stay for the council meeting? It would be my pleasure to have you as my guest.'

Ezok inclined his head until he could control his smile.

'Thank you, sire.'

Romon looked in disgust at the scroll that was handed to him.

'And we have to say this, exactly this, every time?' he sniffed, holding the scroll up by the corner, as if it had been dipped in something foul.

'You will if you want to keep your tongue in your head, and not nailed to a wall somewhere,' the head Berellian bard snapped. 'This is the only saga you perform, no requests for anything else. And you all know the news you have to deliver.'

'But we're bards, for Aroaril's sake! We're supposed to be trusted! If we go around telling these, these ... ridiculous falsehoods, how will our profession be viewed?'

'If we tear out your eyes, how will you be viewed?' the Berellian growled. 'You'll each get a pair of guards to accompany you. Any attempt to perform another saga will result in your arrest — and later punishment. Is that understood?'

Romon had no choice but to nod and attempt a smile.

'Good! Now, you'll each be assigned an area to cover, but we want to keep you moving, so the peasants hear this from several of you. Move to the front and we'll give you a list of towns, and the order in which to visit them.'

Romon found himself in a queue behind Healey, an old friend.

'Can you believe what we're being made to do? First Gello demands we perform his news, then this! It is wrong, my friend!'

'We both know it is, but what choice do we have?' Healey whispered back.

'But what are we doing to the honour of our profession? And what will it do to our country?'

'I'm more concerned about what *not* doing it will mean for my health,' Healey grunted.

Merren looked out over the countryside near Sendric and sighed. Declaring you were going to be a ruler who cared about your people was all very well, but it carried with it an extraordinary amount of work. She was enjoying meeting the people and loved the way they were responding to her, but at the same time it was exhausting.

And her situation was not being helped by Karia. Already upset that she had been left behind by Martil, she'd turned to Merren. That had been fine back at the caves, because Merren had had little to do. But here, with a hundred people wanting her, it was proving impossible to give Karia the time she demanded. And now the little girl was starting to use magic to get attention — a trait that concerned both Merren and Barrett. Twice now Merren had had to call in Barrett because her door had become magically sealed. And several times in the middle of important meetings, one of Karia's dolls had climbed onto the table and 'walked' towards her — the first time, the sight of a seemingly Zorva-possessed toy had almost created a panic.

Karia was confined to her room but that was obviously not a long-term answer. Barrett had suggested a possible solution: reward her for good behaviour. He'd told Karia she could have a ride in the countryside and a picnic, as long as she stopped misbehaving. Merren suspected an ulterior motive for the picnic but in a moment of weakness, no doubt brought on by fatigue, she'd agreed to his plan.

At first the picnic had been almost relaxing, but now she could see her original suspicion was correct.

The picnic had been fine while Karia was with them, but then Barrett persuaded her to walk down to a nearby stream and find some wildlife to bring back to show them. Karia was delighted with the idea but Merren less so — Barrett now had an excuse to try and charm her. Ever since the battle of Sendric he had been clumsily trying to woo her; it was becoming a real concern. Not least because she couldn't afford to offend him — she needed the unique skills that only he could bring to the rebellion. Barrett had obviously seen Martil's absence as an ideal opportunity. It was getting to the point where she would have to say something to him. But what?

'Merren, would you care for a glass of wine?' Barrett asked, producing a bottle with a flourish.

'I took the liberty of borrowing a fine vintage from Sendric's castle stocks.'

'Certainly.' Merren forced a smile. Some alcohol would be very welcome.

'I must say, while they are a vital part of our rebellion, it is nice not to have those Rallorans around.' Barrett smiled as he handed her a glass of the white wine.

Merren took a large mouthful of the wine and nodded. She knew perfectly well Barrett was really referring to Martil — but he also had a point. They needed the Rallorans even though they brought with them plenty of problems. Every one was a troubled man.

'Merren?'

She finished her wine and held out her glass for a refill, then saw Barrett was holding out a bouquet of flowers, obviously grown in an instant.

'White roses — your old favourite, and I perfumed them with your favourite fragrance.'

Merren took them with a fixed smile.

'It's nice here, isn't it?' Barrett said softly.

Merren made a non-committal noise.

'I thought tonight … once you've put Karia to bed … I might cook you a special supper? I think you've been working too hard lately and I would like the chance to spoil you a little …'

'I am the Queen. I am supposed to be working hard!' Merren said, a little more sharply than she intended, and groaned mentally as she saw his face crumple. 'Barrett, I appreciate the offer but I just do not have time …'

Barrett snorted. 'Well, you made time to have a private supper with Martil the night before he left!'

He knew he should not talk to her like that but the

situation was just eating him up inside. She was all that he dreamed of, her face was always on his mind. And after they had both come so close to death in the battle for Sendric, he could not keep his feelings inside any more.

Merren controlled her temper with difficulty. 'That was a farewell supper for Karia, who requested we both be there!'

The anger and jealousy that gripped Barrett's heart vanished as he heard the fury in her voice. Attacking her was not going to work! He had to change tactics.

'My Queen, I am sorry. Forgive me. It's just that you mean so much to me ...'

Merren recognised the danger. Swiftly she leaned in and patted him on the hand. 'You mean a great deal to me, and the rebellion. I do not know what I would do without you and your wise counsel. Now let us call Karia back and we shall finish this picnic together.'

Barrett looked as though he would rather try to articulate his love for her but, Merren was relieved to see, Karia had taken it upon herself to wander back, carrying a bird.

'I've made a new friend,' Karia announced, stroking the crow's glossy head.

She could see that Merren and Barrett were not happy and wondered why. Still, she felt unhappy too. Merren and Barrett seemed to always be finding excuses to send her away. All her life she had been pushed to one side, put in the corner. Father Nott, for all his concern and kindness, had many demands on his time. Her father, Edil, had only cared that she did her chores and kept quiet. Only Martil showed he cared. Only he gave her his time without reservation. Like a flower starved of light and water, she drank in his attention, basked in it, grew on it. To feel wanted, to feel safe, and to feel needed — this was what she had longed for all her life. People always left her. Was it her fault, was there something about her that was strange? But Martil, having his love, it made her feel special, feel safe. She knew she hadn't been behaving too well around Merren and Barrett but having them ignore her was a shock. Suddenly they were like everyone else. It just made her want Martil back more. Only they had sent him away! It was so unfair!

'That's a nice bird you've got there,' Merren said brightly. 'What has he told you?'

Karia smiled. This was more like it! 'Great news! Martil's on his way back here!'

Merren glanced at Barrett, who looked shocked — and probably not just because his plans for getting her alone were ruined. Martil was not supposed to be back for several days.

'Trouble,' she said grimly, not knowing whether to feel anxious or relieved.

Ezok closed the door of his study and prepared to make his report to Brother Onzalez. The idea of filling a shallow bowl with blood and then using the Fearpriest's own magic to summon his image across great distances was a disturbing one, especially to a man who had been taught that everything had to be put into writing. Even now his quill hand itched to write a detailed report. But Onzalez would not wait for coded reports to be smuggled into Berellia.

Ezok summoned Onzalez and tried not to look too deeply into where the Fearpriest's face should be.

'What news?' Onzalez hissed.

'It is all going to plan. These Norstalnes love the new saga. And Gello is delighted with me. The fool even let me sit in on one of his council meetings!'

'But?'

'There is a danger. He is creating a huge army. With our help, the people are becoming loyal to him. He may get to the point where he feels he can turn on us.'

Onzalez considered this for a moment. 'I have sent for help from my homeland. But try to encourage him to move before he is ready. As we know, Rallorans do not die easily. It would be ideal for us if he were to suffer some setbacks. See what you can arrange.'

'As you wish,' Ezok said.

'And see what you can do to get close to the new Archbishop. From what you have said, he may be a valuable ally to us — and could help us turn Gello to Zorva.'

As principal servant to Count Sendric, Gratt had been a respected man in the town. Respected among the servant classes, that is. The richer merchants and business owners regarded him as little more than chattel. Many was the time he had stood in the Count's audience chamber and been regarded as nothing more than a piece of furniture. So now, as he stood in that same audience chamber as the head of the newly elected town council, it was a strange sensation. It was not a warm room, nor an inviting room, but it had a certain presence. He knew it so well, although his place had always been either behind the Count's chair, or at the wall. Sitting at the table, with not just the Count but the Queen — it was a completely different feeling. Helping free the town, helping fight to protect it, nobody could have dreamed a servant would be head of the town council before. He walked around the audience chamber, looking anew at the tapestries on the wall, seeing again the beautifully carved chairs around the huge wooden table.

'Taking the job seriously, my friend?' Conal called, as Gratt ran his hand over the table.

'Just thinking how different it will be, sitting around this table, not waiting on it,' Gratt admitted.

'Well, we may be scum, but I can give you a tip about the other people who used to be here,' Conal said conspiratorially. 'They were just like you and me — except the people want us to be here.'

Gratt smiled. 'I thought you were going to say that old line about how they fart like the rest of us.'

Conal shook his head with a grin. 'No one can fart like me!'

Martil left his men settling back into their camp outside Sendric and brought Nerrin and Kesbury with him into the town. The townspeople were pointing and talking, and he knew they would be wondering what was going on — the Rallorans were not supposed to be back yet. And, when they did return, it was supposed to be with a horde of new recruits. The three Rallorans rode swiftly to the keep, where the Queen would be waiting. He needed to speak to her but, more than this, he needed to see Karia.

On the one night they had camped during the ride back from Gerrin, he had been tortured by dreams again. Previously his dreams of Bellic had taken the form of him wandering streets packed with corpses of townsfolk, their dead faces accusing him. But these new dreams, these were even more disturbing.

The woman and her son he had killed in Bellic, they were there. They stalked him through the streets of the slain, the knife and the spear dripping blood and thirsting for his flesh. Whatever he did, wherever he turned, they were there. He reached the gates of Bellic, tried to break out, but they were impervious to his efforts. He was trapped. He turned to see the woman and boy stalking him, laughing and jeering. He was about to launch one final, desperate attack when something grabbed him around the legs. Glancing down, he looked into the bitter face of the murdered woman from the Ralloran village. The stumps of her arms wept blood as she grabbed him around the leg, her murdered baby lying beside her.

'Your fault. All your fault!' she hissed.

Martil opened his mouth to scream his innocence — only to see the spear and the knife reaching for him. He was tensing himself for the pain of the blows and opening his mouth to cry for — mercy? forgiveness? — when he'd woken.

He sat up, sweating, his heart racing, and almost called for wine, then remembered he had ordered no alcohol be brought — it was causing many of his men problems. He had tried to go back to sleep but was too afraid. The only thing that calmed him was thinking of Karia. She had made the dreams stop once before. She could do so again. With her he could just be himself, not have to worry about being a war captain or a Butcher of Bellic. That all vanished around her. It was a gift beyond price and it was why he wanted to be around her.

So when he clattered into the Count's old audience chamber he gave Merren but the briefest of bows before hurrying over to Karia and hauling her up in his arms, hugging her close.

Karia was delighted to be hugged. She felt safe again. No longer was she the small, annoying child that was being told to be quiet, go to her room, and leave the adults alone. She was the most important person in that room. She hugged him back fiercely.

But the others were not so enthusiastic about Martil's priorities.

Barrett gave a loud snort of disgust and, just in case anyone had missed that, sighed, rolled his eyes and ostentatiously poured himself a goblet of water. 'Anyone?' he offered. 'It seems the news our captain returns with is not so momentous after all!'

Merren ignored Barrett but did try to attract Martil's attention, first with a cough, then finally by calling his name. She had hurriedly summoned the town council, as well as Rocus, Wime, Tarik, Count Sendric, Conal and the town's senior priest, Father Quiller. Quiller had actually been voted on to the new town council by the people but had declined, saying the church should not be involved in politics. Merren had taken to inviting Quiller to every meeting anyway, for the benefit of his advice.

Now she had assembled this council for Martil's arrival — only to have him just want to cuddle Karia.

'Captain Martil!' she barked, her concern coming out as anger. 'What is the meaning of this? Why have you returned so early and without the men of Gerrin and Berry? What has happened?'

Martil was reluctant to put down Karia so he made sure he sat her on his lap, when he took his seat. Barrett had sat himself next to Karia, and had to move his chair across and back to accommodate the large warrior.

Naturally, he did this with as much scraping of chair legs, huffing, sniffing and sighing as he could get away with, to leave everyone in no doubt that Martil was creating all sorts of problems for him. Well, he was not going to be fooled by the man's play for sympathy. *He's just trying to impress Merren*, he thought bitterly.

'Merren, we have a real problem. When we arrived at Gerrin, it was to find the entire town on the walls, ready to fight against us,' Martil said, ignoring Barrett's theatrics.

The entire council exploded with shock, fear, anger, concern and surprise at that sentence and Merren was forced to thump her fist on the table to quieten them down again.

'Do you want to explain?' she said finally.

Martil cleared his throat. 'I'd like a goblet of that water you were offering, Barrett,' he said huskily.

Barrett just stared at him. Did the muscle-bound oaf really think he, Barrett, was going to pour water for him like a servant? Let him get his own water!

'Barrett, if you would please hurry — we need to hear this news,' Merren said impatiently.

Barrett could not believe his ears. If anyone else had asked that, he would have howled at the injustice of it. But as it was Merren, he forced a smile onto his face and poured out a goblet of water for Martil, keeping the glitter of anger off his face as he presented it to him.

Martil nodded his thanks, swallowed half the water in one gulp and then turned to Merren.

'Merren, Gello has sent a bard north to tell everyone that you have hired a thousand murdering barbarians, the Butchers of Bellic, to steal back your throne. They've got the towns so scared of us, the people have actually joined forces with Gello's thugs to oppose us.'

Martil could see his news went through Merren like a knife. Even Barrett forgot his anger as the import of Martil's words sank in.

'Are you sure? Perhaps it was some sort of trick ...' he began.

'It was no trick. We could see the walls were crowded with men and women, waving every sort of weapon they had to hand, screaming hatred at us. That was not faked. People being forced to do something cannot summon that much fear and anger. And then we talked to some of the town council, as well as the militia commander ...'

'Lieutenant Forde. He's a good man, your majesty,' Wime interjected. 'He served with us here for a few years before getting his promotion to Gerrin.'

'What did this good man say?' Merren demanded.

Martil closed his eyes for a moment.

'He said we killed the village! He said we murdered our own people to give us the excuse to go and do the same to Bellic!' Kesbury cried, and everyone turned to him.

Abashed, the big Ralloran sketched a quick bow in Merren's direction. 'Your majesty, I'm sorry, but he said we did that! How could they believe that we would do those things ...' Kesbury's voice trailed off and Martil instinctively tightened his arm around Karia.

'He told us that the bard said we had destroyed Sendric, and that we had crushed an army of Gello's men that had tried to save the town,' Martil said thickly.

Those around the table erupted in disgust and anger; many of them bore scars from the brutal battle fought in the streets outside. It took Merren a moment to calm them down.

'We told him that we would go, to show we meant no harm, and that you would return to prove to him that Sendric was not destroyed. He did not believe us. He said we were Butchers of Bellic and could not be trusted.' Martil cuddled Karia, much as a drowning man would clutch at a rope thrown to him.

Merren gasped, horrified. 'Is that right? That they believe you have been brought here by me to terrify my own country into submission, that I would do that to win back my throne?' She felt sick. Part of her recognised that the Rallorans were devastated to be tarnished with the shame of Bellic once again. This had been their redemption, their chance to begin again — and now their nightmare was being repeated. But a greater part of her was thinking of what was being said about her in towns and villages across the land. That she was so power-hungry she was hiring murdering barbarians to seize back her throne. To think that her own people believed she was capable of such a thing … It was a blow. She had grown used to the adulation here at Sendric. The people loved her. She had begun to dream about the time this would be repeated up and down the country. Now to discover they were terrified of her and thought her some monster, a fiend at the head of a blood-soaked army of occupation: that hurt deeply.

'For centuries, the role of the bard has been sacrosanct. The people believe what they hear from a bard because the profession has been a noble and honourable one for so long,' Quiller sighed. 'Then there is the people's general obsession with sagas.'

'Come now, Father — I agree with you completely about Gello's use of bards to spread lies, but surely the sagas are not to blame here — they are just a harmless diversion,' Barrett protested.

Quiller shook his head. 'For years I have been saying that sagas give people an unrealistic view of the world. Their concepts of good and evil, while admirable in their simplicity, do not present a picture of real life. Take our situation here. Because we are using men dubbed the Butchers of Bellic, we are automatically seen as the side of evil. No matter that these men desperately want to atone. No matter that the dark deed they are responsible for is swamped by the evil emanating from Gello and his backers. Add to this the people's trust in bards and we have a serious problem.'

'Forget good and evil. We have to find these bards, shut them up and then pay our own to start spreading the word about Gello,' Conal snorted.

'My friend, that will not be easy. We do not even control all of the north, let alone the rest of the country. And even if we manage to secure the north, we can do nothing about the areas under Gello's control. We are all agreed that we are not able to challenge him yet,' Sendric countered.

'Well, we don't have to defeat him in battle. My magic can take us around the country and allow us to speak to people in every town and village, if need be. Every time a bard tries to spread lies, we can appear there the next day and tell the people the truth,' Barrett announced. He, too, was incensed at the thought people could believe such falsehoods about Merren. Secretly, he was also a little pleased that the Rallorans had gone from being the rebellion's saviours to their biggest problem. Perhaps he and his powers would now become more important. As the rest of the council continued to argue about what should be done, he daydreamed about taking Merren on a long tour of the country — just the two of them.

Naturally working together so carefully and so long in the campaign to convince the country of her honesty and integrity, they would grow closer ... He was ripped from his fantasy when Nerrin declared he wanted to lead a mission into the heart of Norstalos City to take Gello's head.

'They can't spread any more lies about us if their leader can't talk,' he stated. 'Let the wizard's magic be used for that!'

Barrett pointed out that they had already thought about going after Gello — and rejected the idea because it would not work.

'If anything, it is an even worse idea than before. Not only will he be better guarded but killing him will reinforce the people's fear of the Queen and the Rallorans,' Barrett pointed out, then turned to Merren. 'My Queen, we showed you the pointlessness of this idea weeks ago, back in the forest. Even Captain Martil was against it. Nothing has changed since then.'

'Perhaps we need to call on Captain Martil now,' Nerrin bristled.

'Yes. Captain Martil — what do you think?' Merren asked.

Martil looked up. He had heard little of the debate, instead allowing it to wash over him. But now he saw everyone was looking at him.

'I don't know,' he admitted finally.

The council was more shocked by his words than by many of the things they had heard that afternoon. They had seen Martil angry, they had seen him happy, they had seen him determined, but they had never seen him at a loss before. He had always been sure of the next step in their campaign and, inevitably, it had been the right one.

Merren thought carefully. She could sense the unease around the room. The rebellion had been going so well; now their spirits had been dashed by a combination of the setback at Gerrin and the seemingly intractable problem of the bards and the lies they were spreading. Worse, their talismanic captain, the man who had led them to victory after victory, seemed unable to help. A mood not unlike fear seemed to be permeating the council. But she was not about to give up.

'Right,' she said crisply, jerking their attention back to her. One thing she had learned from the way Martil commanded men was to give them confidence; pretend you knew what you were doing, even if you were not sure yourself. Men are simple creatures, she told herself. Give them direction and they will follow it. Give them nothing and they will confuse themselves.

'We are going to do two things. Firstly, I want Captain Martil and his Ralloran division to march south and take the three passes that give access to the northeast. We need to seal this area off from any other bards or agents of Gello who intend to do mischief up here. Our latest reports are that each pass is held by a full company of troops. Lieutenant Nerrin, how long do you think it will take to have those passes back in our hands?'

Nerrin straightened. 'We can march down there easily enough. We will have the element of surprise and will be able to apply overwhelming force to each pass in turn. It should take no more than a week to have all three passes in our hands, your majesty.'

'Excellent. I want you to prepare to garrison those passes once you have taken them. Let nothing of

Gello's get past. So you will need to be supplied. Captain Martil, will that be a problem?'

Martil sat up, as if awakening from a long sleep. 'The garrisons on each pass will have supplies there. We should be able to capture those. And even with two companies on each pass and roving patrols through the hills, we will have sufficient men to forage — and pay — for supplies from surrounding farms.'

'Excellent. I want you prepared to leave tomorrow.'

'Yes, your majesty,' Martil said, although Karia let out a snort of disappointment. He had only just got back and Merren was sending him away again! She wanted more time with him, not less!

But Merren was not finished.

'The second thing is, we must return to Gerrin, as Martil said we would, as well as visit Berry. Rocus, Wime, Tarik, how many men have we got who are ready to march swiftly? Bear in mind that if our Rallorans are holding the passes, we will not need to keep such a strong garrison to protect Sendric.'

Rocus and Wime exchanged glances.

'I think we could have two companies of men, as well as Tarik's archers, and that's leaving a guard on the town,' Rocus said confidently.

'Excellent. Rocus, you will lead this expedition. Conal, you will look after the town in my absence, as we will need Wime, Tarik, Count Sendric, myself and Barrett to take these companies out and show the people of Gerrin and Berry that we are not the monsters they think we are. You and the council, led by Gratt, will protect the town. In a week's time, we should have both the passes and the northern towns under our control — and then we can think about confronting Gello's lies in his own den. Any questions?'

'I just want to thank you, your majesty,' Conal announced, unable to keep the smile from his face. 'Putting an ex-bandit in charge of a town like this …'

'No thanks are necessary. You have earned the admiration of this town with your actions at the battle and my respect since I have met you. Anyone else?'

Merren looked around the table and was delighted with the change in them all. The men had a fresh purpose and enthusiasm.

'Not bad for some peasant scum, eh?' Gratt nudged Conal, who was flushed with pleasure.

This raised a chuckle, which was broken by Karia.

'I've got a question: who's going to look after me?'

Merren waved down the chuckles.

'You will be coming with us to Gerrin. The passes can be taken by force but we may have need of your magic. Besides, the presence of a small girl will help convince them of our goodwill.'

Martil looked up, realising that he would be without Karia again.

'But, your majesty—' he began.

'I'm sorry, Captain, but our need is greater than yours,' Merren said. 'Besides, night marches and attacks on garrisons is hardly the place for a small girl.' *Also, if she stays with me, I can use her to keep Barrett away*, Merren thought.

Martil wanted to protest more but had to admit Merren had a point. Karia would not only be safer with the Queen, she would also be more useful. And he knew Karia liked Merren. He could not be so selfish as to drag her along.

He nodded. 'As you command, your majesty.'

Merren smiled. The news about Gerrin and Gello's use of bards had stung but she now felt curiously energised, more than ready to fight back. She could see the mood around the table was also different although Karia was looking decidedly put out.

'Gentlemen, you have your tasks. Do not waste time,' she commanded, and they sprang into action.

3

Archbishop Prent dismissed the servant girl and watched with satisfaction as she gathered her clothes from the floor around his bed and hurriedly dressed. There was no doubt about it — power did have its privileges. He thought about asking her to pour him a fresh goblet of wine before leaving but decided against it. She had worked hard enough that afternoon already. Prent stretched before slowly dressing himself and wandering into his office. It was always a thrill to pull on the golden robes of the archbishop. It was a greater thrill to know he did so while their previous wearer, Archbishop Declan, languished in a penitent's cell far beneath him.

Still, he had some concerns that day. He was archbishop in name, and had Gello's backing to be archbishop in deed. But much of the priesthood was fractious. He was owed favours by many senior members of clergy, which was helping keep a lid on any trouble, but there were some, mostly women, who were protesting about some of his decrees. And one bishop, called Gamelon, some hick from the east of the country, was even trying to stir up support against him. Well, it was time to show them once and for all just who was in charge around here.

He had met with King Gello that morning to discuss a new range of sermons, designed to expound on what was already being sung by bards across the country. Gello felt — and Prent agreed with him — that if the priesthood was reinforcing what the bards were saying, then even the doubters would be swayed. 'We need to be all singing from the same hymn book,' was how Gello had described it.

Prent just had to make that reality. It should be simple enough — send out the new sermons with orders they were to be preached over and over. Fight against the Queen, stand with Gello, protect the holy land of Norstalos. Simple enough words, for a bunch of simple peasants. And anyone who refused to preach these sermons would be arrested, securing the priesthood and pleasing Gello in the one action.

He was congratulating himself on how easy it was to be the archbishop when a young servant girl — a different one this time — disturbed him.

'Archbishop, I have two messages here, people requesting a meeting with you,' she said nervously.

'Come in, my dear. Don't be frightened,' Prent smiled wolfishly at her. Archbishop Declan had used recent graduates from the seminary as his secretaries but why, Prent felt, should he be surrounded by those pious fools when there were so many good-looking young women around? King Gello was right: to the strong went the rewards. And Prent knew he deserved every possible reward.

'The first one is from the Berellian ambassador, requesting an audience, the second from a retired priest …' The girl trailed off as Prent waved his hand in dismissal.

'I'll see the Berellian but whoever the old fool of a priest is, fob him off. I don't want to talk to him,' he snapped.

'Yes, but he wants to talk to you,' a man's voice said, and Prent spun to see an elderly priest walk through the back door to his office.

'Who are you and what are you doing here?' Prent blustered. He made a mental note to post guards on that door as well — he thought most people did not know about that way in.

'My name is Father Nott — and I am here to warn you about your immortal soul,' the man said pleasantly. His face was calm as he strolled slowly towards Prent. 'I have been granted a vision by Aroaril and need to talk to you.'

Prent wasted no time; the old man was obviously addled. He rang a bell on his desk.

The sound seemed to animate Nott. 'I come here to help you and you call for guards? Prent, you are even more foolish than you look! While you spend your time abusing servant girls and plundering the church's coffers, there are greater forces at work! The time is coming when you will be forced to make a choice between your life and your soul. Do not make the wrong choice!'

Prent was not really listening to the old man's babble, just looking for the guards. He was relieved to see them burst through the doors, although when they saw the cause of the alarm, they both relaxed, giving Nott a little more time.

'Remember one thing from this, Prent, just one thing. There are worse things than death,' Nott said urgently.

Prent walked over to him, feeling much more confident now his guards were about to haul the old buffoon away.

'Worse things than death? Such as being lectured by a senile fool who can't control his own bladder any more?' Prent sneered. 'Take this idiot away and don't let him in again. Aroaril will be coming to claim him any day now — although I don't know why he would want such a useless lump of whiskers.'

Nott smiled and walked calmly past the guards, back towards the main entrance.

'Next time I come here, it will not be to talk,' he promised.

The squad of criminals was seated in a circle, eating hungrily from a cauldron of stew. Kettering had to admit the food was far better than the slop served to a condemned man. There had been other changes since being drafted into the army. The unrelenting physical work had put muscle on his shoulders and arms and what he had gone through had added new, harder lines around his eyes and mouth. Without access to his expensive hair creams, he had been forced to tie his long hair back with a leather thong. He doubted even his most loyal customers would recognise him now — he barely recognised himself.

'Whaddaya reckon about that bard then, Killer?' Leigh asked through a mouthful of food. 'Wasn't that something? To think we're going to be asked to go north and fight against the Butchers of Bellic! We're the filth you wipe off your boot but our country needs us! We'll be heroes!'

'Dead heroes.' A bearded man who had introduced himself as Hawke had attached himself to the group. Unlike traditional army units, the criminal regiment seemed to be fluid in its composition. As long as nobody ran and no company was dramatically bigger than the next, the sergeants did not seem to worry about who was in each section.

'We won't die! Not when we've got blokes like Killer Kettering leading us,' Leigh declared.

Hawke snorted. 'The other side has Captain Martil, the Butcher of Bellic. You heard the bard! All his men are killers! They probably eat human flesh! I heard that Martil is nine feet tall and has sharpened teeth, like a dog!'

The other men listened in awe, the stew forgotten.

'That is the biggest pack of lies I've heard since my murder trial,' Kettering growled.

'What?' Hawke bristled.

'I know this Martil. He stayed at the inn I worked at. I've talked to him. He was travelling with a small girl, looking after her. The man I met was not the man that bard sang about.'

The other men just stared at him.

'So you reckon the bard was lying?' Hawke mocked.

'Of course he was, you fool! I've worked at inns all my life! Every inn hires Rallorans for protection, because they are the best! How many inns have you gone to when the security on the door was eating babies or starting fights?'

'Maybe they didn't start them, but they sure finished a few,' a tall, hulking man with a broken nose offered.

The other men chuckled at that. They had all seen the inside of a few inns — and been on the wrong end of Ralloran security. Hawke, without any support, looked ready to challenge Kettering again but subsided after a warning look from Leigh.

'Those Rallorans aren't baby-eating barbarians and Captain Martil isn't a monster. The monsters are the men who are against him. They were the ones who set me up, sent me here,' Kettering snarled.

The other men, knowing Kettering's reputation, eased slowly away from him.

'But why would they lie to us, Killer?' Leigh asked nervously.

Kettering thought for a moment. 'We're not being given a second chance. After a few more performances like that, they think we'll just charge right in, kill a few Rallorans before we are all cut to pieces — that way they get rid of us and the Rallorans.'

The other men thought about that — not an easy task for some of them — and none of them liked the prospect of charging battle-hardened warriors, baby-eaters or not.

'So what are we going to do?' Hawke asked.

Kettering sighed and stirred his stew listlessly. 'I don't know — yet.'

'How did it go?'

Nott slipped back into his room and closed the door carefully before answering.

'Anyone around?' he asked softly.

His female companion shook her head. 'Not a one.'

Nott sighed with relief. Sister Milly had been a great help to him over the last few days. A former secretary to Archbishop Declan, she was triply despised by the new regime, being also both rich in Aroaril's favour and a woman.

'It went as expected. Our lecherous archbishop is more concerned about what is in his purse and what is in his pants rather than what is in his heart. I gave him the warning but I fear it will come to naught. At least I survived the meeting.'

'You should not have gone, Father! I should have gone in your place!' Milly burst out.

Nott smiled warmly at her. She reminded him of Mara, his adopted daughter. If she had lived, she would have been a woman like this, he thought. 'No. He thinks I am an old fool who is going senile. You would not be so lucky. How was your expedition?'

Milly sighed. 'It is as we feared. Orders have gone out to remove any priest or priestess who refuses to deliver Prent's sermons. He has had an army of servants clearing out the old penitents' cells in the cellars, so he can fill them with priestesses as well as priests who rail against him, like your old bishop, Gamelon.'

Nott sat down.

'Are you all right, Father?' Milly asked. 'Would you like some tea?'

'As I always say, the day I can't make my own tea is the day I meet my maker. Still, He has told me I have a few more tasks to complete before I finally rest, so boil the kettle and warm the pot.'

'What did He reveal to you?'

'Too much — and not enough. He is not finished with me after all — what I thought was my final task was, in fact, just the beginning of them. He asks a great deal and promises nothing but hard work and the prospect of no reward. It is ironic. I was sure my work here was done and felt disappointed I could not do more. Now I learn I have a greater part to play and I wish my role was ended. Already I have had to lose my daughter, tell my granddaughter that I cannot look after her … My trials have been severe. My years of service are being rewarded with bitterness and pain. And I worry what else I must do before the end. Is the future being hidden from me because it will affect what I have to do? Or because I will baulk at what He requires of me? I do not know.'

Nott paused. 'I do not mean to sound as if I am complaining. I must believe that all I have lost, all I have given up, has been for a greater good. Even though I have not received a sign of hope. All I have seen is that we must be careful but we must start gathering others to help. The time of crisis is upon us.'

He sighed again and Milly felt she would like to embrace the old priest. But she hesitated, and he pushed himself to his feet.

'Now, excuse me, for there is another time of crisis upon me — the time of passing water.' And he offered her an outrageous wink.

Milly stopped preparing the tea and looked over at the old priest.

'How do you do it, Father?'

He shrugged. 'I just have to have faith.'

Sergeant Hutter accepted his plate of food without much enthusiasm. Boiled beef and boiled vegetables — and not much of either. Only water to wash it down. The other men at least got some gravy.

'And that's all you'll eat until you can see your belt again, fatguts,' his trainer told him.

Hutter did not have the energy to argue and made his way slowly to one of the tables. Men made room for him and he nodded gratefully.

'Good show this afternoon, Sarge. I know you love the sagas.' His young constable from Chell, the gangly youth Turen, seemed to enjoy the training but could still annoy Hutter.

'Yes, I did like the sagas but that one made no sense,' Hutter sniffed, trying not to think about stealing Turen's gravy.

'What do you mean, Sarge? Those Rallorans are ripping the north of the country apart, we need to learn how to fight so we can go and stop them. Easy!'

'Constable, how many times have I asked you to use your brain?' Hutter snapped. 'We met Captain Martil back in Chell. That was while the Queen was still on the throne. Why would she hire thousands of Rallorans to put her back on the throne if she wasn't even off it yet? And he spent the night with Father Nott, then left the next day with Nott's granddaughter, the one that Edil wanted back. You knew Father Nott. Would he have let that girl go off with a murdering barbarian?'

'No, Sarge,' Turen mumbled.

'Something stinks — and not just my sweaty tunic. That Martil was a dangerous man but if he was here to slaughter every Norstaline in sight, like the bard said, why didn't he start in Chell?'

'Don't know, Sarge.'

Hutter grunted. 'Me either.'

'So what do we do, Sarge?'

'Do? We do what we're told, lad. For now. But I'm damned if I'm going to sweat so bloody hard for some lying bastard to send me to my death.'

'But why do you have to go? It's not fair!' Karia folded her arms, stamped her foot and pouted her lip at Martil.

He was tempted to agree with her but he didn't think Merren would appreciate him throwing a tantrum. Still, he felt keenly the unfairness of having to explain to Karia something he disagreed with. He also felt guilty about leaving her. He had finally been able to articulate his feelings about Karia but what good was that if he was not around? She needed stability in her life, not more change. How he was going to give her stability in the middle of a war was an impossible question to answer.

'Because I have to. Adults have to do things they don't want to, sometimes, just like children have to do things they don't want to.'

'Like going to bed when I'm not tired?'

'Something like that,' Martil agreed. 'Believe me, I wish I was staying with you.'

'I want to stay with you! You're the only one who really cares for me! The others all want me to be quiet or go away!' Karia declared.

'Well, are we going to argue or are we going to play while I have time?' He was still worried about those dreams of Bellic but, around Karia, the fears seemed to vanish.

'Play! Catch first, then dolls, then you can read me some stories ...'

'Come on then.' Martil smiled as he followed her out of the room. It would be a brief respite. He had Nerrin and Kesbury gathering supplies for the march south. Despite Nerrin's confident words, taking all three passes without significant losses would be difficult. But at least the men seemed pleased to have a purpose — in the short time they had been back, four men were on a charge for sneaking into town and getting drunk, while several fights had broken out. Discipline had been restored but this was not the same proud, confident fighting force he had led out of Sendric just days ago. They needed a victory, and the chance to fight back at those they saw as responsible for spreading the stories about Bellic.

King Gello looked at the map with relish. He had expanded the Royal Council to include his war captains, while the Berellian, Ezok, was now a regular spectator.

'So Lieutenant Bayes in Gerrin reports the Ralloran scum marched away, and Berry has not seen hide nor hair of the creatures. Meanwhile, the performances to our new regiments have them in the right frame of mind to go north and attack. I can see my foolish slut of a cousin now — scurrying here and there like a frightened mouse, not knowing where to turn for help or where to go. We have her surrounded and outwitted and, in a few months, we can go north and crush her like the insignificant ant she is.'

All of the captains immediately applauded his statement and, seeing this, the nobles did too.

'Once our north is secure, we can turn our attention to outside our borders — and the real rewards will flow then, gentlemen! All the riches of the world are there for the taking — to the strong go the spoils! Land, gold, women — we will take them all!'

This time the nobles were among the first to cheer. But a grinning Gello noticed that Ezok did not seem to be joining in the general celebration.

'My dear Ambassador, what is the matter? You have nothing to fear from us — your excellent bards and your brilliant new saga have helped make this possible!' Gello announced.

All eyes turned to Ezok, who smiled in return.

'For that acknowledgement, I thank you, your majesty. But I do have one tiny concern.'

'Out with it, man!'

Ezok sighed. 'Waiting months before heading north to crush this pitiful rebellion seems like excessive caution. Surely we are giving them a chance to escape, or to try something to get out of the clever trap we have placed around them. You have more than enough men, and the country is behind you in your quest to wipe these Rallorans off the map. Why not go now?'

All eyes turned to Gello, who smiled generously.

'Ambassador, I understand you are worried about Captain Martil. He has confused, tricked and defeated your armies repeatedly. But here in Norstalos it is a different matter. He has nowhere to go. The dog still has teeth, however, and I grant you his Rallorans will not be easy opponents. That is why we will not go north until we can send an enormous army into battle. We will only face him when he is outnumbered by at least ten to one — and before I can take that many men north, I need to be sure I can trust them, and that the country is behind me.' He paused. He had failed once before, when he attempted to draw the Dragon Sword. He could not stand the thought of failing again. He would not do anything until he was certain of success.

'Besides, haven't we sent the Berellian Champion out to hunt Martil down? It would be sporting to give him a chance to finish his task! Without him, my idiot cousin won't have a clue what to do. She's a woman! About as useful at leading men as a dog is at painting!'

Gello enjoyed the sycophantic laughter that line provoked from around the table. 'So here is our task, gentlemen. Secure your districts and your regiments. Beq, that means you, as well as Grissum. The archers and the rangers could mean the difference up north. Two thousand bows make an enormously powerful weapon. See to it.'

He watched them go and wondered if he should stop bringing Ezok along to these meetings. After all, having the man question him in front of his council and captains was not to be accepted. Still, it was too early to turn on him. He might yet prove useful.

Captain — now Lieutenant — Kay was wary about being invited to Captain Beq's office. After all, it was Kay's old office. And the last time he had been asked in there, Beq had all but ordered he throw himself on his sword.

But when he was shown in, it was to find Beq in an expansive mood.

'Captain, please, sit down. Can I get you some wine? Juice? It's fresh apples, you know!'

Kay allowed himself to be given a goblet of apple juice and a comfortable chair beside Beq's desk. He was unsure why Beq was no longer calling him 'lieutenant'.

'Tell me, did the men — and did you — enjoy the bard's performance?' Beq asked.

Kay took a sip of juice to cover his confusion. What was all this about?

'Of course. The men were angry and fearful to hear Rallorans were killing people in the north. As was I.'

'Good, good!' Beq smiled, then leaned forwards. 'What if I was to tell you an important secret?'

Intrigued, Kay leaned forwards also.

'King Gello is very concerned about these Rallorans. Knowing they are raping and slaughtering innocent Norstalines in our north upsets him greatly.

We are putting together an army to destroy them before they can do much more damage. Obviously we would like to have the King's Rangers march with us. What do you think?'

'Of course! Every one of them is a loyal Norstaline! Anyone who invades and attacks our country is our enemy!' Kay declared hotly.

Beq nodded. 'I am pleased to hear you feel that way. Once we have secured the north, we will then go south to punish the Rallorans who schemed to let loose their darkest warriors on our people. If we were to do that, well, I will be taking command of one of the new regiments and the King felt that the Rangers would need a new captain — a trustworthy man. Your name was the first that came to mind. But, of course, as we will first be marching against the traitor Queen that you were forced to serve, he does understand if you are not able to agree ...'

'I agree!' Kay almost spilled his goblet in his excitement. He felt alive again — here, at last, was the chance at redemption he had sought. Regain his honour, regain his regiment, defend the people! It was perfect!

Beq's smile grew wider. 'Then we need to train, Captain! The men have to be ready for this test! Now, I have some more good news for you. We will soon be visited by another bard, as well as the Lord of Bellic, the only survivor of the terrible massacre there. On that day, I would like you to join me in welcoming the Lord of Bellic to our barracks and entertaining a man so riven by tragedy.'

4

Martil signalled to his archers and the attack began. This was the third of the passes they had assaulted and they had perfected the technique. Of course, their attacking force was smaller now, as they had left two companies at each of the other two passes. But they still outnumbered the defenders six to one — and Gello's men were light cavalry. As Martil had proved in the forest and at Sendric, they were not up to the task of close-order fighting.

The line of hills across this corner of Norstalos ranged from the impossibly steep to the merely imposing but, in three places, the slope was gentle enough to allow a road to have been constructed. At first glance the passes looked formidable enough. Each was several miles long, with the cavalry at the midpoint, the area where the hills on either side pushed in close. Here, a crude barricade of overturned wagons had been put across the road, with an even cruder battlement of upturned barrels behind that. The cavalry's camp was set up one hundred yards further behind, close enough that they could rush to the barricade swiftly in the event of an attack. A frontal assault on such a structure, with their advantage in odds, would succeed — but not without losses. However, Martil had never seen the sense in a frontal assault when a side assault would do just as well: the cavalry had thought like cavalry, and envisaged a charge up the road into the teeth of their defence at the barricade. Martil, on the other hand, had sent a company around either side of each pass, which had climbed the side of the hills and crept into position unseen. Martil waited at the front with two more companies, as well as his cavalry company and his archers, to draw the defenders' attention.

His tactic had worked at the previous two passes and he saw no reason why it would not succeed now.

'Keep them pinned down! I want them looking at us and nowhere else!' he barked and his lieutenants relayed the orders.

His bowmen were raining arrows down on the barricade now, a steel-tipped hail that had the defenders crouching and ducking for cover. Any that stood were picked off.

'Cavalry to advance! Don't press home the charge!' Martil ordered and his cavalry company formed up into ten lines, a squad per line, and began to advance at a slow walk.

'Now the infantry!'

The two companies advanced at the fast walk, shields held high. Drawn up in a long column of twenty ranks, each rank containing ten men, they were advancing parallel to the cavalry.

Martil waited until he was sure the defenders would be focused on this attack, and wondering how to stop them when to show yourself was a death sentence from his archers — then waved to his trumpeter.

'Now signal the flanking companies to move in and the archers to change their aim!'

He could not help but feel a pulse of pleasure as the companies that had worked their way around the sides of the barricade now stood and charged down. His archers switched their aim to the centre of the barricade, as Rallorans hit either side. Meanwhile, the cavalry spurred into a gallop and the infantry broke into a run. It took an enormous amount of training, as well as trust, to be able to get isolated companies to work together so smoothly, attacks coming in from all directions, so the defenders were given little or no chance to fight back. Martil felt a surge of pride for these men — they were making a highly difficult task look easy. Martil watched his company flags swarm over the barricade, saw swords flashing and heard the sound of metal on metal and metal on flesh as the defenders were torn apart.

Then a Ralloran leaped onto the barricade and waved the Queen's flag, telling everyone that the third, and final, pass was in their hands.

'Right then, let's see what we've got,' Martil announced.

As he urged Tomon forwards, he felt a strange sense of sadness. Planning and executing these attacks had occupied his mind for the last four days. Now he would have nothing to distract him from his dreams. Every night since he had left Sendric, the dreams had returned. Or, rather, the dream had returned; it was now the same one, night after night. As soon as he closed his eyes, the Berellian mother and son he had killed stalked him through the dead streets of Bellic. Each night he tried to get away from them but every time they cornered him. Just as he was about to attack them, the murdered Ralloran mother with the dead baby grabbed him and blamed him for her infant's death and her own torture.

The lack of sleep was beginning to tell on him. Planning these attacks had kept him fresh and his mind alert, but now they were done, he could feel the tiredness steal over him. He wanted to lie down and sleep — really sleep. But he dared not do it. Perhaps if he could get back to Sendric, and Karia...

'We have taken two score prisoners, sir, they've got the same number of wounded and the rest are dead,' Nerrin reported. He had led the flanking attack on the barricade.

Martil, who had begun to doze off in the saddle as he rode to the barricade, roused himself. 'Good work, Lieutenant. And our losses?'

'About what we suffered on the other two: three dead, another eight wounded. All the wounded should be fit to return to duty — the healers and priest are with them now.'

Martil nodded. They had brought two of Sendric's healers, as well as a priest. Thinking about the dead and wounded made him shudder. Not even a dozen men dead — it was a light toll indeed. Back in the wars, securing three vital passes for the loss of a dozen men would have rightly been seen as an astonishing victory. But he could not focus on the positive aspects. The spectre of more dead Rallorans — and more to come — haunted him. Perhaps even worse was a comment he had heard back at the second pass, from a pair of soldiers helping to carry out a body of a comrade: 'At least he's at peace now.'

Martil shivered at the thought.

'Sir — what if people try to get through these passes?'

Martil forced his mind to the problem. 'Well, you should be able to see anyone coming, as long as you post picquets further down the road. If they are potential recruits, or merchants hoping to sell us supplies, for Aroaril's sake let them through. If they are bards, with Gello's men to guard them, I want to talk to them. There might even be a few loose up here already, and when they learn the passes are in our hands, they might try to slip past you. Don't let them. I want to speak to these bastards going around telling this Real Saga of Bellic.'

'That will be our pleasure, sir,' Nerrin said viciously.

The pair of them rode on — they did not even need to dismount, as his men were already pulling apart the arrow-spiked barricade, preparing to move it down the pass, to block access from the south. The pass wound its way around for another mile before emerging in the plains below, although further along there were too many opportunities for an attacking force to slip around the side of a barricade.

'The camp is full of supplies, enough to keep a company of cavalry in food and fodder for at least a month. With what we brought, it will be enough,' Nerrin continued.

They rode towards the camp.

'What about the wounded cavalry, and the prisoners?'

'Same as before.' Martil forced his tired mind to concentrate. 'The healthy can carry the wounded on litters. They leave everything behind — swords, armour and horses. We'll need the lot — once we get enough men.'

They rode in silence for a few moments.

'Will we get enough men, sir?'

Martil did not have the energy to answer that question — and did not want to give voice to his own fears. If those bards were going around to every town and village and turning them against the Rallorans, how could they rally more men to their cause? Instead, he made himself think about their next step.

'Nerrin, I am leaving you in command of the most northerly pass. By leading the attacks on all three, you have proved to me that you are not just a promoted sergeant, you are a captain in the making! I will stay here just long enough to see that Gello does not launch an immediate assault, then will return to Sendric. When I do, you will take command of all the passes.'

The officer's face seemed to flush with pride. 'Sir, I don't know what to say …'

'Say nothing. You deserve every honour that comes your way. Now, these passes are the difference between victory and defeat. With them in our hands, Gello will be fearful of what is happening in the north. If I was him, I would try to take them back and, as we have proved, they are not easily defended. We will have two companies at each pass, with the remaining four companies guarding our flanks, and the space between each pass. You'll need to patrol forwards aggressively as well. Don't let Gello just stroll up the passes the way those dozy bastards let us sneak up on them. Meanwhile we'll take our time and use the supplies that Gello has thoughtfully left for us. I want as many siege engines as you can build. Ballistae, catapults — whatever you can come up with. We have a number of men who served in engineer companies. Use them. But we don't have the men for desperate last stands. If the attack comes when I have gone, fall back rather than stand and die, understand?'

Nerrin nodded, his brow furrowed.

Martil could feel himself flagging and forced himself to blink. 'When I go back to Sendric to plan our next move with the Queen, I'll just take one squad with me: Kesbury and his men. We'll need to work out patrol rosters to keep them off the line. Meanwhile, Barrett supplied us with some of his magicked birds, so you can send word back to us of any developments. Now, I think I'm going to lie down for a little while. Any questions?'

Nerrin watched his captain sway a little in the saddle and thought about asking what was the matter — but decided against it.

'Nothing, sir.'

Karia was not happy about being left. And she was not backwards in letting everyone around her know about it, either. Part of her knew that acting like this was not going to make people want to spend time with her. But she couldn't help herself. It had taken her years to find a daddy, and now people kept taking him away from her. Her fear at being left alone, as well as her loneliness, threatened to overwhelm her. She needed to know that people cared for her but only Martil seemed prepared to show her.

She was riding on her own horse, next to Merren, Rocus, Wime and Barrett. Not that she had ever ridden a horse before but her ability with magic meant she had told it what to do, where to go and to be nice. The horse seemed happy enough and normally she would have enjoyed speaking to it but chose instead to keep a ferocious look on her face and her arms folded. As soon as they were far enough away from the town so that she could be heard, she let out an exasperated snort or an exaggerated sigh at regular intervals.

'Can't you do something about her?' Merren muttered to Barrett.

His heart leaped. His campaign to win her over — or at least interest her as a man, not just a magician — was hardly going well. Looking at it realistically, he knew he was trying too hard. But this was the perfect opportunity to impress her in a different way. So he slowed his horse and let Karia ride up beside him.

'What is the matter?' he asked.

'I'm not happy,' she told him loftily. 'Why couldn't I go with Martil?'

Barrett looked over his shoulder along the path they had travelled. He used the time to control his irritation. With Merren so close — and Martil far enough away — he thought he needed to show his sensitive side. Perhaps Merren would like that.

'We did talk about this. You can be more help to us, and going with Martil might be too dangerous. Besides,' he added, in a burst of inspiration, 'we'd miss you.'

'Really?'

'Absolutely. Now, why don't we see what sort of birds we might be able to summon — we need to see what is happening at Gerrin.'

'All right.' Karia unfolded her arms. The thought that Barrett and Merren would miss her made her feel better. Barrett watched her call down a circling hawk and caught Merren's eye. She smiled at him gratefully and he felt his heart swell. *This was more like it*, he thought. *She just needs time to see me as a suitor, not a servant.*

Merren sighed with relief that she did not have to deal with Karia, or Barrett. She just was not in the mood for talking to either of them. For all her brave words back at the town, she was horribly aware that this was a considerable risk. It was also on her own shoulders. Since she had escaped from the palace, Martil had been there to advise, to plot and finally to fight for her. Now she had sent him off in another direction, with another mission, and all the responsibility rested with her. It was daunting, although it was also exhilarating. She wanted to not just take back the towns for herself but prove she was truly a queen — not merely a woman who was being helped by powerful men. She would be seen to make the decisions, not Martil, Barrett or Sendric. That was the thought that strengthened her when she started to worry about the alternative — that she would fail miserably and not only lose men but also the respect she had earned.

Merren gritted her teeth. *Now is not the time for negative thoughts*, she told herself. *You are a queen and you will succeed. This is what you have trained for since the Dragon Sword refused Gello. Just approach the problem logically, think of what the enemy will probably do — and use Barrett's and Karia's special powers to make sure you know his plan. Then, you can come up with one to defeat it: the best way to defeat an enemy is with the unexpected.*

'What are we going to do?' Baron Gerrin was almost gibbering with fear.

Lieutenant Bayes looked at him with disgust. 'Pull yourself together, man! I thought you nobles were supposed to be touched by Aroaril, not gutless little girls who wet their trews at the first sign of trouble!'

Gerrin staggered over to the window and swung open the wooden shutters. 'Look out there! Call that the first sign of trouble? That's Merren, with Count Sendric and what looks like several companies of Norstalines, all in armour! Men that we said were slaughtered by Rallorans! Forde is not an idiot! If he gets to speak to Count Sendric and the other Norstalines, he's going to ask questions — and we don't have any bloody answers for them! If only we'd just said they were in league with the Rallorans …'

Bayes snorted. 'Forde used to work for Sendric — he's never going to believe that the Count hired Ralloran barbarians to murder his own people. No, our solution is simple — we don't let Forde talk to them. We invite them in for talks, then start a fight before he can speak to them. We'll warn the people that we think these are Rallorans in disguise. Once everyone is attacking each other, they won't know the difference.'

Gerrin licked his lips. 'Will that work? I mean, they outnumber us …'

'If we kill the Queen, the Count and the rest of the leaders, they'll be easy meat.'

'But the risks! So many people could die!'

'Better them than us!'

Gerrin looked out the window again. He shuddered, then nodded. 'All right. We'll do it.'

The change in Kay's regiment was astonishing. Being told they were valued and trusted, rather than being confined to barracks as unworthy of the new King's respect, altered the men's attitudes dramatically. Performance on the archery range improved and the men were drilling with a new spring in their step. Kay was proud of them and Beq was happy with Kay, which was a sufficiently rare event that Kay could enjoy it. He was also eager to head north to tackle those Rallorans ravaging his country — and, if he was honest with himself, eager to see the insignia of a captain back on his tunic.

Still, one thing bothered him. He had known the Queen. Not well, but he had known her. He could not remember her ever seeing a Ralloran, other than the official ambassador. How, then, had she arranged for a thousand of them to spirit her out of the capital and start attacking Norstalines in the far north?

But that was a small concern next to his relief at being able to regain his honour.

The prisoners started to arrive within days. The ones from parishes close to the capital were the first to be dragged before Prent, while the church was full of tales of others being carted across the country in chains.

Father Nott watched them come in, careful to keep to the shadows. All of them were going down to the vacant cells deep under the church's chapter house.

'What do we do?' Sister Milly whispered.

'Nothing publicly. But see if you can't help some of the servant girls. These prisoners will have to be fed — and that is the perfect way to communicate with them. If we win over the servant girls, it will be much safer to pass messages along.'

Merren looked up at the walls of Gerrin. They were packed with people but, unlike the scene Martil had described, these ones were not shrieking hatred or waving weapons. They were watchful, but it seemed more curiosity than anything.

'We must be extremely careful. There will be many innocent men and women in there who have been duped by Gello and his bards. But they are our people and we must ensure they are not hurt,' she warned.

'We shall do everything possible, your majesty,' Rocus promised.

They waited nervously outside the gates as the message from Baron Gerrin had stipulated: Merren and her officers in front, her Norstalines behind in a long column.

Slowly the gates creaked open, and a score of men in red surcoats walked out, led by a mere sergeant. All carried long spears.

'Follow me to talk with Baron Gerrin. Do not start anything, for we shall be watching you carefully,' the sergeant bellowed.

Rocus snarled at the lack of respect being shown to the Queen, but Merren laid a hand on his arm and he subsided.

'Lead on, sergeant of Gello,' she replied in a ringing voice.

The man turned and began walking, and she urged her horse forwards, followed by Rocus and then the others. Her men had left their spears behind, had their swords sheathed and wore no helms, so they looked less threatening. They also did this so they could be recognised, as Rocus had made sure all of the men who had relatives or friends in Gerrin had been brought along.

The only sound in the town was the noise of the horse's hoofs on the cobbles and the jingle of reins and armour as the column rode slowly into the town, towards the central square. The people were eerily silent as they watched the armoured men ride into their town. Just the occasional sound of a baby crying or a child asking a question came from the assembled townsfolk. Quite a few observant children had noticed that the men rode two abreast, and that the man on the left carried a much bigger shield than the man on the right — roughly twice the size, although still painted with the Queen's symbol of the silver dragon.

Merren rode ahead proudly, head held high, looking neither left nor right, although she could see that all watched her. Years of training meant she could mask her feelings and appear as if she was just out for a quiet ride in the country. But the tension was making her insides twist and coil like a nest of snakes. Everything, including her life, was about to be put at risk. Sendric, and particularly Barrett, had argued against her plan. But she had insisted, and they had obeyed. Only time would prove who was right.

Gerrin watched the slow ride through the town with trepidation, Lieutenant Bayes beside him. The pair of them waited in the central square, Forde and the town council some yards behind them — close enough to see what happened but far enough away so that they would not hear what was being plotted. Half of Bayes's men were dressed in ordinary clothes and scattered up and down the route to the central square. At his signal, they were to hurl spears and knives and loose crossbows at the column of men. Once under attack, Bayes had assured him, the soldiers would draw swords and look for enemies — seeing nobody in red surcoats, they would assume that they were being attacked by the townsfolk. At that point, they would attack the people, who would either flee or fight back. Either way the Queen would be denied the town and, at worst, Gello would get the story of a Norstaline massacre at the hands of the Queen to add to his tales of murdering Rallorans. But if all went to plan, he would get a dead Queen. His men would take casualties but, as they had their armour on under their ordinary clothes, they stood a better chance of surviving than the townsfolk. Meanwhile, the men who were leading Merren into this trap would attack and kill the Queen and her officers. The remainder of his men, who were formed up in the square, would use a side street to join the attack. Bayes was confident it would work. After all, in many ways it was similar to the trap Captain Martil had sprung on that hapless fool Havrick — and that had been a success.

'Should we attack now?' Gerrin whispered.

'Wait — we want to be sure they can't escape,' Bayes cautioned. In his opinion, if this cowardly baron copped a knife during the ensuing fight, it could solve a few problems. And offer King Gello an obvious reward to give Bayes when it came time to thank his loyal lieutenant for killing Queen Merren and ending her rebellion.

Gerrin wiped sweat from his brow.

'Nearly,' Bayes muttered, seeing how close the Queen was. The signal for the attack was to be a welcoming salute from a pair of trumpeters. As soon as they finished, the attack would start.

He glanced to where Gerrin stood perspiring, stains showing at his neck and under the arms. Bayes wouldn't be surprised to see a similarly damp stain on the front of his trousers. Someone else deserved the riches that came with this baronetcy — someone like himself.

He glanced up at the Queen and could not help but compare the quivering wreck at his side with the deposed monarch. She looked cool, calm and in control. Shame that was about to end but he had his future glory to think about. He nodded to the trumpeters, who drew a deep breath and began the welcoming fanfare.

The last notes of the trumpet call had barely died away when the sergeant and his squad turned and charged at Merren. In the narrow street, with men crowded behind her and townsfolk to either side, she could not possibly avoid their attack. But she did not even attempt to.

Instead, Karia, riding a few paces behind, threw up her hands. Instantly a huge flock of birds soared down, beaks and talons slashing at the faces and heads of the soldiers. The soldiers tried to cover up and protect themselves from the ferocious assault, unable to press their charge home. Merren glanced at Karia, who was looking determined, but a little pale. This was the part that had upset Barrett and Sendric. Risking her life on the abilities of a small girl — no matter how talented — was terrifying to them. But Merren had a more important task for Barrett. She looked behind her to see what was happening down the street, even as her 'officers' — in reality, Rocus and his men — formed a fighting line in front of her, in case any soldiers got past the birds.

As soon as the trumpets sounded, Bayes's soldiers in the crowd had leaped into action. Half had javelins hidden under their long cloaks, a handful had crossbows and the rest carried throwing knives. All immediately hurled, loosed or threw their weapons, then drew swords and waited to see what the reaction would be.

The men on the left-hand side of the column had ducked down behind their giant shields as soon as the trumpets sounded. Knives, spears and bolts clattered into the shields but few found their mark. One horse was rearing with pain, a javelin deep in its haunch, while a man with a crossbow bolt through his calf was cursing but, as Merren had planned, the large shields had done their job. On the right side of the column, where the men's sword arms were facing the townsfolk, and where they could not have got their shields — especially a large shield — around in time, there was a different outcome. There, the various missiles simply stopped in midair, before dropping harmlessly to the ground.

The soldiers in the crowd stared with shock, while the crowd themselves was gripped with fear — what was happening? Women grabbed their children and thought about running, men grabbed for any weapon they had and hoped they could protect their families — all knew what armoured cavalry could do to them. The soldiers hidden among them prepared to attack. Their ambush had failed but they could feel the fear and tension in the street; it would not take much to trigger a vicious fight. Then they started screaming.

Townsfolk leaped aside as dozens of men fell to the ground, frantically ripping off their long cloaks to reveal the armour beneath — armour that was glowing and steaming with heat. Men rolled on the ground, trying to undo straps. Barrett had been ordered to only give them enough heat to get them out of the crowd, force them to unmask themselves as soldiers, but he was in a foul mood. Not only was he worried about Merren and Karia up the front, but he had had hopes of being able to save Merren's life.

He had argued that was a duty more important than saving the lives of a few soldiers, surely? She had declared otherwise. How could men follow her, when she ensured her own safety with the Queen's Magician, while leaving a small girl to look after one hundred men?

Karia, too, had refused to agree to his suggestion that it was too hard for her. Her confidence and declaration that she could do this 'easily' had been unshakable. True, his protests had ensured that Merren was wearing armour underneath her clothes but that was scant comfort. He wanted to be the hero for once!

His frustration boiled over and the soldiers paid for it, screaming horribly as the metal seared through its leather backing and into skin. Only then did he stop, feeling a little ashamed as men flopped and moaned. *They attacked us, they were the ones who are to blame*, he told himself defiantly.

At the front of the column, Merren could hear the commotion behind but forced it out of her mind. She had to keep going with the plan. She nodded to Karia, who released the birds. They flew away instantly, leaving scratched and bleeding soldiers to search for their spears — only to realise that the Queen was now behind a shield wall of men and horses. Unsure, they turned to Bayes for orders.

'Hold!' Merren's voice, magically amplified by Karia, boomed across the town. 'We mean you no harm! This is a plot by your baron and Gello, to cause slaughter in the streets! They don't care about your lives! They've been lying to you! What that bard told you was false! But we want to help you! Join us, and we will protect you from them!'

The townsfolk looked at the men who had been

hidden among them, now writing on the cobbles in agony, and at the column of armoured men, most of whom had not even drawn swords, and began to mutter.

In the square, Gerrin could see Forde and the rest of the town council advancing towards them. They did not look happy. He was horribly aware that a living and speaking queen was a different person to argue with than a dead one. And he had always been tongue-tied around her. He hated her after she had humiliated him in a council meeting, and belittled every proposal he had brought to the table — admittedly all ones he had been presented with by Gello. But he did not know how to answer her accusations.

'What do we do?' he moaned at Bayes.

The officer was already thinking. Attacking the Queen now was doomed to failure. His men were heavily outnumbered and he could not count on the townsfolk joining him. His only chance was to try and get away — and perhaps try another ambush at Berry. He was under no illusions as to what would happen to him if he went back to Gello and reported failure.

'Prisoners! Grab prisoners!' Bayes bellowed at his sergeant. 'Bring them here!'

The sergeant responded swiftly. His squad hauled screaming women and children back into the square before Rocus and his guardsmen could stop them. Men who tried to protect their families were clubbed or stabbed to the ground.

Bayes drew his own sword and, with the rest of his men, seized the town council and their families.

'What are you doing?' Forde cried, but Bayes bashed him to the ground with the flat of his blade.

The other councillors, being elderly and terrified, put up no struggle.

'Rally!' Bayes called, and his men huddled together, spears pointing outwards, Bayes, Gerrin and more than a score of prisoners in the centre.

'What are we doing?' Gerrin moaned.

'We're getting out of here, you fool! Now shut up and let me do the talking!' Bayes hissed, then waved at the men holding the prisoners. 'Keep the bastards quiet! I need to talk to the Bitch Queen!'

Merren urged Rocus forwards, and a company of her Norstalines rode into the square, spreading out to encircle the small formation of red-coated soldiers. With them came many of the townsfolk, crying out for the men, women and children being held. The side streets were packed, and Merren had to order her men to keep the townsfolk away from Gello's soldiers.

'Surrender the people you have taken! You cannot hope to achieve anything by this!' she called, her voice still magically amplified.

'Free passage! Let us go or we kill every one!' a voice roared back.

The townsfolk sent up such a wail at this that Merren was forced to call for silence.

'You will let these people go if we allow you free passage to the gate?' she called.

'We're taking them with us! They're our guarantee of safety — and don't think we won't hurt them! We'll kill the brats first, then the women!' the officer shouted back.

'How do I know you won't just kill them anyway?'

'The time for talking is over! Move your men aside or the first kid gets its head cut off! Let us get outside and leave us enough horses to ride away!'

'We'll take the horses out now — just don't hurt the children!' Merren called, then signalled for her officers to come closer, Barrett among them.

'My Queen, we can't let them go,' he said urgently.

'I know that — but neither can we see those people killed. Once you and Karia showed me how you can make plants grow tall and hold people — can you do it again?'

Barrett looked mystified. 'Well, yes, but these are cobblestones — there might be a few weeds but hardly enough to ...'

'Not in here! We leave the horses on the grass, outside the walls — when they go to mount, you act. Can you do it?'

Barrett looked at the number of soldiers. 'Might be too many,' he admitted.

'Then just take the ones holding the hostages. Tarik's men can take care of the rest. Understood?'

Barrett and the officers nodded, and hurried off towards the gate.

'No tricks now — or I kill the kids!'

Merren could see that the speaker was the officer, who was carrying a small boy in his left arm, his sword held close to his side. The boy's mother, screaming with fear for her child, was being dragged along by the sergeant, who punched her to stop the cries.

'Stand back! Let them through!' Merren ordered, and the group of soldiers in red made their slow way out of the square, taking their captives with them.

'Your majesty, please! You must save them!'

Merren looked down to see a bloodied man try to push past a pair of her guards.

'Who are you?' she called.

'Forde, your majesty, I was the militia commander in this town before it was abolished. Bayes and Gerrin have my family!'

Merren remembered how Wime had praised this man.

'So you see, Forde, how the men you decided to stand with against me choose to repay you?' she said coolly.

'I regret what I have done and said, your majesty. Save them, I beg of you, and I will be your loyal servant!'

Merren smiled grimly. 'I would have hoped it would not take me saving your family for that to pass. But I do intend to save them.'

Gerrin was almost sobbing as he followed Bayes down the street towards the gate. He could feel the eyes of the townsfolk on him. Every one of them hated him for this. Every one despised him for threatening to kill the town's children in order to escape. The stories of the bard, the call to protect the town from the monstrous Rallorans; they were all forgotten now. No, what every person in the town would remember forever was the image of that long march to the gate. The swords and knives being held at the throats of women and children. How any of the hostages who screamed, or complained, or fainted were either hit into submission or dragged brutally along. Any of the soldiers who might have been inclined to mercy or who might have been tempted to surrender had their intentions changed by seeing what had happened to their comrades who had been hidden down in the crowd. These men were still moaning, or had lapsed into unconsciousness because of the burns they had received from their still-smoking armour.

All the time the people watched.

'Baron! Please! Let us go!'

Gerrin recognised the speaker as Gia, Forde's wife, now being dragged along by Bayes's sergeant. But he just closed his eyes and shook his head at her desperate protest.

It seemed to take forever to make it to the gate and many in the crowd were now shouting threats at them. But they dared not do anything more than threaten, not with the swords so close to so many young necks.

'Ignore them. Once we are on horseback, we will be safe,' Bayes told his sergeant. 'We'll take a few of the women and kids with us, to deter any pursuit. The women can entertain us tonight. If they do it well enough, we might even let them live. But make sure you kill a few of those old councillors — and that idiot Gerrin before we go.'

'Yes, sir!' His sergeant grinned wolfishly, and tightened his hold on Gia.

Merren hurried onto the ramparts, where Tarik and his archers were already waiting. Rocus, Wime and a company of men had left forty horses on a section of grass in front of the tower where Tarik and his men were placed.

'Are you just going to let them go?' Forde cried. 'They'll take our families, do Aroaril knows what to them if you let them get away ...'

'Show the Queen some respect!' Barrett snarled. 'And trust in her wisdom and judgement!'

'Thank you, Barrett,' Merren said calmly. 'Are you and Karia ready?'

Barrett smiled. 'I am, my Queen. Karia?'

The small girl looked a little tired, but she could still smile. 'Easy. Just the way I did to Conal, right?'

Down below, Bayes and his men were now out of the gate, off the dirt road and walking towards the horses. The grass was reasonably short, but still, it brushed their ankles and reached over the hoofs of the waiting horses. Wime, Rocus and their men were a safe distance away, and not barring the way to the road.

'Ready, Tarik?' Barrett asked.

The archer had an arrow ready, as did the men with him. 'When you are,' he grunted.

'Don't hesitate, Tarik. Kill any that might harm the prisoners,' Merren instructed.

'Now, Karia!' Barrett said, and flung out his hand towards the ground.

Forde watched in disbelief. One moment there was a large group of soldiers in red, about half of them dragging or carrying a prisoner, tramping over some small plants towards the horses that would carry them away. The next breath, the same plants had exploded into growth, covering both soldiers and prisoners, gripping arms and legs and holding everyone immobile.

Or not quite everyone. Perhaps a dozen men on the fringes, ones only carrying spears, were left free or were able to tear themselves from the plants.

Before anyone could tell whether they would run, surrender or hurt the helpless prisoners, Tarik and his archers loosed their arrows. All except one were hit, a plump man not in red but in the rich clothes of a noble.

'That's Gerrin! He wasn't a prisoner, he was behind this!' Forde spat.

'We'll take him prisoner,' Merren instructed, as Wime, Rocus and their mounted men rode swiftly in.

But, seeing the men in blue thunder towards him, the Baron turned and ran towards the prisoners.

'Tarik!' Merren snapped.

Bowstrings twanged and the Baron collapsed, just short of the captured soldiers and prisoners, three arrows in his back.

'Thank you, your majesty!' Forde gasped. 'You have saved them all!'

A similar conclusion seemed to have been reached by the rest of the townsfolk, who had crowded onto the walls and packed the space under the gatehouse to see what was happening. Cheers and cries of relief were ringing out across the town.

'It was my pleasure. But I will hold you to your pledge to be my loyal servant.' Merren smiled.

Forde dropped to one knee. 'Your majesty, I will give my life for you.'

Merren raised him to his feet. 'Let us hope it does not come to that. Now go, your family will need to see you.'

She watched him almost sprint down the stairs and turned to Karia. A wave of relief was rushing through her. Not only had she outwitted Bayes and Gerrin, but she had won the town over. She could hear the cheers and screams of delight outside.

A chant of 'Long live the Queen!' was going up around the town, followed by 'Three cheers for the Queen!'. Wime, Rocus and their men cut free the prisoners and returned them to their families, while leaving the soldiers helplessly entwined. Merren felt almost weak at the knees, now the tension was leaving her. At the same time, she felt a wild exultation. She had done it! Done even better than she had dared hope! She hugged Karia, laughing as the little girl hugged her back.

'Tarik, fine work by you and your men! And Barrett — that was brilliant!' she said.

'What about me? Wasn't I brilliant?'

'You were better than that! You saved me and the town!' Merren picked Karia up and hugged her anew. 'Come on, we have to wave to the people!'

She carried Karia to the battlements and together they waved down at the celebrating townsfolk.

'It's the Queen!'

The cry alerted the crowd and the roar that followed was astounding. Earlier that day these people had been prepared to fight her — now they were screaming with joy just to see her.

Barrett watched, a little jealously. After all, it was his skills that had saved the day. Without him, none of this would have been possible. It had been he who had sent birds circling over the town to see the preparations and help work out the trap they were facing, he who had helped turn the trap on Gerrin and Bayes, he who had managed to rescue the prisoners.

'Barrett! Wave to the crowd!' Merren called.

He stepped forwards and half-heartedly waved. It did not seem to provoke a fresh outbreak of cheering. *If only I had been the one to save Merren's life*, he told himself, she might even now be holding me. He could see the image now: the two of them, arm in arm, waving to the crowd. He glanced towards her, a little of the longing he felt inside showing through.

Merren caught sight of the expression on his face and felt a little of her joy leak away. She had enough complications with Martil. And more than enough to deal with just trying to win back her kingdom. Why was it that men could not think with just their brains? She put Karia down and straightened up. If there was one thing that Martil had taught her, it was that the work never finished when the battle was won.

'Let us secure the town,' she ordered. 'We have much to do before we can march on Berry.'

5

Gello's captains were not supposed to meet without him. But this was an emergency. Last to arrive was Grissum, the captain of the archers and now the regiment of criminals. Beq, who'd had the regiment of militia added to his nominal command of the rangers, ushered him inside, to where Livett, the captain of the light cavalry, waited. Livett, who had been seen as one of Gello's favourites but whose regiment had been ruined by Havrick's incompetence, was clutching a goblet of wine, looking as though it was not his first of the day.

'What is this about?' Grissum demanded immediately, accepting a goblet of wine. 'We all know the penalties for being here together …'

'I called this,' Livett announced shakily. 'It is my head already on the chopping block — and yours will follow if we do not work together.'

'Well?'

'I have been training the King's new recruits, the peasants he has scraped together to form the basis of a new army. It's not going well. These men have never held a weapon before. They are useless. Martil's Rallorans would smash them without raising a sweat.'

Grissum drank his wine. 'And how does this affect me?'

'I've had advance word from the north. The passes have fallen — the Rallorans now hold them. The King will hear later today.'

'What!' Grissum forgot his wine and stared instead at Beq, who had obviously heard the news before, since he just looked grim, rather than afraid.

'We won't know what is happening in the north. Worse, that damned Berellian has been getting into the King's ear, telling him he has to attack soon, that to give Martil time is to give him the chance to pull off a miraculous victory. So far the King has ignored him but, after this news …'

Grissum nodded. 'He might order an advance now. Send everything he has north, to smash the Queen before she and her Rallorans can do anything else …'.

'Aye. And there is our problem. Are the men you are training ready?' Livett snapped.

Grissum opened his mouth, closed it again, then shrugged. 'The archers should be all right. They're all proud Norstalines, no matter what. The criminals … they can fight but I don't know as if I'd trust them. There's something funny going on. I mean, after the first bard performed, they seemed excited, ready to help. But with each new performance, there has been less enthusiasm and more muttering—'

'And you, Beq?' Livett interrupted.

'The rangers are keen. The militia … not quite so. I mean, some of them are. But there seems to be an undercurrent in the regiment. Not unlike what Grissum said. As well as the bards, we have had a priest spout the new sermon about the Rallorans to the militia — after all, they're supposed to like that sort of thing. But it seems to have had the opposite effect.'

'Exactly. And what do you think the King's reaction will be if he thinks that we haven't got these men ready to fight when he wants to lead them north?' Livett asked.

Beq and Grissum exchanged looks. 'We'll be replaced, if we're lucky. Dead, if we're not,' Grissum sighed.

'So we must all say the same thing — they are ready and eager to march?'

'Agreed,' Beq said, and Grissum nodded.

But for an accident of birth, I could be down here with these girls, Sister Milly thought as she gathered a dozen servants around her in a quiet corner of the big kitchen. They might be allowed to work for the church but daughters of the lower classes, no matter how devout, were almost never allowed to join the church by their families. Milly's parents had been, while not noble, certainly rich. Her father was a hugely successful saddler and her mother had inherited money from her family, who were still one of the biggest coopers in the country. So when she had felt the call of the church, they were able to indulge her, help her and pay for her training. Seeing these girls, all of them bearing the same scared, haunted look — and at least three of them bearing the marks of Prent's fists on their faces — made her thank Aroaril for her good fortune, as well as cringe with shame that the supposed archbishop of her church was behind this.

The girls were all dressed neatly in church-supplied dresses, all washed and their hair clean and tied back. But their faces told the story. Ordered to do whatever the Archbishop demanded, service here had become a nightmare. It was doubly monstrous — these servant girls, not one of them over twenty, lived at the chapter house, which meant to defy Prent was to lose your home as well as your job. That would put them out on the streets — and they would only have one job option open to them, which was effectively what Prent was forcing them into now.

'I want to help protect you from that monster who calls himself the Archbishop,' Milly told them.

'How can you do that?' one girl, who still sported a fading black eye, asked resentfully.

'By giving you a charm that will make Prent unable to perform around you.' Milly could not help but smile, even though this was hardly a laughing matter.

'Perform?' one of the girls asked.

Milly's smile became a little embarrassed. 'How can I put this? The bird will not rise from its nest, the snake will stay asleep on its rock ...' she hesitated, not sure that her metaphors were quite hitting the mark with these servant girls.

'We understand,' the girl with the black eye said harshly.

The others looked at her with a mixture of relief and suspicion.

Milly found herself glad the darkened kitchen would hide her burning cheeks, not just from her words but from the fact that she had not acted before now.

'Also, I can heal any bruises or ... or other hurts you may have.'

The servants looked a little happier at this but Black-eye stepped forwards.

'So what do you want from us for this?' she asked coolly. 'Everyone wants something.'

Milly nodded. 'You are right. I will want your help. But only to pass messages to the prisoners in the cells below. Messages that will not be seen by any guards, I promise. First, let me prove to you that I can be trusted.'

She waited, while the other girls all looked to Black-eye, who was obviously their leader.

'I don't know. What can you do for us that a bottle of stolen wine and a handful of goose grease can't? And they'll never want anything from us in return.' The defiant words could not mask the pain, Milly knew.

Milly stepped forwards and lifted her hand. Instinctively Black-eye flinched, but Milly just brushed her hand across the girl's face. The others gasped as the bruising and soreness vanished.

Black-eye no more, the girl touched her own face gingerly, then turned to see the reaction on the faces of the other girls. Her face broke into a smile.

'Do that to the rest of us and it's a deal.'

Hutter looked around at the table of men. He had never met these militiamen before but he knew their type: solid, dependable men who had devoted their lives to keeping the people safe. He had spoken to many such groups over the past few days. He had not intended to do so but, as more and more questions were asked of him, he had to come up with answers. Even now he was trying to work out how it had come to this. He had always been one for the quiet life — Chell had supplied all the excitement he needed. But, in recent days, a quote from Father Nott had come back to haunt him: 'We do not get what we want, we get what Aroaril knows we need.' Hutter had ignored the words then but now felt they were somewhat prophetic. He had certainly never wanted this — being dismissed from the militia then effectively kidnapped and ordered to go to war. But perhaps it was what he had needed. Once he had dreamed of wearing the insignia of an officer, even meeting the King. Thanks to what had been done to him, that Hutter was emerging again, appearing out of the extra flesh that was being sweated off him every day. As much as he still wanted the quiet life, he could not sit back, saying and doing nothing.

At first he had spoken to men who approached him but, as his anger and disquiet grew, he had begun to actively seek others out. Men like this group. They were used to finding the truth and uncovering mysteries, which was why they were searching for answers and eager to hear what he said.

'We're being lied to. I've met this Captain Martil and he could not have stolen the Dragon Sword, as the bards and priests are telling us. Nor do I think he was in the country to kill people. He was staying with the local priest, for Aroaril's sake — and he was one of the good priests. He wouldn't have let a maniac stay with him, or given him his granddaughter to look after! And we all know that the Rallorans were here working at inns — and they hadn't slaughtered anyone I'd ever met! So if they are lying about this, what else are they lying about?'

The other militiamen nodded agreement.

'But why are they lying to us?' one man asked.

'Why do people ever lie to us? They lie to cover up a crime,' another rasped. 'Gello's men were stealing anything that didn't move and raping everything that did a few weeks ago — then all of a sudden they stop, we get dragged out here and told we have to fight to save Norstalos from mad Rallorans ravaging the north. Don't know about you but that smells mighty strange to me.'

There was a rumble of agreement this time.

'So what do we do about this? Our officers …'

'Bloody officers! When have we ever listened to officers? All they're good for is wearing shiny armour and writing reports.' Hutter snorted and the militiamen, sergeants to a man, chuckled in appreciation. 'No, lads, we keep quiet, and we keep our eyes and ears open. All criminals make a mistake — and that's when we'll be ready for them.'

'We're being lied to,' Kettering told a cell full of men, all of them scarred, bearded and muscled. A few months ago he would have run a mile rather than walk past a man who looked like this, but now he was actively seeking them out, sharing a cell and a meal with them. Even stranger, they were listening to him. Leigh may not have brains, but he had a certain rat-cunning, as well as a big mouth, and he had ensured that Kettering's tale was spreading through the criminal regiment at a rapid rate. It was helped by the fact a good half of this criminal regiment weren't real criminals at all — just men who had tried to stop Gello's soldiers stealing, raping and killing. Sent to jail on trumped-up charges, they had been scraped out along with the real criminals and dumped into this regiment. They were more than happy to listen to him.

One of them, Kettering had been shocked to learn, was Wollin's celebrated dressmaker, Menner. He had been amazed when he had walked into a cell, expecting to find the usual crop of criminals, only to see Menner sobbing quietly in the corner.

'What are you doing here?' Kettering had asked.

Menner had looked up. He had obviously been beaten recently; his eyes were blackened, crusts of blood lined his nostrils and he had another dark bruise on his chin. But he wiped his eyes before he answered Kettering. 'Gello's men came for me. Said my name was on a list of those who had offended him. Now look at me,' the tubby little tailor had moaned.

Kettering had summoned Hawke and Leigh.

'Keep an eye on him. He doesn't deserve to be here,' he had ordered.

'Do any of us?' Leigh asked.

'Why do we have to look after a crying little baby?' Hawke complained.

Kettering whirled on him. 'Because I said so!'

'But look at him! If I start hanging around him, everyone will think he's my jail-wife!'

'I gave you an order,' Kettering had growled. 'Besides, one day he might save your life.'

'And one day I might sprout wings and fly out of here,' Hawke had snorted but agreed to make sure Menner came to no further harm.

Kettering shuddered to think what would have happened to the dressmaker otherwise. There were many brutal men in the ranks. But, as Kettering was discovering, even they were eager to listen to him.

'We're being lied to,' Kettering repeated.

'What's changed? The bastards always lie to us!' A man with a livid red pit where his left eye used to be was the first to speak up.

'But this is different. This time we can fight back. There will come a time when they plan to send us to our deaths. That's when we strike. It's one thing going to the gallows with your hands tied, and six bastard guards walking around you. It's another being ordered to your death when you've got hundreds of mates with you — and you've all got swords.'

The men in the cell nodded. They may not be the sharpest knives in the drawer — but they all knew what to do with one.

'We'll listen for you, Killer,' One-eye growled. 'You give us the word and we'll be behind you.'

Kettering nodded, although part of him could not help but marvel that he was not only talking to men such as this, but gaining their respect. If he wasn't there seeing it, he would never have believed it himself. Sometimes he had a flash of fear, thinking that they were going to see through the façade of 'Killer' Kettering and turn on him, recognise he was not so different from Menner the dressmaker. But those flashes were coming less often. Inside him was a fire, raging at the injustice done to him and threatening to leap out of control at any moment. That was what the others saw.

The cell they sat in was barely the size of one of the old rooms back at the Crown and Sparrow. Crude piles of straw provided bedding, while a pair of large buckets served as their toilet. They were given half a loaf of bread each, as well as a cauldron of stew, which they scooped out of a communal pot. A few moons ago, he would have rather slit his wrists than live like this. And yet now it seemed so normal. It was things like this that drove him onwards. He would not die before he had his revenge.

Martil woke, his heart pounding painfully, drenched in sweat. He dreaded going to sleep now: every night it was the same. He knew what was coming for him but he did not know how to stop it. Tomorrow he would return to Sendric. He wasn't supposed to, but he had to. He could not stay out here any longer, without Karia. He did not care what that meant for Merren's plan. The last report said they had taken Gerrin and were moving on Berry. He did not know if Karia would be able to help him but he did not know what else to try. He longed for the oblivion of wine but had ordered none be available. Too many of his men had fallen into the same habits he had: using alcohol to numb themselves so they could sleep. If his men were suffering, he would share that, although he had tried to make sure that they did not suffer. He worked them hard from dawn to dusk, strengthening fortifications, building siege engines and patrolling. By nightfall they were exhausted. As for the officers, he had loaded them up with every task he could think of. This meant there was almost nothing for him to do except dread what the night would bring. He poured a goblet of water and drank it slowly, waiting for his heart to slow down and his breathing to return to normal.

'I can't go on like this,' he groaned to himself.

'Captain!'

The familiar call made him leap to his feet, and Sergeant Kesbury was surprised to see his captain already up when he entered the tent a moment later.

'Sir, we've caught a bard trying to sneak past our lines and get back to the south!' Kesbury exclaimed, his face beaming. 'He's a Berellian! Probably the one that performed at Gerrin!'

For the first time in days, a wide smile broke across Martil's face. 'Bring him in — I've been waiting for this!'

Gello was almost beside himself with rage. None had dared go near him until he'd supervised the flogging of one in ten of the men who returned with the news the northeast passes were lost, as well as the execution of any remaining officers and any wounded man judged unable to return to the battleline. He only spared the lives of the others because he needed every man he could get for the coming battle.

When his temper had been soothed a little by watching several painful deaths, he was ready to call in his war captains. But even then, only Ezok dared speak to him.

'My lord King, can I offer my country's deepest sympathies at this setback. As we found to our cost, this Martil is a dangerous, vicious and resourceful enemy.'

Gello ignored the man. He was in no mood to speak to anyone just yet. Why was he surrounded by fools? Did he have to do everything himself around here?

'But, your majesty, I would be remiss not to remind you that I counselled against leaving this Martil alone. As my country knows only too well, he is like a cornered rat, fighting best when his back is against a wall. I suspected—'

This was too much for Gello. 'You suspected he would do this? When no one else did? And now you dare to give me advice?' he roared, leaping off the throne and advancing on Ezok.

But the Berellian did not move, he just offered a short bow and looked Gello in the eye.

'I will give you advice that no other man dares,' he said confidently. 'It is up to your majesty whether you decide to take it.'

That gave Gello pause. Just the fact that Ezok was not frightened of him, seemed prepared to stand up to him in one of his rages, was impressive. Few were prepared to do that. And he was right. Ezok had warned him against leaving Martil alone, said that the Ralloran would do the unexpected, snatch victory from defeat. His own advisers had scoffed at that, had just agreed with him. But if he had listened to the Berellian ... His anger began to drain away.

'My dear Ambassador, you are correct. And I will listen to your advice in the future. As no doubt you have seen, it is a common problem with strong kings such as myself. People are so intimidated by our greatness, they only tell us what we want to hear. Ambassador, you are a brave man and I value that!'

Ezok bowed and smiled. Gello was just like a bully, he reflected. Strong when others allowed him to be but weak when confronted. And this could be turned to Berellia's advantage. Now he was sure his advice would be listened to above the words of even Gello's most trusted men. Excellent. Truly, Onzalez's vision was coming true.

Sister Milly reflected on the resilience of the human spirit. When she had first talked to the servant girls, they had been beaten, abused and ground down. She had met with each one, healing their bodies and offering some support: listening to them talk, explaining to them that it was not their fault, that Prent was wholly to blame for what he had done to them. What she had heard had left her skin crawling. How could you treat another person as an object? Could Prent not realise what he was doing to these young women? Father Nott had spoken to her about the effect power had on certain men, how they came to believe that their position gave them the right to do whatever they wanted.

'That is why we oppose them — because they want Norstalos to act the same way around other countries,' Nott had said.

Milly took comfort from his conviction — and also took comfort from the change she saw in these young women. Rather than looking scared and beaten, the servant girls were defiant and proud as they swapped stories of how Prent had been humiliated in his attempted conquests since she had placed a protective charm on them. Though Milly felt that for some of the girls this was an attempt to prove their toughness not just to each other, but to her. There still had to be deeper feelings for many of them after what they'd been through. She would have liked to work closer with them, try to heal them in spirit as she had in body, but she did not have the time.

Take the bravado of their self-appointed leader, the first girl Milly had healed, who she had learned was called Tiera.

'So he's called three of us in there and when we arrive, he's absolutely starkers, waiting for us. He says: "What do you think of this then?" and, at that moment, your magic works on him again. So while he's looking down, can't see who's saying it, I answer: "I seen a bigger one crawling over the lettuces this morning!"'

The girls all laughed, some more than others.

'He was so shocked, he didn't even punish us for it, just told us to get out of there and not come back!'

Milly smiled, although she noticed there was a shadow behind Tiera's eyes that gave lie to her light-hearted words.

Tiera turned to Milly. 'Sister, tell us what you want us to do.'

Milly took a deep breath. What she was asking them to do could see them dismissed, or lead them to the gallows. But Father Nott had done his part: contacted a man known to be close to Count Sendric, an old priest called Father Quiller. And now she needed to make the other part of the connection, use the powers of the scores of priests and priestesses being held prisoner. Individually, they had been easily captured by Prent but, under the leadership of Declan, they could be a formidable force. These girls were the key to that. She reached into her robe and took out a handful of tiny scrolls.

'You need to give these to as many prisoners as you can,' she said, 'and this is how to do it …'

Merren rode swiftly back to Sendric in an exultant mood. As she reached the shadow of the town's walls, she allowed herself a little self-congratulation. This expedition had gone even better than she dared dream. First there had been the stunning success at Gerrin, then the simple conquest of Berry. Accompanied by Forde, the town council from Gerrin, and Sendric and Wime, she had ridden up to the walls of Berry and shouted that the bards had lied and they were being fooled by Gello. While Baron Berry, a thin, nervous man who, at the Royal Council, had always agreed with the last thing anyone had said, and Gello's officer, a young lieutenant, were arguing about what to do, some of the town's militia, known to both Wime and Forde, opened the gates. At that point Berry and the officer just wanted Merren's promise that they would not be sent back to Gello before they surrendered.

They, along with Bayes and the men captured at Gerrin — once freed from their magical bonds — were being taken north by Rocus and a company of men. The solution of making them work in the mines seemed the best for everyone — they could not spare men to guard them, and the soldiers were terrified of being executed by Gello if they returned to him. The fate of the men injured when Barrett had heated their armour until it burned them was another matter. Barrett had had to use magic to get the twisted metal off their bodies — they would be scarred for life. These men were being sent back to Gello, both as a warning and as a burden to him, although Merren did wonder whether she was sending them to their deaths. She felt guilty about what had been done to those men, and was furious with Barrett for letting it go so far, although the alternative, the deaths of her own men, would have been far worse. She had been only slightly mollified by Barrett's explanation that metal held its heat and, when the capture of the hostages had distracted him, he had lost a little control. She was willing to take responsibility for things done in her name but his claim worried her — she had never seen him lose control before. As far as the people of Gerrin were concerned, the fact the soldiers had been horribly burned was secondary to the hostages being rescued. But how would it look down south, when those men arrived back at their home towns?

Aside from that, there was only good news. Martil

had reported the three passes were all in their hands and Gello had not yet made an attempt to retake them. Capturing the passes had also given them access to more arms and armour, which was important. The two towns, in particular Gerrin, had been enthusiastic about joining the rebellion. Wime and a dozen of his men had stayed behind to help train the new recruits. More than two hundred men had joined up from Gerrin and at least one hundred from Berry. There were not enough arms and armour taken from the defeated soldiers to outfit all the men from Gerrin, so she would have to send wagon-loads of the weapons seized by Martil to the towns, as well as get those red surcoats changed to her colours. As far as food was concerned, the situation looked better. The towns and the surrounding areas had not suffered the depredations of Havrick, so there was plenty of food — in fact, the two towns had stockpiled food in case of siege. So they were able to bring some of that back to Sendric, where only with the help of the local magicians could enough food be grown to feed the town.

Merren was particularly pleased to get so many recruits. Her Norstaline division, which would be under the command of Rocus, had almost doubled in size. Best of all, she had been the one to win them over. She had shown she could lead men. Everywhere she went, people were cheering her. She proved to everyone — not least herself — she was worthy of the crown. Gello's tame bards had not been able to stop her here — if only she could speak to more towns like this, she was sure they would also be won over to her side. Though she still had concerns about how long Martil had before the Dragon Sword started to steal his life …

Her musings were interrupted by the welcoming party that rode out from the town to greet her. She shaded her eyes and saw both Conal and Martil in the group.

'What's he doing back here?' she wondered aloud.

By now, Gello's captains were accustomed to seeing Ezok take a seat next to their King at these war councils. None commented on it, although Livett, Beq and Grissum exchanged careful looks when they saw the map of northern Norstalos that dominated the table.

'Gentlemen, we have a serious problem. That Ralloran dog and his murderers have taken the passes, effectively sealing off the northeast of the country from us.' Gello gestured to the map, where someone had coloured the passes in black. 'We can expect that the towns of Berry and Gerrin will fall also, now that we are unable to help them. Worse, we do not know when my bitch of a cousin might unleash the Rallorans on the rest of the country, or where they might go. She could be planning an attack at any moment!'

'Your majesty, this may not be a problem — we can use it to our advantage to further win over the country. True, we do not know what they are doing in the north, but they are not going to be able to add significant numbers to their army. Even if they did attack, they would be unable to muster more than two thousand men. We could bottle them up with five regiments and, if they do emerge, track them until we can concentrate our men and smash them,' Feld said stolidly. 'That gives us time to train the new recruits further, until we have such a large army there is no possible way they can stand against us.'

The other captains nodded. This was good, sound advice. As far as they could see, it was almost a guarantee of success. No matter how good these Rallorans were, two thousand men could not take on ten thousand or more and hope to win. Given more time, and greater numbers, they could march back into the north with impunity.

Gello scratched his chin and looked at the map.

'Your majesty, if I may?' Ezok asked gently.

'Of course, Ambassador!' Gello immediately said.

'Leaving Martil alone is precisely the thing he wants! It will give him the chance to plot more mischief! As we learned to our cost in the Ralloran Wars, give this twisted criminal time and space and he will use it against you!'

Feld shifted angrily in his seat. As the senior war captain, he was used to his being the only advice accepted. 'But if he's bottled up in the north, how can he do anything? The only way out is through the passes and he cannot gather more men!'

'How do you know he's not going to do anything? Didn't you say he was helpless before? So helpless that he captured those passes and two extra towns! How do you know that he has not sent for help from Rallora? Instead of a thousand of the barbarians, he could have double or triple the number!'

'Thousands of Rallorans would never be able to get this far north!' Feld snorted.

'Really? Like the initial thousand couldn't make it past your patrols?' Ezok fired back.

Feld was outraged to realise Ezok must have been told what had happened at earlier war councils. 'Your majesty!' he appealed.

Gello leaned forwards finally. He always enjoyed watching his supporters squabble amongst themselves.

'Perhaps we should see how far along our training is going. Livett, Beq, Grissum — report now.'

'Training goes well,' Livett began, before his voice choked off a little. He cleared his throat and started again. 'Training goes better than I had hoped. The men are responding well and are eager to fight for Norstalos.'

Beq spoke up next. 'The militia regiment is training strongly. All these men know how to fight, as was shown against our army led by Havrick. Better yet, the rangers are keen to destroy the Rallorans.'

'Good.' Gello nodded. 'Grissum?'

'The archers are ready, sire. As for the criminals, they know how to kill. They are ready to be turned on our enemies now.'

'So we could take them north as soon as possible?' Gello mused.

'Your majesty!' Feld protested. 'Going into battle with a regiment of criminals on our flank is a recipe for disaster! And sending half-trained men against those Rallorans could be a nightmare! This won't be like an open battle, where they can stand at the back, add bulk to the ranks and just watch the experts at work. We'll be assaulting well-defended passes and, after that, walled towns. All our men will lose heart if we are thrown back too often. And those new regiments might be useless for future campaigns if they taste too much defeat.'

'So leave the half-trained men at home! Isn't the Norstaline army the finest in the world? You have thousands of trained men. Surely you can defeat one regiment of Rallorans and a rabble of townsfolk?' Ezok sniffed. Inside, he could barely keep from smiling. This Captain Feld was absolutely right, of course. Captain Martil knew how to conduct a defence of a town. With luck, he could gut half of Gello's troops and leave the Norstaline army a shell, unable to attack Berellia and vulnerable to attack itself.

Gello held up a hand for the debate to stop. He could see some value in both arguments but his greatest fear was to do nothing. He had Norstalos under his thumb — and yet things were slipping out of his grasp. He suddenly wished his mother was here. She always knew what to do. Every time he was confused, she had told him the way forwards. But if she was here, she would be on his throne, she would be accusing him of killing her ... No, he could not think like that! He was a king now and everybody had forgotten the Dragon Sword refusing him! What had happened to his mother had been an accident! He took a deep breath.

'We cannot give this Ralloran and my slut of a cousin any more time than they have had already. This is my throne and they will not take it away from me! It's mine!' He paused for breath, aware that he was sounding a little shrill. 'I want every regular regiment, as well as the militia regiment and the criminals, to form up outside the first pass. The best of the new recruits can be used to make up the numbers we have already lost.'

There was silence around the table; a delighted one from Ezok and a horrified one from the captains.

'Sire, there are many problems with that ...' Feld began.

Gello slammed his fist on the table. 'I have made my decision! I am the King! I will not tolerate failure again! We will assume they will fortify themselves in

Sendric, so we will need supplies for at least a month. Start collecting it now. I want the army at the passes, ready to attack, by the next full moon.'

Gasps echoed around the table as the various captains realised this gave them less than two weeks. Ezok hid his smile carefully.

'You have your orders, gentlemen! To work!'

Ezok stayed just long enough to congratulate Gello on his decision, before hurrying away. He needed to send a report to Brother Onzalez and King Markuz. But he was barely out of the throne room before he bumped into Archbishop Prent.

'Ambassador, I'm so sorry,' Prent said hurriedly.

'No, no, Archbishop, the fault is all mine. Please accept my apologies. Although I must admit, I am glad to have bumped into you. I sent a message requesting an audience with yourself but it must have become misplaced …'

'Not at all, not at all. It's just that I have been … busy. Yes, busy,' Prent mumbled, looking at the floor.

Ezok looked critically at the man. Gone was the arrogance and pride. The man looked as though the weight of the world was upon him. His eyes were darting all over the place and his hands were trembling. A nerve jumped in his cheek every so often. 'Is there anything I can do to help?' he asked carefully.

Prent laughed humourlessly. 'I doubt that. I doubt that very much. This is a problem that is too hard … I mean, it is beyond your help …'

Ezok took the man's arm and steered him carefully to a shadowed corner.

'You might be surprised at what I can do. Although, I suppose, as Aroaril's chosen representative for this country, all you have to do is ask Aroaril for help—'

'Ask Aroaril!' Prent snorted. 'That won't … It's more …'

'I am sorry to hear that.' His heart had jumped at the thought that Prent could not ask Aroaril for help. He looked around carefully and lowered his voice. 'There is an alternative.'

Prent looked up with sudden hope. 'There is?'

Ezok winked. 'Of course. Another way to fix whatever problems you have. A way to appeal to a greater power.'

'A greater power, but I don't …?'

Ezok patted the man on the shoulder. 'Archbishop, I must leave. I am late for an appointment. But I will call by in the next few days to show you what I mean. I guarantee it will solve every problem you have.'

The Archbishop looked up at him with a mixture of hope and fear on his face.

Ezok patted him again and hurried off. It wouldn't do to push the man too much. Let him come to the right conclusion for himself. Besides, he wanted to report the double dose of good news to Onzalez and Markuz. The Archbishop was plainly receiving nothing from Aroaril — no surprise there. But it also seemed he was desperate enough to consider an alternative. Markuz would not care about that, but Onzalez would be overjoyed to think he could pervert the entire church of Aroaril in Norstalos in one stroke.

6

Merren had called a full council meeting for that afternoon to go over the many developments. Martil was not concerned about that, even though he had some important news; he was more interested in seeing Karia. He had arrived back in Sendric just a few turns of the hourglass ahead of the Queen and had had to endure an infuriating wait until Karia returned with Merren.

He wanted the peace that she brought. More than that, she gave him the feeling he was a good man, after all. To have a small child trust him and enjoy being with him … it made him feel better about himself. He could not have explained to anyone else; he just knew she made the dead parts inside his soul come alive.

With her he could forget about being a war captain, forget about the men he had left in the passes, forget about the massive army that was no doubt being assembled now by Gello to strike back — and try to forget about the dream that was waiting for him. It felt like his guilt was growing with every mention of Bellic, and that only made each night's dream worse.

For her part, Karia was delighted to see him. The

last few days had worried her — there had been a distressing lack of attention. Merren had been too busy most of the time, and Barrett had been almost ignoring her, unless Merren was around, then he had been overly kind. Karia did not understand that but she didn't like it. And she could not stop the fear that one day Martil would go away and not come back.

'I don't want to keep leaving you. Why do you keep going off by yourself? Don't you know I miss you?' she demanded.

'Not as much as I miss you,' Martil told her.

Karia nodded her head. That sounded fair enough to her — and more like it. She breathed a little easier. 'So why don't you stay?'

Martil sighed. 'Sometimes I have work to do. I have to do things that take me away from you.'

'But why? Why couldn't you come with us? You should have seen the things I did! I saved Merren by calling down birds, and I helped save some other people by making plants grow, the way I made them grow around Conal that time …'

Martil listened and nodded in the right places. He could feel himself relaxing. After all, if a little girl wanted to be with him, and liked him, he couldn't be as bad as those sagas made him out to be.

When the messenger arrived to summon them to the council meeting, he was reading Karia a saga and was reluctant to go. He made the man wait while he read just one more page.

This meant they were the last to arrive, especially as Martil only just remembered he had to send a message to Kesbury before going into the meeting.

It was obvious they were waiting for him, and Martil was conscious of Barrett's stare as he walked to his seat at the table.

'Now that the captain has decided to honour us with his presence, perhaps we can begin,' Barrett said loudly as Martil sat down, Karia next to him.

Merren cleared her throat and instantly there was silence. 'It has only been a few days since we last met, but there have been great changes. For those who are unaware, Count Sendric, could you outline the success of our efforts to free Gerrin and Berry.'

All eyes turned to Sendric, who described what had happened. When he finished there was much applause from the town council.

'On another note, Lieutenant Rocus should be returning with the gold from the northern mines — gold we can use to further the rebellion and pay the men. Mine production is up, thanks to all the extra workers. It seems they are able to dig almost around the hourglass,' Sendric added. 'This outstanding success is due to the efforts of Queen Merren. As word spreads to the remaining settlements and villages in the north, we expect to bring in even more men — perhaps another company's worth. Now the northeast is ours, with the passes secure, we can look more afield to expand and put further pressure on Gello.'

'It is to decide where we go next that we are here today. To that end, I will ask ...' Merren paused and looked at Martil before deliberately turning away. 'Father Quiller.'

Martil would not have worried about the small snub — he knew she had to make a point after he'd kept her waiting — but the insufferably smug look on Barrett's face made him grit his teeth. However, what came next made him sit up.

'I have been contacted by a priest in the capital. A man known to at least two of those sitting around this table — Father Nott.'

'Father Nott!' Karia squealed, almost jumping off her chair.

Martil's reaction was silent, although no less dramatic. Father Nott! What was he doing? Part of him was delighted to hear the old priest was still alive — and might be able to answer a few questions — while part of him was suddenly terrified that he might want Karia back again.

'This is the priest who is also Karia's grandfather,' Quiller explained.

'How is he? What is he doing?' Karia bounced up and down. 'When can I see him? Did he say he wanted to see me?'

Martil, his throat suddenly feeling uncomfortably tight, tried to make her sit down. 'Let Father Quiller tell us,' he said huskily.

'He is well,' Quiller confirmed. 'Although he did not contact us just to talk about Karia. He and the former secretary to Archbishop Declan, Sister Milly, have been working together against the new Archbishop Prent. They report that scores of priests have been arrested and dragged to the capital for refusing to preach what Gello has ordered — and for still being in Aroaril's good graces. I am afraid the church has been corrupted now. Any of the priests remaining in the villages and towns will be under Prent's control — which means they are under Gello's control. They are telling their flock that the Queen is a bloodthirsty witch with an army of ravening, murdering madmen wreaking havoc on the north and preparing to kill every man, woman and child to the south. The message is almost identical to the one the bards are spreading: we are the monsters, and only by serving Gello can we be stopped. Worse, these so-called priests are telling the people that

Gello is ordained by Aroaril and it is the holy duty of every Norstaline to not just join his army, but to bring Norstaline civilisation to the rest of the world. It is revolting.'

Merren felt the exuberant mood around the table plunge, as if a bucket of icy water had been thrown on their spirits. If the people were hearing this from priests as well as bards — their two most trusted sources — what were the chances they would join the rebellion?

'Did Father Nott have anything positive to say?' Merren asked coolly, forcing her voice to sound unconcerned.

'Yes! Anything about me?' Karia demanded.

Quiller nodded. 'He does send his love to Karia, and he is pleased to know she is still with Martil.'

Martil exhaled with relief.

'Is that it?' Karia huffed.

'He sends a most important message to Queen Merren,' Quiller said gravely. 'He and his helper, Sister Milly, have been in contact with many of the prisoners, including both Bishop Gamelon and Archbishop Declan — they are lightly guarded. Prent is safe in the middle of the capital, and thinks himself impregnable. One old man and a young woman can't manage an escape but, with some help, they could free the prisoners. This could potentially change everything. Once freed ... These are all priests who can use Aroaril's powers. They can not only deal with the guards but also the false Archbishop Prent. Imagine what could happen then. Archbishop Declan still holds enormous respect, while Bishop Gamelon is well known in the east of the country. With the priests freed and restored to their parishes, we could potentially turn the whole east of the country against Gello. The west is his stronghold, Gello is too well-known there. But the east of the country has always suffered poorly in comparison. The priests could help us win them back to our side. Imagine that! We're talking about scores of farming villages, half-a-dozen towns of which the largest is Wollin — thousands of potential recruits. We could even meet Gello on equal terms!'

The mood around the table lifted again. Fresh from seeing two northern towns join their side, they could see the whole east of the country rise for the Queen.

'And how do we achieve that? After all, Prent is within the capital,' Merren pointed out.

Quiller gestured to Barrett. 'With the skills of the Queen's Magician, of course. I know of the proper concerns about travelling to the capital to try to kill Gello. But this is a different situation. Prent is almost unguarded, and the mission is to free allies, all of whom are powerful in their own right. With a small group of elite warriors, they could free the prisoners and leave before Gello even knew what was happening. My Queen, this is literally a gift from Aroaril! With one stroke, we could change the course of the war! We have gathered here to decide our next move. This is it!'

Merren stayed silent for a few moments, judging the reaction from the men around the table. Excitement and anticipation was the main feeling — even Barrett seemed interested. Only Martil was not joining the general approval.

'Captain — it is obvious you have concerns. Share them with us,' she said loudly.

All eyes turned to Martil, who had indeed been looking unhappy, although it was more to do with

Karia's enthusiasm about Father Nott. It took him a few moments to gather his thoughts.

'I don't believe this is the best use of our efforts and time,' he said finally. 'We are asked to risk some of our best men to rescue priests who cannot even guarantee us a single recruit! Do we truly believe that half the country will rise against Gello and join us, just because their priest tells them to? And even if they were somehow able to gather men to our cause, what are we to do with them? Scattered across dozens of villages and towns between here and the Tetran border, how are we to organise them, arm them, train them?'

'I see what you mean,' Barrett agreed. 'Why, we might as well depend on the Dragon Sword to bring men in!'

'And what's that supposed to mean?' Martil snarled.

Barrett stared at him. 'You are the Dragon Sword wielder. By now, there should be a steady stream of men flocking to us, drawn by the Sword's latent magic. But it's not working for you — you're not really good enough. So we have to try something else.'

'This is not—' Merren began but did not get the chance to finish the sentence.

Martil locked eyes with Barrett and tried hard not to imagine punching the mage's insufferable face. 'As it happens, I have another suggestion. A much better one. Sergeant Kesbury!'

The doors to the audience chamber opened and the powerful sergeant appeared, hauling a bedraggled figure with him.

'Who is that?' Barrett exclaimed.

'A chair for our guest.' Martil waved and a Ralloran soldier followed Kesbury in, carrying a stout wooden chair. Everyone turned to watch the Ralloran place the chair in front of the empty fireplace, where all could see it. Grunting a little, Kesbury dumped his captive into the chair, then stood behind the man. The prisoner was not a pretty sight. His face was bruised and bloodied, while his clothes, the traditional bardic costume of red tunic and yellow trews, were also stained with blood and dirt. His hands, which he held gingerly in front of him, were misshapen, many of the fingers twisted and broken.

'I don't like this,' Karia whispered, averting her pale face from the bard and burrowing into Martil.

'Look what you're doing to her!' Barrett cried.

'It's all right, he's a very bad man.' Martil ignored Barrett and spoke only to Karia. 'Would you like to wait outside?'

'No, I want to stay with you.'

'Who is this? What is the meaning of this?' Merren demanded.

'My Queen, this is why I have returned. This is the Berellian bard who performed Gello's lies in Gerrin and Berry, telling them that you would do anything to seize back your throne. We caught him trying to escape south and, after a little persuasion, he told us some very interesting information, which we can use to our advantage.'

'But look at him! What happened?' Barrett gasped.

'It looks like he viciously attacked Martil with his face. Several times,' Conal said dryly.

'And his hands?'

'We had to make him talk.' Martil shrugged. 'And now this liar will not be able to play the lyre for a few months. It is no loss.'

'But you can't do that to prisoners!' Barrett growled.

'Would you prefer I put him in a suit of armour and call you over to burn him?' Martil flared back.

'How dare you! I was trying to save lives, not torture a helpless man!'

'Why don't you tell that to the men being shipped back to Gello in a cart? Men who were still screaming when they went through the passes! We need the information that man had and I made sure we got it!'

'Enough!' Merren thundered, and Barrett, who had been about to fire back another barbed comment, subsided.

'Martil, let us hear what this man has to say, then we can decide whether it was worth torturing him for. I understand how you must feel about the Berellians and the lies this bard has been spreading but, as we have said before, the Dragon Sword expects more of its wielder.'

Martil acknowledged her rebuke, but he did not regret beating the man. It was his fault the dreams had come back. His fault the whole country hated him. These Berellians were evil, and they deserved everything they got. He could not feel a shred of sympathy for the bastard.

'Tell the Queen what you told me,' he instructed the bard.

The man just sat there, cradling his hands in his lap.

'Show some respect to the Queen or I'll show you the colour of your own guts!' Kesbury yelled at him, giving him a slap over the head at the same time.

'And they wonder where the Ralloran reputation

for brutality came from.' The voice that came out of the bleeding, bruised man seemed impossibly silver, smooth and rich, rolling across the room so that everyone could hear it.

He threw his head back and stared directly at the Queen, before letting his gaze sweep across the table. He started to rise, but Kesbury grabbed him by the shoulder and forced him back into the chair.

'Let me stand, curse you! Am I to be made to sit like a dog? If I am to speak, then I will do so on my feet, as a man should.'

'Let him stand. But I warn you, bard, this is not a performance. I want to hear the truth. Tell me what you know and I promise you will not be harmed any more,' Merren said sternly.

The bard slowly stood and, when Kesbury made no further move to stop him, offered a deep and elaborate bow.

'Your majesty, allow me to introduce myself. I am Warnock, member of the Berellian Council of Bards and twice winner of the Bardic World Championships—'

'I didn't know there was a world championship for bards,' Conal interrupted.

'Only Berellians are allowed to enter,' Martil said sourly.

'Do you want me to talk or not? If so, pray refrain from interrupting!' Warnock said dramatically.

'Get on with it,' Kesbury hissed.

Warnock held up his broken hands. 'I have been shown only too well the penalty for not co-operating with your Ralloran barbarians, your majesty,' he announced. 'So here is what I said to them. Doubtless they could have informed you but wished instead to parade their handiwork to you, much like small, ignorant children want to show their mothers a crude painting they have done.'

Kesbury made a rumbling noise in his throat.

'You can talk to us, but I would advise you to stop the insults. You are not in a position to make them, and if you wish to earn my protection, you need to persuade me you are worthy of it,' Merren told him sharply. She had not wanted to see him tortured but this was the man who had been spreading lies about her and inciting her own people to turn on her.

Warnock bowed once more. 'Your majesty, please accept my humblest apologies. The pain from my wounds has made me forget my manners. I was sent to Norstalos, along with many of my brethren, because King Gello requested our presence—'

'*King* Gello? He is not worthy of the title!' Barrett sniffed.

Merren waved him to silence and, after a pause and a disdainful look at Barrett, Warnock continued.

'He wanted to hear the Berellian version of the Saga of Bellic. It seems he felt the saga traditionally performed by his own bards was not providing the full truth to the people. Thus he asked myself and my colleagues to perform this saga to as many people as possible. Your own bards, poor performers that they are, were also given the true saga to recite, as well as the news that King Gello wanted spread to the people. I was sent north, to speak to the towns of Gerrin and Berry, before your Rallorans had a chance to destroy them.'

'I can assure you, the towns are both alive and well — and grateful to be free from Gello,' Merren told him forcefully.

'Ah yes, your majesty, but was it the Rallorans that freed them? I think not. Had they broken through the walls, then the story might be quite different.' Warnock smiled.

'I see little here that is as important as the news we learned earlier …' Merren began.

'Tell her, bard,' Martil ordered.

'Do you mean the news about the rest of the Butchers of Bellic being dead, and you being the only person responsible for that massacre still alive?' Warnock said slyly.

Kesbury drew back his fist but Martil held up his hand and Kesbury stopped.

'Is this true? The rest of them are dead?' Merren asked.

'Thankfully. Only one such murderer remains …' Warnock began but felt Kesbury's hand on the back of his neck and subsided.

'Martil, did you know about this before?' Merren asked.

'It's not important.' Martil shrugged it off. 'I haven't seen any of the other men since … since that day. Anyway, bard, get to the interesting part.'

'What you see as interesting, and what I think is interesting, are, happily, two quite different things,' Warnock said grandly but then Kesbury jabbed him in the back, and he continued.

'King Gello has had us performing to his new recruits, in particular two regiments he has high hopes for. The first is a regiment of militiamen. After the successful use of militia against his own forces, King Gello saw the potential in these men. The second is a regiment of criminals. Killers by vocation, it is hoped they can counter the murderous Rallorans that they will face. Finally, the bards are performing to both the rangers and the archers, showing these loyal Norstalines that their best hope lies with joining King Gello to resist the ravages of the vicious Rallorans. Now we are taking these a step further. To help persuade the regiments, the bards will be backed by a speech from the Lord of Bellic himself, the sole survivor of that hideous massacre upon an innocent …'

'Shut up!' Kesbury bawled at him.

'This is the interesting part,' Martil said urgently, producing a set of scrolls. 'Here are the scrolls we took off this bard. One is the saga, that is unimportant. The second is the news that Gello wants read out, that is also unimportant. But the third is a list of places to be visited by the Lord of Bellic. In two days' time he will go to the ranger barracks and meet with them to help ensure their loyalty. Even better, he will be accompanied by a Norstaline bard. Warnock admitted that the soldiers do not want to hear sagas from Berellians, so they have to use Norstalines on their own soldiers. Better again, it seems some of these Norstaline bards are performing not for love of gold or Gello, but because they are threatened with imprisonment or worse if they do not behave!

'My Queen, you see the possibilities here. We can get to these barracks, get rid of the Lord of Bellic and win over an entire regiment of men! Meanwhile, we can find a Norstaline bard, perhaps even bring him back here, allow him to see what we are doing. Then we can start making appearances of our own at villages around the country! Imagine that — Barrett's powers allow you, me and the bard to appear at a village. He performs the saga he has written about your New Norstalos, you inspire the village with a quick speech and we could return with fifty recruits!' Although Martil wanted the Lord of

Bellic, wanted to catch and kill him so badly he could taste it, he doubted Merren would agree to a plan with the Lord's death as its aim. But if he could dangle the bait of a regiment of loyal men, as well as a bard who could sing her praises, surely that would appeal to her. He added one last temptation. 'The rangers — were they not your regiment?'

Merren leaned back in her chair. 'They are — or were — known as the Queen's Rangers, and from their ranks were drawn the Royal Guard. They will be still commanded, possibly, by Kay, the man who was my guard captain.' She tried to keep her excitement from showing; the idea of appearing in a different village each day, using her own bard to win over the people and bring them back to the safety of the north ... But she had learned from bitter experience over the years not to rush into a decision. Something that was presented as a wonderful idea often turned out to be something worse. She decided to give herself some time to think about it. 'Yes, this regiment is traditionally loyal to the crown but they did not stop Gello when he took over the palace ...'

'How could they? Against a full company of heavy cavalry? They would have been massacred! But now there is the chance to bring them over to our side. An entire regiment of men. And they are bowmen — I tell you, a thousand bowmen and we can hold those passes for years against Gello!' Martil's face was alight with enthusiasm. 'Meanwhile you can win over the rest of the country, using Barrett's skills and a bard!'

'But how do we get them back? I cannot open a gateway for one thousand men — it is not possible,' Barrett argued, although not as strongly as he might.

After all, the Ralloran oaf was actually giving him due credit.

'We march them back. They're rangers, after all. They can split up into companies and re-form at the passes.' Martil dismissed the wizard's question. 'Just think — we arrive just as the bard is preparing to tell his lies to the rangers. You tell them the truth, show them Forde and Wime and whoever's in charge from Berry and we take out the Lord of Bellic, who is obviously the man they are relying on to turn men to their side. Our army is doubled at one stroke!'

'You cannot attack the Lord of Bellic! If you do that —' Warnock shouted, then stopped suddenly.

'You see, the bard is against this plan. This tells me I am right!'

'But the risk is great. What if the men do not turn? Many of the officers will be Gello's men. And what if there are guards with this Lord of Bellic?' Merren pondered aloud.

'Of course there will be guards, but with myself, Sergeant Kesbury and his squad, we can take care of any Berellians they have brought along for protection. As to the rangers — isolate the officers and the men will just sit there. It is risky but the prize is worth it! When we first met you told me yourself, Barrett, that the rangers are loyal to the Queen and not trusted by Gello.' Martil decided to appeal to the wizard. He had complimented the man, the least Barrett could do was offer his support.

'Is that right?' Barrett asked Warnock, not wanting to put his seal of approval on a plan from Martil just yet. Especially as Merren seemed a little unsure …

'Why are you asking him? He's a lying Berellian!' Martil protested. Could the wizard do nothing right?

Warnock stared disdainfully at Martil. 'Even a simpleton could see that the Lord of Bellic is only being asked to speak to these men because they need more reassurance than a bard alone can provide. But I would not expect a Ralloran to understand —'

'Shut up, you filthy little liar!' Kesbury only restrained himself from hitting Warnock with great difficulty, instead giving the man a warning shove.

Merren held up her hands.

'So we have a choice. We can try and free the true Archbishop, as well as the loyal priests, then use them to inspire people to join us, or we attack a bard and some Berellian Lord, with a full regiment of rangers and, perhaps, a bard as the prize. After all, the bard we capture might be one of those eager to help Gello in return for gold. But what then? Even if we have an extra thousand men, are we ready to take on Gello?'

'Well, obviously not,' Martil admitted, 'but those thousand bows will buy us plenty of time to win over more to our cause.'

'How? Through the Dragon Sword — the one that's not working, nor is likely to work any time soon?' Barrett sneered.

'Through the bard we rescue, as I have been saying!' Martil exclaimed.

'The bard that probably won't want to have anything to do with us?'

'Good to see you two are able to work together so well,' Conal commented dryly.

There were a few chuckles at that, although not from Barrett or Martil.

'We are not getting anywhere with this,' Merren said heavily. 'I would like you all, now, to give me an indication which plan you want to pursue. I will think about it and we will meet again tomorrow to decide. I don't think this bard needs to be here to find out what our plans are. Sergeant, please take him down to the cells. But first, Father Quiller, could you see to his wounds?'

Quiller nodded. 'Of course, your majesty. There is no need to let him suffer further.'

The old priest walked across to where Warnock sat, then closed his eyes and placed his hand on the man's shoulder.

'Don't touch me, you old charlatan! What do you creatures want to do to me now?' Warnock shrieked, jerking away from Quiller.

'I will not hurt you, my son,' Quiller said gently.

'Well, I don't want your help! I will take these wounds back to my country and show them what sort of people the Norstalines are. You are quick to tell everyone how wonderful you are, how powerful, how blessed — and then you do this to unarmed men!' Warnock waved his hands, each with three broken fingers.

'Father, heal him and be done with it,' Merren said urgently. She had no desire to have so-called proof of her brutality peddled around Berellia.

'Stay away from me!' Warnock tried to avoid Quiller but Kesbury leaned forwards and held him in place.

'What are you doing to me! Leave me alone!' Warnock's voice held a true note of panic.

Several of those around the table, including Barrett and Merren, turned away from the sight of his fear but Martil stared closely. The man he had interrogated had been stubbornly defiant and barely even made a noise when Kesbury had broken six of his fingers. It was only when he was told his index fingers and thumbs would be next to go — completely ruining his ability to play the lyre — that he had begun to talk. Even then there had been no fear.

'I beseech thee, Aroaril, grant me the power to heal this man,' Quiller intoned softly, laying a hand on Warnock's shoulder.

Karia was watching intently. Magic of all types fascinated her, and she had always liked to see Father Nott perform his healing magic. But nothing seemed to be happening.

'What's going on? Should he ask a bit louder?' she asked Martil, in a quiet voice that penetrated across the silent room.

Quiller stepped away from Warnock, who was cringing away from him.

'Is that it? May I leave now?' the bard asked nervously.

'What happened? He has not been healed,' Merren said.

Quiller gazed down at the man with a mixture of pity and revulsion. 'It seems He does not think you are worthy of healing.' The old priest shrugged. 'I suggest we call a healer, who can splint the fingers and prepare a poultice for the bruises.'

Warnock looked up at him in disgust. 'I told you to leave me alone. But did you listen? Now let me leave this den of torturers and brutes.'

Quiller's face hardened. 'Take him away, Sergeant. Put him in a secure cell.'

'My pleasure, Father.' Kesbury nodded, grabbed Warnock by the collar and hustled him away.

Martil caught a glimpse of the bard's face: it wore a look of relief and fear. It was so strange he almost commented on it. But nobody spoke until the door shut behind the pair of them.

Quiller took his seat with a deep sigh. 'This, as much as anything else, tells me we need to rescue the Archbishop. It is rare for Aroaril not to grant me the power to heal. The only thing I can think of is that the man has come into contact with dark powers. There have been rumours that the Berellians, or at least King Markuz and his top officials, have been dabbling with worship of Zorva. This bard may have been in contact with them. That Gello has chosen such as these as his allies is of deep concern to me. If Gello has made a deal with Berellia, then he has as good as made a deal with the Dark One and we shall need the church to protect us. Aroaril is always careful with the power He grants His priests and priestesses but the Dark God has no such qualms. If, Aroaril forbid, a Fearpriest gets on the loose here … I feel we must act fast. The priests of the Dark God are able to wield enormous power. Even the likes of Barrett may not be able to stand against them.'

'Come now! You can't be serious!' Barrett smiled. 'No man alive can match me at magic!'

'Really? When the man you are facing does not have to worry about using his own energy? Every sacrifice to their foul god that they make — and believe me, they are always covered in gore — gives them power. The magic released by that person's death is available for them to use however they want. How can you fight that?'

Barrett leaned back silently in his chair though his posture and expression conveyed he was still supremely confident of besting a Fearpriest in magical combat.

'Should we not call the bard back, question him further on this?' Martil demanded. He could feel the mood of the room turning back; any sympathy for Warnock after Quiller's failure to heal him had vanished.

'I do not want to see that poor soul tortured further. I will pray on this, but I think it would be better to wait until we have the Archbishop back with us before I talk to the bard. Meanwhile, he can do us no harm while locked in a cell.'

'Then I take it your vote is for rescuing the Archbishop,' Merren said calmly.

'It is, your majesty. I apologise for making such a strong statement —'

'No, it is the sort of argument I want to hear. Now, are there are any others?'

'Before we vote, I want to remind everyone what an extra thousand bowmen means to this rebellion,' Martil said immediately. 'Father Quiller's argument is persuasive, but it misses one vital point: we can rescue the Archbishop at any time. We have one chance, and one chance only, to get rid of the man who is spreading lies about us down south, and at the same time win over a full regiment of troops to our side. Once we have done that, we can go after the Archbishop. We can travel around to other towns and villages, sowing the seeds of rebellion around the country. If the bard we capture along with the Lord of Bellic will not help us, then we find one who will! We can do all that, because we will be protected. I know I have disappointed people, by not being able to unlock the latent magic of the Dragon Sword. But this could give me the time I need! With the rangers, and the Rallorans, those passes will be impregnable. You and your families will be safe. But if we go after the Archbishop first, everything we have won is under threat.'

He looked around the table and saw, with satisfaction, that his argument had struck a chord with many of the others. It made sense, he told himself. That his plan put off seeing Father Nott again and ensured he would get more time with Karia was purely coincidental.

'A show of hands. For rescuing the Archbishop?' Merren looked around the table.

Quiller and Barrett were the only ones who raised their hands.

'I take it the rest of you are for Martil's plan?' she inquired and, when nobody disagreed, she stood.

'There is much to think about here. We shall meet again tomorrow morning and I shall make my decision. In the meanwhile, I would invite you all to join me for dinner this night. With both Gerrin and Berry in our hands, it seems the good townsfolk have kindly sent us a few barrels of wine, in exchange for the swords and armour we sent to them.'

'Well, I'll drink to that deal!' Conal said loudly, as he knew he was expected to.

The meeting relaxed then. Martil used the confusion to slip out with Karia.

'Let's go and play some catch,' he suggested.

'Of course!'

Warnock stayed on his straw pallet until the brutish Ralloran sergeant had bolted the door and left. It took a while for his heart to stop pounding. When that damned priest had tried to help him, he had been terrified. The man could have ruined everything, revealed the full truth. But he had managed to escape the priest's aid, a fact he put down to divine protection. Once he had control of himself again, he looked around. Down here there were no other prisoners, for which he was particularly grateful. The cells were solid stone, with thick wooden doors. The air was foul, a combination of human waste, mould and stale food. But he ignored that. By the standards of most dungeons, it was almost palatial. A large bucket in the corner, a jug of water and a bowl and a straw bed. He got up from his pallet and went around the cell's corners, gathered as many cobwebs as he could and placed them in a small ball on the bed. He listened at the door. Once he was sure he was alone, he drank his small, shallow bowl of water and used his teeth to rip off a small strip of his tunic. Carefully, grunting a little with pain from his broken fingers, he worked open a seam in the tunic and, with great difficulty, he eased out a small, sharp blade. Putting it aside, he placed the empty bowl on the bed and used the blade to make a nick in a vein on his wrist. Holding his arm over the bowl, he hissed with discomfort as blood dripped into it. He did not hinder the flow until the base was covered, then stuffed the little bundle of cobwebs into the cut and used the strip of tunic to tie a crude bandage over the wound. Turning back to the bowl, he whispered the secret name of Brother Onzalez.

The blood whirled into motion, resolving itself into the hooded face of the Fearpriest.

'They will take the bait,' Warnock stated. 'The trap is too tempting for them to avoid. But they are also thinking of trying to free their Archbishop.'

Onzalez was silent for a few heartbeats. 'You have done fine work. Your bravery and sacrifice will be rewarded. We shall try to free you but you must say nothing more. If they come for you …'

'Then I have my blade — and I shall see you in Zorva's blessed realm.' Warnock bowed.

'Until then, my son.'

When Warnock raised his head, the blood in the bowl was gone, as was the image of Onzalez. The bard lay back on the bed, unable to keep the smile of triumph from his face. His tormentors would suffer — and the greater glory of Zorva would be brought closer.

7

Merren found Martil and Karia playing in a quiet corner of the keep's courtyard. Karia was hurling a leather ball at Martil, who was tossing it gently back; she was laughing uproariously every time she managed to throw it far enough away that he could not catch it.

'Mind if I join in?' Merren called.

'Catch!' Karia did not hesitate and hurled the leather ball, about half the size of her head, at the Queen. Merren had not had much time for playing catch as a child — her father had been more insistent she work on economics and law. She reached out instinctively — and the ball flew past her fingers to bounce off her forehead. Her head snapped back and she reeled away, her forehead stinging.

'Merren! Are you all right?' Martil sprinted to her side and prised her fingers away to see a red mark the size of his fist on her head, just below the hairline. He looked over to where Karia stood, shuffling her feet. 'You need to say sorry.'

'But it was an accident!' Karia protested. 'She asked me to throw it!'

Martil shook his head. With a sinking feeling, he recognised the expression on Karia's face. He did not want a fight with her, but he had never backed down from a fight before and he wasn't about to start.

He was saved by Merren, who picked up the ball.

'I'm fine. Really I am. It was just an accident,' she said, bouncing the ball.

'Are you sure you're all right?' Martil asked anxiously.

'I'm fine,' Merren insisted. 'Here — you catch!' Merren tossed the ball at Karia, except it soared high over her head.

'Bad throw! Bad throw!' Karia sang out.

'Well, I don't play catch very much,' Merren admitted, feeling a touch of irritation nevertheless. But as she had a serious motive for joining their game, she swallowed any angry words.

'You'll have to get Martil to teach you. He's very good at it — nearly as good as me, although because I'm younger, when I get older, I'll be better than him,' Karia explained, fetching the ball.

'Then you'd better show me,' Merren said with a laugh.

Martil had not had a chance to be alone with Merren since the battle of Sendric — Barrett had been hanging around like a bad smell, and he always seemed to be inventing ways to get Martil sent out of the town.

'It's pretty easy,' Martil said. 'Throw me the ball first.'

Karia tossed him the ball and he caught it with one hand, unable to resist showing off a little.

'Hold your hands out in front, waist height, then move your hands to the ball as it comes to you,' he instructed Merren, throwing the ball gently to her.

Merren moved her hands automatically as the ball

lobbed in her direction, and they closed around the ball, just before it landed in her stomach.

'Yay! Good catch!' Karia applauded. 'Sorry about my throw earlier.'

'That's fine.' Merren smiled. 'So how do I throw better?'

'Practice. And always point your hand where you want the ball to go,' Martil suggested.

Merren tried but the ball fell short, and to the left.

'Bad throw! Bad throw! Have another go!' Karia sang. 'Martil, you have to show her like you showed me!'

Merren raised an eyebrow, and tried not to flinch at the pain from her forehead. 'You must!'

Martil collected the ball, then handed it to Merren.

'Hold it in your right hand, like this,' he said, standing behind her.

'Closer, Captain, I want to get this right,' Merren insisted.

Martil stepped close behind her and could not help but inhale the light lemon scent of her hair. A lock of it was curling over her ear and he had to force himself to concentrate on the task in hand, rather than brushing it back for her. He took her hand in his, drawing back her arm to make the throw to Karia, who was jumping from foot to foot with impatience.

'Is my stance correct?' Merren asked innocently.

'Feet at about shoulder width, well balanced,' Martil found himself saying.

Merren shifted her right foot across a little, so her hip was now brushing against his.

'Like this?'

Martil's brain, even in its fevered state, could not help but think that she was playing some game —

and it had nothing to do with catch. She had to have some idea of the effect she was having on him. But Karia was over there, bouncing around, waiting for her throw.

'Very good. Now draw back the arm, release the ball at the bottom of the swing, not too high, and finish with your hand pointing towards the target …'

Martil found himself gabbling the instructions, then watching as Merren, with him guiding her hand, completed a perfect throw to Karia.

'Good throw!' Karia applauded. 'See? He's a really good teacher!'

'So, do you feel comfortable about trying it by yourself now?' Martil found himself reluctant to let go of Merren's hand, which would mean breaking contact with her.

Merren smiled at him. 'I think so. But I'll let you know if I need some more instruction.' She eased carefully away from him. It was all too obvious that something was going on with Martil. She needed to know what was the matter with him, and if she could solve it. She'd ensured Father Quiller was keeping Barrett occupied in order to see Martil without other distractions. Despite all the talk of rescuing archbishops and recruiting regiments of rangers, she felt the Dragon Sword was still the key to eventual victory. She had been able to help him before, in the caves, and again after the battle of Sendric. Perhaps a little flirting and charming could help him again. Men were essentially simple creatures, she thought, although Martil appeared to be one of the more complex ones. But his interest in her — she was not keen to acknowledge it as anything more than a fascination just yet — and his obvious love for Karia seemed a constant.

Reminding him of that was her best move, she decided.

Throwing and catching a ball with them was surprisingly relaxing. She had to concentrate — the slowly receding pain in her forehead reminded her of that — but Karia's laugh, as well as her habit of occasionally using magic to try and trick Martil into dropping the ball, made it impossible not to enjoy. Her worries melted away and she wondered why she did not try to spend more time with Karia. It was the ideal counterpoint to the stress of ruling and running a rebellion. Karia's ability to find pleasure in simple things was infectious. Merren had to force herself to remember why she was doing this.

'I need a break!' she declared, after making a particularly difficult catch. 'Karia, how about you run down to the kitchens and ask them to bring us something to eat and drink?'

Karia, always eager for the opportunity to eat something, was off in a flash.

'Here you are, Captain, catch this.' Merren laughed as she threw the ball as hard as she could at him.

Martil caught it deftly, as he had caught all but the most magically bewitched throws to him, and walked over towards her.

'Is there something you want to ask me, Merren?' he said quietly.

'What makes you think that?' she replied innocently.

'Well, you're too busy to do anything but work usually — and you have to make a final decision that could make or break this rebellion — so instead you want to learn how to catch. That could mean that learning to catch has been your secret ambition all

these months — or that you are worried about me.'
He shrugged.

Merren smiled. 'Then you would be right.
Whatever we might plan up there in that room,
unless you can unlock the Dragon Sword's magic, we
are doomed to spend the next fifteen years fighting a
bitter civil war from which Norstalos may never
recover. And, long before then, you will be dead. I
watched that Sword kill my father — I don't want to
lose my Champion.'

'True — where would you find another?'

Merren sighed. 'I don't want another. And I don't
want to see you die. So tell me, what is ripping you
up inside? Is it being the last Butcher of Bellic? I
know you have always felt responsible but to be the
last one, to be the sole survivor, the focus of Gello's
campaign …'

Martil walked away, unable to talk about it. What
would she think of him if he told her the full truth?

Merren followed him. She had had success with
him through physical contact; it broke down the
barriers he was putting up. The strong, powerful war
captain, immune to pain and indefatigable. She knew
that was just the shell and he needed someone to talk
to, he was just unable to say it. How like a man. She
grabbed him by the upper arm and made him turn
around, then stepped close, so their bodies were
almost touching. She could not help but reflect that
this was the sort of thing her tutors had never offered
lessons in. Her father would never have dreamed of
trying to deal with his advisers like this. But then
look what happened to him. She reached up to touch
Martil's face.

'Talk to me. That is a Royal Command,' she said
softly.

Martil's face seemed to crumple at her touch.

'Bellic,' he said simply.

'But surely you don't listen to the lies that bard and his ilk are peddling? Everyone here knows the truth of what happened — the rest of the country will soon understand as well.'

Martil shook his head. 'It's not that simple. The dreams — every night I dream of Bellic.' He took a deep, shuddering breath. How much could he say? Would she still be interested in him? He could not take the risk. He would tell her a little, but no more. 'The people at Gerrin brought it back. Since then, I have been tormented by dreams. I thought — I hoped — that being with Karia would help them stop. She stopped them before. Although they weren't as bad then ...'

Merren felt frustrated. He was holding something back, she could feel it.

'What can we do to help you?' she asked, to give herself time to think. How far could she go to get through to him?

Martil shrugged. 'I hope being with Karia will help me. But one thing is to give me the chance to go after the Lord of Bellic. He's the man who sent troops over the border to murder innocent Ralloran villagers. He's the one who refused to surrender the killers, who forced his people to fight on for so long that when they finally wanted to give up, it was too late. If I can take him, it will be like lifting a weight from my shoulders. He was the one really responsible for all those deaths. I cannot believe he managed to escape from us. I thought nobody had survived ...'

'So the rangers aren't really the prize for you, the prize is killing this Berellian?' Merren moved fractionally away from him, not thinking about his feelings now but more about the decision that waited for her.

'The rangers are the prize,' Martil argued, 'the Berellian is just the cream on top of the cake.'

Merren looked at him sceptically. 'And you are sure of that? Capturing this Berellian will help end those dreams and put you back on the path to becoming a man good enough to truly use all the Sword's power?'

Martil looked into her eyes and remembered his pledge to serve her truthfully at all times. Then he thought about the dreams waiting to haunt his sleep that night.

'I think so, yes,' he said. 'So will you let me go after the rangers before the Archbishop?'

Merren thought frantically. There was truth here — but was it all the truth? And was it enough to risk going deep into the south?

She was saved from answering by Karia returning at a run.

'Come on! They're baking cakes down in the kitchen, if we hurry, we can have them warm out of the oven — and there's fresh milk as well!' she exclaimed.

'In a little while.' Martil tried to slow her down, but she simply grabbed his hand and dragged him along.

'You too, Merren! It'll be a picnic for the three of us!'

Merren followed. She was not sure what she had achieved — certainly not as much as she hoped. There was a problem there, something deep within Martil that was still unresolved. She had got the information about the Lord of Bellic but was unsure if it would alter her thinking — after all, going after the rangers still seemed the better option.

Martil looked longingly at Merren's back. When she had stepped in close to him, he had wanted to take her in his arms, tell her everything. But fear had held him back. It was ironic, really. He could face battle without flinching but, when it came to telling a woman how he really felt, he would rather lie. But the risk of her rejecting him was too great. Fighting was easier. After all, there were worse things than death.

Nerrin peered down at the scores of soldiers working on the plains below the line of hills. The size of the camp they were marking out seemed enormous. He had not seen something that big for years. At a rough guess, there were going to be tent lines, fire pits and latrines for more than ten thousand men.

'You're right,' he told Sergeant Dunner, an old comrade from Macord's division and a friend of Kesbury's. 'It looks like they're bringing up every man they have. Even if we concentrated at one pass, they'd still be able to break through. We'll have to get word to the captain. Keep watching them; I want to know which regiments are coming in, and in what order.'

'Aye, sir.' Dunner looked again at the massive camp. 'Will we take them on, sir?'

Nerrin smiled. 'Nothing to worry about, Sergeant. We've still got the captain! After all, remember Mount Shadar!'

'Aye, sir.'

Dunner waited until Nerrin had hurried away before adding under his breath, 'And I remember the casualty list from his regiment afterwards.'

'It's too nice to stay inside — why don't we go out?' Karia suggested. 'You can give me a piggy back!'

So Martil found himself carrying her out on his back.

'Not too tight,' he grunted, as her arms tightened around his neck.

'I just want to hug you,' she declared, snuggling into his back. 'I love you, Daddy.'

Martil found he could not reply. His throat was tight, and it had nothing to do with the grip she had around him.

He walked slowly through the keep's corridors, with Karia excitedly waving to anyone she saw.

'Come on, faster!' she urged.

'But we have to be careful,' he protested.

'Faster! We'll be fine! You're invincible!' she told him with utter certainty. Nothing could happen to her when he was around.

Martil glanced over his shoulder to see her smile at him, total trust in her eyes. He grinned back at her.

'Hold on!' he said and was off, running down the corridor, deliberately swerving towards decorative pillars, taking steps two at a time and laughing as Karia squealed with delight and clutched on tighter.

'Faster!' she cheered.

They burst out into the sunlight and Karia slid from his back. Puffing a little, but laughing, he followed her into the small kitchen garden.

The afternoon seemed to go on forever. Martil felt like a prisoner released from a dark cell. Everything just melted away — his fears, his guilt — around her it disappeared like mist before the sun. It was a feeling that was worth all the money he had and could ever have. Yes, she could be occasionally annoying but, for a time like this, it was more than worth it. Whether telling stories, playing games or just walking and talking through the kitchen garden, he felt happier than he had in years — it was almost as if he was a child again, through her, with nothing but a bright future and boundless optimism ahead of him. It just felt so good.

Karia revelled in that glorious afternoon. The sun was shining, she was wanted and loved; she was having so much fun, making him laugh and laughing at him. It was perfect. She knew that afternoon would stay in her memory forever. She did not want it to end, and was excited when he suggested they eat dinner in her room, rather than in the audience chamber, where the Queen would preside over the evening meal. Karia thought this was great — she hated having to sit still and quiet at the table while the adults chatted endlessly — boring! And the food always took too long to arrive. The kitchen staff were only too pleased to oblige, having been thoroughly charmed by Karia, and witnessing first-hand how Martil had fought to save them and their families.

So it was a natural extension for Martil to suggest, after they had eaten, that they have a sleepover in her room that night. Part of this was his plan for Karia to keep away the bad dreams, but part was simply not wanting to be without her. She could make him laugh, as nobody since Borin or Tomon had.

Again, Karia thought this sounded just fine. She liked having her own room, with plenty of space for the dolls, but the bed was too big, and the keep made strange noises at night. Plus she felt she didn't get enough sagas read to her, nor songs sung to her. With Martil right there, he would have no excuse for not singing just one more song. And perhaps she would not feel so lonely.

So it proved. After three sagas — including her favourite one about the many princesses who loved to dance every night — two renditions of his 'go to sleep' song and much hair brushing, she reluctantly fell asleep, clutching Dolly.

Martil was exhausted by now — and lying in an awkward position, on his side, squashed up on the edge of the bed with a huge pile of dolls between them. But he was happy.

Looking down at her small face, so peaceful in sleep, he brushed a strand of hair from her eyes and thought how much happiness, how much colour she had brought into his grey life. He smiled. He had not thought about Bellic all the time he was with her.

'Your fault! All your fault!'

Martil sobbed as he scrambled over mounds of bodies. They all seemed to be the murdered Ralloran villagers, although the streets were clearly in Bellic. Worse, even though every one of them bore hideous wounds, they all opened their mouths and spoke with one voice, condemning him as he tried to climb over them, tried to escape the Berellian woman and her son who stalked him remorselessly. Babies, their heads misshapen and smashed, wailed as his hands scrabbled to find purchase on the piles of the dead. Even in the midst of the dream, he found time to wonder where all the Berellian dead had got to. Then he clambered over another pile and discovered them. The side streets were full of the walking dead. Every one of them had wounds ripped into their dead bodies, but the weapons they brandished were clutched tightly in their hands.

'There he goes! It's him! He's the last of them!' the cry went up from a thousand dead mouths, and they rushed forwards.

'I am sorry! I wish I could go back! I wish none of this had ever happened!'

But they ignored his anguished apologies. Instead they hungered for vengeance.

Martil ran as he had never run before. The dead bodies choking the streets had impeded him, but now he just skimmed over the top of them. The dead reached out for him but he was able to evade them. Their moans and screams of hatred pursued him as he sped into the town square — and skidded to a halt.

Here there were no dead bodies lying on the cobbles. Instead, four scaffolds stood in the centre of the square. Hanging from them were the other four war captains from Bellic. Each twisted and choked on the ropes around their necks, while their chests were ripped open, their hearts lying on the cobbles beneath them.

'Your fault, all your fault. You led us to this,' they moaned with one voice.

'No! That's not true!' Martil tried to protest.

'Don't lie to the dead! You are the one! The Butcher of Bellic!'

'Don't call me that!' Martil screamed, but they twisted and turned away from him, writhing endlessly on the ropes that held them.

A roar from behind him made him turn, to see the hordes of the dead rushing forwards, led by the woman and her son, the long knife and the wicked spear lusting for his flesh.

He turned to run once more — the gates were not far away — only to find his legs would not move.

Looking down, dreading what he would find, he stared into the bloodied face of the woman from the Ralloran village, holding her slaughtered baby.

'Your fault! All your fault!' she hissed.

'Daddy! Wake up!'

Martil sat up, the beginning of a scream dying in his throat. His heart was racing and he could feel cold sweat all over his body.

'What's the matter? You were making funny noises in your sleep! You woke me up!' Karia accused.

Martil wiped his face with a shaking hand and tried to calm his hammering heart.

'It was a bad dream,' he managed to say.

Karia carefully moved her dolls aside until she was next to him.

'Lie back down,' she advised.

'I can't …'

'Do what I tell you,' she instructed. 'Lie down and I'll sing you to sleep.'

He allowed her to pat his face and try to sing to him. It was relaxing.

'Now your turn to sing to me,' she declared.

So he managed to sing through a dry mouth, until it was obvious she had fallen asleep again, her small hand resting in his.

He held on to it tightly. He felt that as long as he held her hand, the dream would not come back.

Romon finished his performance, as always, with a bow. He was finding this harder and harder to do, although the presence of a pair of guards meant he had plenty of motivation. But this was ridiculous! Giving a performance in front of a pack of criminals! Murderers and the like — as if they were able to appreciate his art. The thought of what he had been reduced to by Gello left him dispirited. If he had known another trade, he would have snapped his lyre and returned to it. As the audience was ordered back to the training grounds, he turned away, stuffing the official scrolls into his belt pouch.

'Romon! Romon the bard!'

He turned, hearing a vaguely familiar voice, to see a lean man with an angry face hurrying towards him. The man had hard lines around his eyes and, although the top of his head was bald, he had long hair swept back from above both his ears and tied into a ponytail with a crude leather thong. Romon looked around for his guards but, their duty done with the end of another performance given exactly as scripted, they were several paces away, talking. Romon wondered with alarm if this criminal was going to try and kill him in front of so many witnesses.

Romon had never fought a man before, but he did not lack courage. He straightened himself to his full height and held his lyre as if it were some sort of weapon, rather than a small musical instrument.

'What is it?' he said haughtily, putting all his skill into those words and striking a pose that he hoped would show off his fighting qualities.

'Do you not remember me?' the criminal asked, stopping a full pace away.

Romon looked at the man carefully. He had performed to so many people, including some rather fanatical fans who insisted on following him around and sending him strange gifts. There was something about the man that was vaguely familiar — but that was not necessarily a good thing.

'I'm sorry ...' he began.

'It's Kettering, from the Crown and Sparrow at Wollin. I used to book all the bards — you performed for a week straight earlier this year,' the man said urgently.

Romon stared in shock. The Kettering he knew had been a good-hearted, efficient man with all the fearsome reputation of a limp lettuce. What he was doing here, and how he had survived life with this band of cutthroats, Romon shuddered to think.

'You look different,' Romon said automatically. 'Your hair looks good, though.'

Kettering gave him the ghost of a smile. 'It's all I have left of me,' he admitted.

'What happened to you?' Romon blurted.

'There isn't much time. They don't like us talking or thinking,' Kettering said urgently. Part of him registered Romon's reaction but he did not have the luxury of being horrified by it. 'Romon, I know you. You were always a bard to be trusted. Why are you spreading these lies?'

Romon instinctively glanced over to where his two guards were still engrossed in conversation.

'Because I'll be dead otherwise,' he said quietly. 'King Gello is making all this up, he's allied himself to Berellia.'

Kettering nodded. 'As I thought. Thank you. Good luck.'

With that he turned away. He had learned not to attract attention to himself and besides, he needed to think about what this meant.

'Wait! What are you doing here?' Romon called, but Kettering had been swallowed by the crowd of criminals, and Romon had no intention of plunging into them to try and find the man. What was going on in this bloody country?

* * *

'Captain! Wake up!'

Martil cursed as his eyes opened. He had been sleeping, actually sleeping without dreams! He held up his hand and, sure enough, Karia's small hand was still safely enclosed. He let go with the greatest reluctance.

'What is it?' he called.

'A rider from the passes! Urgent message for you, sir!'

Martil groaned and stood. Karia still seemed to be sleeping — she might be tough to get to sleep but, once she was asleep, she was harder to wake. He opened the door to find one of Wime's men, accompanied by a dirty, tired Ralloran scout.

'Message from Lieutenant Nerrin, sir.' The scout handed over a sealed scroll. He was swaying slightly as he stood to attention.

'Take him down to the kitchens, get him food and water, then find him a place to sleep,' Martil instructed the militiaman.

He waited until the pair had walked away before opening the scroll. He read it quickly, feeling his brain wake further with each new word.

'Zorva's ba—' he began before realising Karia was standing behind him in her nightdress, yawning slightly. 'Ba— backside,' he amended hastily.

'What's going on? And when's breakfast?' she asked automatically as he hugged her.

'Let's get dressed — we need to get word to Merren,' he sighed.

It was a hastily assembled council that waited anxiously to hear what he had to say. Outside, the town was just waking up. In the audience chamber, servants placed plates of bread, cheese and honey on the table, and added pots of hot tea and jugs of fresh fruit juice.

Merren waited until the last servant had left. It was not that she distrusted them, but she suspected there might be some bad news that she did not want spreading through the town. There was a general feeling of optimism these days, a feeling the worst of this war had passed, and they were on the winning side. 'What is the news from the passes?'

'We only have a little time: a couple of weeks at best, definitely no more than a month. Nerrin has reported Gello has sent an advance party north; they are setting up a massive camp only ten miles from the most northerly pass. It appears Gello is planning to bring at least ten thousand men north. If we are to act, we must act now.'

'Can we hold those passes?' Merren asked immediately.

'If we concentrate at one pass, we could repulse them for a few days. But they will have cavalry enough to sweep through at least one of the other passes. It will be a delaying tactic, no more.'

'And if we had the rangers as well?'

'We could hold for weeks, but not forever.'

'Can we face them in battle?' Merren made sure her face was impassive. She could see the worry, even the first signs of panic, on the faces of some of the councillors. Barely six hundred of Gello's soldiers had caused carnage in the streets of the town. Now ten thousand were marching north. To show a hint of the concern she was feeling would be deadly. 'I will not allow these towns to be besieged and destroyed. It was my actions that freed them. They are my responsibility. I will not shelter behind innocent people. Whatever happens, it will take place far from these walls, and far from the women and children. If the worst comes, then I will face Gello on the field, alone if necessary.'

'You will never stand alone, my Queen,' Barrett declared immediately.

'You cannot do that! My Queen, you should flee the country,' suggested Sendric. 'Once we are safely away, we can think of returning one day ...'

Merren ignored them. 'Captain, I asked you a question.'

Martil rubbed his face.

'There is one place — about fifteen miles north of the passes. I do not know its name but there is one last, steep hill that overlooks the road—'

'Pilleth,' Gratt interjected. 'It's known as Pilleth.'

Martil nodded his thanks. 'It reminds me of a Ralloran hill, called Mount Shadar. I fought the Berellians there many years ago. We used the angle of the hill to enormous effect. Because of its steepness, our bowmen outranged even their crossbows. With barely two hundred archers, we were able to hold an entire army at bay, simply because they could not advance up a steep slope into an arrow storm. It was not until our arrows ran short that they were able to make progress, but even then the slope gave us an enormous advantage.'

Merren, who had been contemplating a lonely and painful defeat in some muddy field somewhere, snapped back to the conversation instantly.

'With just two hundred archers, you said? So what if you had one thousand — the regiment of rangers?'

Martil forced his face to remain impassive. The story of Mount Shadar was true enough, although he had left out the rather vital fact that only desperate and ferocious hand-to-hand fighting had held the Berellians back until King Tolbert and the rest of the army arrived. His division had inflicted enormous casualties on the Berellians but it had been shattered in the process. His cavalry company, which he had fought with that day, had led several counter-attacks that had saved the lives of many of his men, including Nerrin. But, by the end of the day, barely a dozen still lived. 'With a thousand rangers, as well as my own Ralloran archers and Tarik's company, we could slaughter Gello's men. Half his army is barely trained — men such as that will break rather than advance up a steep hill into certain death. With a little luck, we could actually defeat Gello.'

The reaction around the table was astonishing. One moment everyone had been contemplating a grim future of fighting a last, desperate battle or running for safety. Now Martil — the fabled Captain Martil, the man who had led them to an endless series of victories and who had never lost a battle as a commander — was telling them they could win!

Only Merren did not join in the excited chatter, and the cheers depressed her, rather than lifted her. She had made the decision not to go after the rangers. Martil might think that finding and killing this Lord of Bellic was the best thing for him but she rather doubted that. More importantly, it sounded too good to be true. There was nothing on the surface to arouse her suspicions — it was obvious the information had had to be tortured out of Warnock. But she was wary of committing herself to such a risky venture. Freeing the Archbishop and the priests would be tackling a handful of guards and freeing just enough prisoners who could be transported away by Barrett's magic. As well, they had people on the inside. But the rangers … How many would turn on her? Even if it was just a company, she could lose every man who went down there.

And, even if they could be turned, how could she get them back, especially if most of Gello's army was setting up outside the passes? Persuading men to join her then marching them to their doom was not acceptable. She had been wondering how to tell Martil that. But now it looked as though she had no choice.

With no sign of the talk dying down, she looked quickly around the table. Only Martil did not seem to be joining in the excitement. She caught his gaze and they locked eyes for a moment before he looked away. She felt her heart sink. All those years she had prayed for a Champion to wield the Dragon Sword and now she had one who was both more, and less, than she needed. But she merely slapped her hand on the table to bring silence to the room. This would be a tough decision. But she would make it.

'I have decided we shall attempt to capture this Lord of Bellic, rescue the bard and win over the rangers to our side,' she said heavily. 'I am not convinced this will succeed but I am afraid we must try. The chance to face, and beat, Gello is worth risking everything for. And if we can win over a bard, we could indeed start bringing more men over to our side. With the rangers, perhaps we could hold the passes long enough to give us a chance to try. Because the risk is so great, I will be going. I will not send men to their deaths without risking my own life. For protection, as well as the need to persuade Kay and his rangers that the stories they have been hearing from Gello's bards are all lies, I will take Tarik, Wime, Forde and Rocus, Sendric and Barrett. Wime,

Forde and Rocus can each bring a squad of men to defeat any guards and capture the Lord of Bellic.'

'My Queen, surely that's too many men. Sergeant Kesbury and his squad, along with myself, can handle anything that Berellian has brought along—' Martil began.

'You will not be accompanying us, Captain,' Merren said loudly but calmly.

Martil felt the eyes of everyone on the table upon him.

'I'm sorry, I don't understand, your majesty,' he said carefully. 'Do you not want the Dragon Sword to help bolster your claims?'

'Of course I do. But, as you have said yourself, you are not able yet to master its latent magic.' Merren held his gaze as she spoke. She knew this had to be hurting him, but it had to be done. She had tried the gentle approach, tried to help him without anyone else knowing. But he had refused to talk to her, so now she had to take this action. Her feelings for him were still uncertain but she knew exactly what had to be done to retake her throne. That took precedence over anything else.

Martil flushed as her words hit home. 'If you do not need me—' he began.

'That is not true. I, and this rebellion, need you more than ever, Captain. But we do not need you on this particular mission. My fear is, once confronted with the Lord of Bellic, you and your Rallorans will lose control. I want the man and his accomplices captured, not killed. Dead, he proves nothing except that you are a killer of men.'

Martil felt her words like a blow to the stomach. 'If you are ashamed of my men and me …'

'That is not the case. You and your Rallorans are

a valued part of this campaign. Without you, we are doomed to failure. But in a struggle to convince my countrymen that the sagas they are being told are lies, I cannot afford to have you start a battle. If we do too much fighting at the rangers' barracks, we have lost. Persuasion is our most effective weapon there. But never think I do not value you and your Rallorans. That is why I have a mission for you that is more important.'

Martil struggled to comprehend what was going on. Every time he had tried to work up some indignation, to let his anger free, she had taken the wind out of his sails, catching him off guard. There was a power about her, a strength to go with the softer side she had shown him yesterday. It left him confused. Now she was saying he had a more important duty? What could that be? It had been his idea to go after the rangers!

'It's a twofold task. I need you and Lieutenant Nerrin to start raiding the camp that Gello is setting up. Anything we can do to disrupt his preparations is vital. More than that, did you not tell me of the dangers when too many men camp together? How water must be boiled before it can be drunk, latrine trenches regularly changed, men made to wash and to eat fresh food, or sickness will strike?'

'Aye,' he admitted. 'If Gello does not know his business, within a week he will have as many as one in ten of his men unable to fight.'

'Do whatever you have to. I want his army weakened when he marches against us.'

Martil could feel his head clearing. 'It can be done. They will not be expecting it. We can pollute the water they must drink, taint their supplies of food. We did similar against the Berellians ...'

'Excellent. But for you and Sergeant Kesbury, there is a bigger job yet. I need the two of you and Karia to travel to the capital and free the Archbishop, with the help of Father Nott.'

'We're going to see Father Nott! Yesss!' Karia celebrated beside him.

Martil felt his heart leap into his mouth. What if Karia wanted to stay with Father Nott? What if Nott wanted her back? What would he do without her? How could he stop the dreams then? And Merren. He could not bear to think of something happening to her without him there to protect her. His mind was a whirl of worry. He looked down at Karia's excitement and tried to force a smile onto his face. She was grinning at him, and leaned in to give him a hug.

'I can't wait! Can we go now?' she asked.

Martil knew her long-term happiness and wellbeing were vital. Karia's welfare should be his first concern. But all he could think about was what it would mean to him to lose her, and what his life would be like. He glanced down the table to where Merren was looking at him, an expression of faint concern on her face. He feared for her too but she had shown him in no uncertain terms where he stood. Her words had demonstrated that she might be fond of him, but he was still an asset, to be used and expended when necessary. Just like every other royal. Now he might lose Karia as well. It was too much. He licked dry lips and tried to muster an argument against this plan.

'But Karia isn't powerful enough to open a gateway to allow the Archbishop and others to escape,' he managed to say.

'But she is powerful enough to send a message to me. We will be able to co-ordinate our efforts, so I can make sure the priests get away safely,' Barrett stated. He was struggling to contain his excitement. This was the first time he had heard of Merren's plan but, naturally, he thought it marvellous. He was eager to help in any way that he could to squash Martil's objections.

Martil glared at him. He hoped the useless bastard would do something stupid and get himself killed. That would take the smug expression off his face.

'Won't Kesbury and myself be too conspicuous in the capital?' he tried to ask.

'Kesbury used to work there. He will be a valuable asset in staying hidden,' Merren stated.

'Besides, you will have Father Nott and Sister Milly to help you,' Quiller offered.

Martil stewed in silence, unable to think of another reason against this idea.

'So when can we go?' Karia demanded.

Merren cleared her throat. 'We need to act swiftly. Barrett, we need Wime, Rocus and Forde here as soon as possible. Father, you need to contact Father Nott and tell him to expect a dozen new pilgrims, who will need to be hidden. Aroaril willing, we shall all leave in the morning.'

'I can't wait!' Karia exclaimed.

I can, Martil thought gloomily. The only bright spot was at least Karia would be with him.

8

In his former life, Hutter had been a huge fan of the sagas. He had often made a special trip to Wollin to hear a really good one. He had lost some interest in them now, especially the Real Saga of Bellic, which was beginning to grate. Luckily this was to be the last performance before they marched north to end the slaughter the Rallorans were visiting on the towns there. Or so he had been told. But when he saw the bard was the famous Romon, he could not help but look forward to the performance. He had seen him twice before and thoroughly enjoyed both appearances.

Sadly, however, this one was something of a disappointment. Not only was it the same damned saga, but there was none of the spark, the showmanship, that had set apart Romon's earlier performances. Still, it was not every day that you were able to meet a bard who had performed at court, so he lined up to speak to the great man.

Romon was signing scraps of parchment and shaking hands, and this was the only time he actually looked animated. Hutter wondered at the two guards who had watched his performance but who now were rolling dice.

Finally it was his turn.

'So where are you from?' Romon asked warmly.

'Chell — a little village just outside Wollin. I saw you perform there twice, at the Crown and Sparrow.' Hutter smiled.

Romon looked at the man. That was the second mention of the Crown and Sparrow he had had recently.

'I can't help but feel your performance today was not up to that standard,' Hutter continued.

Romon looked around carefully. This time, given his audience was militiamen, he had been allowed to mingle with them, and his guards were even less interested in what was happening with him.

'Why do you ask?' he said carefully.

Hutter shrugged. 'Let's just say I made a career out of telling the difference between truth and lies.'

Romon rubbed his ear. What was it about people from that part of the world? What was going on? 'I just perform what I'm told. Or else,' he said quietly, gesturing over his shoulder towards his guards.

Hutter's face hardened. 'I understand. Thank you. Aroaril go with you.'

And with that he was gone, before Romon could ask him if he knew Kettering, and why they were both suspicious about this saga. There was a story in here, Romon felt. If only he could have the chance to find out what it was. But there was no time. After he had spoken to the other men standing in line, he would have to ride hard with his guards. Apparently tomorrow he had to perform at the barracks of the King's Rangers. Some Berellian dignitary, a lord no less, was to address the men before they marched north, and he was required to back this up with another bloody recital of this cursed saga.

*   *   *

'What's the matter?' Karia asked.

Martil looked down at her in surprise. 'Why do you ask?'

She shrugged. 'You've been really quiet today. I wondered why.'

Martil was literally lost for words. What could he say? Where could he start? And what would she understand of his problems, his concerns? It would not be fair to burden her. Besides, what could she do?

'Would a hug help?'

Not trusting himself to speak, Martil just nodded, and she immediately grabbed him around the chest, squeezing him tight, as if she would never let go. He hugged her back, smelling the fresh scent of her hair, lemony, like Merren's. He kissed the top of her head. Something in him wanted to tell her about his dreams but his fear kept him from doing so. After all, they were about to go off and see Father Nott. This was not the time to be telling her the truth, or she might want to stay with Father Nott.

For her part, Karia was also feeling concerned. She was excited about seeing Father Nott again, especially as he had said such a thing was impossible. But there was also a fear within her. Father Nott had given her up to Edil; Edil had not wanted her. Martil had tried to return her to Father Nott and he had sent her away again. She was enjoying life with Martil but what if he did not want her any more? Would he try and give her back to Father Nott? But she did not dare ask Martil. She did not think she could bear that.

'Do you want me to hold your hand again tonight?' Karia looked up.

Martil hugged her fiercely. 'Yes, I do,' he admitted.

Martil sat up, the beginnings of a scream dying in his throat, the sweat thick and clammy on his body.

'You bloody idiot,' he told himself softly. He must have let go of Karia's hand in the night, giving the dream a chance to take hold.

Then he looked down to see Karia's small hand in his own.

'What am I going to do now?' he whispered into the darkness.

Tiera had proved to be an extraordinarily valuable ally for both Milly and Nott. As well as being able to pass on messages to the prisoners, to warn and prepare them for a rescue attempt, she had smuggled a dozen robes out of the laundry: Nott had decided to disguise Martil and his men as novice priests. A few weeks ago such a disguise could not have succeeded but many of the novices being recruited by Prent were far more muscular than the usual crop. Besides, it would only have to be effective for a day or two.

Now Nott, Milly and Tiera were waiting in a city park, near the huge oak tree that was the meeting point. Not many people were around this early — the mornings were beginning to have a definite chill and the city's denizens usually waited for the day to warm up. But they had already seen a few children and wanted to be careful. Tiera and Milly kept watch while Nott checked the tree.

'There they are,' Nott said urgently.

The end of a wizard's staff was suddenly poking out of the seemingly solid trunk of the oak tree.

'Anyone around?' Nott asked.

'All clear, Father,' Tiera reported.

Nott tapped thrice on the end of the staff, the pre-arranged signal, then stepped back.

A large Ralloran soldier walked out of the tree trunk, holding on to the oaken staff, followed in quick succession by nine more soldiers, then out came Karia and Martil. As soon as they were clear of the tree, Martil knocked three times on the staff and it was withdrawn.

'Father, where are you?' Martil turned. Kesbury and his squad were spread out defensively around the tree, just in case.

'I am here.' Nott stepped around the bulky Kesbury and Karia let go of Martil's hand to sprint to him, almost knocking him over in her excitement.

'Father!' she squealed.

Martil watched her run over and hug the old priest and felt a sensation not unlike pain in his chest.

'Karia!' Nott hugged her back and kissed her.

But Martil had no time for their reunion. 'Father, we should not stay here,' he said urgently. 'Who are your companions?'

Nott straightened up with some difficulty, as Karia was still hanging on to him.

'Sister Milly, former secretary to Archbishop Declan and my eyes and ears in the church. And Tiera, one of the church's servants and a loyal friend. She has secured us these robes, which we will use to disguise you.'

Tiera immediately began handing out the large brown robes, which came with a deep cowl. Martil nodded approvingly. He had forbidden his men to bring their mail shirts, for the sound and smell of them was impossible to hide. Instead, each man was wearing a boiled leather breastplate and carried sword and dagger, all of which were sure to arouse suspicion on the streets of the capital.

Tiera, who had long red hair and wide green eyes and whose shapely body could not be disguised by the modest uniform she wore, was attracting plenty of approving glances from Kesbury and his men as they pulled on the robes. She stepped close to Milly, under the pretence of picking up more robes. The young priestess had been expecting this. After all, Tiera had just escaped the unwanted attentions of Prent. The last thing she wanted was to have a bunch of burly soldiers ogling her.

'It's all right. They are good men,' she said softly.

Tiera nodded and smiled, a little uncertainly. 'I am fine,' she lied confidently, then started handing out more robes. Milly sighed. A girl like Tiera should have been able to flirt and laugh with these men, for it was obvious they meant no harm, they were just reacting normally to a pretty girl. But instead her eyes were downcast and her body language nervous. Prent had so much to answer for.

'How are you?' Nott crossed to Martil and gripped his arm. The old priest had been delighted to see the change in Karia. She had put on some weight, her hair was clean and brushed, her skin fresh and clear of bruises, her face happy. But not much had changed with the warrior since Nott had seen him last. In fact, judging from the deep circles under his eyes, Martil was even worse than before.

'I am fine, Father.' Martil did not want to discuss anything with the priest.

'I am sorry I could not tell you what was going to happen. The state you were in, I feared you would have simply run.' Nott tried to joke about it.

'How about you just tell me how it ends, and we'll call it even?' Martil suggested, trying to make it seem as if he was also joking.

Nott sighed. 'My son, I do not know how it will end. In fact, I fear even Aroaril does not know how it will end.'

'Then what use is He?' Martil said unthinkingly.

Nott's grip on his arm tightened. 'I have told you not to speak like that! And, given what we are about to do, I suggest we need all the help we can get.'

Martil pulled his arm free. 'Let's get somewhere safe and you can tell me all about your plan.' He accepted a robe from Tiera and pulled it over his head.

Nott stared at him coolly. 'I hope you remember I am not your enemy,' he said softly, then turned to the others. 'Follow me, all of you. If we are stopped, you are all under a vow of silence. Tiera, I need you to take Karia's hand and walk with her, a little way ahead of us. If you see a patrol, stop and pick her up, understand?'

Milly opened her mouth to volunteer for the job instead but Tiera was quick to step forwards.

'I can do that, Father,' she said confidently.

Karia was a little reluctant to be parted from Nott but, reassured that she would see him back at the chapter house, she skipped happily enough alongside Tiera.

'Follow the Father — and for Aroaril's sake keep those swords out of sight,' Martil instructed his soldiers. He had had enough practice over the long years of the Ralloran Wars to put aside his personal feelings in order to get the job done. He would do so again, although watching Karia skip away from him was putting that ability to its sternest test.

* * *

The ranger barracks was several miles from any villages or towns. On one side was a long series of archery ranges, from the basic series of targets to the more advanced, complete with trees, walls and even houses. On the other side was a small wood, which was also used as a training ground. There was no wall around the barracks, and getting in was obviously not going to be an issue. It remained to be seen if getting out again would be. The woods, with the undergrowth trodden flat by years of training exercises, had three oak trees, one of which they had arrived through, any of which could be used as an escape route. But Merren prayed it would not come to that.

'Your majesty?' Rocus gestured at the model of the barracks they stood around. Thanks to Barrett's magic, some twigs and mud had become miniature buildings on the forest floor.

'We'll go in as a small group, and we'll be relying on you, Barrett, to make it a dramatic entrance,' Merren announced.

She was not happy about this whole mission.

They had managed to get some accurate information about the upcoming performance by sending one of Wime's men in to pose as a tinker. He had been generous with a couple of bottles of brandy, sharpened a few knives and come back with a fair idea of what was going to happen.

After all she had risked, and faced, it seemed ridiculous to gamble so much on this. But she knew there was no choice. Still, giving the final order to go in there was not easy.

'Wime, we are sure of the information from your man?' Merren looked at the dependable militiaman.

'On my life, your majesty.' Wime nodded.

'It will be on all our lives,' Merren reminded them. 'So the companies of rangers will be seated across from the archery range, facing towards the targets. The bard will be standing with the targets to his back, facing the men, while the officers, the Berellians and other dignitaries will be seated to the right of the rangers, closest to the barracks' offices, where they will return for refreshments after the performance.' She marked out the positions in the dirt.

'We must secure the officers, the Berellians and the dignitaries at the same time as we confront the bard and speak directly to the rangers. Tarik, Wime and Forde will lead most of the men there. Because they are out of a direct sight, we can have them in hand before anyone realises what is happening. Without their officers, the rangers will not act — and myself, Barrett, Sendric and Rocus can win them over, along with the bard. Questions?'

There was a short pause.

'If it all goes wrong?' Rocus asked.

Merren smiled grimly. 'We'll meet back here. Get here any way you can and don't go back for anyone, including me — understood?'

'It won't come to that, your majesty. We will be triumphant!' Barrett said immediately.

She nodded. 'We move when we see the companies start to assemble on the archery range.'

Kay had to admit to being a little underwhelmed on meeting the Lord of Bellic. The man was not particularly tall and was remarkably nondescript. His face was clean-shaven and seemed to have no distinguishing features at all. He was dressed in black, with the only hint as to his rank being a golden crest featuring a lion over his left breast. He did not even carry a sword; instead, a pair of daggers was sheathed at his belt, which seemed to feature an unusually large buckle. He also had a strangely shaped belt pouch, both wide and tall. To a bowman such as Kay, it reminded him of a half-size arrow bag. The man was also rather rude, merely nodding when introduced to Kay.

'You must be a remarkable man, to not only have survived such an infamous massacre, but to be able to talk about it,' Kay said, trying to make conversation. It was an art he had worked on while captain of the Royal Guard.

'Luck, nothing more,' the Berellian said in a cold voice. 'Now, if you will excuse me.'

Kay inclined his head, expecting the Berellian to circle around the room, speaking to the other officers, but instead the man walked over to the window, where he stopped, watching the nearby archery training range.

His entourage, a dozen men, were likewise dressed in black, and less than talkative. They were also well armed, carrying several throwing knives as well as swords and belt pouches similar to their lord's. Just what they were expecting, Kay did not know.

'They're a proud people,' Beq explained with a shrug. 'They might be our allies but no doubt they don't trust us. And besides, they probably fear that Rallorans are going to descend on them at any moment! Looking forward to the show?'

'Indeed, sir!'

If the Berellian lord was a disappointment, then the bard was a welcome relief. Kay had long admired the work of Romon, and had seen him perform numerous times at court. They were soon talking about old acquaintances and laughing, until Beq stepped between them.

'Well, I think it's about time we started the performance, don't you? After all, we need to prepare for the march north tomorrow!'

'Yes, sir. I'll give the orders,' Kay agreed, then grinned at Romon. 'Sorry to interrupt the memories, my friend.'

'Perhaps I'll see you afterwards?'

One of Tiera's younger sisters was about the same age as Karia, so she had enjoyed chatting with her on the way back to the chapter house. It was early in the morning and there were few patrols about, so Karia, after being initially shy, had been free to talk about Father Nott, about Martil, 'the greatest warrior dad in the world!' and about her teacher, the Queen's Magician Barrett.

'I wish I had a life as interesting as yours,' Tiera said ruefully. 'All I do is wash dishes, wash clothes and clean up after the novices and priests. They might be holy but they're still smelly.'

Karia thought that hilarious.

'But that's all I'll ever do,' Tiera sighed.

'You should come back with us,' Karia said. 'Merren's always saying that good people are needed. She says that it's not who your parents are but what you can do that's important.'

Tiera almost stopped walking then. 'Merren? As in, Queen Merren?'

'That's her. Do you know her as well?'

Now it was Tiera's turn to laugh. 'Not exactly. Maybe I should come back with you. There's not much for me here. Aroaril knows, King Gello and

Archbishop Prent believe the people beneath them should literally be beneath them,' she added bitterly.

'What does that mean?'

'That they're not very nice.' Tiera hastily decided to change the subject. 'So, what could I do there?'

'Well, you could work for Barrett. He's the Queen's Magician, which means he needs people to cook and clean for him because he has to keep all his strength for working magic. Then you could play with me when you get bored.'

'We'll see,' Tiera said, her attention drifting from the conversation as they neared the chapter house. The front and back entrances were guarded but the door to the servants' quarters was ignored. After all, the servants were beneath notice.

She waited for Father Nott and Sister Milly to catch up.

'We'll go in the front and distract the guards, then you take Martil and his Rallorans up to my room,' Nott instructed. 'The guards know me, know that Milly accompanies me out on a walk every morning. I'll have a chat with them, give you the time to get around the corner.'

Tiera led the men in through the side entrance unseen, past the washrooms and storerooms and up the back stairs to Nott's room. She was happy to help, and grateful to both Milly and Nott, but still felt uncomfortable walking up the stairs; she could sense the Rallorans' eyes as they followed her.

A pair of novices walked past and bowed their heads. Tiera bobbed hers in return and was relieved to see the Rallorans clumsily copy the move. A quick walk down a corridor and she opened the door to Nott's room, ushering the soldiers inside to where Nott and Milly waited. The entrance of eleven large men made even the spacious room suddenly seem crowded.

'I have to get back to my duties, the other girls are covering for me. But call for me if you need help and I'll be back,' she said.

The Ralloran that Father Nott had called Martil pushed back his cowl.

'It might be too dangerous for you,' he warned.

'I'm happy to risk my life. It wouldn't be worth living if it wasn't for Sister Milly,' Tiera said defiantly. 'Besides, Karia said I could come back with you.'

Martil turned to Karia, who was trying to look innocent. 'We shall discuss that later,' was all he said.

He waited until the door was shut before pulling off his robe. 'Can we be sure we won't be disturbed here?'

Nott smiled. 'There are no other residents in this block of rooms; it is for older priests who have come back to the chapter house to live out their last. But it seems Aroaril has other plans for me — I am not required to join Him just yet. You can spread out and use as many rooms as you want, but I would advise keeping the doors locked and opening only to either myself or Sister Milly. Tiera and the other servants will keep you well supplied. When do you think you will effect the rescue?'

'Can I get something to eat first?' Karia interrupted.

'I can find you something,' Milly offered.

'Karia, I need to talk with Martil and his men,' Nott said gently.

'More talk! All right, I'll wait,' Karia sighed with great care, and accepted a cup of milk.

Nott waved for the soldiers to sit down, and

Kesbury and his men perched on every available surface.

'So where is the wizard, Barrett? And what of Father Quiller? I thought this was to involve both of them …' Nott asked delicately.

Martil scratched his chin. 'There has been a change in plan. We learned that Gello is preparing to march a massive army north. The Queen, as well as Barrett, are on another mission: to win over the regiment of rangers to our side, as well as bring back a Norstaline bard and capture the Lord of Bellic, the man really responsible for that infamy. They have to do this today, as it is the only time we know the Lord of Bellic will be at our mercy. As we do not need to worry about time, we can wait for Barrett to be finished with the rangers. That will be tomorrow at the earliest. So we strike then. Once we know Barrett is ready, we'll all leave and make for the park. We should be out of the capital before anyone even realises anything is wrong. That is the plan but it all depends on taking the building without Prent or any of his accomplices getting away. That's up to you.'

Nott nodded. 'Milly, the drawings if you please,' he said.

The young priestess stepped forwards and unrolled a series of scrolls. The Rallorans looked at her, but not the same way they had looked at Tiera.

For the first time, she wished that were different, only so she could protect Tiera. The young woman might offer the world a hard-bitten, tough exterior, but her treatment at Prent's hands had damaged her. Perhaps going back with them all to the north was the best thing for her. Milly made a mental note to speak to Father Nott about that, as she unrolled the first of the scrolls for the Rallorans to see.

'This is the plan of the chapter house. We are up here on the first floor, above the kitchens. Down the stairs you came up, and past the storerooms, is more stairs to the cells where Archbishop Declan, Bishop Gamelon and the others are being held. Once penitents' cells, they were used for more stores, but now these have been cleared away — or given away, not to the poor but to Gello's soldiers.

'One cell has been converted into a guardroom, but there are never more than four men on duty there, as well as two on the door to Prent's office, two at the front door and another pair at the back. The off-duty squad sleeps on the ground floor, in here. But I can take care of them.'

Martil smiled at the young priestess. Her black hair was cut short and she had serious grey eyes, as well as a generous mouth and a snub nose with a scattering of freckles. 'And how will you do that?'

'Easily, with Tiera's help. We shall serve them a meal that will put them to sleep.'

Several of the Rallorans chuckled. 'So, we get the word the off-duty squad is out of the way, then we'll free the prisoners. Once we know we have them, we'll take the guards at the front and back of the building — and go and visit Prent. The treacherous bastard betrayed the Queen to Gello when he was just a priest; I'm sure the Queen would like to see him again.'

'So how will we know when we are to make this rescue?' Milly asked.

'When Barrett returns to the north, Father Quiller will contact you with instructions. Not sure how, but I gather you are familiar with his methods.' Martil shrugged.

'Aye. Thanks to Aroaril, His priests can talk to each other across long distances,' Nott said. 'But I would have thought it safer to wait until you had finished with one mission before starting another …'

'It was felt that Barrett would have been too tired after his efforts with the rangers to send us both ways,' Martil said carefully. That had been one of just many points he had argued about. 'Besides, there was the fear that winning over a regiment of rangers and capturing a key ally of Gello's and a bard in one stroke would cause Gello to fly into a rage and lock the capital down.'

'So, we just need to wait until we hear from them tomorrow? Nothing to do but rest, eat …'

'And play with me,' Karia finished, a milk moustache on her face.

The small band of Norstalines was able to walk right up to the barracks without being challenged or even seen. Everyone had been sent out to the archery ranges, where the bard was warming up — they could hear the sounds of a lyre across the quiet buildings.

'We should be able to come out right behind the main party,' Tarik reported, returning from scouting the area. 'But I don't know how you are going to appear behind the bard without being seen, your majesty.'

'Leave that to me,' Barrett said importantly. 'As long as we don't talk, and move quietly, we shall not be seen. I shall use my powers to disguise us. A keen observer might spot a shadow, or think he can sense our presence, but we will seem as if a wind is passing them.'

'Someone sounds like they're passing wind now,' Wime murmured to Rocus, who fought to keep a straight face.

'One thing: I can't pick out the Lord of Bellic. There's a dozen men dressed all in black — he could be any of them,' Tarik said with a shrug. 'There's certainly nobody dressed in a golden surcoat, or court finery.'

Merren bit her lip. Identifying the Berellian Lord, and capturing him immediately, had been an important part of the plan. With a knife at their Lord's throat, the other Berellians would be far more amenable.

'If only Captain Martil was here, he could tell us which one it was. He met the bastard, apparently,' Rocus offered.

'Yes, but Martil is not here. We are,' Merren said sharply, a little too sharply, she knew. 'We shall just have to be quick. You all know what to do. I don't want unnecessary bloodshed — after all, many of those officers are men we want to serve with us. Call on them to surrender. We shall outnumber them, after all, and if they are isolated, away from their men, they will soon realise that and give up. But, if they fight, then of course you can fight back.'

Wime, Forde and Tarik nodded agreement.

'We shall not let you down, your majesty,' Forde said fervently.

Summoned from Gerrin by Barrett's magic, he had leaped at the chance to prove his worth to the Queen, and to her rebellion. He and his men were proud to be wearing the blue surcoat with the silver dragon crest.

'Then Aroaril be with us,' Merren said heavily.

Each bard brought his own interpretation to the saga, and used movement, the cadence of their voice and their lyre to add dramatic effect. Kay liked this kept to a minimum, personally. He felt watching a grown man prance around plucking a lyre was disrespectful to the saga. Romon obviously agreed with him, as he used his voice to great effect while standing still. Kay had been enjoying the performance but was now distracted by something in his peripheral vision. However, whenever he turned his head to see it properly, it disappeared. As a ranger, he knew the value of peripheral vision, as it caught movement even in low light. But here the sun was shining and there should be nothing moving behind the bard, surely?

Then a burst of golden light behind the bard made everyone blink, and gasp. Six figures were standing behind Romon facing the ranks of rangers.

Three were in armour, wearing a strange blue surcoat with what looked like a dragon crest on the front. The fourth was obviously a wizard, judging by his deep purple trousers and tunic, as well as the staff he carried. The fifth seemed to be a noble, who looked strangely familiar to Kay. But the last ... Kay gasped. The last was Queen Merren! She was wearing a blue robe, with a sleeveless jerkin of mail over the top. The mail was impossibly bright, while the crown on her head shone incredibly golden.

At first, many of the rangers thought this was all just part of the show, and a few had even started applauding. But quite a number had served in the Royal Guard, and they recognised the Queen instantly. Whispers went up and down the ranks.

'Soldiers of Norstalos! I give you your rightful Queen!' the wizard roared, his voice louder than even a bard could manage. Not that he had any competition. Romon was just standing there, mouth open.

Kay glanced left and right. Nobody seemed to know what to do. The sudden appearance of Queen Merren had been so shocking — and unexpected — that everyone was hoping someone else would be able to explain it. The rangers were glancing at their officers for orders, the officers were looking at Beq, while Beq, for some reason, was looking at the Lord of Bellic. Kay wondered if he should stand and take control of the situation. But what should he do? Why had she come here — and arrived in such a manner?

A noise made him turn and he saw armed men in blue surcoats, at least thirty, clatter out from the office building and form up around where he and the other officers sat.

'Nobody move! We're not here to hurt you, just to tell you the truth about the Berellians and the lies they have been feeding you!' Queen Merren's voice, magically amplified, boomed across the archery range. Even more impressive, she was seemingly lit from behind by the golden light.

A tough-looking man in blue, with a scarred face, told them, more quietly: 'That goes for you as well. Listen to what the Queen has to say and not one of you will be hurt, not even the Berellians. Where is the Lord of Bellic?'

Kay saw the Berellian stand from his seat.

The leader of the Queen's men signalled to two of his companions. 'Bring him here and guard him well. We are all Norstalines, there will be no need for bloodshed. Listen to the Queen and learn how these Berellians and Duke Gello have tricked you.'

The men hurried over to where the Lord of Bellic stood, relaxed. The Queen was speaking but Kay was focused on what was happening here, his mind awhirl.

Then the Lord of Bellic signalled to his companions and exploded into action.

Merren surveyed the assembled rangers with a growing feeling of hope.

'The usurper, my cousin Duke Gello, has tricked and lied to you. There are no Rallorans attacking and killing people in the north! I have here Count Sendric, as well as leaders from the towns of Sendric and Gerrin, who can tell you that it was not the Rallorans who were killing people but the soldiers of Duke Gello! Gello wants to ally himself with Berellia, our traditional enemy, and start a war that will conquer the world! The Real Saga of Bellic is a lie, and we will prove it! As for the Lord of Bellic ...'

She glanced over to where the Berellian sat — and gasped in horror.

Wime's men reached out to grab the arms of the Berellian — only for him to draw a pair of daggers in one fluid movement, then slam them into the men's throats.

'Stop him!' Wime roared but the Lord's hand went to his belt — the buckle came away to form a throwing knife. His hand flicked out and Wime collapsed, the knife buried in his eye socket.

'No!' Merren cried, but there was nothing she could do. She was standing barely twenty paces away but she was gripped with a feeling of unreality — surely this could not be happening.

The other black-clad Berellians drew swords — one tossing a pair of blades to their Lord — and attacked her men, who seemed dazed by the loss of Wime.

Having seen Martil in action against Havrick's soldiers, Merren had both rejoiced and been horrified at how he had carved a bloody path through their ranks. This was like watching that day again, only in a nightmarish reverse. Her men tried to fight back — Tarik sent one black-clad man flying back with an arrow through the chest — but the Berellians were in another class entirely. Forde and his squad from Gerrin charged into the attack but these half-trained men were cut to pieces.

Black-clad Berellians spun, ducked, leaped and darted, using throwing knives and short swords to cut down man after man.

Meanwhile a short man in the rich uniform of a war captain had leaped onto his chair.

'Attack them! Seize them! It is the traitor Queen! Kill her!' he screamed at the ranger officers.

There were about thirty ranger officers seated with the Berellians. About half of them drew swords and joined in attacking Merren's men, while the other half backed away, looking instead at an officer that she saw, with a shocking jolt of recognition, was Captain Kay, the former commander of her Royal Guard. He was not joining the attack, but nor was he helping her men, who were trying to form a rudimentary shield wall against the incessant attack.

Rocus roared in rage and frustration and started to run over to help but the thunder of hoofs made him pause. From the far side of the archery ranges galloped a squadron of light cavalry in the red of Gello.

'It's a trap! We have to get out of here!' Merren bellowed.

'My Queen, we have to get back to the oak, and escape! And we have to go through the barracks or those cavalry will cut us to pieces!' Barrett cried.

'Give us some time!' she ordered him. 'Rocus! Get

176

over there and take command — take us back into the barracks. We'll use that as cover to get to the woods. Move!'

Rocus raced towards where the Queen's men were desperately defending themselves against the Berellians and ranger officers. Barrett hesitated for a few heartbeats, then turned. He looked around wildly, then his gaze fell on the archery targets. Each was the height of a man, twice a man's width and made of thick wood, padded and painted. With a gesture, he uprooted target after target and sent them flying across the field at the height of the horses' knees. Each one scythed down three or four horses, and threw the charge into confusion.

Sweating now, he turned with a smile to see Sendric and the Queen hurrying towards the one-sided battle. He ran after them, only to have the bard rush towards him. He prepared to use his staff on the man, but the bard waved his arms.

'You are right! The saga we're being made to sing is all lies! I want to find the truth for myself — take me with you!' Romon shouted.

'Are you a madman? We're likely to all be killed or captured!' Barrett growled.

'Then I'll claim you took me against my will. But I'll risk it!'

Barrett stared at him, baffled. 'Well, come with me if you're that crazy!'

And without checking to see if the bard was coming, he sprinted to catch up with the Queen. If they were going to get out, he was going to have to do something special. It was a dire situation but it was also an opportunity to impress Merren.

Tarik had always been a quiet man, reluctant to yell orders, but with Wime lying dead two paces away, he knew he had to do something if they were to get away. He nocked and loosed, sending another black-clad devil tumbling to the ground, although they were proving immensely hard to hit. Each one was incredibly skilful, and the various militiamen and guardsmen seemed unable to cope. Although Martil had trained them to fight together he usually launched them from ambush. Now they were the ambushed, and their talismanic captain, who could turn a battle on his own, was not even there — and the result was very different.

'Hold steady! Lock shields!' Tarik shoved two men together, the sergeants took up his call and there was finally a rough line. The last man outside it, one of Forde's militia, was chopped down by a pair of the Berellians but the line easily held a charge of ranger officers, throwing them back so they got in the Berellians' way. Tarik glanced over at the rangers. Luckily they seemed to be just sitting there. Without weapons, without orders, they were at a loss as to what to do. Tarik was grateful none had brought a bow to the bard's performance. Even a dozen archers would have destroyed the shield wall in an instant. As it was, they had enough problems with the Berellians. Stuck behind the enthusiastic but futile attacks of the ranger officers, they were throwing darts, not the tiny, flimsy things used in the harmless tavern game, but heavy metal spikes the length of a man's hand, each with a wickedly barbed head. Most could be blocked with a shield but one man was already down, his throat torn out by a dart.

Then Rocus and the Queen were there.

'Where is Martil? Come and face me, you coward!' the Lord of Bellic challenged.

'He's not here! If he was, he'd cut your black heart out, Bellic!' Merren yelled back, wishing it were true.

The Berellian spat. 'The Lord of Bellic is long dead. I am the Berellian Champion, Cezar — and I shall have to take your heart, instead!'

Tarik loosed an arrow at the man, but he batted it away with a blade.

'Time to go, your majesty!' Rocus said.

The rangers were at last moving — their commanding officer had roused the closest company, and they were obviously heading for the armoury and their bows. Meanwhile, the cavalry were advancing again, and the ranger officers continued to be thrown back by Tarik's men.

'Back! Keep your line! Through the barracks!' Rocus cried.

They backed away but holding a shield wall together while retreating was incredibly difficult. With the Berellians hurling their darts, the right-hand side was savagely attacked. Two men went down, and for an instant it looked as though the whole line would collapse. But Barrett — his staff now the size of a small tree — waded in, sending both ranger officers and Berellians in all directions. Men flew screaming through the air and, in the confusion, Rocus gathered the Queen's men and sent them running between two buildings.

Tarik led the way. He could hear the roar of orders and knew it would not be long before the rangers were hunting them through these buildings.

Merren could see her men were already gasping and puffing for air; the mail hauberks they wore were weighing them down and the exertion of fleeing after fighting was exhausting them.

'Stop! Get those mail shirts off! We need more speed!' she ordered.

'My Queen?' Forde was among many who turned and gaped at her.

'Those hauberks are slowing us down. Get out of them if you want to live!' she snapped.

Immediately most of the men began to tear at buckles and straps.

'You heard the Queen! Move your stupid arses!' Rocus spat at the few laggards.

Men paired up, tugging the heavy, unwieldy shirts over the heads of their fellows.

'Hurry! Hurry!' Merren urged. She had ditched her own shirt and felt much lighter for it. They had lost time here, given their pursuers an opportunity to spread the net. But without it they would have been run down, too tired to fight.

Just as she was congratulating herself on a winning gamble, a squad of rangers ran around the side of the building and almost fell over them. The rangers had no bows but had swords in their hands.

'Kill them!' their sergeant shouted, and raced forwards.

Tarik sent an arrow through his throat.

The other rangers had hesitated, despite the order, and the death of the sergeant sent them running back the way they had come.

Tarik looked at Merren quizzically.

'We'll worry about their loyalty later. Run!' She waved them on.

And they were off again, breath sawing harshly in their throats. They could hear horns sounding, and Merren worried just what orders they conveyed. The buildings seemed to go on forever — run past one, and there was another. Tarik led the way; the veteran hunter had brought them in and she was confident if anyone could lead them out, he could.

At the corner of one of the barracks buildings, they stopped to catch their breath.

'Just past this last one, there is the gate, beyond that is the wood,' Tarik said, and gestured. 'Not much further.'

'Where are those Berellians?' Barrett asked, worried.

'They know they can't stop us,' Rocus said.

'We don't have time to worry about them! Come on!' Merren waved them forwards.

Tarik looked around the corner, cursed, and ducked back. An instant later, an arrow thumped into the wall.

'They've got about a score of archers lined up fifty paces away — they'll spit any man who goes round that corner,' he snarled.

'Is there another way?' Merren asked.

The hunter just shook his head.

'We'll just go round with shields up — we'll lose a few but we have to do it,' Sendric suggested.

'I've got a better idea.' Barrett smiled at Merren, then calmly stepped out into the open.

'Barrett!' Merren cried.

He felt his blood sing a little when she called his name with such concern, but his concentration had to be on the line of rangers, who immediately loosed their arrows. Reaching into the magic, he increased the natural heat and friction each arrow was experiencing as it flew through the air, multiplying it until the arrows simply burst into flames and fell at his feet as ashes. He felt his breathing quicken, the sweat stand out on his face, but it had been worth it.

'Quick!' He waved. 'I will protect you!'

Without argument, the men rushed out, shields high, Forde and his last two men making it their business to protect Merren.

More arrows poured in, as the rangers nocked and loosed as fast as their trained hands could draw back the strings. Barrett sent each burning to the ground then, when the men were past, increased the size of his staff and used it to catch the last two arrows, before waving at the rangers and stepping into cover.

Men cheered and patted him on the back, and he used that to give him time to slow his breathing, mop his brow and take a drink from his waterskin. When he saw Merren, he was under control, almost.

'You need to conserve your energy,' she chided him, albeit with a smile.

'I will do whatever is necessary to get us away,' he declared. Her earlier comment about how she had wished Martil was here had stung a little. Certainly the muscle-bound oaf — or rather, the Dragon Sword — would be of use, but he was going to show her just how valuable he was.

'Not far now! Keep going!' Merren encouraged the men, and they lengthened their strides as they ran past the last building.

Tarik waved them on. 'Just around the corner is the gate!'

'Slow down! Stay together!' Rocus called.

A door burst open to their left and rangers poured out, swords in hands. Unlike the other squad, this one ran to the attack without pause. They hit in the middle of the group, bowling over two men, one of them Sendric, who took a blow to the head that drove him to the ground.

Rocus bellowed orders to lock shields but Barrett saw that was not going to work.

'Leave them to me!' he roared, and sprang to the attack. He could feel the tiredness starting to build up but he willed himself to ignore it.

In a moment his staff was the size of a small tree, and he smashed it into the rangers as though it were as light as a twig. With his first blow, two men were flung high into the air, to crash into the side of the building. The reverse sweep sent three more cartwheeling across to the other side. Immediately the momentum changed; Rocus and Tarik were there, calling to their men to stand together and hold the attack. Barrett ignored them, and gestured towards the open door, behind which more rangers massed. The huge double wooden doors slammed shut and, for good measure, he made the wood grow so the doors were sealed shut forever. There were still a dozen rangers outside, fighting against the Queen's men, and he ran to finish them off, happy that the Queen would be watching him win the battle for her.

'Now I have you, bitch!'

Merren had backed away from the little battle, but now she spun to see the Berellians emerge from the opposite building, and she saw how they had sprung the trap.

'Barrett!' she cried, knowing that no normal man could get there in time to save her.

Barrett whipped the end of his staff around, sending the last three rangers flying, and turned with a smile on his face, expecting to see Merren's grateful face. Instead he saw the remaining Berellians hurl darts at her.

'Nooo!' he screamed and sent out his magic, creating a blast of wind strong enough to deflect the barbed darts, so they slammed into the building instead of Merren's flesh. But the exertion took its toll. His legs felt rubbery and his vision swam. He fell to his knees to see the Berellian leader snarl in fury that his first attempt had failed, then draw his sword and leap forwards. To Barrett's horror and anguish, he knew he could not reach her in time.

9

Martil had tried to play with Karia, but she was only interested in Father Nott. She wanted Nott to talk to her, read to her, and play with her. The fact they were playing with the dolls he had bought her only made Martil feel more irritable.

With nothing to do, his thoughts turned dark. There was the nightmare waiting for him that night; the fear of being in the capital, surrounded by soldiers loyal to Gello, with no possible way of escape; the massive field army Gello was assembling; and, worst, the thought that Merren expected him to be able to defeat it, with no more than a few companies of half-trained townsfolk, a regiment of archers and a regiment of his Rallorans.

He had lied to her, lied to all of them, just so he could finally capture the Lord of Bellic and have the chance to end the nightmares that still plagued him. Ironically, Martil was not sure what he was going to do with the Lord of Bellic if and when he had him. Forcing the man to publicly confess how he had slaughtered a village then ordered his town to fight to the death was hardly going to result in a song to wash away the Real Saga of Bellic.

And, after all that, Merren had not wanted him to go along on the attempt to capture the Lord of Bellic. Instead, he was sitting in this room, with nothing to do but try not to hear the sound of Karia's laughter coming from next door. He could not even sharpen his sword, to give himself something to do. The bloody Dragon Sword never needed sharpening. Never needed anything, except something he could not supply. He gripped the still-cold hilt and stared into the expressionless eyes of its dragon carving. Why wasn't it working for him? Why could he not unlock its power?

He sighed. It was obvious. A good man did not have nightmares about killing women and children, did not bear the sole responsibility for the most infamous massacre in the continent's bloody history. And a good man did not lie to the woman he cherished an impossible love for.

He sheathed the Dragon Sword violently and contemplated the next few hours. They promised to be just as bleak. He felt if he stayed in this room for much longer he would surely go crazy. He had to get out. But where? The capital was crawling with soldiers, although they could not be in every tavern in the place. What if he went and had a few drinks? He might even hear a bard in action, be able to plausibly say that was part of the mission. He struggled to think if they had passed a likely looking place as he fumbled in his belt pouch, to check he had some money. There was a bit of gold still in there, and something else — an obscenely-shaped wooden token. He hauled it out. The Golden Gate. Now there was an idea.

He tried to tell himself it was a bad one, that he should just wait in his room — there was too much depending on this mission. He could not jeopardise it. But the thought of Lahra — and her ample charms — blotted everything else out from his mind. He could slip out, pay a quick visit and be back by dark. Perfect. He knew better than to ask Father Nott for directions. The old priest was too canny, and would be sure to catch on. And Karia might even ask awkward questions. After all, that was her specialty.

But that Sister Milly ... surely she could be bluffed?

'Sister, how do I get to the Church of the Sun from here? I need to sit in the peace there. You understand?' Martil said casually. 'Obviously it would be too dangerous to try it in here, but at the church, I will go unrecognised.'

Milly looked up from writing out a series of messages which Tiera would slip to the prisoners that night.

'Don't you think it dangerous to go out?' she asked simply.

Martil shrugged. 'Perhaps, but I still need to. You of all people should know how much a person needs to speak quietly to Aroaril.'

'And your room is not good enough?'

Martil tried a smile. 'I'm afraid I'm a traditionalist. It has to be inside a church.'

Milly looked hard at him, then sighed. 'I cannot stop a man from wanting to connect with Aroaril. I would caution against it, however. You are essential to the success of this rescue.'

'Nothing will happen,' Martil assured her.

'Go out the side entrance, then head up the street. Take the second left, and you will be in the road that leads you to the Church of the Sun. How long will you be? If I know when to expect you back, I can alert Tiera to help you get upstairs without being seen.'

Martil thought quickly. There was no harm in the question, and she seemed to be accepting his story, which, he had to admit, did not have the ring of truth. What the Dragon Sword thought of it, he neither knew nor cared.

'I'll be back at nightfall,' he promised, before ducking away, just in case she had more questions.

Creeping down the stairs and out the side door was easy enough, and he lost himself in the crush of people on the street by the time he walked past the front door with its bored guards. With the thought of what awaited driving him on, his step was eager and strong.

Milly silently watched Martil sneak down the stairs, then walked up the corridor to the room where she knew Sergeant Kesbury was relaxing. Nott had warned her that Martil was a man on the edge, and she did not for a moment believe his story of wanting to spend a few hours of quiet worship in the Church of the Sun. But, as a daughter of the city, she knew that the notorious brothel the Golden Gate was near the church. If she had stopped Martil leaving, she knew he would have tried to slip out of his room unseen. At least this way she could follow him, and ensure he did not end up getting killed. But she would need help.

Kesbury was sitting down, feet up on the table, alternating between running a sharpening stone down his sword blade and chewing on some bread and cheese.

'Sifthter,' he said through a mouthful, and jumped to his feet.

'Sergeant, I need your help,' she said crisply. 'The captain has slipped out to visit a brothel and we need to watch his back.'

'Watch his back …?' Kesbury said in confusion, flushing a little.

Milly sighed. 'Poor choice of words. He's gone to the Golden Gate, do you know it?'

'Know it? I used to work there!' Kesbury snorted, before hastily adding, 'As a guard, Sister.'

'Well, we need to make sure he gets there and back safely. Come with me.'

'Of course, Sister.' Kesbury sheathed his sword and grabbed a last piece of cheese. 'I'm ready.'

Martil found the Golden Gate easily enough, even though it did look a little different in the light. Gone were the torches and men standing on guard outside. But when he stepped though the gate, a pair of guards in the unusual pink surcoats appeared out of the foliage, lead-tipped staves at the ready.

'Do you know where you are going, sir?' one asked gruffly.

Martil sighed. There were no Ralloran accents here now. But he did not need to speak, he just held out the token. The guards inspected it carefully, then moved aside.

'Welcome back, sir,' the guard grunted.

Martil hurried down the carriage driveway, his boots crunching on the gravel. This stupid little token was going to prove it was worth some of the gold he had spent on it. The guards on the front door were likewise impressed by the token, and waved him inside.

He entered into the light and the warmth with a delightful air of anticipation. It was just as he remembered it, with the colourful divans and rugs — and the exotic paintings on the walls. At this time of day, there were only a couple of other men in the room, both of them drinking and both with half-naked women on their laps.

'Welcome, sir,' Sillat, the brothel owner, appeared at Martil's left elbow. 'What can we do for you today?'

Martil flashed the token at her, and she smiled broadly, before taking it from his hand. Producing a small knife from under her dress, she carefully carved a notch in the side before handing it back with a flourish. Martil pocketed it again, relaxing a little that she had not commented on him. Obviously a brothel this size would have many clients but not to be recognised was nevertheless a relief.

'So, who would you like to see today?' she inquired, opening the cupboard behind the counter which held the coloured bellpulls.

'Is Lahra free?' he asked casually, hoping she would be and wondering what he would do if she was not. Still, there would be other women …

Sillat winked. 'Can you be swift?'

'What?' Martil flushed.

Sillat chuckled throatily. 'It's just that she has to leave for another appointment in a half-turn of the hourglass. If you want your full turn, there are other ladies, but if the half-turn is sufficient for you, I'm sure Lahra can … fit you in,' she suggested, with a raise of an eyebrow.

Martil knew he was supposed to smile at that, but it was an effort.

He nodded 'A half-turn of the hourglass is fine.'

'Excellent! Wait there.'

Sillat tugged Lahra's bellpull, and then gestured to her door.

Martil walked over, past the over-stuffed divans and chairs, dimly registering that a carriage was arriving, judging by the crunch of gravel, the cracks of a whip and the shouts of coachmen. Probably a nobleman, he guessed. Well, even if he were also for Lahra, he had the first turn. Let the noble wait.

Lahra opened the door almost as soon as he got there, and he saw her dull eyes widen in surprise and recognition.

Not wanting her to blurt out his name, or what he had done there on his last visit, he stepped through the door, shutting it behind him.

'You!' Lahra hissed angrily. 'You've got some nerve! After what happened last time!'

Martil remembered, with a guilty surge, that his last visit had seen her tricked into impersonating the Queen, and probably resulted in her being imprisoned for a while. He had thought she might have forgotten by now, or at least forgiven. Still, she worked for gold, didn't she?

'Sssh! I can explain! And I have gold!' Martil uttered what he hoped were the magic words. He had spent enough on the bloody token already to not want to hand more over to this whore, but if that was what it took …

'I never got my two gold pieces!' she almost howled.

Desperately, Martil fumbled in his pouch and came out with three gold coins and a couple of silver.

'Look! Let's just go in your room and talk about it,' he suggested, tucking the coins away again.

Lahra's expression softened a little at the sight of the gold. 'Right, follow me,' she ordered.

He hurried behind her as she stormed down the passage. The combination of high-heeled shoes and short dress focused his mind away from the gold and onto something else entirely.

She held open the door.

'So tell me why I had to spend two turns of the hourglass in the dungeon, why I lost my two gold pieces, and why Sillat only gave me half the usual fee for appearing at King Gello's birthday party and coronation party!' she ranted.

'Well, you must realise what is going on in the country,' Martil began, not sure if he should try to have a political discussion with her and not really wanting to waste any time, either. The sand in the hourglass was trickling away.

'I know that the King himself calls for me! I know that I appear at the finest parties in the land!' she declared. 'And you put all that at risk!'

'He's not the King, he's a usurper, and he's just using you to humiliate the real Queen! As soon as he has control of the country, he will lose his interest in you — surely you see that?' Martil argued.

He realised, with a sinking feeling, that she was not going to listen to reason. If he had apologised profusely and offered her a pouch of gold, it might have been a different matter. But, looking at the expression on her face, that was probably out of the question now.

'So you're still with that Queen? The one who was rude to me?'

'Well …' Martil temporised, unsure of what to say.

'Are you here to kidnap me again?' she demanded.

'I never kidnapped you! And I'm only here to …' Martil trailed off as she walked across to a red bellpull and hauled on it with all her strength. 'What was that? Are you calling for another girl to replace you?' Even as he spoke, he knew with a sinking feeling that was not going to be the case.

'The King himself is on his way here to see me! I know where my loyalties lie — I am a servant of the Crown!' Lahra declared defiantly.

Martil swore. 'That bellpull was for the guards, wasn't it?'

The pounding of feet in the passage answered his question for him. Cursing, he ducked out of the room. He was angry; with himself for not handling this better and doubly angry that he would not be able to handle her at all now.

A pair of burly men in the brothel's signature pink surcoats charged at him, the lead guard swinging a lead-tipped stave at his head. Martil dodged the staff and it slammed into the doorframe. He used his left arm to lock the staff against the wall, then brought his right elbow up into the man's face. Blood spurted and Martil heard the nose break but as soon as the man reeled away, hands clutching at his face, he grabbed the staff. He had never used a quarterstaff before but he hefted it confidently enough.

The second guard hesitated and made the fateful mistake of glancing at where his moaning companion was attempting to stem the flow of blood from his face. Martil pounced at him. Before the man could bring his own staff down to block it, Martil jabbed the heavy tip into the guard's stomach and, when he folded over, slammed the other end into his temple. The man went down like a sack of carrots.

Lahra watched this from the doorway, open-mouthed. Martil decided to keep hold of the staff. He was feeling in a bloody mood now and rather hoped he would get the chance to use it. He guessed that more guards would be arriving at any moment, so pulled a pair of gold pieces from his pouch and tossed them to her.

'That's the payment I promised you for helping rescue the Queen. Enjoy your fame while it lasts, because I will kill Gello and every noble who supports him,' he swore.

She just stared at him, incapable of speech.

Furious, Martil stormed back down the passage to the over-decorated entrance room. He did not just walk through — he jerked open the door and stepped back, staff held low. A howling guard in a pink surcoat leaped through the door, not wielding a staff but a short club. Coldly, Martil measured his approach and jabbed the end of his staff into the man's throat. Choking and gasping, the man flew backwards and Martil stepped over him and into the main room, staff at the ready.

Three guards were waiting for him, all with the lead-tipped staves. Martil bellowed with rage, using the noise to startle them, then leaped to the attack. One end of his staff buried itself in the groin of the man to his left, who collapsed, a silent scream contorting his face. The man to his right caught the other end in his stomach, then the staff came up to block a blow from the man in front. Martil recovered from the block and rammed an end on the last man's foot before belting him across the face as he jumped in agony.

Martil looked around the room before throwing the staff down. Nobody said anything as they watched the moaning, bleeding guards flop around on the floor.

'I'm leaving now. You can use the gold you owe me to pay the healer's bill for your useless guards,' he told a stunned Sillat. 'I would advise no one else to try to stop me.'

He walked across the room and opened the door. He had downed six men inside — he doubted there would be any more around and, even if there was a pair still on the gate, they would not pose much of a problem. If he had faced six Rallorans, now that would have been a different matter, but these soft Norstalines couldn't fight their way out of a church school playground. However, the satisfaction of having downed six men was not exactly making up for missing out on an afternoon in bed with Lahra. Now what was he going to do? Return to the chapter house?

He slammed the door behind him, still unsure what to do, and turned to see a full squad of heavy cavalrymen encircle him. Behind them was an officer in a red surcoat. And behind him was what Martil remembered as the Royal Carriage — obviously now being used by Gello.

'So what do we have here?' the officer sneered. 'Planning an attempt on the King's life, were you? Take him!'

All thought vanished from Martil's mind and, before he even realised what he was doing, his hands had flashed down to his swords.

'Come on then, you bastards!' he roared.

The ten men, all in heavy mail hauberks, and carrying sword and shield, slowly closed in.

'Captain Kay! Get your men into action or you will never hold rank in the King's army again!' Beq screamed the order, spittle spraying into the air.

Kay was struggling to keep up. First the Queen had appeared, then all these armed men, then the Lord of

Bellic had turned out to be a Berellian assassin, then Romon the bard — who had been hand-picked to tell Kay and his men why they should fight for Gello — had gone with the Queen, and now everyone was running around in confusion. The Queen and her men were lost in the maze of barracks buildings, and the Berellians were after them. Beq had already mustered Company One, which was made up of men who had sworn the loyalty pledge to Gello, and sent them chasing after the Queen. Kay's instinct was to get his men under control — sending companies of men chasing into the barracks was just likely to get them killed. But Beq was bellowing that he wanted the Queen stopped and killed.

'Now, Kay!'

Kay's mind cleared. He would capture the Queen, and ask her what was going on. Something was not right here. But he would find the answers.

'Companies to me!' he bellowed.

Merren had instinctively flinched as the Berellians hurled their evil-looking darts at her, cringing as she waited for them to rip home. Instead, they all flew past her and she realised with a shock of relief that Barrett must have intervened to make them miss. Her relief was short-lived, however, as the Berellian Champion snarled in fury, drew his sword and leaped at her. She had seen him kill four of her men so far, including Wime, and even as she drew the dagger at her belt, knew there was no way to defend against him.

'Die, you Bitch Queen!' the Berellian howled as he sprang at her. 'Die for Zorva!'

Merren brought up her dagger, determined to at least go down fighting.

196

Time seemed to slow, the Berellian's leap seemed to take forever — and then a man hurled himself at the Berellian. The pair went over in a crash, and Merren recognised Forde. Before she could do anything else, she saw the Berellian's short sword bite deep into Forde's side, saw the blood spurt out and the shock and pain register on the militiaman's face. But Forde just wrapped his arms around the Berellian, hanging on as the assassin plunged his sword home again.

'Run, my Queen!' Forde cried, then choked.

'Help him!' Merren appealed, but Rocus was there now, the big guardsman grabbing her arm.

'It's too late for him, my Queen — and if we stay, too late for us!'

Even as he spoke, a pair of the Berellians threw darts at her, which slammed viciously into Rocus's shield.

Merren allowed herself to be pulled away, and forced her legs to start running, as the Berellian tried to free himself from Forde who, even in death, clung tightly to the assassin.

'Move it!' Rocus shouted at his men.

The rangers had been dealt with by Barrett, but the exhausted wizard was now being dragged along by a pair of men. A dazed Sendric was being supported by the bard.

'Not far now!' Tarik urged them on through the gate.

Merren, hoping to remain unseen, wiped away a tear.

'He died well, my Queen,' Rocus said softly. 'A death we can all envy. He swore he would save your life one day, and he did.'

'I didn't want anyone to have to die for me,' Merren said thickly.

'I'm not too keen on it myself, but some things are worth dying for. Now we just have to make his sacrifice worthwhile,' Rocus puffed as they ran out of the gate.

The wooded training grounds with the oak which was their escape route was barely fifty paces away. Barrett, who had been swigging water and stuffing honey treats into his mouth, was now able to run unaided and Merren began to hope they would get away without any more losses.

When she worried about being able to help Martil, Sister Milly drew comfort from the sheer bulk of Kesbury. He was very reassuring. The crowds on the street parted to go around him, even though he was covered from head to foot in the robe of a novice priest. They were not able to keep Martil in sight but Milly was confident he would be going straight to the brothel.

'How do we get inside without the guards knowing? They might believe a novice priest wants to pay them a visit but they'll never believe that of me,' she hissed, as they watched from across the road.

'Easy,' Kesbury said confidently, 'follow me.'

He led her down the street, to a much smaller gate, this one hidden by some thick bushes.

'Anyone around?' Kesbury asked softly.

Milly looked around carefully then clutched at Kesbury's arm.

'What is it?'

She gestured wordlessly as the Royal Carriage clattered past them and swung into the driveway of the Golden Gate, accompanied by a squad of cavalrymen in full armour.

'Aroaril's beard! Do you think Gello himself is in there?' Kesbury breathed.

Milly shook her head. 'Not enough guards. He is always accompanied by a full squadron. It seems he wants the support of the people but he does not have their love.'

'Still, we'd better get in there. That could put the captain off a bit.' Kesbury took the thin chain that locked the gate, and grunted with the effort of hauling at it until a link stretched enough for him to slip it off, open the gate and lead her inside.

'They probably won't go inside — it'd upset the paying customers — but they'll be waiting when the captain steps out. And if he sees a bunch of troopers standing around, he's just as likely to take them on as he is to try and slip past,' Kesbury whispered, as he led the way through the lush gardens.

'Really?'

'Aye. He always was a mad bastard.' Kesbury grinned. He seemed to be enjoying himself.

Milly found that strange. For herself, she was sure the pounding of her heart was loud enough to give them away. She was acutely conscious of how dangerous this was. She had seen her Archbishop seized and arrested in front of her; now Father Nott had placed Martil into her responsibility and she felt acutely the pressure of such a charge. Irrationally, she wondered how someone as large as Kesbury could move so quietly.

He led her to a small, hedged arbour that had a wide, cushion-filled bench, then used a dagger to trim a small hole in the hedge, allowing them to see the main building.

'What is this?' Milly kneeled on a cushion to peer at the troopers standing casually beside the parked coach.

Kesbury coughed. 'On a warm night, some of the ladies, er, entertain out here …'

'Of course.' Milly almost laughed as she saw his embarrassment. It was strange, but she felt comfortable around him.

'What brought you here, Kesbury?'

The big man shrugged. 'Bellic, I guess. It all leads back to there. What I saw at the murdered village, what I saw, what I did in the town — I could not stay in my own country. I had to come somewhere where people did not spit at you in the street. We did our duty, we followed our orders, and half the country hated us for it. Now the Berellians and Gello are trying to do the same to us here.'

'But there are terrible stories from Bellic,' Milly said gently.

'I would like to make up for it. Of course I would. But I could spend the rest of my life helping others and never balance the scales.'

'But you still live by the sword …'

Kesbury shrugged. 'It is the only skill I have. What craftsman wants an apprentice older than he is? And I do not fight so much for a country as Captain Martil. Him and the Queen. I fight for them and the mates around me.'

'You are a good man,' Milly told him softly.

Kesbury grinned. 'You haven't seen me with a few ales inside me, Sister.'

'There's still time.' Milly smiled back.

The sound of a bell clanging by the gate made Kesbury sit up.

'What is it?'

'That's the alarm,' Kesbury said grimly.

Sure enough, the two gate guards raced down the drive and into the main house, while the troopers now leaped to attention, drawing their swords and facing the door.

Kesbury pulled off his robe. 'We need to get closer,' he whispered, and led her down a series of paths, until they were crouched in the bushes just a few paces from where the troopers stood waiting. Milly's mind was racing. What could she ask Aroaril to do to help save Martil? She had covered this in theory extensively during her training but was horribly aware she had never asked for those sorts of powers. Her palms were sweaty, her mouth dry and she had an intense urge to relieve herself.

She felt a touch on her shoulder and nearly jumped. Kesbury leaned in close and placed his mouth against her ear. His warm breath tickled her and, for a moment, she forgot about her fear.

'When the captain comes out, you take care of as many of the ones on the far side as you can, I'll take the pair nearest to us and we'll leave the rest to the captain. Understand?'

She nodded. Talk of taking care of ten armoured men seemed madness, yet Kesbury exuded confidence; she felt herself relaxing a little, even thinking about how his lips had felt against her ear, for Aroaril's sake! Thinking about such things at a time like this seemed perverse, but she could not help it. Besides, it was better than worrying about how she was going to 'take care' of as many troopers as she could.

Then the door opened and she saw Martil walk out, saw the officer challenge him.

'Come on then, you bastards!' he roared, swords flashing into his hands.

As if in a dream she watched the troopers advance carefully, shields high and swords out. Surely this could not be real and she would not have to stop them …

Then she felt Kesbury's hand raise her up and jumped when he gave a war cry, drew his sword and dagger and charged forwards.

Somehow she followed him and saw the first troopers turn to meet this new attack. Her mind cleared as she saw what she had to do.

'Hold them, Aroaril!' she cried, gesturing towards the troopers furthest away from her.

Instantly she felt the warmth and surge of power that came from divine help. The four troopers on the far side of the yard froze in place, the expressions on their faces almost comical.

Then Kesbury struck the side of the line closest to them. The troopers had their backs turned and although his war cry had alerted them, they did not turn before he was on top of them. His sword took one in the back of the neck and, almost before that trooper had fallen, he had rammed his dagger into the side of the second.

The next two in line moved to deal with this threat, and Milly reacted to that, as well.

'Make them sleep, Aroaril!' she prayed — and the pair toppled over in front of an astonished Kesbury.

'Surrender now, or die,' Martil told the last two troopers and the officer.

With their comrades all down, and a pair of Rallorans advancing on them, the troopers backed nervously away.

'Attack, you fools! The King will have us killed otherwise!' the officer cried desperately, running forwards and aiming a blow at Martil.

He never even got close. The Dragon Sword lopped off half the officer's blade and cut his head from his shoulders with one wicked blow.

That was enough for the last two troopers, who threw down their swords.

'We give up! Just do one thing for us — hit us before you go!' one pleaded.

Kesbury and Martil exchanged looks.

'The King will kill us if you don't,' the second added.

Martil sheathed the Dragon Sword and gestured to Kesbury. The sergeant reversed his bloodied dagger and, with a pair of carefully judged blows, struck the men with the pommel.

'Good work, Sergeant. Sister, I thank you for your help.' Martil smiled. Only now he was safe did he bother to think about the danger he had been in.

'I appreciate your thanks, but this is hardly the Church of the Sun, is it? Perhaps next time you decide to lie to me about your carnal urges, you will listen to my advice!' Milly snapped, the adrenalin rush of the close encounter and her use of Aroaril's power flowing through her.

'I wouldn't expect a priestess to understand carnal urges,' Martil growled back, only too aware this little trip had been a flop in more ways than one, while the guilt and self-loathing he was feeling about it was hovering close to anger.

'Perhaps we could continue this discussion back at the chapter house?' Kesbury suggested delicately.

'Aye. Well, thank you anyway. I will not forget it.' Martil was determined not to be ungrateful. Besides, if he was quick with the apologies, he might even be able to persuade her not to tell Father Nott about this.

* * *

'How much have you got left, Barrett?' Merren asked urgently.

The wizard gave her a tired grin around a full mouth. 'Plenty, my Queen,' he mumbled.

The deep shadows under his eyes, the sweat stains on his tunic and the way his hands shook as he washed down food with water told a different tale, but she had to hope his strength would be equal to his ambition to be the hero. Out of the more than thirty men that had accompanied her, barely half were left. They were stumbling towards the safety of the trees but that was almost a false hope — about two hundred paces away she could see rangers darting into the cover already. These were men who trained among this wood regularly; they would hunt her small band down if they could. But the bigger concern was the cavalry, which was charging to the attack just fifty paces away. There was no way they were all going to get away in time, especially with Sendric and another wounded man being dragged along.

Then Barrett raised his free hand to the sky. Instantly a score of birds took flight from the trees, soaring high then swooping down to attack the cavalry horses. These beasts had been schooled to charge home into a packed body of men but they reared away from sharp claws and beaks raking at their eyes. In a heartbeat the charge was a shambles: horses falling, men shouting, horses screaming, men toppling.

'Quickly now!' Merren took Barrett's arm to help him, as the wizard was struggling badly now.

The trees gave the illusion of safety, and the exhausted band paused there for a few moments, sucking in deep breaths.

'Not far now! But we must keep moving!' Merren said encouragingly. To the best of her memory, the oak tree was barely fifty paces away, almost straight ahead.

''Ware right!' Tarik cried, nocking and loosing in one fluid movement.

One ranger stood from his hiding place and Tarik's arrow took him in the chest, sending him flying backwards. But then a second revealed himself, and an arrow soared towards Merren. Before he could duck back into cover, another of Tarik's arrows took him in the throat and he disappeared into the bushes.

Rocus leaped forwards, the arrow meant for Merren shattering on his shield, but his desperate dive sent him stumbling forwards, where he smashed his head into a tree. He struggled to get up, his eyes glazed.

'Help him!' Merren snapped. 'Come on!'

Dragging their wounded, the little band staggered through the trees, Tarik leading the way

'I see the oak!' he called.

Almost as soon as he spoke, arrows started falling around them — there was obviously a line of rangers waiting to their right. One man was hit in the upper arm, but the rest of the arrows wasted themselves on trees or on shields.

'Into cover!' Merren ordered, although there was precious little of that to be found.

'We have to keep going! They'll be moving men around us!' Tarik cried.

Merren glanced over at Barrett, but the wizard looked exhausted — and he still had to transport them away from here through the oak tree.

'We have to try. Two men with Barrett, Rocus and Sendric. Tarik, can you keep their heads down?'

'I'll try, my Queen.' Tarik grinned at her and she breathed a sigh of relief that he was still here. He stood and loosed three arrows in quick succession.

'Move!' Merren called and they struggled to their feet, hauling along their dazed or exhausted companions. She thanked Aroaril she had ordered them to leave their mail shirts behind. Even without them the men were tired; with them, they would have been caught by now.

Arrows flew in and men tried to duck behind shields. One man swore as an arrowhead scraped a bloody trail along his side, then Tarik choked as one sank deep into his chest. He struggled to draw his bow but another two arrows struck him and he fell backwards, writhed once, and then was still.

Without waiting for orders, the rest of the band dived to the ground.

'Tarik? Tarik?' Merren screamed, feeling the beginning of panic touch her. Wime and Forde dead, now Tarik too — Rocus and Sendric unable to help …

She crushed the panic ruthlessly. She would escape from here. She would not lose.

One of Forde's men, one of only two left alive, was lying next to her, tears trickling down his cheeks.

'We're all going to die,' he moaned softly. 'We're all going to die!'

Before she even knew what she had done, Merren slapped him across the face.

'We are *not* going to die!' she snarled. 'I will not allow it!'

Shocked, the man just nodded at her.

'What is your name?'

'Jaret, your majesty,' the man mumbled.

'Well, Jaret, we shall get away, and I shall make

sure that when we return to Sendric, you and your family will dine with me. Agreed?'

'Y-yes, your majesty!'

'And for Aroaril's sake, call me Merren!'

Leaving Jaret gaping at her, Merren crawled over to where Barrett lay gasping for breath. Arrows flew in every few moments, but none of the rangers were keen to show themselves long enough to aim properly. She knew that would not last. She had to do something to get them out of there. What she was decided on would cause problems later — but if she did not do it, there may not be a later.

'Barrett, how are you feeling?' She stroked his cheek tenderly.

'Give me a moment and I'll be fine.' Barrett smiled up at her devotedly.

She leaned in and kissed him gently on the forehead. 'I need you. You know I would not ask you normally, for I love you and would not want to see you hurt. But we have to get to that oak tree safely. And we have to do it now.'

Barrett felt the tiredness drop away from his spirit, although his body was still telling him it had had enough. Her words were like fire within him, and his forehead still burned from the touch of her soft lips. She'd said she loved him and cared for him! He used his staff to haul himself to his feet.

'Watch out!' Romon called. He could scarce believe he was still there — on at least three occasions he had wanted to hide, to stay behind, but had kept going instead. He put it down to reading too many sagas. He had to see if there was a happy ending to this one.

Barrett waved away the concern. He had to know where the rangers hid.

Sure enough, eight arrows soared towards him. Concentrating fiercely, he stopped their flight, then sent them back down the exact same path they had flown. With a meaty thump, all eight buried themselves in the men who had released them.

'We're clear now!' Barrett gasped, clinging on to his staff to stop himself from falling. All the strength was gone from his legs and he felt dizzy. He barely noticed as arms helped him onwards.

'Quickly now!' Merren urged them on. She felt guilty for what she had done to Barrett but could not afford to think about it now. Once they were back in the north, she could explain to him.

The desperate little band raced to the oak tree, making sure Barrett was at the centre. One arrow hitting the wizard now would trap them all.

'We're here! Barrett, get us away!' Merren slapped Jaret on the back and grinned at the remaining men.

Barrett reached out to touch the tree. He struggled to control his mind. His legs were shaking uncontrollably and there seemed to be two trees in front of him.

'Come on, Barrett! I believe in you!' Merren touched his shoulder, her lips brushing his cheek.

The words, and especially the touch, seemed to clear his mind. Barrett squared his shoulders and reached out to the tree. *One last effort*, he told himself. *One more and I can rest*. He reached into the tree, then jumped to the next, held that one in place and jumped to another, then another, then one more. But he could feel them slipping, struggling to get free.

'I cannot take us all the way — I am losing it!' he moaned.

'Just get us as far away as you can, then we can wait until you are rested,' Merren said urgently.

Barrett swayed a little. Desperately he grabbed at the trees, adding another six, seven — no, that was all he had. He thrust his staff into the tree.

'Quick!' he urged. His heart was thumping painfully and the breath was rasping in his throat.

Swiftly, supporting their wounded while keeping a hand on the staff, the men rushed through the tree, until there was just Merren and Barrett

'Thank you,' she said softly, kissing his cheek before darting through.

Once again, her touch gave Barrett a surge of energy, and he clawed his way along his staff until he was through the tree and out. Then he smiled at Merren and collapsed.

10

Kay had his rangers sweep through the woods three times before he reported back to Beq. They found the body of one of the Queen's men, as well as those of ten rangers, but nothing else. It was a mystery. The whole thing was a mystery. Romon had disappeared with them, which confused Kay even further. The bard had not been a prisoner, so why go with the Queen? Unless she was telling the truth when she said Gello and the Berellians were lying ... That seemed almost impossible, until you thought that the man who had been introduced as the Lord of Bellic turned out to be the Berellian Champion, and the leader of a band of killers. None of it was making sense.

Kay went down to one of the storerooms where the bodies were being laid out, ready for burial. Six of his brother officers had died in the fighting, with another five injured. All had been appointed to the rangers from other regiments, brought in because they were friends of Beq, but nevertheless, they were men he had known and he wanted to say farewell. As he entered the storeroom, he was shocked to find a pair of Berellians cutting the ears off the bodies of the Queen's men.

'What is the meaning of this?' Kay thundered. Desecrating the bodies of men who had fought bravely was revolting to him.

The Berellians did not even look up. 'Trophies. We have permission,' one said laconically.

Furious, Kay stormed off to look for Beq. This was an outrage and he would put a stop to it.

He paused outside the open door to Beq's office, where he could hear Beq talking to the Berellian Champion.

'I hope you will convey to your ambassador that we did everything that was required of us,' Beq was saying. 'That the Queen and the remnants of her band escaped was not our fault.'

'Their wizard saved them,' the Berellian agreed. 'And, of course, that the cursed Captain Martil was not with the Bitch Queen was not your fault.'

Kay was intrigued by the conversation — why would a Norstaline war captain be at all concerned with a report to the Berellian ambassador — but he was also aware that every moment he delayed was potentially another body desecrated by those Berellians, so he rapped on the door and pushed it open.

Beq and the Berellian turned to face him. 'What is it, Kay?' Beq snapped.

'Sir, some of the Berellians are cutting the ears off the bodies of the dead! When questioned, they claimed they had permission to do so!' Kay exploded.

The Berellian stared at him coldly. 'And they do have permission. Besides, what is the problem? The taking of trophies is a traditional right of the victor.'

Kay ignored him. 'Sir, with your permission, I wish to arrest these Berellians and see that the dead are buried with all due ceremony.'

'Permission denied,' Beq mumbled, refusing to meet Kay's eye. 'You are to let the Berellians continue.'

Kay gaped at him. 'Sir, I must protest! Whatever foul customs the Berellians insist on using, this is Norstaline soil and the dead being despoiled, whatever their faults, were Norstaline!'

Finally Beq showed some emotion. 'That is enough! You are to return to your duties, *Lieutenant* Kay, and if you mention this again, I can assure you that you will never hold command in the King's army! That is a direct order!'

Kay saluted stiffly and marched out of the room, seething inside. Everything had seemed so simple a few hours ago. Lead his men north, defeat a rabble of barbarous Rallorans and regain his honour, as well as his rank. Now it was all mixed up.

'Where have you been?' Karia demanded.

Martil stopped in his tracks. They had returned to the chapter house without incident and slipped back upstairs again without being seen. If his men's safety had not depended on the chapter house guards being so useless, he would have been angered by their incompetence.

He had been mentally rehearsing his story for Nott, going through several possible excuses on the way back. He expected Sister Milly to tell tales to Father Nott, so he thought he had better get in first. But no sooner had he walked in the room, than Karia had run over and confronted him.

'Nowhere,' he said defensively.

Karia was on edge. It had been lovely to see Father Nott again, and she had enjoyed her time with him but it had left her feeling uncertain. Father Nott had seemed preoccupied with other things — she had

had to remind him of their place in the story they were reading at least six times! Then there was Martil. He had been acting funny the last couple of days, and now he had gone off by himself. What if he left her behind, and Father Nott did not want her? She had made up her mind to make Martil feel guilty so he would spend more time with her.

'Why didn't you take me with you?'

Had Nott put her up to this? Martil felt his anger rise.

He tried to cut her off. 'You couldn't come. I had to go alone.'

'Why?'

'Because I said so!' Martil roared in her face.

Karia burst into tears and ran away, jumping onto the bed at the back of the room and covering her head with her arms.

'Martil ...' Nott began.

'I don't want to hear it!' Martil bellowed, and stormed from the room.

Gello only just contained his temper. First came the news from Ezok that the trap to kill his cousin and her Ralloran mongrel had failed, then a report the Ralloran had been waiting for him at the Golden Gate! The report from his guards, who had been there to escort Lahra back to the palace for the night's entertainment, was rather garbled. A session with the torturer's knives had failed to get much more sense out of them, either. But, according to Lahra herself, the Ralloran had planned to be there to kill him. And, judging by the incompetence of his men, may well have succeeded if Gello had not remained at the palace!

'How did he know I was going there?' Gello asked grimly.

Ezok spread his hands. Cezar's failure had left him seething. Still, he recognised this was an excellent opportunity to get further inside Gello's trust.

'Well, sire,' he began carefully, 'you have mentioned Lahra many times. All the nobles know you visit her. It may be that one or more of them still bear some allegiance to the former Queen. Or, perhaps jealous of you, they think they might do better under her rule.'

'The bastards!' Gello breathed.

'It is the curse of great rulers such as yourself. The nobles can be compared to a pack of jackals, squabbling for scraps from the table of a lion. But, like all jackals, they cannot be trusted.'

Gello nodded thoughtfully. He had been battling a growing dread these past few days — he was so close to wiping away the stain of his past dishonour but he feared another failure. Without his mother to talk to, he was eager for good advice from a source that would not try to take his throne, or accuse him of strangling her. With some difficulty, he forced his mind away from that train of thought. 'There is much sense in what you say. What do you suggest?'

'Obviously you must be careful as to what you say before them, sire.' Ezok shrugged, inviting Gello to take it to the obvious conclusion.

'Indeed. And I shall keep them under my eye at all times. I want them with me, not in their estates, plotting. If they are all in the capital, under my control, they will find it hard to try anything!'

'A brilliant plan, sire!' Ezok applauded. 'But what about the Ralloran, Martil? If the Queen's Magician helped the Queen escape, he is unlikely to be in the capital. So Martil will have been unable to escape.

He might be lying low, waiting for the traitor to contact him again.'

'You are right!' Gello exclaimed. 'I will have the guards doubled on all gates, as well as on the palace. And I'll have the nobles followed. Anything suspicious and I'll have them on the rack faster than they can beg for mercy!'

Ezok bowed. 'As always, your majesty is a man of wisdom,' he intoned. With the nobles not to be trusted, and the war captains sidelined, he would be the only person Gello would listen to now. Just as Onzalez had prophesied. He would have liked to spend some more time just reinforcing that, but he had another appointment this evening. The new Archbishop was sending begging notes, asking for a meeting. Snaring the Norstaline archbishop for Zorva on the same day he had secured his hold on the King — that would be a success to put against the failure of Cezar.

'What is it that ails you, my son?' Nott asked gently.

Martil, who had been ready for anger and accusations, was caught off-guard. He had half expected Nott to walk in, declare he was no longer a fit guardian for Karia and walk out again. Now Nott had wrong-footed him by sitting down and asking a concerned question.

'What makes you think there is something wrong?' Martil countered.

Nott smiled. 'I worked in a farming village long enough to recognise the smell of dung, so don't try to offer me some. You sneak out in search of a whore and almost get yourself killed, then, on your return, yell at Karia. Now, I know you are not a complete idiot, so there must be something bothering you.'

Martil did not know what to say.

'Bellic,' he said thickly. 'I am haunted by dreams of Bellic.'

Nott nodded. 'What makes these different?'

Martil hesitated again. If he told the priest everything, would he be sympathetic, or disappointed?

'You need to talk — whatever it is, it is obviously eating you up inside,' Nott said softly.

The lack of sleep, the fear, the anguish, it all seemed to well up inside Martil and he had to get it out. 'Every night I am back there — in Bellic. The dead hunt me through the streets, led by a woman and a boy — both of whom I killed. I run over piles of bodies, not Berellians but Rallorans and Norstalines who have died under my command. The other four war captains are there; they blame me for their torture. But when I try to escape, the thing that stops me is this woman from Rallora — she and her baby were killed by the Berellians. They did … terrible things to her, then left her to die, just letting her stay alive long enough to see her baby murdered.' He looked into Nott's kindly face, trying to make him understand.

'My regiment was the one guarding the border when the Berellians crossed and destroyed her village. She says it's all my fault — and she's right! If we had stopped them at the border, she and her baby would be alive, there would be no Bellic …' Martil's voice trailed off. He looked away.

Nott patted Martil's shoulder gently. Now was not the time to tell the man that, without Bellic, Martil would not be here now and Norstalos would have no Champion to take up the Dragon Sword. Sometimes he felt the weight of his years and, more importantly, the weight of responsibility that he bore. But he had faith that what he was doing was right; he had to.

'A guilty conscience is a good thing,' he told Martil. 'But this is more than that. You need to fight back against this dream.'

'How?' Martil looked up, a desperate hope in his eyes.

Nott scratched his chin. 'I believe the Dragon Sword is behind these dreams.'

'The Dragon Sword?' Martil stared down at the hilt in revulsion.

'To have such strong, vivid dreams — it smacks of the Sword's magic.'

'Bastard dragons!' Martil growled but Nott laid a hand on his shoulder.

'Relax, my son. It is trying to help you.'

'Help me? If this is its help, I'd be bloody terrified if it doesn't like me!' Martil spat.

Nott smiled. 'I think it wants you to overcome your past, so you can become its true wielder. It is forcing you to face your deepest fears, the darkest parts within you. To overcome it, you need to find your best parts.'

Martil just looked at him blankly.

'Your love for Karia. You need to bring her into the dream,' Nott explained.

'But I don't want her anywhere near that place!'

'I know,' Nott said patiently. 'She won't be. She will be your weapon against the dream — you must make her your way out. To escape from your past, you have to escape from this dream. Do that, and not only will the dreams stop, but you will become the true wielder of the Sword.'

Martil ignored Nott's final words; his only thought was making the dreams stop.

'But how can I get out of the dream?'

Nott sighed. 'It is not my dream. It is your mind that is trapped in Bellic — only your mind can find a way out of it. Besides, if I tell you the way out, how does that help you? The dream, the memories, the past — however you want to describe it — will only catch up with you again.'

Martil wished the bloody priest would just tell him how to do it or, better yet, pray up some magical solution from Aroaril. No, of course it could never be that easy. It had to be a mysterious puzzle to solve, just like in those cursed sagas. Still, there was a shred of hope. He could make the dreams stop. He sat up straighter. Since Nott had tried to help him, he thought he should be magnanimous.

'Father, about the brothel business, I'm sorry ...' he began.

Nott waved him to silence. 'That is in the past. It is the future I am worried about. That you escaped from Gello's men will have warned him that you are in the capital. No doubt he will think firstly about himself but his thoughts will eventually turn to other avenues. It is only a matter of time before he discovers you are here to free the Archbishop and the other imprisoned priests. With the advantage of surprise, we should be successful. Without it, we are lost.'

'But we have to wait for Father Quiller to let us know Barrett and the Queen are back with the rangers. Without Barrett, we have no escape,' Martil argued.

'I have heard from Father Quiller — there has been no word from Barrett or the Queen,' Nott said. 'That might mean they are still with the rangers, trying to get them all north. Or it might mean something more ominous. Nevertheless, it matters not. We must free the Archbishop tonight.'

'And what then?'

'We can wait here, once we have control of the building, and hope to hear from the north, or we can try to get out of the city by ourselves. We can decide once we have the Archbishop free and Prent in our power.'

Martil looked into the priest's eyes and saw there was no persuading him.

'Fine. We'd better tell that servant girl. Get a message to the prisoners and we'll strike after that.'

'There is one more task …'

Martil sighed. 'I know. I'll apologise to Karia.'

Merren looked around and tried to think. They had stepped out of the oak tree into a small wood, seemingly in the middle of nowhere. It was getting dark and she had wounded men, as well as the dazed Rocus and Sendric and the unconscious Barrett. The wizard had saved them but would they be able to save him?

Barrett lay on the ground, along with Rocus and Sendric, while the two wounded men sat beside them, pain etched on their faces.

'Where in Aroaril's name are we?' one man cried.

'This is not the north — I can't even see the hills! We're just in another part of the country!' another man, one of Rocus's former guardsmen, groaned. 'We're all dead men!'

No one seemed immediately willing to disagree with that pronouncement until Jaret stepped forwards.

'We won't die. You can't lose hope,' he declared.

'That's great coming from you! You were nearly pissing yourself back in the barracks — and you can't fight if we are found — you and your mates were about as useful as tits on a bull!' the guardsman snorted. 'Bloody militia! I knew we couldn't trust you bastards!'

'I left my mates dead back there! Don't you tell me they weren't worthy!' Jaret snarled.

'If they'd been any good, we wouldn't be in this mess!' the guardsman growled. 'Don't you understand? Gello's going to hunt us down and kill us all!'

'Afraid, are you?' Jaret was drawing strength from the other militiamen, not just his companion from Gerrin but the remnants of Wime's men, who were now behind him, looking grim. The other men, all guardsmen, lined up behind their spokesman.

Romon was amazed to see these men still seemed ready to fight. He prepared to run. Surely nothing could stop a bloodbath now.

'Why, you little …!' The guardsman drew his sword and instantly other men went for their blades.

Then Merren stepped in between the two groups, Barrett's staff in her hands. She rammed one end into the guardsman's stomach and then reversed it, swinging it in a sharp arc that made Jaret step back and let go of his sword hilt.

'Enough!' she bellowed.

They all stared at her in shock.

'Put your blades down! We will not fight amongst ourselves! And we will not die!' she roared. Part of her thought she should be afraid, but this was swamped by her anger and determination not to be defeated, especially not like this.

'Our real enemies planned a trap to kill us all and they failed! We escaped! This is a victory, not a reason to fight among ourselves! Sheathe your blades or face me!'

Romon watched in awe. She was half the size of many of the men, all of whom were blood-spattered and had both sword and shield. All she had was a staff and her will. But she turned them from warriors into small boys, abashed at being caught doing something wrong. Blades disappeared into scabbards.

'Good! Now, do you want to know how we shall get back home, or do you want me to send you away, and then tell your families you were too scared to see them again?'

The men, their rage swiftly cooling, were all looking at her, hope, fear and not a little desperation in their faces. They clearly expected her to come up with a way to save them. Romon eased a parchment out of his belt pouch and began to take notes.

Merren had acted to stop a fight without thinking about consequences, much less how they were to escape from here. All the men who might have offered her help were either dead, not there or incapable of speech or thought. It was all up to her. She took a deep breath. *Just think this through aloud*, she told herself.

'Right. They'll think we have escaped to the north, so we won't have to worry about pursuit,' she mused. 'We just have to stay hidden until Barrett has recovered his strength, then we can resume our trip home. So we will need shelter, warmth and food, as well as help for the men with wounds. Jaret?'

'Here, your majesty,' the man said.

'I told you, call me Merren.' She smiled.

'What is your name, guardsman?' She turned to the man who was only now regaining his feet.

'Wilsen, your majesty,' he gasped.

'Give me your hands, both of you!'

They held out their hands, looking like boys about to receive the punishment cane from a teacher.

Merren drew her dagger with her free hand and made a small cut on each man's palm. Both flinched but, with her watching, neither said anything nor drew his hand away.

'You two are now sword-brothers. It is on your honour to see that your companion stays alive. Now shake on it!'

Sheepishly, the two men clasped hands, wrist to wrist in the warrior's grip, their blood mingling.

'If I see one of you without the other, you will answer to me,' she told them. 'As your first duty, I want the pair of you to find a village. Go there and buy us some supplies, enough for, say, two days. We shall not stay here long. After what we have all been through, there is no need for us to fight. Every man has proved their worth. We must not give in to despair. Our friends gave their lives so we might live and breathe now. To use that to argue with each other is a betrayal of their memory. Understand?'

The men nodded, and Merren could feel the mood had changed. They were thinking about what they had escaped, and how they might make it home. She dug into her belt pouch and produced a pair of gold coins, which she dropped into Jaret's and Wilsen's hands. 'That should be enough for food and maybe an old horse or a donkey to help carry it. You can even keep the change! But make sure you bring back a skin of wine.'

They stared at her, wondering why, until she smiled.

'We must send our friends off. A toast to the dead and thanks for our survival.'

'Aye.' Wilsen nodded. 'You are right, your majesty. Come on, Jaret. Sooner we start, the sooner we're back. How good are you at bargaining?'

That was the way, she told herself. Instead of thinking about their fight, or even how far they would have to walk, or what sort of reception they would get from a strange village, they would be thinking about how much money they could come back with. Now for the rest of them.

'You and you.' She pointed to a pair of big guardsmen. 'Find a stream and refill the waterskins. The rest of you, we need to make some sort of shelter for the wounded, and a place where we can light a fire without being seen. We don't have much daylight left, so let's get moving!'

Romon the bard walked over and gave a short bow.

'Your majesty, may I compliment you. I thought we would all be dead!'

'There's still time for that. Save your congratulations for when we are safely back at Sendric,' Merren told him, but with a smile. 'Are you still thinking you made the right decision in coming with us?'

Romon grinned. 'I regretted it from the first. But I would rather be anywhere than debasing my noble profession for the glory of Gello.'

'I see you have the bard's gift,' Merren said wryly.

'I want to find out the truth, and tell people what is really happening in their country, as I have always done,' he said simply.

'Then you will be welcome. And now, perhaps, you could try to get some water into the wounded?'

'A pleasure, your majesty,' he bowed.

Merren was pleased with the cheerful activity around her. The trick was now not to think too much about what she was going to do when she returned to the north without the help her rebellion so desperately needed, what she was going to say to Wime's wife Louise, Forde's wife Gia and the families of the other dead men — how Martil was going to free the Archbishop when there was no possibility of help from Barrett.

Tiera brought them the news while Martil was reading another sickly saga about a girl whose soldier doll came magically to life and helped her defeat an army of evil mice. It had taken surprisingly very little to appease Karia — she had been happy that he had wanted to read to her. Martil was not interested in finding out why she had calmed down so quickly, but he was keen for Nott to see that he and Karia did get along well. If only Nott had seen them together back at Sendric's keep, he thought bitterly.

Karia, for her part, had been afraid he would just leave and not come back. When he offered to read her a story, she had leaped at the chance. If he was thinking of leaving, it would not do to upset him further.

'I have passed the messages to the Archbishop, the Bishop and a handful of others,' Tiera reported. 'They are all ready. But one thing. The Berellian ambassador, along with two guards, has arrived and is dining with Prent now. Lilith is serving them in Prent's apartments.'

'This could be a complication,' Nott mused.

224

'I don't like Lilith being alone with Prent. Perhaps we should change the plans and go for Prent first ...' Milly said.

Martil laughed. 'This is not a complication — it is a bonus! We will snap up a Berellian along with Prent! No, we keep to the plan. Once we have the priests with us, there is nothing Prent can do. But if we get him first, what's to say an alarm is not sounded for the guards to start killing the priests and priestesses? Besides, what is Prent going to do in front of the Berellian ambassador?'

Nott and Milly reluctantly agreed.

'So when do we go?' Tiera asked.

'I just have to finish this saga — three more pages.' Martil held up the book apologetically. Karia was sitting comfortably on his lap and showed no signs of wanting to move.

'I'll get Kesbury and your men then, shall I?' Milly said with a smile.

'And this will solve my problem?' Prent asked, half hopefully, half suspiciously.

Ezok spread his hands. 'It is the only thing that can possibly help you, my friend. You are an educated man, you know about the power of opposites. If Aroaril has used His power on someone or something, then there is only one being that can oppose that.'

Prent shifted his grip on the knife nervously. 'But, still ...'

Ezok controlled his anger through the ease of long practice. 'My friend, you heard the words from the mouth of the girl. One of the priestesses here has placed a charm on you. You cannot perform with a woman until it is removed. And there is only one

God who can break a charm from Aroaril. So you can either wait here impotently—' Ezok added a heavy emphasis to that word '—or you can do this.'

Prent was sweating now, and he licked his lips before glancing down, to where the naked young servant girl was tied across his desk, her mouth gagged, her terrified eyes pleading up at him.

'Think of it. The power to break the charm that ensnares you, the power to do what you will. He grants His loyal followers many abilities. You will be even stronger than if you had been the Archbishop of the weaker god.'

Prent groaned. 'I don't know if I can!'

'Then you will go through the rest of your life humiliated, as half a man, mocked by the women of Aroaril,' Ezok said coolly.

'Stop!' Prent almost shouted. His hands were shaking but he used the sharp knife to open a vein on the servant girl's wrist. Fumbling a little as she thrashed and tried to cry out, he caught the steady drip of blood in a silver bowl that had once held fruit.

'Seal the cut now, we don't want her to bleed to death too soon,' Ezok ordered. 'Now give me the bowl and we shall begin.'

Guard duty was boring — and Ward loved that. The more boring it was, the better he liked it. Chasing rebels through forests, forming up in the battleline to take on a regiment of ravening Rallorans — these were excitements he could do without. No, he was content with a row of cells filled with quiet prisoners, three good meals a day and a warm bed. Better yet was when he was on guard duty with men who shared his love of gambling. He was three silvers up — and tomorrow was his day off. Now, if he could just win a couple more, he would have enough for drinks all night and the best whore in the tavern. He chuckled to himself — he had been dealt three queens. Carefully he pushed a pile of coins towards the middle of the table.

'This will be the killer, lads,' he told the other five men.

'No, this will be,' a cold voice interrupted and Ward looked up to see the guardroom was full of armoured men, led by a warrior with a shining sword. 'Stay where you are if you want to live.'

'It's the Rallorans!' One of Ward's friends, a lean man called Tam, the furthest from the door, started to rise.

Another of the armoured men swung his sword once, viciously, and Tam slumped back, his head half severed.

'Anyone else?' the big warrior snarled.

Ward, spattered with Tam's blood, kept his hands on the table and prayed everyone else would do the same.

'Sergeant Kesbury! Even men to watch these guards, odd men on me,' the leader snapped. 'Where are the keys to the cells?'

When nobody moved, he hefted his sword. 'Don't make me do this the hard way,' he warned.

'There!' Ward pointed to the thick bundle of keys on a nail beside the door.

'Thank you.' The leader took the keys and walked out, followed by every second man.

'Just sit quiet now, lads, and you'll be fine,' the big warrior called Kesbury announced.

Ward had no intention of moving. He could see his luck had changed — although at least it was not as bad as Tam's luck.

Martil hurried down towards the cells, ripping the keys off the ring as he went, handing them to his men. This had been easy so far. Thanks to Tiera, they had been able to slip down here unseen. But speed was vital. Just one man escaping onto the street could ruin everything. Gello could not know that they were here.

'Spread out and start unlocking doors! Soon as we find the Bishop or Archbishop, let me know. Once we have a couple of cells clear, we start bringing the prisoners down,' he ordered.

'Captain Martil! Over here!' a fine voice called out and Martil peered down the dingy passageway. These old cells were dry enough — otherwise they would have been useless for storing produce — but Prent had obviously decided not to worry about spending much on lamps. All he could see was endless stone walls and solid metal doors, each with a small grate with bars set close together.

'Archbishop? Where are you? I can't see!' Martil called in frustration.

Next moment the passage was as brightly lit as day and Martil and his men had to cover their eyes for a moment until they could adjust.

'Does that help?'

Martil now saw a cell door two down on his right had a hand poking out of it.

'Thank you!' he called as he hurried over.

Within moments the Archbishop was free, shaking Martil and his men warmly by the hand and stretching. His robes were grubby, his face unshaven and his hair greasy but he looked well enough and was smiling broadly.

'I cannot tell you what a pleasure it is to be free,' he said warmly. 'I understand your plan is to seize this building and hold it until there is an opportunity to escape north?'

'Absolutely, your grace.' Martil nodded. 'But we must hurry …'

'Of course, my son.'

The Archbishop closed his eyes for a moment, murmured something and, next moment, the keys flew out of Ralloran hands to the doors. With a giant click, every door in the passageway swung open and a collection of dirty and dishevelled priests and priestesses poured out, smiling and embracing each other and the Rallorans. Martil noticed they tended to be either women or old men.

'Those cells weren't built for comfort, but at least we had some time to pray, and reflect.' A white-bearded priest patted Martil on the back.

'Is everyone out?' the Archbishop called.

A quick check later and it was confirmed. Martil guessed there were almost one hundred priests and priestesses now crowded in the corridor.

'Then let us go and find the false archbishop, there is a great deal Prent needs to account for,' the Archbishop called, which brought a rumble of approval.

'He will have guards, as well as the Berellian ambassador,' Martil warned.

'So much the better!' A plump man in the dirtied robes of a bishop joined them. 'I understand my old friend Father Nott is behind all this?'

'Well, the Queen is also behind this,' Martil said carefully.

'Ah, yes, the Queen! I am sorry to say I did not do much to keep her on the throne — but I can make up for that now!' Archbishop Declan was rubbing his hands together. 'Let us waste no more time! I have spent far too long in that damned cell. What say we keep it for Prent, eh, Gamelon?'

'My thoughts exactly, your grace.' Gamelon grinned.

Borne along on a tide of excited priests and priestesses, Martil frantically signalled for Kesbury to bring out the prisoners.

'Let's move!' he called. 'We'll take the guards on the doors next, then visit Prent!'

Securing the building was ridiculously easy. Archbishop Declan asked Aroaril for the power to hold the guards, then a couple of Rallorans walked out and carried them in, before taking their place. The unfrozen guards were then marched down to the cellars. The freed priests and priestesses, with the able assistance of Bishop Gamelon and the guidance of Father Nott and Sister Milly, were removing Prent's new students from their rooms and taking them down to the cellars. Martil judged that barely half a turn of the hourglass passed before the chapter house was entirely theirs — except for the Archbishop's quarters, where a pair of guards still stood, and where Prent and his guest were no doubt enjoying afternoon tea.

'That was easy enough! Now for the fun part!' Declan announced. 'Coming, my dear bishop?'

'Me too!' Karia, who had been waiting upstairs with Tiera, was determined not to be left out. The whole enterprise had turned into something of a joke. There were so many priests and priestesses there, all eager to call on Aroaril for His power, that Martil could not bring himself to refuse her.

11

Prent had, at first, been terrified when Ezok had rasped out strange words in a guttural language — and when a Fearpriest had appeared in the bowl of the girl's blood. But what the man said began to drive the fear from his mind and replace it with heady thoughts of glory.

'You have opened the door to a world of unimagined power. Whatever you want can be yours — and there will be no useless guilt or pointless conscience to stop you. If you want strength and power, all you have to do is follow my instructions,' the Fearpriest, who introduced himself as Onzalez, told Prent. 'Follow my instructions and then call upon Zorva for whatever you will. He will grant it.'

Fascinated, Prent had nodded assent.

'You must sacrifice the girl to Zorva. I will preside over the ceremony, but you must make haste. This gate you have opened to me will not last long.'

Prent looked down at the girl, whose terrified eyes almost bulged out of her head. He felt his spirit quail again. Seizing power was one thing, telling people to do things on his behalf was another. But to actually sacrifice a young woman by his own hand …

'You must cut out her heart, then hold it over the ceremonial cup while I speak the words of the initiation rite. Then you must drink the blood from her heart and offer both her heart and your soul to Zorva. It is a simple process,' the Fearpriest went on. 'You will then be initiated into Zorva, as is Ezok. I shall also speak the words that induct you into the priesthood but to seal that, to actually begin to wield power on His behalf, He will then need at least another death, preferably more. You must offer lives in exchange for power. Virgin girls are best and priestesses of Aroaril would be better yet. Ezok will be able to help you again. The men with him are pledged to Zorva and will help you prepare any of the captives that you require.'

But Prent was having second thoughts. Certainly, he had perhaps bent a few of the church's rules over the past few years — particularly in the last few months. But to actually convert to Zorva and kill, not just a frightened girl but more …

'You have to act now,' Onzalez told him. 'The magic that allows me to talk to you is running out.'

'Prent, if you want to be a man, you must commit to Zorva,' Ezok urged.

But Prent was unable to act. He opened his mouth to say so, when his guards burst through the door, one racing over, the other slamming the locking bar into place.

'Rallorans! In the building! And they have freed the Archbishop and all the priests! Now they're coming up the stairs for us!' the guard shrieked.

Prent gaped at him, unable to comprehend how that could have happened.

'Rallorans! They'll kill us all, even if the Archbishop does not!' Ezok gasped. 'Prent, you are the only one who can save us!'

The words cut through the terror, and Prent's

mind cleared. The choice was simple — there was no choice. 'Begin the ritual,' he said crisply.

'Once you have done this, you must sacrifice more lives to begin to use power. Every life you give to Zorva, he will return to you as power, the magic to use as you will. Ezok, your guards — they will have to be sacrificed. Prent, use their hearts — call upon Zorva and they will be infused with His power, and become mighty weapons to turn on the servants of Aroaril. Finally, call upon Him to turn the sacrifices into unholy warriors,' Onzalez said urgently. 'If all else fails, call on Zorva's protection. May He be with you.'

Then he began to chant something in the same language Ezok had used to summon Onzalez. Prent was barely listening to the words anyway. Instead, he gripped the knife.

Ezok's two bodyguards clubbed Prent's pair of guards down and dragged them over, ripping open their tunics to expose their torsos.

'Sacrifice them, then we will offer ourselves up next,' one of the bodyguards stated, as if he were talking about going out for a walk.

Prent wiped sweat from his eyes and focused on the bound, thrashing young woman who would be his first victim. As Onzalez spoke, Prent could feel a definite chill in the air, and the bright sunlight streaming in through the windows now seemed to be dull, clouding over almost, as the room darkened. Beneath him, the girl was desperately struggling, trying to scream through her gag. Prent ignored her. His future, his survival, was more important.

'It is done! Strike now, then lift the heart high, offer it and your soul to Zorva!' Onzalez cried out.

Prent gripped the long dagger tightly, then brought it high above his head.

The walk up the stairs to the Archbishop's quarters seemed more like a triumphal procession to Martil. His instinct would have been to creep up the stairs and surprise the guards but Declan had taken over. And he seemed to want to make a statement about retaking his position.

'The time for hiding is past — we must show everyone Aroaril's true power,' Declan declared grandly.

The Archbishop led the way, priests and priestesses laughing and chattering behind; it was the strangest military advance Martil had been in. But Martil's only involvement since freeing Declan had been to insist Gamelon, along with a score of priests, Kesbury and half the Rallorans, go around the back way to block the other exit. He was thankful he had insisted on that when Prent's guards spotted this parade. As soon as they glimpsed the implacable advance up the stairs, they turned and ran. Martil cursed when they vanished into the room, slamming the doors behind them.

'Not to worry, my son, we can open any locks,' Declan announced confidently.

'But they'll warn Prent and the Berellian — they could escape!' Martil growled.

'They'll just run into Gamelon. There are only two ways out of the room — and the street is a long way down!'

Martil bit his lip. This all went against his instincts, and he could feel the hair on the back of his neck stand up.

'Do you feel that?' Declan asked suddenly, as his slow, triumphal march up the stairs stopped.

'What?' Martil knew he was on edge.

The other priests and priestesses had also stopped.

'What is it?' Martil asked again.

'I can feel a great evil gathering. There is something dark going on in that room!' Declan exclaimed. 'Quickly!'

Martil ignored the temptation to point out he had been right and simply followed the Archbishop as he bounded up the last few stairs to the doors.

'Open in the name of Aroaril!' Declan said grandly and Martil heard the locking bar clatter to the floor on the other side, watched the huge, gilded doors glide gently open.

To reveal a scene from a nightmare.

Declan gasped in horror, while Martil just gripped the Dragon Sword tighter.

Firstly he saw four men lying on the floor in front of the Archbishop's giant desk, a bloody, gaping gash under each ribcage and their faces glazed in death. Worse was the young girl tied to the desk, her torso likewise ripped open. Prent stood beside her, laughing. In his hands he cradled bloody hearts, while blood stained his lips and was splashed all over his golden robe. A tall Berellian was behind him, a cruel smile on his lips. Beyond them, Gamelon, Kesbury and a group of other priests and priestesses, including Sister Milly, burst through the other door.

'You are too late, fools! I have power that you can only dream of!' Prent shrieked.

'Prent, what have you done?' Declan found his voice. 'I thought you foolish but never in my wildest dreams did I think you would convert to Zorva! You realise you will have to hang for this?'

Prent laughed again. 'Wrong! It is you who will die! Taste the power of my God!'

'Hold!' Declan bellowed, pointing at the bloodstained man.

But Prent just laughed. 'You cannot affect me. I have Zorva's protection! Now taste His anger!'

And he hefted the bloody hearts, which burst into a strange flame, too red and bright to be natural. One after another he hurled them at Declan, a stream of fiery missiles.

Martil, just behind and to the side of the Archbishop, instinctively dived for cover.

But Declan stood his ground.

'Aroaril protect me!' the Archbishop thundered, and held up his hands. A shimmer of light, tinged with gold, appeared in front of him, just as the first heart flashed across the room to strike against it in a thunderous explosion. Fire burst out across the front of the shield the Archbishop had created and he took an involuntary step backwards. The second, third and fourth hearts struck, each one driving the Archbishop back and down with the force of their impact, until he was on his knees. The last one seemed to gather pace and struck with redoubled force; while Declan was untouched by the fury of the fire, the force of the impact flung him back and up to smash into the edge of the open door. Martil heard the crack of breaking bones and Archbishop Declan fell to the ground limp as a rag doll.

Prent laughed in the horrified silence that followed.

'Now, rise! Rise and defend me, warriors of Zorva!' he commanded.

Martil was baffled for a moment — then saw the four dead men stand jerkily and pick up their swords. For a moment he thought they must have been feigning death, in order to surprise him, but he saw clearly the bloody wounds on their bodies, and the vacant look in their eyes and realised they had been given some form of twisted half life.

'We shall give you a chance to serve your weakling God in a more personal way,' Prent taunted, then signalled for the zombie guards to clear the way — through Gamelon, Milly, Kesbury and the others.

'You shall not escape!' Bishop Gamelon charged forwards. 'You will pay for your evil, Prent!'

Martil scrambled to his feet and raced across the huge room to help.

'Begone, fiend of Zorva!' Gamelon thrust out a hand at the zombie warriors, who shambled to the attack, swords held high for the first blow.

The first of them, a guard in Gello's red, stopped cold in his tracks, although his legs still tried to walk forwards and his sword arm beat impotently on an invisible barrier. But the other three strode on unimpeded.

'Stop, I said!' Gamelon thrust out his other hand at the second, one of Ezok's former men in Berellian black and gold, and he was blocked. But the other two kept coming, urged on by Prent. Sweating now, Gamelon stopped the third — but in doing so, the first was freed and began his advance again.

'Hold on, Bishop!' Kesbury roared, running to help, Sister Milly beside him. She had seen the body of poor Lilith stretched out across the desk, bloody and dead. She wanted to help but she also wanted revenge.

The sensible thing would have been for Gamelon to run backwards, to where other priests and indeed Kesbury's swordsmen could have helped him. But, like his archbishop, Gamelon was a man who believed utterly in the power of his position. He switched his holding spell back to the first, as Kesbury arrived in time to block a blow from another. But the last zombie hacked down with his sword.

'Protect —' Gamelon began but could not finish, as the sword opened his throat.

Kesbury gave a howl of anger and swung his sword in a massive blow that beheaded the second Berellian zombie. But the creature did not fall. It simply stepped forwards and slashed blindly with its sword. Revolted, Kesbury backed away but now all four were turning to him, swords lashing out wildly.

'Hold!' Milly blocked one, then Martil arrived, confident the Dragon Sword would make short work of these diabolical monstrosities. He slashed down viciously, hacking off the sword arm of the beheaded creature. But still it did not give up. Instead, it kneeled down and fumbled for the fallen sword with its other arm, while the severed arm thrashed around, fingers opening and closing as it tried to grab at Martil's leg.

Revolted, he slashed off its other arm, only to see them both inch towards him, while the truncated torso was still walking. Horror, disgust and fear warred within him as he hacked at the closest arm. Fighting a normal man was one thing but fighting these creatures of darkness …

Prent laughed as Martil and Kesbury defended themselves against the three remaining zombies, while trying to avoid being grabbed by the pieces they chopped off the ghoulish creatures. The thrill that had coursed through him as he had used Zorva's power — it had been so many years since Aroaril had granted him any power that he had forgotten the feeling. But surely it could not have been any better than this. He wanted more; he would truly do anything for it now. Killing the girl had been difficult, but when he had offered her heart and his soul to Zorva, ecstasy had flooded his body and he had been eager to use the knife on the men, wanting to feel that sensation again. He would have liked the unholy warriors to have grabbed more sacrifices for him but it looked as if the cursed Rallorans would be too strong for them. Still, at least they would let him escape.

'This way!' Prent and Ezok abandoned their twisted creations and ran instead towards the main entrance, where shocked priests and priestesses stood over the broken body of their archbishop. Martil's remaining Rallorans rushed forwards but Prent was equal to the task.

'Hold them, Zorva!' Prent roared, and they froze helplessly.

For a moment their way looked clear, then two figures stepped around the door, an old man and a small girl.

'Karia!' Martil bellowed. He slashed one zombie in half and tried to run over to help, only to be tripped by a disembodied arm.

'Out of the way, you old fool! The girl we shall take with us!' Prent laughed.

'No, you will never do that,' Nott said firmly. 'Ready, Karia?'

'When you are, Father,' she said calmly. She trusted him absolutely, and was also eager to show him some of the things she had learned.

Nott held out his hands, and a thick wall of thorns appeared in front of Prent and Ezok. Before Prent could summon the power to clear them away, Karia set fire to the thorns, forming an impenetrable barrier of rippling flames.

'You cannot dispel that now, for that is natural magic allied to that of my God, you filthy Fearpriest!' Nott roared. He bent down and hugged Karia.

Prent tried, but the flaming thorns stayed where they were, a formidable barrier.

'Back! Back!' Ezok grabbed at Prent and they raced across the room, to where their zombies were all in pieces but still fighting.

'Milly! The fire of purification! It is the only thing that will stop them!' Nott bellowed.

Milly, who had been trying, as Gamelon had, to keep the foul zombies at bay by holding them in a magical grip with little success, understood instantly.

'Purify!' she prayed aloud, then pointed at the last recognisable creature, which had lost an arm but was still slashing furiously at Kesbury. Instantly the creature burst into flames. Desperately it tried to keep attacking but the fire consumed it rapidly, forcing it to its knees, then to the floor, where it was reduced to ash.

Prent and Ezok skidded to a halt, and now backed away towards the massive windows that looked out onto the street below.

'Now we'll have you, Berellian!' Martil snarled.

'Not this time!' Ezok called back. 'And when we return with the King's guards, it is you who will be screaming!'

He hurled one of the gilded chairs at the nearest window, which promptly shattered, then he and Prent raced towards the gap.

'Stop them!' Martil yelled in frustration, but Nott and Karia's barrier was effectively preventing anyone from that side of the room from getting in, and the remnants of the zombies were slowing everyone else down.

Arm in arm, the Berellian and the newly converted Fearpriest leaped out of the window — and floated gently down to the ground.

Martil kicked an arm away towards where Milly was burning up every part she could see, and sprinted towards the window. He arrived just in time to see the pair of them land fifty yards down the street and immediately race away. Cursing, he struck at one of the shards of window glass, then stalked away. How could that have gone so wrong? And what were they going to do now?

Once they were safely around a corner, Prent and Ezok slowed to a stop.

'Both the Archbishop and his lackey Gamelon dead — not too bad,' Prent panted.

And the religious leader in this land is now a Fearpriest, a very good result, Ezok thought.

'We must hurry. We need to raise the alarm so we can catch them all — especially that Butcher of Bellic!' he said.

'We can do that easily — there's a church nearby, we can ring the bells there. That's our traditional alarm and how I nearly caught the Queen before.' Prent smiled.

Ezok coughed. 'I think we had better find a patrol, instead. I'm afraid neither of us is going to be able to enter a church of Aroaril.'

Prent stopped, then realised what Ezok meant. For a moment he was shocked, then he shrugged.

'And perhaps it would be best not to mention how we got away to the King just yet,' Ezok suggested delicately.

'Why not? Won't he be glad his ally has power now?' Prent demanded.

Ezok smiled. 'He wants powerful allies, to be sure. But he might think that someone as powerful as you is not so much an ally but more of a rival. Sadly, kings are often jealous of others with power. No doubt you have seen his temper. It would be best if we were to keep this between ourselves, for now.'

Prent reluctantly agreed. 'Agreed. It will be our little secret for now.'

'They're both dead,' Nott confirmed. 'Looks like the Archbishop broke his neck and back when he took the force of that explosion.'

'So we managed to lose both the men we were sent here to save?' Martil spat. 'And, worse than that — we have to try and get out of the city now, before Barrett is even ready?'

'There has still been no word from the Queen,' Nott confirmed. 'Quiller has heard nothing.'

'It is not a total loss, we still have nearly one hundred priests and priestesses here,' Milly argued.

'But we needed the authority of the Archbishop, or at least a bishop,' Martil groaned. 'Without them, how are we going to persuade the people to join the Queen's rebellion?'

They were all still in the Archbishop's chambers, with the bodies of Declan, Gamelon and the poor, sacrificed Lilith laid out together, and covered by curtains.

'We can still have an archbishop,' Milly stated firmly.

'How?' Martil asked sarcastically. 'Do we just invent one?'

'No, we vote for one. What we have here, in this room, is the entire remaining church of Aroaril in

242

Norstalos. We shall vote, and then we shall have a new archbishop. And that man will be Father Nott.'

Everyone turned to look at Father Nott, who merely bowed his head as the assembled priests and priestesses broke into applause.

'We do not have the time for prevarication or modesty. So I will take on this heavy duty. And my first act will be to appoint Sister Milly, Bishop Milly.'

'Father!' Milly began, then corrected herself. 'Your grace, I am not worthy. I have not even attained the rank of mother, or held a parish!'

'I shall decide who is and isn't worthy, and believe me, you are!' Nott snapped. 'Now to our escape — we could hold the guards at one of the gates but I fear they would just come after us with cavalry.'

'They will seal the gates before we can even get there,' Martil predicted. 'We need to get out by magic. Can you replicate that trick of Barrett's, where you open up a gateway through the trees?'

Nott sighed. 'No, we cannot. But Karia can.'

All eyes turned to the small girl, who immediately hid behind Martil's leg.

'No! She is not strong enough to hold open a gateway for so long!' Martil growled. 'I will not allow her to be used like that!'

Nott smiled gently. 'I know. But she can do it — for a few of us. Most of the priests, priestesses, Rallorans and servants in this room can hide in the city overnight and then slip out of the capital over the next few days.' Nott turned to the priests and priestesses. 'By staying at inns, and not wearing robes, you will be able to escape this city. Once out, here is your duty: Head for your parishes and spread the word about the evil that has taken root here. Encourage the people to join the rebellion. Bishop

Milly and I will be in the north, at Sendric. Contact us there and we will bring help. There is a Fearpriest loose in this country — and unless he is stopped quickly, a wave of evil such as we have not even dreamed about will engulf our people. Get clothes out of the storerooms, equip yourselves with funds and hide yourselves in the city before the alarm is raised. Martil, myself, Milly, Tiera and Sergeant Kesbury: Karia will be able to get us out of the city and at least partway towards the north. That is my decision; I ask you to hold to it. We cannot afford to wait any longer. Go now, and go with Aroaril.'

Martil ensured his men all had some gold, thanks to the Archbishop's funds, and promised to see them back at the passes. The city would be sealed tight for the next day but this was the capital — soon they would have to relax the restrictions and it should be easy enough to get out.

He doubted they would see many of the servant girls again. They were each given two years' wages in gold and most of them were almost overcome with shock to see so much money. They all embraced Bishop Milly before leaving, however. Martil did wonder why Tiera was to stay with them but there was no chance to ask Nott why. The new Archbishop was embracing the priests and priestesses as they came to see him dressed in a variety of tunics and dresses, and giving them final instructions.

The chapter house emptied swiftly, until it was just the six of them.

'To the park, then!' Nott waved his new flock on.

And then the alarm horns began to sound, first one, then more, until they were blaring out all over the capital.

12

Barrett slowly came to consciousness as a gentle hand helped lift his head up, and someone trickled water into his parched mouth. He wanted to sit up but he felt as weak as a kitten. He could barely summon the strength to swallow the water. It was deliciously cool and soothing and he luxuriated in several mouthfuls before he felt able to speak. Whoever was feeding him was being both patient and caring, and he knew who it was.

'Merren?' he croaked.

'The Queen is busy. But I will call her over when you have eaten something,' a strangely familiar voice said, one Barrett could not place immediately. With a sinking feeling, he realised it was the bard, Romon. Still, the Queen wanted to see him once he had eaten. That was a good sign. He was exhausted but the thought of her was a bright flame within him. He opened his eyes to see he was lying in a crude shelter, roofed with sticks and leaves, only just big enough for a man to sit upright inside.

'What have we got to eat?' he asked. 'And where are we?'

'We got some supplies from a nearby village. Nobody knows we are here, for the moment, and the

Queen wants to keep it that way, at least until you are well enough to take us all back north. So for the sake of all of us, eat up.'

Barrett was famished but did not have the strength to feed himself. Romon fed him a simple stew, washing it down with plenty of water. Barrett ate and ate, not stopping until his stomach was actually pushing against his belt.

'That was supposed to be my dinner as well, but at least it went in a good cause,' Romon said wryly.

Barrett ignored him. 'Now I've eaten, where is Merren?' he asked eagerly.

'She's just talking to Sendric and Rocus. They were both hurt but seem to be recovering now,' Romon said flatly.

'Can you go and get her?'

Romon shrugged. At least he could get away from this ungrateful wizard and perhaps even grab some dinner for himself. 'I'll see if she's free,' he said.

Barrett eagerly watched him go and arranged himself carefully, so he would look like a wounded warrior. He could feel the strength slowly returning to his legs but he guessed it would be a day or two before he was ready to make the trip home. Plenty of time for Merren to show how grateful she was. Besides, she had told him she loved him! He had put his life on the line for her, showed her how valuable he was, and now she had realised her true feelings for him! All his favourite daydreams came rushing back and he ran through them. He was so lost in these happy thoughts that he started almost guiltily when Merren ducked into the low shelter.

Merren had quailed inwardly when Romon told her Barrett was awake, had eaten and was asking for her. She had been occupied with making this little camp as secure as possible. Thanks to Jaret and Wilsen, they had an old horse as well as plenty of supplies. Rocus and Sendric were just about back on their feet and she was confident they would be able to wait here for a day or two longer without fear of being discovered.

But looming over all these concerns was the issue of what she had said to Barrett, how she had driven him beyond his limits so they could escape. That needed a reckoning. While she had been quick to take charge of these men, she found herself trying to find an excuse not to go and hurt Barrett. For that is what she had to do. He would be impossible otherwise. But how would it affect him? Would he go so far as to leave her service?

She thought about this and wondered, for a moment, whether to ask Romon to tell Barrett she was too busy, and would see him later. But she had been raised to meet her duties, no matter how unpleasant. And leaving him any longer would probably just make matters worse. So she squared her shoulders and marched over. Still, her heart was pounding a little and she had to pause and take a deep breath before she went into the shelter.

'How are you, Barrett?' she asked warmly.

'I am recovering, Merren. I will be back on my feet by tomorrow and able to take us all home either tomorrow night or the day after.' He smiled. 'Luckily I work hard at training — I doubt there would be a dozen mages in this world who could have done that much magic and survived.' As he spoke he pulled up his tunic to show her his chest, every muscle clearly defined after he had burned off every scrap of fat on his body.

Merren had thought to show her — genuine — concern for him before moving on to the issue of what she had said at the ranger barracks but, when he flashed his chest at her, she thought she better move on to it immediately before he did something they would both regret.

'Barrett, I am glad to hear that. But I need to talk to you about an important matter.'

'Of course, Merren. What is it?' Barrett almost held his breath. This was it! This was going to be the moment when she confessed her love for him!

'Barrett, when I said to you that I loved you, it was not what you might think.'

He liked the first half of the sentence but the second half did not sound right. Neither did her voice. There did not appear to be as much warmth in it as he expected.

'Oh?'

'I love you like a brother, like a friend. Not in any other way.' She said it in a rush, knowing she had to get it out before it was too late. 'I know what you are hoping for but I cannot return those feelings. I said that to you back in the wood because I knew it would revive you, and we needed you to escape. I used you and I am sorry.'

Barrett could barely hear her for the pounding of the blood in his head. His stomach seemed to have turned into a lead weight and the stew he had eaten was burning his throat. He struggled to breathe and he did not know where to look.

'But … but …' He struggled to find something to say, some hope he could extract from this.

'There is no possibility my mind will change,' she said gently, almost hating herself for doing this to him but knowing she had to finish it. 'You will

248

always be a friend, always be a trusted counsellor. I could never forget what you have done for me over the past few years but I can never be anything more than a queen to you.'

Barrett's throat was choking him and his eyes were burning. But he had his pride.

'You must be mistaken, my Queen,' he managed to squeeze out past the huge lump in his throat. 'I never thought that way about you. I have never been anything more than a loyal servant.'

Merren could hear — and see — the pain in his voice and on his face that gave lie to those words. She reached out to pat him on the shoulder but he jerked away from her.

'I am sorry,' she said, as gently as she could.

'Nothing to apologise for. Nothing at all. Now, if you will excuse me, I need some rest,' he said thickly.

Merren sighed. Staying here would achieve nothing.

'Come and talk to me when you feel better. I need suggestions as to what we can do now,' she offered, hoping that might give him something to work towards.

Barrett did not answer. He could not trust himself to speak and, after a long pause, she ducked out of the shelter and took a deep breath.

Well, that had gone about as badly as she expected. She knew their relationship would never be quite the same but if he could learn to work though this, it would be enough. She hoped.

Barrett lay in the shelter and wished for his heart to stop, so it would not hurt so much. He felt sick to the stomach and his eyes were stinging. But he would not cry. He was stronger than that. How could she tell him she could never love him? Emotions warred within him. Hurt at the way she had refused him, anguish at the way he had wasted so many years carrying a secret, futile love. Then there was anger; anger at his own foolishness. Why had he been so stupid as to dream a queen could ever be interested in him? What an idiot he had been! And finally there was bitterness, aimed at Martil. If that over-muscled oaf had not turned up, waving the Dragon Sword and trying to charm her, maybe she would have discovered her true feelings for him!

The bitterness and anger merged. He could not be angry at Merren, he did not want to be angry at himself, but Martil — Martil was a wonderful target for everything he was feeling, so he concentrated on that.

The streets were emptying fast. The city folk had heard the alarm horns and wisely decided they needed to get home and off the streets. The little group of six tried to hide within the rushing crowds; the park was not far away but the number of horns blowing the alarm seemed to indicate that they would be lucky to get there without seeing any of Gello's men.

Martil guessed Gello would send the bulk of his forces to the gates, seal them off, and then start to work inwards. That should give them enough time to escape — as long as Karia was indeed able to get them out. And that was a big if, as far as he was concerned.

The more the streets emptied, the more exposed he felt.

'There they are!' A patrol of six men rushed across the street, drawing their swords. They should have watched and followed until they met another patrol, but two warriors, two women, a young child and an old man looked like an easy target.

It was a fatal mistake.

Battle had always freed Martil's mind of worries, so he was almost glad to draw the Dragon Sword and leap to the attack, Kesbury at his shoulder. Two soldiers tried to fight back and were cut down by Martil, a third was picked up and slammed into a wall by Kesbury, then Nott and Milly called on Aroaril to hold the others in place, as much for their own protection as for Martil's.

'Is it just me, or is this getting easier now?' Milly wondered aloud.

'You are right. It is easier. Now you ask with the authority of bishop,' Nott said. 'We can discuss it more later but, for now, there's the park. Quickly!'

Martil looked at him carefully. When he had first met Nott, he had been sure the man was not long for this world, he had seemed so frail and old. But, particularly since he had taken on the duty of archbishop, he seemed to be stronger and, if possible, younger. A little divine intervention was the obvious conclusion but Martil did wonder how this would affect Karia — and himself.

The park was quiet, its small lake empty and the many walking paths deserted. Anyone who had been enjoying the late afternoon sunshine on its grassy lawns had quickly run for cover when the alarms started. So it was easy to walk swiftly to the oak tree they had arrived through, although Martil felt faintly ridiculous, standing around a tree, watching a little girl expectantly.

'So what do we need, Karia?' he asked, trying to focus. After all, hundreds of soldiers could pour into the park after them at any moment.

'We need an oaken staff first!' Karia declared.

So Martil drew the Dragon Sword and sliced through a length of branch about the width of his hand, and easily his height. He handed it to her and she smiled nervously back.

'Are you sure you want to do this? It's not too late to try something else,' Martil said, knowing that was a lie but more concerned that she would be hurt.

'No, I can do this,' Karia said, with a mixture of confidence and nervousness.

'Of course you can. I'm proud of you and I know you can do it.' He smiled and she glowed a little at that.

'We all believe in you, Karia,' Milly said encouragingly.

She was enjoying this, being the centre of attention. And she was sure it would not be hard. After all, she had seen Barrett do it many times, and made him explain how he did it just as often. *The magic will guide you, just keep your destination in mind as you travel from tree to tree. And don't let them get out of order.* Well, that was silly! As if she was ever going to forget anything! She never forgot things.

'Ready now!' she announced, then took the branch in one hand and touched the tree with the other. 'Here we go!' she announced. 'Tree to tree to tree to tree to tree …'

'You're doing it! You're jumping across the country!' Tiera cheered.

Martil looked across but, as usual, could not see anything unusual. So what could Tiera see? He glanced up at Nott but the old priest's face was giving nothing away.

A horn's blast, closer than the others, made Martil

crane his neck — a patrol of Gello's soldiers stood at the far side of the park. Again there were only six of them, and they were making no move to attack, instead blowing a series of short, sharp blasts on a horn, to summon more pursuers.

'Maybe that's enough now, Karia, just take us through,' Martil suggested.

'It's easy, I feel fine!' Karia exclaimed, although sweat was now trickling from her hairline and her face was reddening.

'Here, hold my hand,' Martil told her, not sure what he was going to do to help but knowing she was not ready for this, wanting to protect her.

Karia, her attention on the tree, dropped the staff and reached up blindly — and grabbed his hand that held the Dragon Sword. As she did so, the hilt of the Dragon Sword suddenly grew warm.

'It's working easier now!' she exclaimed delightedly.

'Stay like that! Keep her hand on the Sword!' Father Nott thundered.

Martil was so surprised he nearly did the opposite, but recovered just in time.

'Why? What's happening?' he hissed.

'She's drawing on the power of the Dragon Sword! She's using the Sword's magic, rather than her own! Keep it going — don't let her stop!' Nott ordered.

Easier said than done. A thunder of hoofs made the rest of them turn, and they saw a squadron of cavalry canter into the park and form up into two lines on the lawns.

'We have to go now. Anywhere is better than here!' Martil said urgently. 'Stop at the next tree, Karia!'

'But I could keep going!'

'No, that's far enough!' Martil said, trying not to give an order.

She nodded, then glanced to where the staff had fallen to the ground. 'Help me with the staff!'

Before Martil could reach down, Tiera grabbed the end of the oaken branch and helped Karia thrust the long staff into the tree and hold it there.

'Quick now! Hold onto the staff and don't let go as you go through!' Nott urged, although nobody seemed that eager to be the first to get away. Martil could not entirely blame them — this mode of travel was very different with a small girl, rather than the Queen's Magician.

'Follow me!' Milly declared, grabbing the staff and walking through the tree, hauling herself along the staff, hand over hand. She vanished and the group paused.

Milly's head appeared out of the tree.

'Hurry up!' she snapped.

'Father! You should go first, you are too valuable to lose!' Martil jerked his head at Nott, then remembered he should be calling him by his official title. Too late now.

Nott just smiled. 'My flock will go first. The shepherd should always see to their safety before his own,' he said calmly.

Martil signalled to Kesbury, who gulped, then walked through, keeping hold of the staff.

'Hold it steady when you get through!' Martil told him, then took Tiera's place beside Karia, letting the young woman hurry through.

The first rank of cavalry spurred themselves to the gallop and the second rank followed; the ground was starting to tremble now from their hoofs. Worse, he could see men flitting among the trees — infantry had obviously followed the alarm call as well, coming into the park from a different way.

'Father, get through there, for Aroaril's sake!'

'What's happening?' Karia asked nervously, still facing the tree. He could hear her breathing now, fast and harsh, and knew they had to hurry — even without the approaching cavalry.

A pair of men in Gello's red, both holding swords, had stepped out from behind a tree about a dozen yards away, and were stalking towards them purposefully.

'Don't worry about anything, just concentrate on what you are doing,' Martil said, trying to keep his voice calm as Nott moved slowly into the tree.

The nearest cavalry were only twenty paces away now, and had lifted their swords ready for the first stroke, while the infantrymen had split up, ready to rush at them from two sides.

'Let's go now,' Martil gritted, trying to keep his voice even. Scaring Karia would do more harm than good — and he had no wish to escape a sword blow only to spend the rest of his life encased in some tree.

He tried to grasp both her hand and the Sword, while holding the staff firmly. He closed his eyes and stepped forwards, as she did.

Someone was pulling the staff, gently, so as not to dislodge their grip, and they walked on a step at a time, emerging on the other side to cheers from those anxiously awaiting them.

'We're through, you can let go now,' Martil told her, for he could hear the cavalry closing in — and a shouted challenge coming through what should be a solid tree.

'All right!' Karia blinked and stepped away from the tree, dropping the branch as she did so.

Martil thought he heard a faint scream, which was cut off suddenly.

He looked over at Nott, who nodded. 'That will be a nasty surprise for a woodsman one day,' was all the new Archbishop said.

'You did it!' Tiera cheered Karia, giving her a hug and twirling her around.

'And you helped! You must be able to do magic too!' Karia laughed, enjoying the praise and the applause from the assembled group. 'You'll have to study with Barrett, like me!'

'Where are we?' Kesbury asked, getting to the point.

'I just need to rest a bit, then I'll get a bird to tell us,' Karia yawned.

Martil picked her up as she wobbled on unsteady legs.

'Water — and some food!' he snapped.

Kesbury pulled out a waterskin while Tiera opened the bag she had filled from the kitchen stores before they left.

After making sure Karia had drunk most of a waterskin and eaten a hunk of cheese and a large honeycake, Martil felt able to look around. They'd come out in a small wood overlooking farmland. A flock of sheep was grazing beneath them and recently ploughed fields stretched beyond them. Presumably there was a farmhouse nearby but Martil could not see one.

'I would think we are about halfway to the north,' Milly said quietly.

'Long enough away from the capital that we should be able to relax tonight,' Nott acknowledged. 'And tomorrow, we can return to Sendric when Karia has more energy.'

'I'm fine now!' Karia insisted, stifling a yawn.

'How about you sit with me and I read you a story?' Nott suggested.

'I'd love that!' Karia exclaimed.

'Martil — when we reach Sendric, I wonder if I could ask you a favour?' Nott said quietly.

'Of course.'

'I would like to spend a couple of days with Karia.'

Martil felt a sinking feeling, but how could he refuse? 'Certainly,' he managed to reply.

'Excellent. Now, I suggest we eat some of the supplies that Tiera has thoughtfully brought, then get some sleep — although perhaps, Martil, you and the sergeant could keep a watch, just in case?'

Martil nodded. He was afraid of sleeping tonight anyway. He was supposed to be using Nott's idea to fight against his dreams. But he had no idea how he was going to persuade his mind to rescue himself by using Karia. Especially as he was afraid Nott was going to take her back.

Gello had to see this for himself.

'That's how they got away, sire,' Feld told him. 'We sealed the gates, then tracked them to this park. They were walking through the tree, so two of our men tried to follow and, well, you can see for yourself.'

Gello stared at the huge oak tree. The backs of two men, including both legs of one and the leg of another, were sticking out of the tree, just hanging limply.

'They were moving for a short while, then they just stopped. We could not pull them out or push them further in,' Feld said flatly.

Gello sniffed. It was an unpleasant face but one he was tempted to mete out to a few others.

'We had them in our power and they managed to escape!' he growled. 'I thought you said the wizard was not with them?'

Nobody seemed eager to offer an answer until Ezok coughed gently. It was time to move to the next stage, to use this opportunity to actually bring him around to the worship of Zorva.

'Normally, sire, priests are not able to do something like that. But there have been disturbing developments. It seems Aroaril may be giving them more help than normal.'

'What! Why?'

Ezok spread his hands. 'I suspect it may be due to the pleas of your cousin and her followers. After all, you have taken actions that some could see as attacking the church of Aroaril. Whatever the reason, it does present you with a unique problem, sire.'

'Oh?'

Ezok gestured delicately towards the trees and Gello followed him immediately.

'Sire, if Aroaril is indeed giving special powers to his priests, then you may need to combat that. If Aroaril has set Himself against you, then you need to balance that power with another, similar power …'

Gello glanced over his shoulder to where his captains stood.

'What do you mean?'

'There is only one who can oppose Aroaril, who is more powerful than Aroaril. The Great God himself — Zorva.'

Gello recoiled. 'You cannot be serious!'

Ezok smiled gently. 'I have sworn to always give you the advice you need to hear, not the advice you want to hear. You do want to be victorious, carve your name in history, do you not?'

'Of course!'

'Your cousin and her Ralloran dog are trying to use Aroaril against you. They think it is the only thing that can stop you. And perhaps it might …'

'No! I shall not be stopped again!' Gello breathed.

'Then you will need to call on Zorva. The enemy of your enemy must be your friend,' Ezok offered.

Gello shuddered. He hated religion at the best of times. And was not Zorva reputedly the source of all evil? He had just won the people back again — and he was under no illusions as to how most of conservative, God-fearing Norstalos would regard a deal with Zorva.

'Concepts of good and evil are pointless for men such as yourself. There is only power, and nothing has more power than Zorva,' Ezok said softly.

Gello could only agree with that sentiment but he did not want to consider such a radical step now. He had faced a few setbacks but he was still in control.

'I do not wish to talk about this now! I don't need Zorva, I don't need Mother, I don't need anyone!'

'Of course, sire. We can wait. But I would caution — you cannot leave it too long. If Aroaril is indeed against you …'

'Enough! I have made my decision!' Gello said violently.

'I shall say no more, sire, for now. Just consider my words, for the time may come when you need to act.'

'I shall think on it. No more than that!' Gello stalked back to where everyone else waited.

'Is it even worth ordering a search of the surrounding countryside?' he snarled.

'I would suggest, sire, that instead we redouble our efforts to send our men north, to stamp out the

Queen's rebellion before they try anything else,' Ezok said delicately.

Gello looked at the ambassador. He could see the angry looks many of his captains were sending Ezok and Prent.

'But you can confirm both Archbishop Declan and Bishop Gamelon are dead?' he said darkly.

'Naturally, sire. We can show you the bodies,' Prent added.

Gello nodded. 'Then not too much damage done. A bunch of country priests have escaped. So what? A proclamation from the old Archbishop, or a prominent bishop might have concerned us but the peasants are not going to take notice of a pack of aged priests and women! Increase our efforts to get the men north, though. I have had enough surprises from my bitch of a cousin and her Ralloran dog.'

The streets of Bellic were choked with corpses.

Martil tried to hide but only had a moment before the horde of howling dead spotted him again.

'Kill him!' The cry was taken up by a score of ripped-out throats.

Martil did not waste his breath pleading with them. He knew by now that they would not listen. He saved his apologies for the bodies he clambered over in his desperate attempt to escape. He recognised many of their faces — and was horrified to see new ones among the familiar. Men — and women — he thought he had forgotten but had dragged here, seemingly, to haunt him.

Ahead was the town square, with its tortured display of his fellow war captains; beyond that was the gate. He had a growing conviction that if he could just reach the gate, Karia would be able to open it, and he could get away.

But perhaps the twisted inhabitants of Bellic had also come to that conclusion, because their pursuit was fierce and deadly that night. Normally they seemed content to hunt him through the streets, were happy for the woman and her son to move in for the kill. Not tonight.

A screaming woman, her intestines bulging out of a wicked wound, raced out of a doorway and sliced a butcher's knife at his face. Instinctively he leaned back, and his sword lashed out, taking off her head in an instant.

'Over here! He's over here!' the head screeched from where it had come to rest on the cobbles, while the body still stumbled after Martil, the knife cutting through the air.

Martil backed away in horror. He had to get away. Karia was waiting for him.

But more dead were appearing all the time, reaching out to grab him, slow him down or drag him into darkened homes, where flames roared and strange voices gibbered hate.

Desperate now, he slashed and hacked to either side as he ran; a trail of severed limbs and heads still tried to follow him, while their owners staggered to catch up. Broken corpses pawed at him, and jabbed spears and swords at his legs. His swords rose and fell, trying to cut himself loose from their clutches.

Now he was in the town square, where the other four war captains writhed and twisted on their endless gallows.

'This is all your fault! Your fault!' they hissed at him as he ran past, but he dared not stop. If he slowed down for a moment they would have him.

'You cannot escape us!' the leader of the dead, the woman he had killed, capered on a battlement over the gate. 'You don't deserve to!'

But Martil ignored her. The gate was ahead — he knew he could escape now. At full pace he hurled himself at the massive wooden gate, then beat on it with his sword hilt.

'Too late!' a voice taunted and he turned to see the host of the dead arrayed in a semi-circle around him. Many of them were missing limbs or heads, although, as he watched, some of these crawled or wiggled to join their owners. At their head were the woman and her son. The spear and the long knife were ready and seemed to have grown wicked barbs.

Martil crouched, swords ready, and was prepared to throw himself forwards in a last attack when a creaking noise made him glance over his shoulder.

The gates were opening!

He looked again, a wild, outrageous hope rising in his chest. Through the gates, in the distance, was a small hill that overlooked Bellic. On that hill stood a small figure, which beckoned to him.

It was Karia!

'No! You must not escape!' the dead howled.

It was too late. The host of the dead were not going to stop him. He turned and stepped forwards, wanting to run through the gates.

But something grabbed him around the legs and he looked down in horror to see the woman from the Ralloran village, still cradling her dead baby.

'Your fault! All your fault!' she hissed.

He tried to break free but her grip was unyielding. He looked up to the hill where the small figure waited for him — and saw the gates *beginning to close now, heard the insane laughter of the dead …*

'Captain!'

Martil sat up, a scream dying in his throat.

'Captain, you were thrashing around — I thought you were going to call out!' Kesbury whispered.

Martil ran a shaking hand over his face.

'I'm fine now, Sergeant. Just a bad dream,' he managed to say.

'Bellic, sir?'

A quick glance told him that everyone else was asleep. With a pang, he saw that Karia was cuddled up with Father Nott — or Archbishop Nott, as he should be thought of now. 'Aye. But I'm fine now.'

Kesbury thought he did not look fine but he was not about to say that.

'I'll stand watch now, Sergeant. You get some sleep.'

Again, Kesbury thought it would be better if his captain rested but he would not contradict an order. He lay down on the ground and closed his eyes.

Martil watched him for a moment, then stood and began to pace around carefully. He would not sleep again that night. He could not face that dream again.

He looked down at Nott, sleeping peacefully next to Karia, and sighed. Maybe she would be better off with him after all. Thanks to Aroaril, it looked as though the old man still had quite a few years left in him. And, although Martil was younger, he had no guarantee of a long life with the Dragon Sword refusing to work for him — and that was even before you thought about Gello's massive army coming for him.

* * *

263

'What are we going to do now?' Sendric asked.

He, Merren, Rocus, Romon and Barrett were sitting around, eating the last of the bread and cheese.

They had been unable to go back to the village to get more supplies, even though both Merren and Sendric had more coin. The dust of marching men had been seen on the road, and Merren had ordered them to stay hidden. She had personally led a patrol out to look at the advance, keeping hidden as the regiment of rangers had hurried past on the main road. By now the men trusted her implicitly — although Sendric had chided her privately for taking too much of a risk — and accepted her orders without question, although it meant discomfort for them. The only one spared from rationing was Barrett, who had rested frequently and eaten prodigiously over the last day and a half and had announced he was ready to take everyone back north the next morning.

'I mean,' Sendric continued, 'not only did we fail to win over the rangers but we also lost many valuable men, including both Wime and Tarik, two of the three leaders of this little rebellion who have been with us from the start. We also lost Forde, who gallantly saved you, my Queen, but without him, it is going to make it more difficult to bring on the men from Gerrin and Berry.'

Merren swallowed a mouthful of bread. 'We shall return to Sendric. I am confident that Captain Martil will have rescued the Archbishop, and the rest of the priests. Once we have them safely back, we can use them to rally the ordinary people. With the towns rebelling behind him, Gello will not be able to lead his army north, and we shall have the time we need,' she said calmly, injecting a confidence she did not feel into her words.

'Merren, you have shown you are willing to make the hard decisions. Therefore, I beg you to consider making one now,' Barrett said flatly. 'The people are afraid of Gello, but, thanks to the bards and his tame priests, also afraid of the Rallorans. We need to make the choice easier for them.'

Merren considered him carefully. Since their little talk, he had seemed normal — too normal. She had expected more from him: more anger, more hurt, more tears even. Not that she had wanted that but seeing him apparently take rejection so well — it was a little disconcerting.

'How do we achieve that?'

'We need to remove the Rallorans from the decision. Send them south, to attack Gello. His army will take months to recover from the damage they can inflict.'

Merren stared at him. 'And the Rallorans?'

'Well, obviously they will be wiped out. But I can save Martil, as the Dragon Sword wielder. With the Rallorans gone, the people will have nothing to fear, and will be happy to join us. Meanwhile, their sacrifice will have given us the time we need to recruit a Norstaline army.'

Barrett decided he needed to clarify those comments, in the light of the stunned look on Merren's face. 'We are all agreed that there is no way we can defeat Gello's army? Then we have to make a tough choice. Do we all die, or do we make a necessary sacrifice so Gello can be defeated? The Rallorans knew what they were letting themselves in for when they joined us. They, more than any of us here, know that wars cannot be won easily. Besides, they are men with no end of problems. In some ways, we shall be doing them a favour. And, in the same action, we save ourselves.'

Merren just stared at him. 'So we just tell them to march south and keep killing Gello's soldiers until they are all dead?'

'Of course not!' Barrett laughed briefly. 'We shall tell them that we are planning a surprise night attack on Gello's camp and that the Norstaline companies will cause a diversion, allowing them to break free and retreat. Only we shall not provide that diversion. Already deep in the enemy camp, the Rallorans will have to keep fighting, for Gello won't offer them surrender. Warriors like that, fighting to the death — they could easily take out three or four times their number — perhaps even a little more. Gello will be unable to assault the passes with more than a third of his army dead or wounded. He will be forced to retreat and we can gather a new army, a Norstaline army. It is dishonourable, it is even contemptible. But when the alternative is our death and Gello triumphant, what choice do we have?'

Merren just sat there, unable to speak. Part of her could see the logic of his argument but there was no way she could possibly agree to this. Even if it regained her the throne, it was something she could never come to terms with. And then there was Martil. If he survived, he would never accept the death of his men.

'Your majesty, he does have a point. The Rallorans have been as much a hindrance as a help. With them, we have earned ourselves a breathing space. Without them, we could attract a much larger army of volunteers,' Sendric offered.

Merren turned to look at Romon, who sat silent.

'Do you have anything to add, bard?' she asked.

Romon smiled. 'I am a bard, I am a recorder of history, not a maker of history. Do what you will; I seek to merely tell the people about it.'

'Well, you can tell them I would rather die than betray men who have sworn an oath to me. There will be no sacrifice of the Rallorans. If there is no hope, I would rather walk away from the country. With me gone, there will be no need for Gello to destroy the towns — he can afford to be generous. And I refuse to let people suffer in this struggle between Gello and myself ...'

'Your majesty! You can't walk away!' Barrett gasped.

'Leaving the country would only cause more problems — do not forget that Gello is allying himself with the Berellians and now Fearpriests! Without you, Gello would be able to do what he liked!' Sendric protested.

Merren gazed at them. 'I do not want to walk away. I truly believe I am better for this country than my cousin. But if it ever got to the point where I had to do things I hated, things I could never live with, then I would walk away rather than destroy the fabric of this country.'

Nobody answered her, although Romon's quill was busy.

'So,' she continued, 'I must believe Martil has succeeded in his mission. We must trust in him to give us more time.'

The barracks was still in a mess, and the companies were in disarray because Kay had had to promote a number of sergeants to replace all the officers who had died trying to apprehend the Queen. But the orders were unequivocal: March north with all speed. Food and supplies will be waiting at the camp, so travel light, with only the basics. Kay was still seething about the Berellians but he was also eager to get back his captaincy by destroying the vicious Rallorans. He had decided that, despite his feelings about Berellians, he could fight against Rallorans with a clear conscience.

The criminals were grumbling, and Kettering was hearing it all. They were hungry, they were footsore and they were tired.

'We should cut and run — take out the sergeants and officers and scatter,' was one suggestion that gained a fair bit of support.

'We stay together. We run too early, then they'll hunt us down. When we take control, we do it when the time is right.' Kettering sent the order out and was not in the least bit surprised when it was obeyed. The political prisoners, the ones who had found themselves in jail on trumped-up charges, they were happy to obey him. And even the real criminals respected him. Now he just had to repay that trust, by not allowing them to be led to their deaths.

Nerrin laughed and clapped his men on the back as they passed him, sweaty, soot-stained and grinning in the darkness. Behind them, a huge pile of supplies in Gello's camp was going up in smoke and flames.

'It was too easy, sir.' Dunner chuckled. 'They had one squad of sentries on! The lazy bastards! We had the place alight before they even worked out what was going on!'

Nerrin smiled. 'They'll have a full company on each night from now. But it's too late.' He glanced back to where several hundred newly woken soldiers were frantically trying to save casks and barrels from the flames. They were trying in vain. The Rallorans had soaked many of the wooden casks in lamp oil, to help the flames along.

'An army goes through supplies faster than a two-copper whore goes through customers. They can't sustain a long siege now. Once those rangers get here, there's no way Gello will be coming north this year,' Nerrin said loudly, wanting that message spread among the men as widely as possible.

13

Martil was in a foul mood. Not only had he been haunted by exactly the same dream for two nights in a row — where Karia opened the gates of Bellic yet he could not escape the clutches of the murdered Ralloran mother — but he had been forced to watch Nott laugh and play with Karia. The new Archbishop was with her the whole time, not even giving Martil the chance to play with her. As the others had found ways to occupy themselves while they waited for rescue — Milly walked the countryside with Kesbury for protection and Tiera stayed well away when they were out — Martil was left to sit and brood.

Nott had taken time out from reading a saga to Karia to tell him that the Queen was safe and would be returning to the town that day, as they had planned too. But Martil also worried that his men back in the capital would not be able to escape. And that the priests and priestesses might not bring in volunteers. There were so many uncertainties. Above them all, though, was the fear that Nott was preparing to take Karia back. As much as he tried to tell himself that would be great, that he could get on with his life, could relax and finally get the chance to never read another saga again, he felt sick inside.

There were only two things that let him clear his mind: battle, and being with Karia. But while fighting and killing only gave him more bad memories, Karia gave him a feeling of peace. She could drive him crazy but she also made him feel more alive than ever before, gave him an appreciation for life he had not thought possible.

The thought of losing her filled him so full of rage and hurt that he needed an outlet or he would surely explode. The return of Kesbury and Milly, who had been off walking, provided the perfect opportunity.

'Next time, Sergeant, I want to know your proposed route, and a series of warning calls, so we know how to rescue you, if necessary,' he growled, knowing he was being ridiculous. But he also knew Kesbury would never argue back. 'And what are you doing spending so much time with a bishop, anyway? People might talk!'

'Yes, sir, sorry, sir,' Kesbury said woodenly.

'We're staying away, because otherwise you bully him,' Milly said.

Martil saw the chance to release some anger and took it gratefully. 'I bully him? Sister, he is a soldier, and I am his commanding officer! This isn't the church, and I advise you to keep your nose out of it!'

Milly swelled with outrage. 'Did you advise me to keep my nose away when I was saving your miserable life back in the capital, when you decided that seeing a whore was more important than saving the Archbishop?'

'What's going on?' Karia asked, wandering over.

Martil was bubbling with rage, and knowing that Karia would now be asking him about whores as soon as she could added guilt to the potent mix.

'None of your business! Now go away!' he roared at her.

'But what did she mean …'

'I said enough!' Martil turned, his fist clenched.

Karia squealed in fear and sprinted away into the bushes.

Martil watched her go and realised his hand was raised against her. The anger drained out of him, replaced by horror and loathing. He spun about and ran, crashing through bushes and bouncing off trees, running blindly in an effort to get away.

Milly started after him, but Kesbury caught her arm.

'You should let him go, Milly,' he said softly.

The return to Sendric was worse than Merren had dreamed.

The people were used to seeing her return triumphant and had been confidently expecting her to be at the head of a Norstaline regiment, the famous Queen's Rangers. At worst, they expected her to be bringing back a bard and a Berellian lord, the latter in chains.

So when she arrived back with just a bard — and barely half the men she left with — it sent the town into shock. Fear and rumour ran through the streets. She knew she would have to stop it, but there were things she needed to do first.

She made a point of seeing all the wives, starting with Louise, Wime's wife, then moving on to Forde's wife Gia. Romon had wanted to come in with her, but she had refused him. She would not use the grief of widows to make her look better for a saga. She cried with them when she described their deaths, how she would have been killed by the Berellian Champion if it was not for Forde's sacrifice.

'I want you to take the place on my war council that your husbands had,' she told them.

'I cannot!' Louise was the first to refuse.

'You must. All we have suffered for, all we have lost loved ones for — it is all threatened. I need your help and advice, when you are ready to give it.'

She had received their agreement, although she was not sure when they would be able to help. Nor did she notice Romon slipping in to talk to them after she had left.

'Your majesty, we must talk to you.' Quiller and Conal, who had looked after the north in her absence, had waited with ever-decreasing patience until she'd finished seeing every one of the wives and families of the men who had died — and that was just the men from Sendric. The ones from Gerrin and Berry had been sent for but would not arrive for a day or two.

After speaking to so many devastated women and children, she needed to sit for a moment. But it looked as though she was unlikely to get time alone. Merren made Quiller and Conal wait until she had at least poured herself a goblet of wine, then waved them to a seat.

'We need to give the people some good news. By Aroaril, I need some good news! Tell me of Martil.'

Quiller cleared his throat.

'Not much good news, I am afraid. He rescued the Archbishop and the Bishop but, when they went to arrest Prent, they discovered him with the Berellian ambassador. They were sacrificing a girl to Zorva.'

'What?' Merren gasped.

'It gets worse,' Quiller said grimly. 'It seems Prent is now a Fearpriest, of sorts. He was able to call on the power of the Dark One and, in the ensuing battle, both the Archbishop and the Bishop were killed, and Prent escaped.'

Merren dropped her goblet. She ignored the spreading lake of wine on the tabletop. 'So where are they now?'

'They sent the priests and priestesses off in all directions, to tell their parishes that Gello is allied with Zorva, and to call for volunteers to fight the evil. Karia used her magic to get the new Archbishop and Bishop, as well as Martil and Kesbury, out of the capital. They will be travelling back here tonight.'

'Prent a Fearpriest?' Merren tried to make sense of this. 'A new archbishop and bishop?'

'Voted in. Archbishop Nott and Bishop Milly,' Quiller said flatly. 'I am afraid that neither of them is known. Obviously Nott is well regarded in a small part of eastern Norstalos but Milly was the former secretary to Archbishop Declan and would be familiar only to those in the church. A proclamation from either of them will not carry any of the weight that one from Declan or Gamelon would have carried. Some might take notice, just because it comes from the Archbishop of Norstalos, but I fear it will be easy for Gello to discredit them. As for Prent, he is new to his powers. But he must not be allowed to develop them. Already he has accounted for two of the most powerful men in the church. It cannot be long before he will be ordering pyramids built; pyramids topped with bloodstained altars to the Dark One.

'There is a silver lining. It will be impossible to hide what he is for long: the Dark One insists on regular blood sacrifice. And when the people learn that their supposed Archbishop is a Fearpriest, they will rush to join us.'

'Only we do not have enough time for that to happen,' Conal interrupted. 'I have the latest reports from Captain Nerrin, at the passes. Already two regiments of Gello's men have arrived and more are coming in every day. Worse, Nerrin reports that he has destroyed perhaps half the supplies that Gello had stockpiled at the camp.'

'Worse?'

Conal shrugged. 'Nerrin was trying to ensure they could not lay siege to the passes. But, without supplies, Gello will not be able to stay in his camp for long. That would have been ideal if we had the rangers, to help us hold the passes. But now he must attack as soon as possible — and we cannot stop him. We have not revealed this to the people, for obvious reasons. The town council also wants to speak to you, to get assurances of safety for the town. The people are afraid for the future.'

Merren absorbed those blows and fought to keep her face impassive. When she was sure she had control of her voice, she asked: 'Is there any good news?'

'The training of the new men goes well. Mixed in with our experienced troops, they should hold,' Conal offered.

Merren nodded. 'You have both done well in my absence. I thank you for your work. Before I see the town council, I have something I must discuss with you. Barrett, with some support from Sendric, suggests we sacrifice the Rallorans for our own survival. Have them attack Gello's camp and hope they do so much damage that he has to crawl away, licking his wounds, giving us enough time to build up a Norstaline army.'

'I understand what Barrett is saying and it could work,' Quiller said slowly. 'But it is a move of

275

desperation and will, ultimately, destroy what we are trying to build here. You have said it matters not where a man was born but what he does. Sending good men to their deaths because they were not born in this country will prove that a lie.'

Merren smiled. 'Well said, Quiller. And you, Conal?'

'My Queen, you know what I always say about a choice. On the one hand we have something we do not want to do, but on the other hand — ah, look, I don't have another hand.' He waved his stump theatrically and, despite herself, she smiled.

Then Conal stopped smiling and held up his remaining hand. 'This is your only choice, my Queen. Men follow you because they know you care about what happens to them. You are not just using them to bring yourself land and riches. But to sacrifice so many men like that — people will not be able to trust you again,' he said passionately.

Merren paused for a moment.

'There is another option. We could find ships, sail away from here. My feud with Gello has put everyone's life at risk in the north. But without me …'

'Without you, Gello and his Fearpriests will be free to rule!' Quiller snarled. 'You cannot walk away from here and leave the country to fall to Zorva!'

'Your majesty, it would be a noble gesture — but it would not save one life and might cost many more,' Conal agreed.

Merren stood and walked across to them. The thought of giving up and walking away was a hard one to contemplate — and the thought of seeing all these people suffer for her actions was harder still. Ultimately, though, she felt Quiller was right.

Abandoning the people would not save them from Gello.

'Thank you,' she said gravely. 'The time for hard decisions is here but there is a difference between hard decisions, and foolish ones. Send word to me when Martil arrives. I will be walking among the people, talking to them. They have to know they will be safe.'

'Captain!'

Martil reflected that, whenever people called him captain, trouble followed. He had been sitting on a fallen log, lost in self-loathing. Somehow he managed to do exactly the wrong thing at the worst moment. Joining the army, sacking Bellic, falling in love with an untouchable queen and now doing the one thing he had promised never to do, raising a hand in anger to his daughter. Karia, his way back from the pit of despair. Karia, the one person who Nott had said could help him escape from his nightmares. Karia, the little girl he was already desperately afraid of losing. How could he have done that to her? How could he have been so stupid?

'Captain!'

Kesbury's voice cut through the mist in his head.

'What is it, Sergeant?' he snapped.

Nott had wanted to go and find Martil but Kesbury had insisted it was his duty. Kesbury had not really known Martil during the wars, except as his commander, although Martil had saved his life. He had spoken to him only a handful of times. Actually spending so much time with him, discovering the fabled Captain Martil was a man with many faults, had been difficult. But, in some ways, it made him more likeable.

'Sir, we're ready to go. We're just waiting on you.'

Martil sighed. He felt a shame so great it threatened to overwhelm him. No wonder the Sword still refused to reveal its power to him. No wonder Karia preferred spending time with Nott. He had to face it, he did not deserve her. She was too good for him.

'Sir, Karia knows it was an accident and you did not mean it. The Archbishop explained it to her. She says if you come back, you can read her a story.' Kesbury's voice was flat, matter-of-fact.

Martil closed his eyes as they suddenly burned. It took him a few moments to bring his voice under control.

'I'll be right there.' He paused, knowing more had to be said. 'And, Sergeant?'

'Yes, sir?'

'Forget what I said earlier about you and the Bishop. Although, I would suggest you need to be a little careful when we are back at Sendric. A bishop is greatly respected but there are many, especially older Norstalines, who are not so keen on women in the priesthood. They will seize on any gossip they can to undermine Milly's authority, you understand?'

'Of course, sir.'

'Excellent.' Martil decided to pretend that everything was normal. 'Let's go then.'

The others were waiting patiently by the oak tree, Karia had the staff ready and was bouncing up and down with excitement at the thought of showing off her magical abilities once more. She saw Martil and looked away nervously.

Martil felt the pain of that like a knife in the heart but took a deep breath and prepared to walk over, to

278

fall to his knees and apologise to her, swear to all that was holy that he would never have hit her, never. But Nott stepped in front of him.

'Not just yet,' the old priest said softly. 'She needs to maintain her concentration for this. You cannot make her think about anything else, understand?'

Martil opened his mouth to disagree but saw the sense in Nott's words.

'All right.'

'Good. And, when we get out the other side, I need to talk to you about Karia,' Nott whispered.

Martil nodded but, inside, he had turned to ice.

Gello made sure his tent was properly put up, and Lahra installed in a smaller version just behind, before joining his captains, the nobles, Prent and Ambassador Ezok. After she had helped save his life from the plot of that Ralloran butcher, he had decided to keep Lahra close. Besides, he wanted Merren to see Lahra by his side, when his cousin was dragged before him after her defeat. He had plenty of time. Regiments were still marching into camp, while the families of the nobles were being installed in a smaller camp, to the south, where they would be safely under his thumb. He had no intention of rushing there. The men had to be given time to recover from the hard march. Then the passes had to be scouted and, finally, his victory had to be savoured. He was on the cusp of success and there would be no more failure. Not again. After all the years of plotting and planning, it all came down to this: His overwhelming force against the pitiful rabble Merren had managed to scrape up. Certainly the Rallorans would be formidable but there were not enough of them to stop his army.

True, there were other problems on the horizon. His captains were muttering against him, and it seemed at least one of his nobles was already plotting his downfall. But these were small concerns. The important thing was to restore his honour, his legend forever enshrined — and the humiliation of the Dragon Sword's rejection forgotten.

So when he swaggered into the huge tent, lined with servants and filled with his captains and nobles, he expected the treatment given to a conquering hero. Certainly the applause as he walked to his place at the head of the tent and sat down on a makeshift throne was welcome. But when he waved for the war council to begin, it all went wrong. Everyone had a complaint.

'Sire, we are desperately short of supplies,' Feld said immediately. 'The Rallorans raided the camp when all the food had arrived, and after the guards had been lulled into a false sense of security. I took the liberty of having the guards flogged but the problem remains. Our regiments hurried here with only enough supplies for the march. Once all are here, we shall eat through the remaining supplies in three days, no more.'

'What?' Gello slammed his fist on the arm of the throne in frustration. Why was he surrounded by idiots?

'We can be ready to assault in three days, sire, but it will mean a direct attack. We cannot afford any extravagant flanking manoeuvres that will leave our troops hungry and tired,' Feld added.

'And the march to Sendric? Do we have enough for that?'

'Not really,' Feld admitted. 'But once through the passes we can split up, live off the land long enough to take the towns. And we can send some regiments back for more supplies then. But a frontal assault will cost us plenty of men. The Rallorans have the high ground, and can see what we are doing. Once it is obvious we are aiming a hammer blow at one pass, they will concentrate there.'

'All the better!' Gello grinned. 'We can destroy the bastards in one effort. We'll send in the criminals first, the militia behind them and then our regulars. It doesn't matter if the first two thousand men are slaughtered, as long as our regulars are preserved. We'll chase those vermin until we have exterminated the last of them from our country. Does anyone really think they can turn us back?'

'No, sire,' Feld agreed. 'They can hurt us but they cannot stop us. The Dragon Sword has done nothing, so only divine intervention could save them!'

The assembly joined in Feld's laughter — which was cut off as Gello leaned forwards, his face like thunder, and said, 'What did you say?'

'The Dragon Sword has done nothing, the only thing that can save them is divine intervention, sire,' Feld repeated, mystified.

Gello leaned back, chewing on a nail. Feld was right about the Dragon Sword. It had not even been a factor. The Ralloran dog was obviously unworthy of it and unable to unlock its magic. He had virtually forgotten about it and could safely put it out of his mind now. But Feld had also touched on the only thing that could stop him. He had not thought about divine intervention before, now it seemed everyone was mentioning it. He did not really think Aroaril would send fiery bolts from the sky to destroy his army but, still … This close to victory, he could not help but remember how he had been thwarted at the last moment before. He could not let that happen again, even if it meant a deal with dark powers. He became aware that everyone was staring at him.

'Are there any real problems?' he demanded, to cover himself.

Immediately the nobles began complaining about the way they were being treated, about their accommodation and about not getting their promised rewards.

Gello sighed. Sometimes he felt it would be easier if he just had them all killed.

'Make a note of everything that is said,' he ordered a scribe. 'Ambassador, walk with me.'

Ezok was at his side in a moment but Gello waited until they were safely out of earshot.

'I have been thinking about what you said back at the capital. This business with Aroaril — how sure are you that He is helping my cousin?' Gello asked. 'That is the only thing I fear now, for surely there is no other way for Merren to save herself.'

'I am afraid there is a concern there, sire,' Ezok said carefully. 'After all, as your captain pointed out, the only thing that can stop you now is divine intervention. And Aroaril's power is strong in the north. We had an agent inside the town but he was found and destroyed by a priest of Aroaril.'

'An agent? Who?'

'You remember, sire? The bard? The one we used to lead your cousin into Cezar's trap?'

Gello nodded. He hesitated to go any further down this path, but the thought of failing again drove him onwards. 'I do not want to have any concerns heading into this battle. The business with the nobles, the lack of supplies — they are easily controlled. But Aroaril … My cousin's Ralloran dog freed many priests of Aroaril from the capital. What if they were to intervene in the coming battle?'

'You would like the reassurance that Zorva stands ready to help you, while not committing yourself to Him?' Ezok suggested.

'You have it exactly, Ambassador!' Gello said with relief.

'Well, as it happens, sire, I think I may have an answer there for you. I have been speaking to Archbishop Prent, who does not have the favour of Aroaril. But he would be ideal for this purpose. After all, he is your spiritual adviser already. Surely it makes sense to have him able to wield actual power, should the worst happen.'

Gello smiled wickedly. 'Excellent idea! Should I speak to him?'

'No need, sire. He and I have already spoken on this subject and he is eager to help. You may rest easy on this matter. Although, when you see what Zorva can do —'

'This is far enough for me at the moment,' Gello interrupted.

'Of course, sire.' Ezok bowed and smiled. It was almost too easy to manipulate Gello now. 'There is one thing: Prent will need to make a few sacrifices.'

'I don't care if he has to give up his old house and robes!' Gello snorted.

Ezok coughed gently. 'No, sire. I meant blood sacrifices. Might I suggest some of your disloyal nobles?'

Gello had no doubt there would be a thick sheaf of complaints from the nobles waiting for him when he returned to his quarters. 'They are all disloyal, all but Worick and Cessor. Take any you need — but hide the bodies. And tell me what you discover from them in the process.'

'As always, your majesty is wise.' Ezok bowed.

Merren had been cheered by the people she talked to. They were worried, but she promised them, time and again, that the town would never face a siege. In turn, they told her how happy they were to be living under her rule, how they would never go back to Gello's rule. She had brought along Jaret and Wilsen as guards, not so much because she feared for her life, but more because the crush of people eager to talk to her made it hard to move through the narrow streets, and a couple of large men in armour was an effective way of parting the way. Merren felt she and the people were drawing strength and encouragement from each other. She certainly did not mention she had ever considered walking away from the country.

She was working her way down one street, talking to stall owners and residents alike, when the press of people lessened suddenly.

'Where's everyone going?' she asked.

'The Archbishop! Back with Captain Martil!' someone cried.

Merren and her guards cut down a side street to where people were trying to catch a glimpse of the Archbishop, who had only visited Sendric once before.

'He's a bit older than I expected,' one woman said critically, only to be hushed by her friends.

'And where's the rest of the captain's men? I thought he left here with a dozen of them?' someone else muttered.

Merren pushed closer to see Karia walking hand in hand with an elderly man in the robes of an archbishop, followed by a woman in the robes of a bishop, what looked like a serving girl, and Martil with Kesbury walking behind. She wanted to get through, but the press of people was too great. She gestured to Wilsen.

'Make way for the Queen!' he bellowed, and the crowd parted as if by magic.

'Merren!' Karia cried and ran over to her, gave her a hug, then took her by the hand and led her across to the new Archbishop.

'Archbishop Nott, I presume?' Merren forced a smile for the benefit of the crowd.

'Your majesty.' He bowed.

'Let us give the people a little encouragement,' she said softly, then turned to the gathering.

'We have Aroaril on our side! We have the Dragon Sword on our side! Nothing can stop us now!' she shouted, gesturing at Nott and Martil, and hoping it was true.

14

Martil had taken his place at the council table dully. He spoke to Louise and Gia, who sat in their husbands' places at the table, but ignored the bard.

Karia was not there; Nott said she was playing with Tiera. He did not argue — the old priest had made sure Martil was not alone with Karia since that outburst in the forest and he could not blame the man.

But he was driven out of his torpor by rage when he learned what had happened at the ranger barracks, and how the Queen had only just escaped an elaborate trap that had killed Forde, Wime and Tarik. Losing them was a bitter blow.

'If only I had been there! I could have killed that weasel of a Berellian!' he growled when Barrett had finished outlining everything that had happened.

'Well, you weren't there, and we cannot change what is done — we must focus on what we can do,' Barrett snapped.

Martil ignored him. 'We must gut that Berellian bard that lied through his teeth to us. He was sent here to tempt us into that trap!'

'Too late,' Conal said and shrugged. 'When we learned what had happened to the Queen, Quiller and I took a squad of guards down to the cells. He had opened his veins with a sharp blade obviously hidden on his person.'

'He had scars on his arms that were only half-healed. I would say he was using his blood to communicate with a Fearpriest and tell him what we were doing,' Quiller confirmed. 'I heard followers of the Dark One are able to do that.'

'It all ties in with what we learned,' Nott agreed. 'It seems Gello is being helped by a Fearpriest, whether he realises it or not. But the real danger, of course, is that a Fearpriest would not be content with merely helping. He will want control, eventually.'

'I am more concerned with what is happening now,' Merren said sharply. 'We have lost valued friends and companions and all we have to show for it is a new archbishop and a bard. What do we do now? Would it be better for the people if I went into exile?'

'No!' Nott said vehemently. 'Not with Fearpriests loose in this land. Now is not the time to run — now is the time to stand and fight! I have high hopes for the priests and priestesses we freed. They will spread word of the evil that has taken hold of Gello. Once they get word to us, we can go and bring back recruits, plenty of them.'

'It's too late, Father — I mean, Archbishop,' Martil said tiredly. 'Even if we could bring back hundreds of men, we would not have time to train them. Gello does not have enough supplies to lay siege to the passes. He must mass his men and smash through, within a few days. To send untrained farmers and townsfolk into battle will only see a massacre.'

'So what are we going to do? Barricade ourselves behind these walls and try to wait Gello out?' Louise exclaimed. 'We can hold for weeks, maybe months, but I know you cannot hold the walls forever. They will get in here — and what happens then?'

'I will not allow that,' Merren said immediately. 'Whatever happens, I will not subject the people of this town to another street battle that will see many of them killed. This will be decided on a field far from the town, so that Gello will not get a chance to destroy Sendric, Gerrin or Berry. We will accept every man we can get, of course we will. Several hundred extra men, even if they are untrained, could prove the difference. We proved that in the victory we enjoyed in this very town. We shall use the Battle plan that Martil recommended at our last council meeting — tactics he used successfully at the Battle of Mount Shadar. With Aroaril's help, and a little luck, we shall hurt Gello so badly that he withdraws to lick his wounds. To that end, I expect Captain Martil to draw up a detailed battle plan, and present it here by tomorrow at the latest, so we can make a final decision.'

Martil bowed his head, which also had the desired effect of hiding the horrified expression on his face.

Mount Shadar had been classed as a victory, but he had kept from her the fact it had only come about when the Berellians had retreated rather than face the Ralloran reinforcements. Another turn of the hourglass and his brave defence would have ended in the utter destruction of his men.

How in Aroaril's name was he going to defeat an army even bigger than the Berellian force he had faced, with little more than what he had at Mount Shadar?

Barrett watched Martil suspiciously. The man had been acting strangely ever since his return. He was not telling the truth, Barrett was sure of it. And if he could prove Martil was lying, then there was still time to persuade Merren to abandon this futile battle outside the passes and adopt his brilliant idea to sacrifice the Rallorans. He made a mental note to dig through Count Sendric's papers. Surely there was an account of the Battle of Mount Shadar there.

'Barrett, may I have a word?' Archbishop Nott patted him on the shoulder as the council broke up.

'Yes, Archbishop?'

'I have a young woman, a serving girl we rescued from the chapter house. Her bravery helped us greatly but she also revealed some ability with magic. Apparently she could see what was happening when Karia helped us escape. I think it would help her greatly if she were to study with you.'

'Really? While I recognise that I have a duty to help other magic-users find their way, I already have a student — an exceedingly talented student. This girl is obviously only mildly gifted, or her talent would have shown itself before now. Surely she would be better off working with one of the two wizards in town …'

'She has already developed a relationship with Karia. But, more importantly, she was … abused by Prent. She is a brave woman but it has obviously affected her greatly. I would like to see her learn with a man I can trust, a man of honour. Not casting aspersions on the other wizards, but I do not know them. You, on the other hand, I know by reputation. You would not think of taking advantage of the natural bond that a teacher and student develop, the undoubted respect she will have for someone of your ability—'

'Absolutely not! I would never dream of hurting a woman, or pressing my suit on another,' Barrett declared. He cleared his throat. 'A serving girl, probably from a poor family — perhaps she never had the chance to study. I'd be happy to run her through a few tests tomorrow. Obviously Karia must be my priority — I mean, to think she actually managed to help you escape by opening an oaken gateway! She may have had a better teacher than I but I do not think I could have duplicated that feat at her age! She already has more control and power than most of the wizards in this country and she's not officially allowed to sit her test for the First Circle for another four years!'

'She is a wonder,' Nott agreed. 'Every day I look at her and feel pride. She is a special child. What you have done to unlock her talent is inspiring. It is partly why I feel so confident entrusting Tiera to your hands.'

Nott shook hands with Barrett and left.

Barrett watched him go. It was strange, but he did not feel quite so angry and hurt inside now. Had the old man done something to him? He knew how natural magic worked and would have detected that in an instant but the new Archbishop had the full power of Aroaril available to him. All he had been thinking about was a way to humiliate Martil, now he was starting to think about how he might be able to teach this young woman.

Nott caught up with Martil before the warrior could escape.

'We need to have that talk now,' he said firmly, steering Martil into a side chamber.

Martil could not even muster the energy to rage at the man. For the first time, he was ready to surrender. The Dragon Sword had given up on him, and the Queen thought he had a winning battle plan, when all he had was a creative way to get them killed. But, most importantly, he had proved himself unworthy of Karia.

He sat, subdued, waiting for the axe to fall.

'I have to apologise to you, Martil,' Nott said sadly.

Here it comes, Martil thought.

'I have been monopolising Karia for the past few days. It has been at a time when you have been under a great deal of pressure, and I know how much you enjoy time with her.'

Martil just looked at him. He wished the old man would hurry up and get it over with, then he could go out and crawl into a wineskin somewhere.

'But, you see, it was an old man's vanity. My God has forced me to give up many things but to give up my granddaughter, once to that bastard Edil and now to you, seems to have been the hardest thing. I have a greater duty now and I cannot take the time to look after Karia. I'll be going to tell her that now, and I will need you to comfort her and take care of her, because she will be upset. But knowing she means so much to you will be my comfort. I can go out and do what my God requires, because I have faith that she will be better off with you. So, you see, I have treated the last couple of days as a farewell. Of course I will be able to see her from time to time but she needs to have some certainty of where she is and I cannot provide that. You can. I know being shut away from her for the past few days has been hard on you. I ask you to forgive me for that, and thank you for indulging an old man.'

Martil stared at Nott. His brain was having trouble digesting what he had just heard.

'You don't want to take her away from me?' he said stupidly.

'Aroaril's beard, no! She needs someone who can devote time to her. She needs you.'

'But, but — what happened in the forest! I don't deserve her!' Martil cried.

Nott sighed. 'She knows you did not mean that and she saw how upset you were. She is also feeling a little fragile. She fears that neither of us wants her, when the truth is we both do. But it will be better for her, on many levels, if she is with you. With your blessing, I would like to look after her for one last night.'

Martil did not know what to think or feel. He was still awash with self-loathing over raising his hand to Karia. He had been so sure that Nott would take her away that he could not comprehend she would stay with him.

'I think we should both go to Karia, and tell her together,' Nott said calmly.

Martil slumped in his chair. 'I don't deserve her,' he groaned. 'Why are you leaving her with me?'

Nott grabbed him by the shoulders and Martil was struck anew by the force in his grip. 'You are a better man than you think. You need Karia's help to free yourself from the horrors of your past, as Karia needs you to do the same for her. No, you don't deserve her. But if you think that every day, and resolve to be the best dad you can for her, then that is enough. Now come on. She is waiting, and worrying about what we are going to say to her.'

Nott almost dragged him up and out of the room. Martil shambled along beside the priest, trying to get his head around what had just happened. By rights he should have been ecstatic that Karia was to stay with him but he had been so worked up about losing her that all that was inside him was a dull ache. And in his brain was the repeated thought that he was unworthy, that Nott might want him to look after her but why would she want to stay with him?

Karia had set all her dolls up carefully, and inspected them for the fourth time. She was too nervous to play with them. She had been playing with Tiera but then Bishop Milly had arrived and taken Tiera away, saying that Tiera was going to meet Barrett and learn how to be a wizard, too. That was all very exciting but now she was alone, and she knew Father Nott and Martil were coming, to talk to her about who she would like to live with. They were taking a long time, and she had all these butterflies swirling around in her stomach.

She wanted to stay with Martil but after the way he had raised his hand and yelled at her, her fear was he did not really want her. She had not really been afraid of him but it had been a shock to see him act like that. He had yelled at her before, the first time she had met him, at Father Nott's house. Now they had met up with Father Nott again, he was yelling again. She did not know what that meant but she did know she didn't like it. But the Martil she knew, that was the one she wanted to stay with.

She cuddled Dolly close and found herself wondering if they wanted her to make the choice. If so, who would she choose? Martil or Father Nott? Her first impulse was Father Nott; after all, she had known him for so much longer, but then she thought harder. Life with Martil was definitely more interesting and, truth be told, more fun. She wanted to say that she wanted to live with both of them — that way they could both take care of her. But she realised that she would choose Martil and immediately felt anew the fear that he would not want her.

When the door opened, she almost jumped. Then she leaped to her feet, as Nott and Martil walked in.

'What's happening?' she demanded.

Nott smiled at her. 'Martil and I have been talking about you. You know we both love you very much, and we would both like to look after you. But I am afraid my new job will take me away from you after tonight, so you will be staying with Martil.'

She looked at Martil, who appeared anything but happy, and she knew her fears were real.

'Doesn't he really want me?' she asked, trying to keep the quiver out of her voice.

Martil looked up then. 'Of course I do! I just don't think I deserve you!' he cried.

'I thought you didn't want me any more,' she accused.

'I'm sorry if you thought that. I love being with you. I want to make you happy.' He fell to his knees. 'I am so sorry for what happened back in the forest. I swear to you it will never happen again. Do you want to stay with me?'

She rushed over and hugged him. 'Yes!'

When he felt her small arms around his neck, holding him close, he felt something break within him and, moments later, they were both crying.

Nott wiped a tear away himself. This had sadly been necessary. And not just for Martil to be able to escape his dreams. Aroaril was going to ask a great deal of both of them. Apart, they were never going to be able to handle it. He hoped what he had done, while hurting them, had made them realise that their future lay together. At least he knew they would be happy, as long as they lived. Now he had another task to fulfil.

Gello and his captains left the plains and rode up through the hills, closer to the first pass, the most northerly one. With them, as was his wont, was Ezok, and with him was the Berellian Champion, Cezar. Ezok knew the captains were frightened of him and that, in battle, it was easy for accidents to happen. Cezar was there to make sure the accidents happened to other people.

The pass they were inspecting was the one most used by traffic heading north and, while the middle pass was actually a little wider, the road here was far better, the climb upwards gentler. It also offered the most direct route to Sendric. Looking up the hill to the pass itself, the Ralloran barricade appeared daunting — felled trees had added to the basic wagons-and-barrels barricade they had started with. There were also plenty of men manning the makeshift ramparts.

'At least a company, with more on the valley walls, and probably archers hidden behind,' Feld announced. 'But they have been busy, as well.'

As he spoke, a strange noise made several of the horses start, and a large rock arced through the air.

'Quick now!' Feld snapped, and they spurred their horses off to the side. The rock landed with a thump about twenty yards short of the group and bounced and rolled down towards the plains below.

'Catapults. They've got a decent range on them — and our scouts have seen ballistae as well. They will take a toll before we can close with them,' Feld warned.

'Won't matter. Once we are within bowshot, we can overwhelm them with archers, then send in the infantry to finish them off, eh, Beq?' Gello said cheerily.

'Indeed, sire.' Beq bowed.

'How long?' Gello demanded of the others.

'The last regiments will be here by tomorrow night. Give them two days to rest and eat, then we can assault, sire,' Feld promised.

'Excellent! See it is no longer, or you will be in the front rank.'

'Shall we give them a full volley of ballistae, sir?' Dunner asked, pointing towards the siege engines that looked like giant crossbows and hurled a spear twice the height of a man.

Nerrin shook his head. 'Let's keep a few surprises for them. My gut tells me they are coming straight for us. No feints, no fancy business, just mass the men and roll through us.'

'It'll be slaughter, sir!'

'Aye, it will. But it will also work. Is the last of Kesbury's squad back in our lines?'

'Yes, sir, the final pair just got in.'

'Good. Send two of them back to Sendric with word for Captain Martil. We'll concentrate the men here, and send horses to the other passes to drag their ballistae down here.'

'Just the ballistae, sir?'

'Aye. The catapults will be too heavy. It'd take too long — we have two, maybe three days before they march.'

Merren set herself a frenetic pace. The fear that a massive army was about to loom over the horizon was working not just on the townsfolk but also on the soldiers she had recruited. Losing Wime, Tarik and Forde, as well as a dozen of their best men, had shaken confidence. The people had grown too used to victories — to suffer two setbacks in quick succession had the mutterers and naysayers out in force.

But Merren refused to give in to that. She spoke to small groups, anything from a squad of men to a few families in a street. Every time her message was the same. *I will not allow you to be hurt. We must have faith. Aroaril and the Dragon Sword are both on our side. And our army will be led by Captain Martil, the man who beat the Berellians, who was never defeated in battle. How then can we possibly lose?*

Martil knew he should feel better, but he actually felt worse. Knowing Karia would be staying with him and, even better, that she wanted to stay with him, should have made him ecstatic. He had been so worried about losing her. But he could not shake the feeling that he was not worthy of her. Worse, as he tried to draw up a battle plan, he felt as though he was letting everybody down. It was simple enough. He would use his Rallorans as bait, putting them on the hillside, with every flag they could muster, to draw Gello's attention.

Because of the hill, his archers would outrange Gello's men by thirty paces. As well, he would have every ballistae they could drag up the hill. They would cut huge gaps in the Norstaline archers as they advanced. But they would be able to struggle uphill; there were just too many to stop with only one hundred and twenty archers. At that point, Rocus and the Norstalines, who would all be mounted, could be brought from the back of the hill and out through a cutting to strike Gello's men in the flank. They would drive them back the first time easily. But each time after that would get harder. Eventually the Norstalines' superior numbers would win out, barring some miracle.

He threw down the plan in disgust. If only he could get the Dragon Sword to work! That had been the key to victory all along. But he had been unable to do anything more than use it to cut hapless soldiers apart in battle. If he had been a better man, Merren and the others would not be in this mess! He was going to lead them all to their deaths, he was sure of it. They would follow him, trusting him, believing that the fabled Captain Martil could not be defeated. Then they would all be slaughtered.

Even if he somehow survived, he would be forever haunted by the deaths he had caused. There would be a new saga sung around the continent. Of how the last Butcher of Bellic led a trusting queen to her doom. Throughout the ages, men would spit on hearing his name.

Now, how was that a better future for Karia? How in Aroaril's name could Nott let him look after her, when that was what she had to look forward to?

'Now, call for the worms to come up to you,' Barrett urged Tiera.

They were out in the small kitchen garden attached to the keep, where fresh herbs were grown. Barrett always liked to use this test to distinguish how magical a person was. Tiera, who was almost twenty, was too old to fully develop her powers, such as they were. By the time she had done enough study to reach the upper echelons, it would be too late — she would be too old. But there was certainly enough time for her to make the Third Circle, at least, which would ensure her a decent living in any town.

He told himself he would have been happy to supply instruction to her even if she had not been so attractive. Of course, not that he was going to encourage anything of that sort. He had been told, first by Nott and then by this fierce-looking Bishop Milly, that Tiera had been deeply affected by the abuse she had suffered from Prent.

'Although her body has been healed, her spirit is still wounded. This training will help her regain her self-confidence and self-respect,' Milly had told him. 'Do not do anything that will hurt her.'

Barrett had drawn himself up to his full height and made sure he gave her every last bit of his best withering look.

'Bishop, you need have no fear on that score. I would never harm a woman. I am not some mindless warrior who thinks women were created for one purpose only! You may rest assured that Tiera will have nothing to fear from me!'

'Excellent. And I thank you for this. Tiera did us a great service back in the capital and she deserves more than to return to a life of drudgery.'

So now he was going to see just what sort of life she could have.

'Here they come!' Tiera laughed, her eyes closed, her fingers dug into the earth. 'I can feel them! This is wonderful!'

Barrett watched carefully but only saw about half-a-dozen worms wriggle to the surface. His heart fell a little. Third Circle was probably the best Tiera could ever hope for, even with rigorous training and dedication. She had nothing like Karia's talent. But he kept all that from his voice.

'Excellent!' He applauded her. 'Now, send them back. Good work! You have taken a big step into your new life! You certainly have magic ability. Now, we should go up to my study …' He stopped talking when he saw something flash behind her eyes, and cursed himself for saying that. 'I mean, we shall go into the hall and I shall show you a variety of exercises to clear your mind and focus your thoughts, which you can practise by yourself. Then tomorrow we can begin to work on your control of the magic.'

'Why not today?'

'I have to go and search through some old papers — you'd probably find that boring.' He shrugged.

'I could help you,' Tiera offered.

Barrett hesitated. Two sets of eyes would be better than one. 'That would be wonderful,' he said, thinking he had better give her an opportunity to avoid it. 'But only if you want to help me. It might be very boring. And you need to conserve strength for magic tomorrow.'

Tiera smiled at him and he felt something jump a little in his chest.

'I would like to help,' she told him.

Kettering walked around the lines of what he now thought of as his men. He went to his most loyal followers first, who were mainly the men who had been arrested for defying Gello, although it also included a number of career criminals. He made sure Menner was still all right, although the march north seemed to have exhausted the little tailor. Hawke had ended up carrying Menner's pack and sword.

'Killer, do I really have to keep looking after him? Some of the boys are saying things about us,' Hawke growled. 'Couldn't we just leave him somewhere? I mean, he's not likely to do much in battle but get himself killed. He can barely hold a sword!'

Kettering stared at Hawke until the big man groaned and threw up his hands.

'Fine, then! But don't say I didn't warn you!'

Kettering kept up his mission to spread the word, speaking to the hardened criminals, men who listened to him with a wary respect, seeing in Kettering a man whose iron purpose might just free them.

The criminals had been given bare rations — more like the food they had been used to in their original dungeons. Accepting that had been hard as they watched the cavalry regiments nearby gorge themselves. Resentment and hunger made them eager to listen to what Kettering had to say.

Inside him, the fire was almost out of control. He had seen the man who had set him up, who had killed that stableboy and then left him to hang for a crime he had not committed. The bastard was not even skulking around — he was riding with the King! Dining with the King! That, more than anything, made Kettering determined not just to escape but to somehow gain his revenge on those who had put him here. Part of him recognised that the old Kettering was long gone; that man had been burned off by the fire of adversity he'd been put through. Everything he had once thought important, all he had once held dear, was gone.

Meanwhile, his anger lent strength to his words, helped drive them into the minds of the men he spoke to.

'They've brought us here for their reason. But we are our own men. We shall choose our moment.

Listen for my orders. Ignore the men who claim to be our sergeants and officers. Obey only me or the men I have chosen,' Kettering told them.

He had decided he needed to extend his control over the regiment. He'd chosen men he could trust or, at least, men who were willing to follow him. Mainly men like himself, who had once been respected and even loved, until Gello and his ilk had taken all that away, but also criminals like Leigh and even Hawke. Each had a squad or company to command.

'We shall have our revenge, somehow,' Kettering said.

And they all believed him.

'Sarge! Have a look there!'

Hutter still found Turen annoying but the young constable — now private — had seemingly appointed himself as Hutter's personal servant. With all the demands on his time, it had been a great help not to worry about the mundane things, like his tent and his food.

'What?'

'It's that bloke who came into our village, asking for Martil. He's with the King!'

Hutter turned to see the King and his captains riding past, surrounded by a troop of guards. At the back rode two men in black, one of them the evil little bastard who had terrified him back in Chell.

'What's he doing with the King?' Hutter wondered aloud.

'Can't be anything good,' Turen opined.

Hutter had to agree with him. Perhaps Turen was finally getting his brain working. 'Looks like we've got a vital piece of evidence in our case, lad. Get the sergeants in. I need to talk to them.'

'Are we going to arrest the King, Sarge?'

Hutter sighed. No, the boy was still an idiot.

Barrett was acutely aware of Tiera as they both worked in Sendric's records room. The room smelled of dust and mouse droppings and, with all the shelves, there was little space. It was simply a small storeroom that had shelves lining every wall, filled with books and scrolls. No doubt there was some order but he was yet to decipher it.

He knew he was not supposed to be alone with Tiera but the door was open, at least. Still, in case Bishop Milly or someone else walked in, he was trying to keep half an eye on her, so he could always be at the point of the room furthest away from her.

They had looked yesterday afternoon without success, then met down here soon after breakfast and started searching again. The council meeting was going to begin soon and he knew they would have to leave the search to attend it.

Tiera, on the other hand, was oblivious of time passing. This task was no different to many of the meaningless, boring duties she had done every day as a servant. She recognised that Barrett was a kind and gentle man, albeit rather pompous, and actually felt relaxed in his company. She would not have been able to stay in a room this size with, say, one of those Rallorans for such a time.

But she was aware that Barrett was being very careful not to come near her. The existence of an invisible barrier that she was not allowed to cross was both reassuring and a little amusing. She tested it by taking a pace closer, and was rewarded by seeing him edge away, keeping a decent distance between them. She had always had a sense of mischief, so she carefully, and slowly, pursued him around the room, until she had him almost backed up in a corner, where he would have to brush past her to get out. What was he going to do then? That would be the real test of who he was, she decided.

Barrett was wondering how to get out of the corner he had been backed into. He could no longer smell the dusty books or even the mouse droppings — only the lemon scent of her hair. He was wondering if a little magic might not be in order here when a scroll caught his eye.

'This is it!' he cried, grabbing it down and ignoring a shower of mouse droppings. 'An account of the Battle of Mount Shadar! We did it! Come on, we have to get this to the council meeting!'

Tiera stepped aside for the excited wizard, feeling almost a little disappointed. It was strange. She had thought she could never feel comfortable alone with a man again.

'Archbishop, I am always glad to see you. But I do have a council meeting starting soon — perhaps we could speak afterwards?' Merren suggested, as she tried to brush her hair. Normally she had maids for this sort of thing but Nott had asked for a private word.

Nott sighed. 'I am afraid this cannot wait. It is about Martil.'

'What about Martil?' Merren tugged the reluctant brush through a knot and swore under her breath. Why did people always judge a queen on her appearance? Her grandfather had reputedly regularly turned up at court spattered in mud and blood from the hunt and nobody had said a thing. But if a queen wore an old outfit or appeared without her hair done, everyone started whispering.

'I need you to trust him.'

Merren looked at the Archbishop. 'What is going on?' she demanded.

'Martil is the only way you can defeat Gello and the Fearpriest menace. I need you to firstly remember that, and secondly to ensure that he is the man we need,' Nott said steadily.

Merren laid down the brush carefully. 'Why don't you just explain, to save us both time?'

Nott smiled wistfully. 'I wish I could tell you everything. But I do not know everything — indeed, such a thing is impossible. Even Aroaril cannot say what will happen, because there is another power, a dark power, striving to make sure its vision comes to pass. I can tell you this much: At this council meeting, you will be given reason, good reason, to doubt Martil and his ability to win this battle. One of your most trusted advisers will ask you to abandon the Rallorans. You must not do this. Martil is the only way you can win. Everything in his life — and I do mean everything — has prepared him for this. I have not taken a church service with you; I do not know if you truly believe or just nod in Aroaril's direction. So I will ask you to have faith in Martil. You must do that.'

Merren listened with growing disquiet. Putting her trust in an old priest's words, no matter how heartfelt, was something she was reluctant to do.

'You may say Martil is the only way for victory but you have to admit that he is deeply troubled. I have doubts about his state of mind and I do not blame anyone else for having them also! Putting not just my throne but the lives of all who trust me into his hands —'

'I ask more than that. You must put your trust in Martil but you are the only one who can make him ready to live up to that trust. You must do whatever it takes to ensure he is able to use the Dragon Sword.'

Merren shook her head in exasperation. 'What do you think we have been doing? If we could help him unlock the Dragon Sword's magic, don't you think we would have done it by now?'

Nott took her hands in his. This was a breach of royal protocol and Merren was so taken aback by the move that she did nothing. Nott stared at her.

'There is something that you, only you, can do to save Martil, so he in turn can save you.'

Merren jerked her hands free as she realised what he meant. 'What! For a priest, you ask a great deal! Do you really think that—'

'Do you think I would be telling you this if there was another way?' Nott's eyes bored into hers. The effect was almost hypnotic. She found herself unable to look, or move, away.

'There are so many reasons for you not to do this. You are a queen, he is a common Ralloran. You need to preserve yourself for a political marriage. He is in love with you, and this will only create problems for your people, for yourself and for the likes of Barrett, who you recently rebuffed. And you cannot just give yourself to him, like some sort of ceremonial sacrifice, to lie back and think only of Norstalos. You have to want to. Only then can he become the man you need to wield the Dragon Sword and save your country.'

'And if I do not do this?'

'Then you will either flee or be destroyed. There is no way to defeat Gello's army in the time you have left,' Nott said calmly.

Merren stood abruptly, breaking the spell between them.

'I never thought to hear such a thing from the Archbishop! You do know what you are asking of me?' Her mind, her emotions, were in a whirl. She was part horrified, part terrified — and somewhere there was a frisson of excitement.

'I would not ask it unless I knew there was something between you both,' he said.

'You presume too much!' Merren snapped back.

'Perhaps,' he agreed. 'Although I do know there is something. Ultimately, you are a woman and he is a man. Whether you are what the other needs, whether you are meant for each other, I cannot answer. Only you two can. I have told you what I must — that only through Martil can you defeat Gello and only through you can Martil become the man who can lead you to that victory. What you choose to do with that information is up to you.'

Merren laughed harshly. 'You do not leave me much of a choice!'

'On the contrary!' Nott thundered. 'You have a choice! You can flee this country, try to escape to Rallora, or Aviland, or Tetril, rally support against Gello there. You can hope Gello's embrace of the Dark One so horrifies Norstalos that he loses his support here. Putting your trust in Martil does not guarantee you victory. You could save him and still lose the battle; you are massively outnumbered.'

'I wish you would give me a straight answer!' Merren snarled at him.

'Life is about making choices, and having the courage to live with the choices you have made. You can stay and fight, or run and hide. But if you want to stay and fight, then Martil is your only hope of success. You are the Queen. Nobody can make that decision for you. I am sorry to put you in this position. I wish we had met in the capital, where we could have both spent our lives working to improve the lot of the people. But we have met like this and I have given you the best advice I can. Do with it what you will.'

Merren wanted to rage at him, wanted to grab the old man by the shoulders and shake him. But instead she took a deep breath.

'Leave me now. I have much to think about.'

Nott bowed. 'Of course. Incidentally, I must thank you for also taking care of my granddaughter, Karia. She speaks most highly of you.'

Merren inclined her head, not trusting herself to speak, and Nott bowed again, before walking out.

Outside, he sighed. He regretted having to do that to her. Merren was a fine young woman, and had held this rebellion together. He would never have wanted to force her to do something against her will. But time was running out; he had to nudge her down a path she was already considering.

This was why Aroaril could never guarantee victory. He was relying on people and, more than that, relying on people's emotions and relationships. Nott knew there was a power in love but to entrust the fate of the whole world to it? He was glad he was just his God's instrument.

Merren had to force her mind to consider Nott's words. Part of her wanted to ignore everything; to stay and fight but find another way to defeat Gello. The thought of running, of leaving Gello triumphant — she had flirted with the idea but now could not bring herself to do it.

She had always known that she and Gello were

locked in a competition for Norstalos, a competition where there could be but one victor. She had never imagined the cost to the country would be as great, of course. That price was the one thing that made her think of running away. Her head told her it might be time to go, that leaving might save lives. But her heart would not let her. Giving up was not in her nature. Besides, only Gello's mercy would decide if her departure would save lives — and he had shown precious little of that. But there was more to it. She could argue, convincingly, that what she was doing was better for the country, that Gello would bring Norstalos to ruin. Her plan for Norstalos would significantly improve life for the people. That was true, but not all of the truth. At the core of things, she had to admit she wanted to beat her cousin.

So it all came back to Martil. Until now, all her emotions had been focused on first holding, then winning back, her throne. But she remembered the kiss they had shared back at the caves; the effect she had on him. She had enjoyed flirting with him, teasing him a little but had refused to let herself consider taking her relationship with him further, despite her attraction. Her duty was clear — a marriage of political convenience, not love.

She could tell herself it would be for her country, that it was to save her people but the truth was, she found the thought as intriguing as he was. And a little bit exciting.

If she had been an ordinary woman ... but the problem was, she was never going to be an ordinary woman. She was a queen.

15

Martil looked and felt terrible. His nightmares about Bellic never seemed to end and he could not shake the feeling that he did not deserve Karia. She was sitting next to him, chattering away; he did his best to talk to her but was barely aware of what she was saying. He was trying to concentrate on the battle plan he had in front of him, and hoping nobody would see the flaws in it. The situation was not being helped by Barrett, seated opposite him with a ridiculously wide grin on his face. He was getting on Martil's nerves.

The chatter around the table seemed to be going on for a long time and he vaguely registered that Merren was not there yet. When she finally did arrive, she looked as if she would rather be elsewhere.

'Your majesty, if I could start proceedings by telling you what has happened since we set free the priests and priestesses,' Bishop Milly announced, as Merren finally sat down, signifying that the council had begun.

Merren waved for her to continue.

'I am afraid there is no good news. It took many of them days to journey to their parishes. And when they arrived there, they found the people scared and confused. Gello's use of bards and tame priests to spread a message of hate has left the people unsure who to trust. We are countering his lies with the message that Gello has turned to evil but it will take days, if not weeks, to win the people back,' Milly said regretfully. 'It appears we are on our own.'

Many around the table exchanged worried looks but Merren merely nodded, as if she had been expecting this news.

Barrett leaped out of his seat in his eagerness to speak next.

'Your majesty, I have discovered something of importance that I must share with you,' he gabbled, staring at Martil the whole time.

'Go ahead, Barrett,' Merren said, tiredly.

'This is an account of the Battle of Mount Shadar, the one that Captain Martil proposes to base our strategy on. It lists how many of his men were killed or wounded in the battle — and explains in detail how Martil's regiment was saved by the arrival of King Tolbert and reinforcements. Had they not arrived, he would have been defeated and his regiment destroyed. Captain Martil is a liar and he is leading us all to our doom!'

Barrett spat the words out, an expression of fierce triumph on his face.

If he had had more energy, Martil would have drawn his sword and leaped across the table. But he knew the wizard, pompously annoying as he was, spoke the truth.

The rest of the table erupted in shock and anger. Some were yelling for Barrett to withdraw his comments, others were voicing their fear that the mage was right, their soldiers were doomed and Gello would be triumphant.

'Silence!' Merren's voice cut through the hubbub.

She stared around the table, until her eyes met Nott's. He nodded knowingly at her and she forced herself to look elsewhere.

'If you do not agree with Captain Martil's plan, do you have an alternative?' Merren forced herself to say.

Barrett looked away from Martil finally.

'I do. I have already proposed it to you.'

Merren shook her head. 'If you mean tricking the Rallorans so they sacrifice themselves, their deaths buying us time to build an army, then I have already told you I shall never agree to that.'

Again the table erupted, this time with Martil joining in, and Barrett looked somewhat abashed, albeit a little defiant.

'Enough!' Again Merren was able to silence the room.

She took a deep breath. Every eye was upon her and she could feel the weight of the decision pressing down on her. She stood at a branch in the path — whichever way she chose now, there was no going back. History would be the only judge as to whether she chose correctly. But she had been told for years it was her duty to make decisions. She hesitated only a moment longer, then let out the breath and made her choice.

'This is what we shall do,' she began. 'And there will be no debate about this. Any of you who do not like my decision, or do not agree, will be free to leave my service, with my blessing, to make what they can of their lives.'

She looked carefully around the table. Most were

hanging on her every word, although Martil was just staring at the table and Barrett concentrated on Martil, as if determined to drink in every moment of his downfall. Nott was smiling gently at her.

'I shall not leave. I shall put my trust in Captain Martil. He outwitted Gello's men in the forest, won the battle of Sendric and took the passes for us. His plan is undoubtedly risky but the alternatives are unacceptable. I will not leave this country to the excesses of Gello and his Fearpriests. I could not come back and take the Crown if I left my people to suffer while I lived in safety. Nor will I subject this town to a siege. We shall fight Gello in the field. If we are defeated, there will be time enough for the town to escape. I will go out and face Gello and his lackeys, even if I am alone. I do not order you to follow me. I only ask that you help me finish what we started, to make a New Norstalos, a country where we can all be proud and free, and where you will be valued for what you can do, not where you were born. So who will stand with me?'

Almost before she had finished speaking, Louise and Gia had stood, closely followed by Rocus, Nott, Conal, Gratt and more. Quiller was quick to begin but a little slow actually getting up, while Sendric seemed to give it a moment's thought before rising. Romon was standing, scratching furiously onto a piece of parchment. Karia leaped onto her chair, until only Barrett and Martil remained seated.

'Barrett?' she asked, gently.

He turned a stricken face towards her, and seemed ready to either run or cry. Then Tiera, who was standing next to him, touched him on the arm. Barrett took a deep, shuddering breath, then pushed back his chair and stood.

'I swore an oath never to leave your side,' he said, at first throatily, then with more power. 'I would never break that oath.'

She smiled at him, then looked at Martil.

'Come on!' Karia was tugging at his arm by now, wanting him to join what looked like a fun game, and slowly, in response to her urging, he stood.

Next moment people were clapping and cheering.

'To victory!' Merren called.

'The Queen!' Conal roared, and the chant was taken up.

She looked around the table then, knowing not all of these people would survive the coming battle, hoping at least some of them would and feeling the weight of those lives on her shoulders. But she kept herself smiling as they clapped and cheered. Half of her work was done. The most difficult half lay ahead, she judged, looking at Martil, who was still staring at the table.

Martil had been almost relieved when Barrett had delivered his accusations — he would not have to lead more men to their deaths. He could go away and die peacefully, forget about queens and Dragon Swords. Then Merren told them all she would ignore Barrett and put her trust in him. For the second time in as many days, someone was putting their trust in him and he felt he did not deserve it. They were all clapping and cheering now; he thought it was probably for Merren but it still made him cringe. She was so brave, so strong — and he was going to lead her to destruction. It was almost too much to bear.

'Captain Martil, I need to talk to you alone,' he heard Merren say, before she addressed the meeting once more. 'I shall summon you again to discuss the battle plan.'

Martil barely registered that people were now filing out of the audience chamber.

'Karia, why don't you come with me for a little while,' Nott said softly.

Martil realised he was alone with Merren.

Ezok could feel the thrill of power surging through his veins, stronger than any drug, more intoxicating than the finest wine, more thrilling than the most beautiful woman. The King of Norstalos now danced to his tune. He was the one pulling the strings here, making a vain and arrogant man do almost whatever he wanted. Norstalos was his in all but name. For instance, it had taken but a few simple suggestions about traitors among the nobles for Gello to give Ezok and Prent the right to question — and torture — any minor nobles they wished, in order to ensure Gello's safety. This gave Prent every opportunity to make sacrifices to Zorva and build his power — and Ezok every opportunity to find weaknesses in Norstalos he might be able to exploit. It was a heady feeling but it was only the beginning: Berellia would be next. After all, Markuz was but a puppet now. He did what Brother Onzalez ordered. And surely Ezok's reward for delivering this fat, prosperous country to Zorva would be one throne — perhaps two.

Happy thoughts such as these warmed him as he sat in Gello's war council, feeling the hate and anger coming towards him from the assembled war captains. He needed these fools to give Gello a victory — but not too convincing a victory. Ideally, Gello should suffer massive losses, so his expansion plans were crippled and the captains were disgraced, to further entrench Ezok's influence. Already the nobles were an irrelevance — only a handful had been invited to this meeting and these were not even seated at the table, filling chairs placed against the walls instead.

'So, we are all ready?' Gello said, snapping Ezok's attention back again.

'The men have had a chance to rest, and fill their bellies. The horses could use more time — there was little enough hay here and the march north was hard for them,' Feld reported.

'It won't come down to the cavalry anyway. It'll be close work to force the pass, then the cavalry can chase the survivors down like rats,' Gello dismissed. 'I want nothing to stop our march to glory. Beq, Grissum, can we trust the archers and rangers to fight and die?'

'Absolutely, sire!' Grissum said immediately, and Beq nodded his agreement enthusiastically. Neither wanted to be the one blamed for stopping Gello's so-called march to glory.

'And the volunteer regiments, the criminals and the militia — we can trust them?'

'Without a doubt, sire,' Beq said hastily and Grissum echoed his sentiments.

'Good, good! And, Livett, how are the new recruits going?'

With Livett's Light Horse regiment shattered at the battle of Sendric, his numbers had been made up from among the infantry. Their numbers had been bolstered by the recruits Gello had assembled for his grand army of conquest and who Livett had assured him were ready for battle.

'The cavalry is back to full strength, sire — we stand ready to turn an opening into victory for you!' Livett declared. In truth he was happy with having his regiment brought back to life. And the men chosen to serve with him — seen as being the best and most loyal infantry — were excellent. Certainly the infantry regiments had suffered a little as a result, but one company of half-trained recruits scattered through each regiment was not excessive.

'And what of our opponents?'

'The Rallorans have concentrated at the one pass. They are barely one thousand, although they do seem to have built a score of ballistae and a pair of catapults to help the defence,' Feld said.

'We shall let the archers and rangers whittle them down. A full arrow sheaf per archer — that will be forty thousand arrows for one thousand Rallorans. After that, we'll send in the infantry to clean them up and the cavalry to chase them away,' Gello stated.

That brought a rumble of approval from the table. All could see a demoralised, broken enemy.

Gello smiled at the men seated around the table. This was what he had dreamed of. This was the moment his mother had promised him would arrive. He was poised to become the absolute ruler of his country. He wished his mother was here to see it, so he could prove to her that he was worthy after all. Of course, if she had been, she would have been interfering, telling him what to do. Well, she had never taken the throne — he had! This triumph would be his alone. And it would be the first of many, until the whole world knew of Emperor Gello the Great — and everyone had forgotten about how the Dragon Sword had refused him.

'Gentlemen, we stand on the brink of utter victory. And this will be but the first of many! This army will roll on through the southern countries, until we are all draped in plunder and women!'

His captains all tapped the table in approval, while even the nobles were moved to applaud.

Gello signalled, and servants brought out wine for them all.

'To victory!' he toasted.

'Come with me, Captain.'

Martil followed, unresisting, wondering what Merren was going to say to him. He had no doubt she had some sort of inspiring speech planned, to fire him up and get him ready to lead her army to victory. But he was so tired, his spirits so low, he could not see how anything she could say would help him.

He was vaguely aware that they were now in Merren's private chambers but it was only when he heard her bolt the door that he really started to take notice.

'What's the matter?' he asked, his instinct for danger beginning to kick in.

Merren almost laughed. 'Where do we start?'

Getting Martil into her room had been easy enough. But even now she was not sure how she was going to take it further. One step at a time, she told herself.

'Sit down. Do you want a drink?'

Martil looked longingly at the decanter of wine but managed to refuse.

'Well, I do,' Merren said with feeling, and poured herself a large goblet, took a swig, then topped up the goblet once more before sitting down next to him. Where to begin?

'You once swore an oath, on Karia's life, to serve me and obey me without question,' she stated.

'I did.' Martil straightened up automatically.

'Then I command you now to tell me what is wrong with you. You sit at the most important war council meeting we have ever held, staring at the table! You propose a battle plan that is flawed at best but refuse to admit it. I hear you have been shouting at Karia. And, worst of all, you don't even fight with Barrett when he gives you every reason to want to! Where is the Martil I first met?'

Martil opened and closed his mouth. Where could he start? There were so many thoughts whirling around in his exhausted brain that he felt it was a miracle his head had not already exploded.

She tried again. 'Martil, whatever else, you are the Queen's Champion and the wielder of the Dragon Sword. You freed me from Gello's palace, built me an army, gave me victories and this town. You won me a battle and saved my life. Nothing you can say can change that, or the respect I have for you.'

But still he could not answer. There was too much inside him to actually get out. He turned to her with anguish all too apparent on his face.

Words were not enough, she decided; stronger measures were called for. She took a gulp of wine then leaned in, grabbed his face and kissed him as hard as she could on the lips.

It was like someone had thrown a bucket of cold water on him. Before he knew what he was doing, he was kissing her back, until she broke it off, keeping her face close to his, holding his cheeks in her hands.

'Will you tell me now?' she demanded.

'I don't deserve you. I don't deserve Karia. I don't deserve people cheering me,' he said hoarsely.

'Good. Go on,' she urged him.

And out it all came, like poison pouring from an infected wound. How he should have stopped the Berellians from torturing and mutilating a Ralloran village. How it was his fault, how his guilt at their fate made him destroy Bellic. How he had killed a woman and child there, how his order had seen the whole town razed. How the dead stalked him through the streets of Bellic every night and no matter what he did, he could not escape them. How he thought he was going to lose Karia, and then had raised a hand to her. How Nott wanted him to look after her but he could never be good enough. How he was terrified that his plan was going to lead everyone to their deaths and he would be haunted forevermore, despised through the ages: the last Butcher of Bellic, who worked his evil on a young queen and led her to her doom.

'Karia loves you,' she suggested.

'Karia is a little girl! She was treated like a slave by her real father — anything would look good to her, compared to him! If she knew the truth, she would run away from me!'

'But still—'

'I am not a good man! Everyone thinks I must be, because I drew the Dragon Sword, but it won't work for me! It's going to kill me for what I have done and what I keep doing!' His last cry was almost torn from him.

Merren kissed him again, but lightly this time. Listening to his torment, and understanding just what he had been going through, evoked in her a wash of tenderness and sympathy. He had come north looking for peace but, because he drew the Dragon Sword, she had asked him to do the very things he hated.

'There is a good man in there,' she said softly. 'The Dragon Sword does not make mistakes. It can see into your heart. We just have to help you find the good man and break clear of your past.'

Martil almost laughed and tried to tear himself away from her, but she held his face firm.

'If I knew how to do that, don't you think I would have already done so?' he groaned.

'You need proof that you are a good man. I know how to show you,' she said softly.

Until now, she had not been sure she could go through with this. For weeks she had been wondering whether she actually felt something for him. Now she knew she did. If Nott had not come to talk to her, to ask her to do this, she would never have acted, she knew that. But now she wanted to. This was not just about the Dragon Sword, about winning back her throne or even saving her people. This was about Merren, a woman, and Martil, a man.

She let go of his face and took his hand.

'Come with me,' she told him and led him back into her bedroom.

That was all she needed to do, she thought. After all, he would know what to do after that.

With an anguished howl, Martil rolled to the side of the bed and sat up, his head in his hands.

'What is it?' Merren sat up beside him and rubbed his shoulders.

'I don't know! I can't do anything right! I'm just no good!' Martil cried, not caring that he was now thumping his forehead with his hands. 'I'm not good enough for you — look at me, I'm useless! I can't even make love to the woman I love! Just leave me, let me go and die!'

She watched the tears running down his face and knew it could not end like this. She grabbed his hands then and forced him to turn and face her.

'I won't do that. Ever. And you are good enough. Martil, I love you. And if you can't make love to me, then I shall to you.'

Stunned, Martil did not resist as she pushed him back onto the bed.

This time, and the time after, it worked.

The howling dead had spotted him again.

'Kill him!' The cry was taken up by a score of ripped-out throats.

Martil did not waste his breath pleading with them. He saved his apologies for the bodies he clambered over in his desperate attempt to escape.

Ahead was the town square, with its tortured display of his fellow war captains; beyond that was the gate. The gate! Night after night it had drawn him, haunting him with its false promise of safety. He hated it. But there was no choice. The streets held nothing but death.

'You cannot escape us!' the leader of the dead, the woman he had killed, capered on a battlement over the gate. 'You don't deserve to!'

But Martil ignored her. At full pace he hurled himself at the massive wooden gate, then beat on it with his swords.

'Too late!' a voice taunted and he turned to see the host of the dead arrayed in a semicircle around him. Martil crouched, swords ready, and prepared to throw himself forwards in a last attack, when a creaking noise made him glance over his shoulder.

The gates were opening!

He looked again. Even though he knew there was no hope, he had to look. Through the gates, in the distance, was a small hill that overlooked Bellic.

On that hill stood a small figure, which beckoned to him. Karia!

'No! You must not escape!' the dead screamed.

He turned and stepped forwards, wanting to run through the gates. He had never wanted anything more.

But something grabbed him around the legs and he looked down in horror to see the woman from the Ralloran village, still clutching her dead baby.

'Your fault! All your fault!' she hissed.

He tried to break free but her grip was unyielding. He heard the insane laughter of the dead ...

'Let him go!'

The power of the voice, the command it held, was unstoppable. The Ralloran woman released him, the desperate, impossible strength she had commanded now gone. Martil stepped past her and staggered towards the gate, almost unable to believe this was happening.

'No! You must not escape!' the dead howled and rushed at him.

'Leave him! You no longer have power over him!' The voice was, if possible, even stronger.

It stopped the howling monstrosities in their tracks.

'Martil, take our hands,' the voice ordered. 'You are too good a man to stay there.'

He stretched out his hands and felt a warm, strong woman's hand grab one, a small child's hand clutch the other. Together they pulled him clear of the shadow of the gates. He looked up to see Merren and Karia standing there.

'You can let go of the gates now, Karia,' Merren said.

The little girl waved her hand and the gates slammed shut, trapping the dead in that town. The *shrieks and howls of hate and anger were cut off in an instant.*

'Stand with us now, Martil,' Merren told him.

'Stay with us,' Karia agreed.

'While ever I have life,' Martil said.

He turned, to see Bellic was gone. They were standing alone in a field, where flowers were beginning to bloom, forming a shape in the green grass. It was odd, but it looked like a dragon.

'I like this better,' Karia told him. 'If you rest here, the flowers will make you a bed. Try it!'

'Come on!' Merren beckoned to him. She and Karia were lying on a colourful bed of flowers.

Martil smiled. He lay down …

And slept.

Nerrin called for riders in the dawn.

'Deliver this message to the Queen or Captain Martil — no other,' he ordered. 'The Norstaline army is preparing to march. Make sure you are back here by nightfall, or you might miss out on our victory!'

'Are we going to stand here, sir? We'll hurt them but we can't stop them,' Dunner said anxiously.

'Don't worry. Captain Martil will have a plan. He won't leave us to die,' Nerrin said, with a confidence he did not entirely feel.

Martil woke up slowly. It took him a long time to work out where he was. It was an unfamiliar bed, but he had slept in enough of those over the years. It was more an unfamiliar feeling. He felt good. He felt rested. He felt calm. For the first time in he didn't know how long, his mind was clear and ready to think. Better still, the memories of Bellic, the knowledge of what he had done, was not haunting him. It was there, but it was as if it had happened to another man, as if it was separated from him now. He would not forget, but he felt he could at last leave the horror behind him.

He almost shook his head at the wonder of it all. Merren. She had done this to him. She had told him she loved him, she had — well, she had proved it, last night! Thanks to Merren. Well, Merren and Karia. With them, he had done it, he had escaped from his dream! And it could never haunt him again. Karia had opened the gates but it had taken the love of Merren for him to be able to step through them. He almost felt like shouting for joy. He looked over but saw he was alone in the bed.

The joy slipped away a little, then. He may have escaped his past, but how was he going to escape the future? A massive army was marching towards them and everyone expected him to come up with a plan to stop them. Obviously his strategy from Mount Shadar was going to hurt Gello, but not stop him.

For the first time in weeks, his mind began to hunt for a solution. He cast his mind back to Pilleth, the hill outside the passes. It had a stand of trees on its summit, as well as more on its rearward-facing flank, which would help to hide the cavalry. Other than a small stand of trees back from its base, the rest of the countryside was open ... trees! Perhaps he could use them to transport warriors to attack Gello and his commanders. Without Gello and his captains, the army would dissolve. But whoever went would have to be both a brilliant warrior, and insane. There was no way back from there.

He was about to discard that idea, then almost laughed. It was so obvious! He would go! With the

Dragon Sword in his hand and Barrett's magic protection on his skin, Gello's guards would not be able to stop him. He could kill Gello, every Berellian and every man with the gold braid of a captain hanging off him. By the time they cut him down, Gello's army would be leaderless and Merren could simply walk down Pilleth's slope and take control of the country. It was so easy!

He paused then. Obviously Merren would never approve of it. But Barrett would help him. The wizard would be delighted to send him on a suicide mission. Best of all, he would not have to kill hundreds of Gello's soldiers, or lead men who trusted him to their death. He would take the battle to the man who had started it all.

But he could not lie to Merren. So he had to tell her a sort of truth — that he and Barrett would travel there together to kill Gello. After all, it was a version of the plan she had suggested so long ago, back in the caves. Only he and Barrett would know the real truth of it.

But what about Karia? For a moment he went back on his idea. He could not leave Karia alone, after what he had promised her. But then he remembered all the men outside, the Norstalines and the Rallorans, who would die for him. He remembered how Louise had looked when he had talked to her about Wime's death. There were many other people who loved Karia. Merren, for instance. Aroaril knew, the girl needed a mother more than she needed a scarred guardian. He could not let other men die when a way to save them all, and win the battle, required just his death. He would entrust Karia to Merren and then do what he must.

He would talk to Merren, then find both Barrett

and Rocus and get word to Nerrin to pull back to Pilleth. He glanced out of the window and swore. It looked like it was almost midday! He must have slept for a day and a half! He swung his legs off the bed and thought he had better at least pull on some clothes before he went looking for her. He should also wash his mouth out. And he definitely needed to use her privy.

'Good morning — or should I say, good afternoon.' Merren smiled at him as he walked out of her bedroom to find her going through papers. 'I would have stayed but there was too much work. The maids brought me extra bread and cheese, as well as fresh juice, if you are hungry.'

Martil was, but he could see Merren was trying a little too hard to be casual. Yesterday he would not have known what to say or do to reassure her but, this morning, everything seemed clear.

He took her hand and lifted her up into an embrace. The scent, the feel of her hair, was wonderful on his face. She felt warm, beautiful in his arms. The memory of last night rose within him and it was only with an effort of will that he stopped himself from picking her up and carrying her back into the bedroom. He could wish for nothing more than to stay in her arms forever. But that would be too cruel, for both of them.

'What you did for me ... You rescued me,' he said hoarsely. 'Last night, you and Karia opened the gates of my nightmare for me, let me walk free. I know you are a queen and cannot follow your heart, but I will be forever in love with you. Whatever you are prepared to offer me, even if it is nothing more than last night, will be enough. I wish I could spend forever with you but I know that is too much to ask.

We do not have much time. I must find Barrett and Rocus, get word to Nerrin and then I will take you through our battle plan. Gello could be marching even as we speak. We can decide what last night means when we have won the battle.'

Merren was astonished by the change in him. The Martil of yesterday was gone; in his place stood a different man. She had been sitting here, trying to immerse herself in boring papers but desperately thinking what to do about him. She had been worried he would come out of the bedroom demanding her hand in marriage. Last night had started badly but finished wonderfully. But the real question was, where to from here? She had not thought about that; she had not thought past seducing him. When he had walked out, she had been torn between a rush of feelings towards him and a wave of nerves. But he seemed to be saying all the right things.

'You are sure?' she asked.

He kissed her then, long and deeply.

'I know what I am doing and where I am going now. Last night was the greatest gift anyone could give me. I will never be the same again.' He stroked her face and looked deep into her eyes. 'But I must go. I cannot let my feelings for you risk this rebellion.'

Merren watched him go and felt more confused than before. She had thought to gently tell him that they could never be together and certainly could never marry. After all, even if they defeated Gello, she would become queen of a divided country — a country that had been taught to hate Rallorans. But now she wanted to be with him more than before.

Martil shut the door and leaned against it for a

moment, closing his eyes. What he had wanted to do was take her in his arms and never let go. He wanted more than anything to make a life away from this, with Merren and Karia. But he could not leave men to die, even if it meant sacrificing his happiness. Speaking to Merren like that had been difficult. But clinging to her would have been worse. He just hoped she would not remember him too badly, when she learned the truth.

Barrett was taking Tiera carefully through a series of mental exercises to focus and sharpen the mind. It was slow work, especially when compared to Karia, but he found it enjoyable to be with her. His enjoyment was soured, however, by seeing Martil striding towards him, as if he owned the whole world. Barrett hoped the Ralloran oaf would go away.

'Barrett! We need to talk!'

Barrett tensed, his hand stealing down to his staff. Did he want revenge for yesterday? If Martil tried anything, he would be ready.

'What is it? Can't you see I'm busy?' Barrett snapped.

'We need to talk about the battle plan,' Martil told him. 'Alone.'

Barrett gripped his staff tighter. 'Why not here?' he said suspiciously.

Martil looked around, then leaned forwards carefully. 'Because I want you to help me die,' he hissed.

Barrett almost dropped his staff. He looked for some sign of jest, but Martil's face was impassive.

'What?'

'You heard me. But Merren cannot know about this.'

Barrett turned to Tiera. 'Take a break, get yourself something to eat. The mind is like any muscle, and must be exercised regularly — but it also needs rest. Good work this morning!'

Tiera smiled her thanks and, as soon as she was out of earshot, Martil grabbed Barrett's arm and hustled him over to a quiet corner.

'What is all this about?' Barrett demanded.

'You were right, wizard. The battle plan is flawed. We can hold them off for a while but it is not a winning plan, not with the few archers we have. But I have thought of a way to win. You will create that magical protection for me, then help me use an oak tree to appear next to Gello. By the time his guards stop me, Gello, his Berellian friends and his commanders will be dead. Then Merren can just walk down the hill and take control of Gello's army.'

Barrett just stared at him.

'Are you serious?' he finally managed to say.

'This is not a time for jests!' Martil growled. 'Will you help me with this, and one other thing?'

'What's the other thing?'

'Karia. She will need plenty of help after I am … gone.'

Barrett looked at Martil anew. He thought he hated the man, but he could not do so any longer. 'You would do this to save us all?'

Martil held his gaze. 'Yes, I would.'

Barrett held out his hand. 'It is a noble gesture,' he admitted. 'Of course I shall help you, in any way I can. But what of Merren? I can't see her approving this plan.'

'We tell her that we are both going, me to kill Gello, you to bring us back afterwards. But in reality, there could be no chance of return. She does not need to know that.'

Barrett nodded. It was clever, and it had just enough truth to be plausible. There were only advantages in this plan but he found himself regretting that Martil had to die. He would miss arguing with him. Not that he was about to say anything like that, however.

'I will do it. What next?'

'We have to find Rocus, and explain to him that the Queen will be expecting him to make several charges to clear our front line but he is to ignore all orders from the Queen. Leading a charge will only get men killed needlessly. Only you can tell him to advance, which you will do when you see that I have killed Gello.'

Barrett hesitated. 'You are sure of this course of action?'

Martil recognised that Barrett was, delicately, asking him if he wanted to die.

'I'd rather live, but this is the only way we can win.' He shrugged.

Barrett was prevented from making a further plea by the arrival of a sweating rider.

'Captain Nerrin's compliments, sir. The Norstalines are leaving their camp and forming up for an assault on the pass. The captain expects them to reach the pass tonight, and assault either during the night or at first light.'

'It'll be first light,' Martil predicted. 'He won't want to try a night attack with inexperienced troops. And, after what we did to Havrick, he'll march during the day and give them a night to recover before the attack. Get back to Nerrin and tell him to fall back to Pilleth. Leave the cavalry company to give the impression we plan to make a stand but have them slip away during the night. Meanwhile, use every other horse he has to drag as many of the ballistae as he possibly can up Pilleth. If we don't have enough archers, we can at least give Gello's men a nasty surprise.' Martil clapped the man on the shoulder.

The Ralloran saluted.

'Do you have a plan, sir?' he asked hopefully.

'It'll be like Mount Shadar, only better,' Martil told him and the Ralloran hurried off with a smile.

'I can send a bird with those instructions to Nerrin, if you like,' Barrett offered.

'Excellent. I'm off to find Rocus, then we'd better brief the Queen. We have to get down to Pilleth as fast as possible. Gello won't get there until late tomorrow but we need to be ready in case he sends his cavalry through.' Martil paused. 'I can trust you to help me, can't I? This is the only way to save the Queen.'

Barrett extended a hand. 'You have my word,' he said simply.

Martil could not help but smile as he clasped the wizard's hand in the warrior's grip, wrist to wrist. 'Shame it was only a desire to see me die that brought us together,' he offered.

'I might want to help you die, but that doesn't mean I'm a friend of yours,' Barrett replied with a wink. 'Now we'd better find the Queen. If Merren sees us shaking hands, she'll know there's something strange going on.'

16

Gello was not about to make the same mistakes as that idiot Havrick. His men were ordered to make the eight-mile march up the pass at a slow pace, with rests every turn of the hourglass. When they arrived in midafternoon, the men were stood down and ordered to eat and drink. They would be on half-rations after this day, but he wanted to make sure they were well fed for the battle tomorrow — although calling it a battle was hardly fair. He had learned the way Martil had taken the passes and decided to copy it. Archers would pin down the defenders while a three-pronged attack would curl in and crush the defenders. Then he could release his cavalry to chase the Rallorans down.

But the cavalry would not be making the initial assault, so he ordered they provide the sentries for the night's guard. He wanted his men to be rested but would not put it past the Rallorans to try a night attack.

Not that they seemed to be doing much. He could see their banners were still flying, and they had men on the ramparts, but they were hiding.

Cowering, more like it, he decided. Cowering like the dogs they were.

He thought about touring the campfires, talking to the men, inspiring them and encouraging them to fight like lions in the morning. But he could not be bothered. The scum had better fight, or he would have the backs flogged off them.

He ordered his tent constructed, then called for wine, food and Lahra — in that order.

'And you are certain of this?' Merren said suspiciously.

Martil and Barrett had explained their plan to occupy Gello's forces, then spring a trap on him by using a magical gateway. But it sounded too good to her.

'Your majesty, you wanted him dead earlier. This is just a variation of that plan.' Barrett shrugged.

'Merren, I ask you to trust me. I will deliver you victory,' Martil promised.

Merren paused at that. It was eerily close to the words Nott had spoken to her about Martil.

'But why did you not think of this before?' she asked.

'My mind was occupied with Bellic, and my nightmares,' Martil sighed. 'I was too tired to think straight. This morning, I could think again, and the plan came to me.'

Again, Merren was struck by the similarity of his words to the prediction Nott had made. They had no time to come up with a different plan, anyway. She nodded.

'Then we shall do it. Draw the men up for the ride south. Thank Aroaril we have taken so many horses from Gello since the fighting began! But, before we leave, I want to speak to the men.'

*   *   *

Ezok put aside the now empty bowl and looked up at Cezar and Prent. They had spoken with Brother Onzalez, but had received little useful information. The Fearpriest had only been able to say that the next few days were going to be vital. They had to be ready for the unexpected, and seize control of any situation that presented itself.

'Tomorrow, we need to stay close to the King. He needs to win, but the victory needs to come at a high price. That is what Zorva wants, and that is what He shall get,' Ezok instructed.

'Certainly. But now can we get on with the sacrifice?' Prent asked petulantly.

Ezok sighed. The new Fearpriest's eagerness for blood and power was understandable, but getting a little tiresome. Luckily there were plenty of minor nobles that Gello did not care about. And Zorva would appreciate a taste of noble blood.

'Who are these?' Ezok gestured at the bound man and woman.

'Baron Wollin and his wife.' Prent grinned down at the elderly couple, who were writhing in their bonds. The Baron had already supplied the blood they had used to contact Onzalez.

'Then let the ceremony begin,' Ezok said wearily.

Eagerly, Prent began to chant, and Ezok forced himself to pay attention, rather than think about his plans for the morrow.

'Do we stay or do we go, Sarge?' Turen asked as they sat around eating a rather tasteless stew. There wasn't even much of it.

'We stay, for now,' Hutter replied. 'But there's something else going on here. Have you noticed there's fewer nobles than what we started out with?'

Turen looked at him, wide-eyed. 'No, Sarge.'

'Well, I have. Pass the word for a couple of the lads to get themselves put on latrine duty. If I was going to dump a body, I'd put it in an old latrine trench. Nobody's going to go digging there.'

Kay had been feeling much happier about things. He had attended a brief war council and, although he was standing at the back, he had been able to see the King, and hear him order the archers and rangers to take the lead.

'The enemy will assault you with siege engines, and they have a company of archers as well. But you must stand firm and overwhelm him.'

Kay had saluted then. It had felt good.

'Soldiers of the Queen! We march now to fight the enemy and defend our homes, our families and our very way of life! If we don't win, then our country will be ruled by Berellians and Fearpriests! They want to sacrifice your wives and children to their Dark God! It is up to you to stop them. Remember that! And you *will* stop them! The battle will be hard, I will not lie to you. But we will have the advantage of the high ground. We shall trick them, outwit them and defeat them! Remember, we not only have the Dragon Sword, wielded by a man who has never been defeated, but Aroaril is with us!'

Merren's voice, magically amplified, boomed out across the keep's courtyard, where her Norstaline companies, all in blue surcoats — some dyed more crudely than others — stood in crisp lines. They cheered her then.

'I will go with you, I will stand with you and I will share your joy when we win a victory that will resound through the ages and stand next to anything even the fabled King Riel achieved!'

'The Queen!'

Someone started the cry, others took it up until it echoed off the walls. Outside the courtyard, the streets were lined with townspeople, ready to wave their soldiers off. They too took up the cry, screaming it out, until the afternoon air rang with the chant.

'Are they ready now?' Merren asked.

'As ready as they can be,' Martil agreed.

'Soldiers of Norstalos, follow me to victory!' Merren called.

She and Martil walked down the stairs of the gatehouse to where horses were waiting, along with Barrett, Rocus, Nott, Milly, Quiller, Conal and Karia. Gratt had been left in charge of the town while they were gone, with instructions to get out and head north if things went bad.

Martil waited until Merren had climbed into the saddle, then he mounted Tomon and followed her out of the gatehouse tunnel, into streets lined with cheering and crying women and children, tossing flowers in their path.

He felt at peace. He knew what he was going to do and he knew it would work. For once, the fact he had been unable to get the Dragon Sword to work was unimportant. It would kill for him. That was enough. He had not looked at the hilt for days, and even Merren had given up on asking him to inspect it for signs of life. That was a relief in itself.

Gello could feel the tingle of anticipation as he sat on his horse, watching his regiments march smoothly up the road into the pass. The criminals and the militia were ragged compared to his regulars but that was to be expected.

'Any moment now,' he murmured, as the archers marched swiftly toward the Ralloran blockade.

Last night had been uneventful. The Rallorans had not tried anything. He had almost been disappointed with them. Perhaps their reputation was overblown.

Still, he would be able to rewrite his own reputation soon. His destruction of a regiment of elite Rallorans in his first battle would be a fine beginning to his legend.

He noticed the archers were within range of the catapults but the huge siege engines would take so long to reload that they would be lucky to get off three volleys before they were overrun.

But nothing happened. He sat forwards in the saddle when the archers marched into range of the ballistae. He wanted to see if the archers would take the punishment and keep going — only then could he judge how loyal they really were.

Again, nothing happened. This was curious — and the lack of activity on the barricades even more so. He could only see a handful of helmets above the makeshift ramparts.

Now the archers were within bowshot, and they smoothly deployed, nocking and loosing as swiftly as they could. A never-ending stream of white-tipped arrows soared down onto the barricade — but nothing was coming back in return. Suspicion began to nag at him, a suspicion reinforced when he saw a mounted officer gallop back from the front.

'They've gone, sire!' Beq roared, as soon as he got close enough. 'There's nobody on the ramparts!'

Gello chewed his lip. Order a general advance?

'It could be a trap, sire,' Ezok warned.

'Indeed. Send a company of rangers in to look. That is what they are trained for, and if they die, then it is no great loss,' Gello decreed.

Beq turned his horse and galloped back.

Gello and his captains watched in silence as a company of rangers eventually ran forwards, bows drawn, and raced up to the barricade After just a few moments, their officer ran back to Beq, who immediately heeled his horse around and galloped furiously back down for a second time.

'They've gone. Pulled back to Sendric,' Gello snarled. 'Get the cavalry ready for pursuit. Livett!'

'Sire, my men stood guard all night — they will mount up as soon as possible but it will be at least a turn of the hourglass before the horses are saddled and ready,' Livett stuttered. 'Then we have to bring them up the pass, through the other men.'

Gello clenched his fists. He was tempted to have the man dismissed but it had been his orders that saw the cavalry on night watch.

'As fast as you can! Every moment we waste, they march further north!' he bellowed.

Kay stood by the barricade, trying to get his thoughts in order. He had been shocked when Beq had ordered a company up to the barricade. If the Rallorans were trying to spring an ambush, it was a certain death sentence.

'Don't argue, Kay, the King himself commands it!' Beq had spat.

'But, sir, this is ridiculous! Sending a company when one squad could do the same — and would not be nearly so tempting a target,' Kay had argued.

'This is the King's order! Do you dare disobey it?' Beq had exclaimed.

'I question it, if it makes no sense and endangers my men!' Kay protested.

Beq softened his tone. 'Look, Kay, it's just one company. They do not matter. They're easily replaced. But the King's memory is long — just obey the order.'

But Kay was having none of that.

'That's a hundred mens lives! Why sacrifice them for nothing? I'll send a squad forwards instead,' he had insisted. 'I will not order men to their deaths like that!'

'Then you can lead them!' Beq snarled. 'Take a company forwards, now!'

'You can't be serious, sir!'

'I mean it! Lead a company forwards now, or I shall have you arrested and court-martialled for cowardice and desertion!'

So Kay had run forwards. He and his men were alive because the Rallorans were gone. No thanks to the King or Beq. It was galling. Their lives — his life — were worth nothing. It had been like a bucket of cold water dashing into his face, waking him up from a strange dream. Serving the King, restoring his reputation, winning back his regiment — these were all things he had been dreaming of but he had woken to a nightmare. How could he have been so foolish? How could he have listened to someone like Beq? He could see clearly now. The Queen's sudden appearance at the barracks all made sense now. He thanked Aroaril that she had been there. Otherwise he might still be following Gello and Beq, still thinking that they were offering him a way to regain his honour. They were giving him nothing — other

340

than a way to see his men killed to bring them honour and riches.

But knowing that did not help much. How was he to do anything now? He watched as Beq returned, full of anger.

'Form your men up, Kay — we march in pursuit of the cowardly Ralloran dogs. Luckily for you the King did not see your hesitation. But it will not go unpunished. You can expect guard duty tonight. At the latrines.'

Livett had a thick screen of scouts out — a full company riding as much as a mile ahead of the main body of troops. He had heard all the reports of how skilled these Rallorans were at ambushes, and as a result his progress was less the bold pursuit that Gello had demanded and more an attempt to sneak through the pass without loss.

Even outside of the pass, the pursuit was less than dashing. Luckily they did not have far to go.

'We've found them, sir!' one of his sergeants reported breathlessly, and Livett spurred his horse forwards to the foot of a nearby hill from where he had been riding in safety at the back of the column.

'I found a lad from around here — he tells me the locals call the hill Pilleth,' the sergeant reported. 'It's deceptively steep, sir. Because the slope is so long, it doesn't look too bad — but a cavalry charge will lose all momentum by the time they are halfway up, and infantry will be exhausted.'

But Livett was not really listening. Instead he was inspecting the dominating hill, massively wide but probably only two hundred yards in height at the summit, which was crowned with a small stand of trees. Here the Rallorans were drawn up in battle formation, flags flying. Perhaps a score of ballistae stood just in front of their lines.

'A full regiment, I'd say, wouldn't you, Sergeant?' Livett asked hesitantly.

'Yes, sir.'

'Good. Send a squad back to the King, inform him the Rallorans are making a stand. Send a company to ride around the back, to see if there's anyone else around.'

'Yes, sir.'

Martil watched the light cavalry company start their ride around the hill with relief. They had only arrived a turn of the hourglass ago, having ridden hard through the night to get here. Luckily the pursuit had been slower than expected, a fact reported to them by Barrett's feathered scouting system, and allowed them to arrive in a rush before the light cavalry reached Pilleth. Now the troopers would report the Rallorans were seemingly isolated on this hill, for the Norstalines who had ridden so hard to get here were sleeping, hidden in the wooded cutting to his left, as he looked down the hill. To those standing below, the wooded valley started on Pilleth's right flank, and wrapped around to the rear, covering the far slope of the hill thickly in trees. That in itself would discourage cavalry from coming too close, but half of Martil's Ralloran archers were in the treeline, along with every Norstaline archer they had, so any of Gello's men who tried to investigate too closely would receive an unpleasant surprise.

'They'll take the bait,' Martil announced. 'We make too tempting a target to ignore. Just like the Berellians.'

Merren stifled a yawn. 'When can we expect an attack?'

'It'll take him most of the day to bring his men forward, to funnel them through the pass. If he's a fool, he'll attack late today. Otherwise, he'll wait until the morning, when they've had a chance to rest and eat. Which means we have a chance to do just that.' He smiled.

'It's good to see you smile again,' she told him. He had seemed imbued with a renewed energy since their night together, although with Barrett, Sendric and a dozen others just a few paces away, she was not going to refer to it. She had known a relationship with him would only cause problems. But, afterwards, such cold, calculating statements were hard to justify. On the ride south, she had begun to think about life with him, and what it might mean. These were complicated thoughts; luckily there was so much else going on she could put them aside and tell herself there was time for that later. She could almost believe it, too.

'Are you sure your plan will work?'

'As sure as I can be,' he admitted. 'The only concern is if Gello does not set up his command post by those trees. But he will. The only shade around — I cannot see him giving that to his men or even his officers.'

'Then all we have to do is wait?'

'Aye. Wait and rest. If you will excuse me, I want to go and see Karia.'

'Of course.' Merren watched him go, and tried not to think about him. Not that everyone was going to give her the time to do so. What she really wanted to do was go to sleep but she could not — there were too many of her supporters gathered around wanting to speak with her and her brain was too full of worries and fear. Tomorrow, hundreds of men who trusted her could be dead. She could be dead. And, no matter what, her country would never be the same again. She had almost too many thoughts to fit into her mind. And it seemed everyone else just wanted to give her more.

'My queen, if you have a moment …?' Nott asked, before anyone else could speak to her.

'Yes, Archbishop?' She tried to concentrate.

'Why don't you sit down here, underneath your flag,' he suggested.

Gratefully she sat down, beneath where her silver dragon standard had been sunk into the soft grass. Local farmers must graze sheep up here, she thought, to keep it so short.

'I think you need to rest, your majesty,' Nott said softly.

'Rest? I can't rest! There's too much to do, too much to organise — these men are here because of me, I cannot let them down! What if I missed something because I was resting?'

'I know, your majesty,' Nott agreed. 'Sleep now.'

He touched her arm and, almost instantly, she fell into a dreamless sleep. Carefully he covered her with a cloak, then stood with a groan.

'She needs to sleep. You can't order a queen to rest but, as an archbishop and a grandfather, I can bend the rules,' he announced loudly. 'Come back later. Sergeant Kesbury — I order you to stand guard over the Queen. No one is to wake her, whatever the reason. Understood?'

Kesbury, who had been standing just behind the Ralloran battle line, a few paces away, saluted and brought his squad over.

'Yes, sir!' He signalled and the sleeping Queen was surrounded by a ring of armed Rallorans.

Nott addressed the others, who had all been waiting to talk to Merren. 'I think we should all rest. The morrow is likely to bring rather more excitement than we wanted, and we shall need all our strength for that.'

He kept the smile on his face until all had turned away. They all thought this one battle would finish things — but he knew it would just be the start. He had done all he could to prepare these people. Now it was up to them.

'Captain!'

Martil reflected he would have to change his rank soon. That title was infuriating him now.

'What is it, Conal?' He kept walking.

The ex-bandit stepped close, and put his hand on Martil's arm to stop him.

'I just wanted to talk to you about your plan,' he said quietly.

'Yes?' Martil looked meaningfully at the hand.

Conal swapped it for his stump. 'Threaten to cut off my hand if I don't remove it now. You can't — because I haven't laid a hand on you.' He smiled.

Martil shook his head. 'I don't have time for games, Conal. What is it?'

'Your plan. You and Barrett taking on Gello and his captains. The Queen might have agreed to it but I've been a skilled liar for years and I know when you're trying to pull the wool over her eyes. And Barrett supporting you! That wizard would claim the sky was orange if you said it was blue. You're not coming back from this, are you?'

Martil forced a laugh. 'Good jest, my friend. But I intend to come back.'

Conal did not smile. 'You need to. You might be thinking no further than winning this battle but some of us have to consider what comes after, if we do win. This country is in a mess. We need you. This one battle will not wrap everything up neatly — this isn't a saga. And what about Karia? You have to come back for her.'

Something must have shown in Martil's eyes then, because Conal reached out and grabbed him with his one good hand.

'Don't do it, man! There has to be another way!'

Martil stared into the ex-bandit's eyes. 'There isn't.'

After a long moment, Conal looked away.

Martil patted him on the shoulder. 'Merren doesn't need me. She's got men like you. That day I threw a tankard of piss over you was a lucky one for Norstalos.'

'Well, not everyone can boast about that,' Conal replied with a smile, which quickly faded. 'Listen, if you don't come back, I'll do what I can for Karia.'

Martil nodded. 'There is something else as well. I want you to stay with Rocus. The Queen might want him to charge out too early — if he does, many of those Norstalines are going to die. They'll bite deeply into Gello's men but then they'll be stuck there and chewed to pieces. He won't be able to see what's going on, so make sure he ignores any orders from the Queen. Barrett can tell you when it's time to attack. Understand? Don't ride out until Barrett orders you, or, so help me, I'll come back and kill you in your dreams!'

'You can count on me,' Conal whispered.

Martil smiled. 'I know I can.'

*　*　*

All day Gello's army straggled in, forming up below Pilleth. As Martil had predicted, Gello ensured his tent was placed beneath the trees, while his men had to find whatever space they could. There was a small stream that ran beneath Pilleth, and the men could at least drink their fill, although the rations were short.

'Let them rest. Tomorrow we shall assault,' Gello ordered lazily. 'Make the preparations.'

The regimental doctors sharpened their instruments, and prepared themselves with many a fortifying drink of the alcohol that was supposed to cleanse wounds. No priests had been found who could accompany the army and were actually able to heal. It was a concern to the captains, although not to Gello.

'Sire, we will need all our men for our invasion of the south. If we could save our injured, it could prove vital,' Feld insisted.

'Oh, very well. See what you can do.' Gello yawned. 'Get the camp set up. I don't want the latrines so close this time, in case the wind changes.'

'But, sire, they are already dug!'

'Captain, do I have to think of everything myself? Get some of the criminals to dig a new one! And don't bother me with stupid questions again!'

Up on Pilleth, Nerrin made sure the men got as much rest and food as possible. The size of Gello's army made for an imposing sight, and he was glad the Norstalines were hidden below, unable to see it. Even to veterans such as himself, it was daunting to see their sheer numbers. Twelve thousand men, near enough, facing about sixteen hundred. They might have the advantage of the heights, but that seemed scant comfort at the moment. But men who were resting were not men who were worrying about the enemy, so he made sure no more than one company was on duty at any time. He also kept a runner close, to send for Captain Martil if anything happened. The highest rank he had held was sergeant and, frankly, he preferred it that way. Being a captain was just too much responsibility. He wondered what Martil was doing.

'So the princess married the miller's son, who was really a prince, and they lived happily ever after,' Martil read, and closed the saga with a sigh of relief.

'That was good. And I can even read parts of it myself now, can't I?' Karia said happily.

'Your reading is getting very good indeed,' he agreed. 'I'm very proud of you.'

'How about a quick game of catch, then maybe we can play with dolls?' Karia suggested. Now she knew she was going to be staying with Martil, it was a relief, although she had seen little of him over the last few days. In her view, that meant it was important to make up for lost time.

'We need to have a little talk first,' Martil said carefully.

Karia pretended not to have heard him. 'Little talks' had never brought anything good in the past and she doubted this was going to be any better. If she carried on as if she did not hear him, and started getting out her dolls, perhaps it would never happen.

But he picked her up and sat her on his lap as he leaned back against a tree. He had made sure there was nobody close. He had faced death before but even that did not scare him as much as the prospect of trying to say goodbye to her.

'Karia, I want you to stay with me, I want us to have a little farm, where you can ride, help me look after the animals and show me how to play dolls like Merren does.'

Karia nodded. That all sounded good, but surely he did not have a sad look on his face to tell her something happy.

'But I've got to fight in a battle tomorrow. Something might happen to me.'

'No! I can protect you, like I did before! Just keep me close, and I'll make sure nothing happens to you!' she cried.

'I have to do something dangerous — go and fight some bad people — and I can't take you with me.'

'Why? Why do you have to do that?' She did not really understand what he was saying to her, but the way he was saying it scared her.

'Because of the Dragon Sword. I'm the only one who can use it.'

'So use it to make everyone help us, instead of fight us!' She thought if she could argue hard enough, he might stop being silly and go back to playing with her.

Martil bit his lip. 'I wish I could. But I cannot get it to work. It doesn't like me, or the way I am using it.'

'Well, it's silly! I'll tell it to like you!'

'It won't work like that.' He tried to soothe her, because he could sense tears were not far away. This was hard enough as it was.

'Then tell it you'll change! Look, you have two swords, why not just use the Dragon Sword to protect yourself, and use the other one to attack people? That way it will like you!'

Martil stared at her. He had been about to tell her that was impossible, when it occurred to him that it might just work. If the Dragon Sword did not like killing, then he could stop using it to cut people in half, and use it to cut swords in half instead. Unfortunately, her suggestion had come too late to have much effect, especially as his plan was to use the Dragon Sword to kill as many as possible before he himself was cut down.

'It's too late for that, I'm afraid,' he sighed. 'But that was a brilliant idea. I wish I could say to you that I will come back —'

'Then tell me! Promise it, swear it to Aroaril!' She beat her fists against his tunic-covered chest.

'I can't swear to Aroaril, because that would be wrong. I can't lie to you,' he said, as gently as he could, but she burst into tears.

'It's not fair! It's not fair! I just found my daddy and now he's going to leave me!'

He grabbed her and hugged her close, feeling her small body shake with the force of her sobs. It took him a long time to be able to speak again, and he could feel the tears running down his face.

'Karia, you saved me from my nightmares. You saved my life. I want nothing more than to spend the rest of my life looking after you. But there is something I can do that will win this battle, and will save the lives of all our friends. I cannot let people like Nerrin, Rocus and Conal die, just because I want to be with you, because I love you. I wish —' he tried to go on but his voice failed him. He cleared his throat, blinked his eyes until he could almost see again and tried to speak. He was not sure if she could even hear him, because she was crying into his shoulder. But he had to tell her this. Perhaps, in years to come, she might remember it and gain some comfort. 'I will be waiting for you on the other side. We will be together again some day.'

'I don't want you to die!' she cried. She wished she could find the words to make him stay. She wished she could think of some magical way she could make him stay. But all she could think of was how happy she had been.

'I want you to live,' he said thickly. 'I want you to grow up strong, and happy and free. And if my death can give you that, I will consider it a fair trade.'

He could say no more. The thought of leaving her was giving him second thoughts about his plan to sacrifice himself. But there was no other way. He had to go through with it. He owed Merren, and everyone else, at least that much. Especially Merren. He held Karia close until, worn out by crying, she fell asleep in his arms. He could have put her down and tried to get some sleep himself, but he did not want to let her go while he still had breath in his body.

17

'Sire, I can heal the men,' Prent announced.

Gello, who had been entertaining Lahra, looked up in surprise at being interrupted.

'What are you doing here?' he snarled.

'Your captains were looking for priests who could heal the wounded. I can help,' Prent repeated.

'And you call on me to tell me that?' Gello growled.

'It is important, sire. Because the way I can do it is by offering blood for blood. It will heal the men but I do need to explain it to you first.' His voice was eager but Gello could see his eyes kept straying to where the half-naked Lahra stood nearby.

Gello sighed. 'Leave us,' he told Lahra.

She wrapped what looked to Prent like the Royal Cloak around her shoulders, before ducking into the back of the tent.

Gello watched her go, then swung to face Prent. 'What are you blathering about, priest? I thought you told me Aroaril had refused to answer your prayers for years?'

Prent smiled viciously. 'He has. But I gain strength from another source now. A more powerful one. I do Zorva's bidding and He rewards me with power.'

Gello stared at him. 'Are you serious, priest?'

'It was the only way I could survive, the only way I could defeat the old Archbishop and his lackey. I can now provide you with power, as long as you allow me to offer blood to my God.'

'Whose?'

'Noble blood is best. And there are many you do not trust ... We have been discovering many hate you and have been plotting against you.' Prent looked over at Ezok, who had followed him into the King's tent. The ambassador nodded. They had learned some interesting things about Gello from some of the older nobles, and decided to embellish them, to further manipulate Gello. 'They remember the Dragon Sword refusing you. They talk about it still — get together and laugh at how you cried when the Dragon Sword refused you, how you ran from the throne room.'

'What!' Gello stormed from his seat and grabbed hold of Prent's collar. 'How dare you, priest!'

Ezok saw Prent gathering himself to do something to Gello, so he jumped in between them, laying a cautioning hand on both their shoulders.

'He is just telling you the truth, sire; the truth everyone else has tried to keep from you. We seek to help you, no more than that. With Zorva's help, you can wipe clean your history, and revenge yourself on those who have laughed at you behind your back all these years,' Ezok said into Gello's ear.

Gello turned furious eyes on Ezok.

'And how do you know all this?'

'As you commanded, we have been questioning those nobles whose loyalty is suspect, in order to find the traitor.' Ezok bowed his head.

'We can help you, sire! Zorva can give you everything you ever wanted!' Prent said eagerly. 'I have felt the power that flows when you spill blood! Let us rid you of the nobles who hate and fear you and, in return, we can both save your men's lives and begin to heal your past!'

Gello slowly let go of Prent, but did not step away.

'So you cut a few lying throats, and Zorva gives you the power to heal my men?' he said harshly.

'Not quite. The wounded men must convert to Zorva first. But to a man who is dying, that is surely not too much to ask.'

Gello hesitated. He wanted the nobles dead. The thought of people talking behind his back, laughing as they remembered his humiliation, was too much for him. But having his men worshipping Zorva …

'These men will be restored to full strength, and become fanatically loyal to you.'

'They already are!'

'They will become more so,' Prent insisted. 'Nothing will appear to change, it is just that you will gain all the benefits of having a god on our side. Believe me, sire, this is the path for you. My life has not been the same since I converted!'

Gello still hesitated, for his life was feeling pretty good now. He was King of Norstalos, he was about to destroy his cousin once and for all and then begin on his conquest of the rest of the continent. Why did he need a god's help when he could do it all himself? Silencing the nobles was one thing, introducing the worship of Zorva in pious, conservative Norstalos was another …

'Are you finished? Only I'm gettin' cold out 'ere!' Lahra called from the sleeping area of the tent.

Gello swore. He did not have time for this! He wanted to finish with Lahra, then meet with his captains and finalise a strategy for tomorrow. Tomorrow! He had to be sure he would win.

'Do what you want, priest. But if it causes problems, I'll have you killed,' he growled. 'Now leave me!'

'As you wish, sire. You will not regret this.' Prent smiled.

'We will need the cavalry for the invasion of the south,' Gello said. 'A charge up the hill will be useless, so we shall hold them in reserve for pursuing the beaten rabble and riding them into bloody shreds. So what is our plan of attack?'

Feld gestured towards the rough map drawn by a pair of scribes, using a long stick to illustrate his words.

'Similar to the planned assault on the pass: We send the archers up first, to soften the Ralloran line, then a massive assault led by our conscript regiments, so they take the brunt of the casualties,' he explained. 'Our line will be both wider and deeper than their shield wall, so it should be a simple matter to wrap around and crush them.'

Gello nodded with satisfaction. That was exactly what he wanted to hear — but he looked around when there was a hiss of disapproval.

'What?' he demanded.

Ezok smiled, almost apologetically.

'I am sorry, sire, but I do have my concerns about this plan.'

'Well, tell me!'

'There was a similar battle in the Ralloran Wars, one at which Captain Martil commanded a regiment. Mount Shadar, it was called, and he used a hill such as this one to great effect to hold up our men. Firstly, your archers will be outranged, by forty or even fifty paces. You will find they will do little damage to the Ralloran lines. Then, when you get close to their shield wall, a second force will strike from the flank, to disrupt your lines and cramp your advance, so you cannot use numbers to overlap them. As we found to our cost, attacks can be broken up and pushed back down the hill with surprising ease.'

'Mount Shadar! Of course! That is why they have chosen this place, rather than face us in the pass!' Gello exclaimed. His studies had included all the major battles of the Ralloran Wars, and the memory of the battle leaped out, now it had been pointed out to him. He felt a surge of relief — then a flare of anger that nobody else had realised what the Rallorans planned. 'Ambassador, again you have proved your worth to me! And does anyone want to suggest why the combined intelligence of my best men was not able to detect the trap the Rallorans had laid for us?'

There was a deathly silence.

Ezok just enjoyed it. He had been debating whether or not to reveal what he knew about Mount Shadar. He had recognised the similarities at once. If he said nothing, Gello's men would be hurt by one surprise attack, before their superior numbers ensured victory. If he told all, Gello would win a little easier, albeit still with heavy losses. But Ezok would supplant Gello's captains completely.

Onzalez would be happier with the first result but Ezok was starting to think about his future, as well. The more powerful he was, the harder it would be for the Fearpriest to decide his usefulness was over.

'There is no excuse, sire. We should have realised what the Rallorans intended. Our scouts reported no other forces at the back of the hill, although they were unable to get close to a wooded valley that comes out halfway up the hill,' Feld finally said, breaking Ezok's thoughts.

Gello smiled wolfishly. 'You are correct, Feld. There is no excuse. Tomorrow, you will all command your regiments, rather than stay with me. How your men perform tomorrow will then tell me whether you can still be trusted to give me the best advice.'

Several of the captains looked horrified at the prospect, but none was prepared to say anything.

'And the battle plan, sire?' Feld's face was impassive but inside he was seething.

'The archers will advance, as before. Beq, Grissum, I want you to lead those men in personally. I don't want them staying safe and wasting arrows on the grass. Take them close, take your losses and keep going, understand?'

'Yes, sire,' they chorused.

Beq glanced at Grissum, who nodded almost imperceptibly. They both knew walking those forty or fifty paces would probably see them dead. But refusing would see them killed now.

'We will need a force out on our right flank to face a cavalry charge, take some losses and protect our main attack. So we shall put the conscripts out there. Who cares if they are torn apart? Then our regulars will lead the main attack. Ezok, what think you of that plan?'

Ezok bowed his head. Gello's archers would be slaughtered and his best men would be decimated by fighting veteran Rallorans before achieving victory. Perfect.

'I could not have thought of a better plan myself, sire. Only divine intervention can save your cousin.'

Gello sank back in his chair. There it was again! At least he had Prent working for him. And, judging by the lack of complaints he was being presented with, Zorva was happy with noble blood. But he did not want to rely on that for victory — he wanted the triumph to be his alone! Still, better to be safe than sorry …

'Captains, to your regiments. Ambassador, would you like to dine with me tonight? And of course I will require your company by my side for the battle tomorrow.'

'It will be a pleasure, sire.' Ezok watched the captains file out of the tent and bowed again, so Gello would not see the fierce triumph on his face.

'Halt! What are you men doing over there?' Kay had been at turns infuriated and humiliated by guard duty at the latrines but he was also determined to do the best job possible. It was not easy. The latrines were some distance from the camp, and sparsely lit. He had already been distracted once this night, by no less than the Archbishop, who had wanted to talk to Kay and his men about how Aroaril had betrayed them and let them down. It had been quite the strangest sermon he had ever heard from a priest but, out of respect, he had listened politely as the man rambled on about Aroaril's mistakes. Then, seemingly without reaching a conclusion, the Archbishop had turned and walked away. It had been most mysterious and, worryingly, had prevented him from completing his patrol of the area.

So when he saw a small group of men creeping furtively towards the latrines, he ran over with his squad of men.

'Identify yourselves or we'll cut you down!' he demanded.

'Calm down, soldier. I'm Sergeant Hutter, First King's Conscripts. Who're you?'

'First Lieutenant Kay of the Que— I mean, King's Rangers. And I'm asking the questions here. What are you doing?'

'Here, I'll show you.' Hutter gestured to one of his men, a tall, gangly youth, who held up a torch, waving it over the trench.

'Sarge, look at this. Here's another one.'

Kay peered reluctantly into the foul-smelling trench, and recoiled in surprise and horror.

'There's two naked bodies in there! What do you know about this?'

Hutter smiled grimly. 'I'm a militiaman. It's my job — or at least it was — to investigate this sort of thing. We've noticed that there aren't as many nobles about as there were. We wanted to know why — and I think we have just found our answer.'

Kay stared at him.

'What do you mean? Are you saying someone is killing our nobles?'

Hutter gestured at the bodies. 'Well, I don't think they just choked to death on the smell out here. Turen, turn one over.'

The youth with the torch handed it to another, then leaned in and grabbed an arm. Grunting with the effort, he managed to flip the body over, releasing a fresh stench into the air.

'That looks like Baron Wells! But his heart's been cut out!' Kay gasped. His mind seemed unable to grasp what was going on. He knew the southern town of Wells — his uncle lived there. Why was its ruler lying dead in a latrine trench, with his heart cut out?

'What is happening here?'

It was a question Kay would have liked to ask, if he could have thought of it, but instead a lean man with fierce eyes and long hair tied back in a ponytail had said it. He and his companions, a scruffy-looking bunch, all carrying shovels, were wandering over.

'And who are you?' Kay felt his grasp of the situation had slipped badly. 'What are you doing here?'

'Private Kettering, Second King's Conscripts. We're here to fill in the latrine trench and dig another.'

'Yeah, we always get the shit jobs,' one of Kettering's companions, a big, bearded man, rumbled.

'What's happening here?' Kettering ignored his companion, as well as Kay, and addressed Hutter, instead.

'We'd noticed the nobles seemed to be disappearing. This seemed to be the obvious hiding place, so we decided to come and have a look,' Hutter explained. 'We found these two, then the soldiers turned up.'

'Why would you bother looking? Who cares if the nobles live or die?' Kettering spat.

'I don't care for the nobility myself, but I do care when people try to lie to me. There are dark forces at work here. This is the sort of thing you associate with worshipping Zorva. Something smells — and not just this trench.' Hutter straightened up.

Kay had the feeling he was just irrelevant here; nobody seemed to be worried by the fact he had a squad of armed men with him. He wanted to take control of the situation — but he was also interested to hear what was going on.

'We're all being lied to. The Berellians with the

King are the ones that set me up for a murder I did not commit. They are the real power in this army,' Kettering said coldly.

'Is that a fact?' Hutter exclaimed.

'He's right!' Kay blurted, then gulped as everyone turned towards him. 'My own captain took orders from the Berellian Champion, I saw it. And, just before I noticed you, the Archbishop kept me talking and away from this area!'

Hutter took a torch and stepped closer to Kay.

'That adds up to a right unpleasant conclusion: that we're about to fight for Zorva.'

'But that's monstrous! The people won't stand for that! We should go to the remaining nobles, go to the senior officers — warn them, tell them what is going on!' Kay exclaimed.

Hutter turned a world-weary eye on him.

'And you think that'll do any good? We'll just end up in a shit pit with our hearts cut out. The King's obviously the one behind all this. Do you think he'll listen to us over his archbishop and his friends?'

'But we can't just sit here and do nothing!' Kay argued.

'Never said we would,' Hutter sniffed, then turned away from the soldier. 'Kettering, wasn't it? How many of your fellows think the way you do?'

'We all do. Killer Kettering is the real power in our regiment,' a lean youth declared.

'But how about you, Hutter? Are the militia still interested only in getting free beer and locking up innocent men?' Kettering asked.

'The officers are. But all the sergeants are with me.' Hutter assessed Kettering with a careful eye. 'We've been told we will be posted out on the right flank, to watch the main advance. How about you?'

'The same.' Kettering nodded.

'I'm thinking we could work together.'

'Are you mad, you militia shit-slinger? We'd walk a mile just to spit in your face!' a bearded criminal rumbled, stepping forwards. Instantly the atmosphere tensed.

Kettering held up his hand and his companions subsided.

'Two regiments would be better than one. We should see to it that we can speak to each other, perhaps even work together,' Kettering said calmly.

'Wait! But what about these bodies!' Kay cried.

'Go away, soldier boy. Don't meddle in what you don't understand. We're going to fill in this trench, like we were ordered, then we're all going to go back to our camps,' Kettering said.

'What about him? Won't he just go running to the King? Maybe we should make sure he and his men are deep in this trench before we go,' the bearded criminal warned.

'I have never betrayed anyone in my life!' Kay growled. 'What can I do to help you?'

'You can help us dig the trench, if you want,' the lean criminal offered.

'I meant about the Berellians infesting our country!'

'What makes you think we need your help? You don't control your regiment, or you wouldn't be patrolling a latrine the night before the biggest battle Norstalos has seen in centuries. Now get going, before I find myself agreeing with the criminals over there that we need to silence you,' Hutter said with contempt.

Kay stood for a moment, torn by indecision, but when the criminals and militiamen picked up shovels and got to work, turning their backs on him, he abruptly walked away, followed by his men.

He only stopped when he was safely in the darkness again. He would never betray anyone, but what of his men?

'Don't worry, sir. We all think like you — and most of the regiment does as well,' his sergeant said, echoing his unspoken worries.

Kay glanced at the man. Sergeant Ryder had been part of the Royal Guard as well.

'What should we do then, Ryder?' he asked.

'Well, we can't desert. We'd be ridden down and killed. We can't not fight, because we'd be killed. We're in a tight corner here, sir. That's why they pay you extra to be an officer.'

Kay tried to smile. The truth was, he had no idea what to do. He had been so blinded by his disgrace, and his desire to redeem his career, that he had committed a terrible mistake by agreeing to support the King.

'I'll have to think about it. Perhaps there will be a way we can avoid fighting against the Queen,' he said, more in hope than anything.

'I need a knife,' Tiera said.

'Why? We don't use our energy fighting, we use it in magic.' Barrett smiled.

He was trying to show her how to heal, using magic. It was relatively simple, just a matter of imagining a person as they should be, not cut open by a sword or axe or spear. And if she could help that way, she could save a few lives.

'No, I mean if the worst happens tomorrow, and we lose, I don't want to be taken alive by Gello's men. Apart from what they would do, I dread being dragged in front of Prent again …' her voice trailed off, and Barrett had to restrain an impulse to offer her a hug.

'It won't come to that,' he promised.

'You don't know that!'

Barrett hesitated, then settled for holding her hand. 'If the worst happens, I'll get you to safety. I promise, on my life.'

She smiled wanly. 'Thank you. You must think me foolish …'

'Don't talk about it. You are safe now. And soon you will be a qualified wizard, allowed to set up your own business wherever you want!'

In truth, her skills were developing slowly. He doubted anyone would be prepared to pay much for her work. But she was responding well to his praise, even if she could not complete all the tasks he set.

'I know I will never see him again but, still, I can't get the memories out of my head. I wake sometimes, at nights. That must sound ridiculous to you. You are probably wondering why you bother to teach me magic. I've seen Karia at work, and she can do things I can only dream of — and she's just a little girl! Sometimes I worry that you're only doing this because you think I might sleep with you—'

'That's not true!' he said hotly. 'I have a duty to magic, to help teach it to others. You are a brave woman who went through a terrible ordeal, yet still had the courage to help us. And I am not looking for a partner, or a companion. In truth, I bear my own hurts.'

'You? I thought women would be falling over each other to throw themselves at you! A rich, powerful, young wizard! Many of the women I grew up with could only dream of snaring a husband like that!'

Barrett smiled ruefully. Partly because he wanted her to trust him, partly because he wanted to speak about it, he decided to share a secret with her. 'In truth, I always dreamed of the Queen. I cherished a secret love for her, for many years. But when I tried to confess it, she told me she could never love me back.' He shrugged.

'Truly?'

'Truly.'

She smiled. 'More fool her, then. Why don't you show me that healing trick again?'

Karia woke up first, and her moving made Martil wake up — then groan as blood flowed back into the arm she had been resting on. He moved, and she grasped him around the neck.

'Don't go! Don't leave me!' she begged.

Martil blinked the sleep out of his eyes. It was before dawn.

'I'm not going away yet. You can stay with me. How about we get something to eat, together?' he suggested.

She decided not to mention anything about last night. She thought that if she said nothing, but made sure she did not let him out of her sight, then she could protect him. Because, without him, who was going to look after her? She could not let him go.

'I need a piggyback!' she told him.

So he made his way slowly back up the hill of Pilleth, Karia comfortable on his back, her head on his shoulder. He wanted to get some food, but he also wanted to see a few people.

Down below, fires were burning, hundreds of them, as Gello's army was slowly coming awake. Up on the hill, fires were being teased back to life and cauldrons of tea and porridge were being hung over the top. Martil walked past several, aiming for where he recognised Nerrin, Dunner and others.

'Captain! We'll have some food ready soon, you and your daughter should help yourselves,' Nerrin greeted him.

Martil knew he would not get rid of Karia, so simply sank to one knee, and eased her off his back, although keeping hold of her hand. He stayed on one knee.

'I am sorry. Sorry to all of you,' he called loudly.

'What do you mean, Captain?' Nerrin asked, baffled.

Other Rallorans were leaving similar fires and drifting over, both confused and intrigued by the tableau.

'You men are all here because I gave the order to destroy Bellic. If it wasn't for me, you would all be at home, in Rallora, with wives and children and hope in your lives,' Martil called out. 'I am sorry for what I did, sorry for what it has meant for you. But I promise you this. You will not pay for my mistakes with your lives. At the end of the day, I want you all to go home, find some peace, find some happiness.'

Silence greeted his words. Many of the men seemed embarrassed by what he was saying, others could not understand it.

'We shall stand with you to the end, Captain,' Nerrin said finally. 'We swore an oath to serve you, and we would never break that.'

'Then I free you from your oath. Any of you who wish to go, should go now, with my blessing. Don't die for nothing,' Martil implored.

By now, hundreds of Rallorans had wandered

over, and the latecomers were being filled in by their fellows. But none made a move to go.

'We shall not run. We shall not even take a step back. We are Rallorans, and we shall fight to our last breath for freedom!' Dunner suddenly bellowed.

Martil bowed his head. That was the rallying cry he had used before Mount Shadar. He opened his mouth to tell them this was not Shadar, there was no rescue coming — when Nerrin shouted it out again. This time it was taken up by every man, swelling in volume as they all joined in, then echoing across the entire hillside as a thousand men repeated it at the top of their voices.

Martil closed his mouth. He could not trust himself to speak.

'Did you think we would forget, Captain?' Nerrin stepped closer and held out his hand.

Martil had to take it, and allow himself to be pulled to his feet. He kept his head bowed, until he had control of his eyes again. Why could he not stop weeping? He hated himself for that weakness, even as he could not stop it.

'Nerrin, form your archers up a good fifty paces in front of our lines. As soon as Gello's archers get into range of you, step back. Keep your men alive for as long as possible.'

'Aye, sir.'

'Everything else ready?'

'Yes, sir. We have three spears for each ballistae, and we have dug range markers for our archers.'

'Good work.' Martil shook hands with him and moved off.

Nerrin was by now thoroughly mystified by his captain's behaviour. Perhaps it was some way of inspiring the men? He supposed that must be it — he could see men clapping each other on the back and repeating the battle cry from Mount Shadar to each other. What had been quiet, concerned faces were now grinning at each other with pride. Yes, that must be it, he decided.

Martil accepted a mug of tea from one fire, a bowl of porridge from another, while Karia made sure she accepted every single offer of some hoarded sugar for her porridge, until Martil swore it was more sugar than oats. Yet he could not tell her off. Not that morning.

'What was that all about?' Conal asked, wandering over.

'I tried to say I was sorry, that they didn't need to fight. And they should leave now, go home and find some happiness.'

Conal looked over at where the Rallorans were laughing and joking, sharpening swords and eating.

'Good to see that speech was up to your usual excellent standard,' he said dryly. 'Especially as the Rallorans are the only chance we have of winning.' He glanced over his shoulder. 'Are you still resolved to throw your life away?'

'I will not let men die needlessly for me. Not when my life can save them. Once the archers are engaged, and Gello's attention is on them, I shall go and kill him. He and his Berellians. And that will be the end.'

They paused for a long moment then, both looking down the hill to where the trees were still in darkness — Gello was sleeping in.

Then Martil turned away. 'Are you and Rocus ready? Because the Queen may well order you to charge. But you must not. You must do whatever you can to stop her, to protect those men down there. Remember, you need to give me enough time to do my job, and enough time for Barrett to tell you it's done. Can I trust you to do this? Because men's lives depend on it.'

'You can depend on me,' Conal assured him, a little alarmed by the intensity in Martil's eyes.

Martil smiled then. 'I know I can. Any man who could stay beside me through that gate tunnel will be able to do something like this.'

Conal chuckled then, relaxing. 'Indeed! Well, you know what I always say — any time you need a hand ...'

Martil clapped him on the shoulder and walked on to where Merren stood with Romon, Nott, Milly, Quiller and Sendric. The Count was dressed in full armour, and running a sharpening stone up and down his blade.

'Do be careful, Count. This battle will not be the end. We shall need you, afterwards,' Merren was saying.

'I could not miss this opportunity. Gello tortured and killed my daughter. This is my chance for revenge.' Sendric finished rasping the stone along the blade and slammed his sword back into its scabbard. 'I would kill every man down there, if I had the chance.'

Merren bit her tongue. She did not need another middle-aged, unfit warrior with a shoulder that had not healed properly after the Battle of Sendric. What she needed was an experienced administrator to whom she could delegate a whole host of problems. But logic was not working on him. She would have to put him where he could do little damage, and where he might just survive the battle.

'Very well, Sendric. You may ride with Rocus. But you will not command. You will ride as a common soldier, under the orders of Rocus and Conal. Is that agreed?'

Sendric dropped to one knee.

'My Queen, my inaction helped bring us to this point. If I had only supported you in the Royal Council against Gello … I owe you a debt I cannot repay. I owe my country a debt I cannot even begin to comprehend. Today, I hope to start balancing the scales. If we survive, I will do whatever you wish.'

Merren smiled grimly. 'Be sure I will hold you to that, Count. I will walk down and address the Norstaline companies soon. Captain Martil seems to have done most of my job for me with the Rallorans.'

'What was that battle cry, Captain?' Romon asked, quill in hand.

'It was from a speech I gave at Mount Shadar.' Martil shrugged.

The bard was scribbling furiously. 'Well, I can tell you this is going to make a great saga!'

'As long as we win!' Quiller added.

Romon sniffed. 'Either way, it is going to be entertaining. That is the important thing.' He was excited. This promised to be the most pivotal battle in the history of Norstalos, and he would be the only bard there! He had never seen a battle and was looking forward to seeing the honour, the courage and the nobility of war that he had sung about so much. He had offered his services to Nott, to help bring the wounded back to the priests — the chance to talk with the gallant wounded as he helped them back was priceless.

Martil ignored him. He was not sure if the bard was really on their side or not. He certainly had done little to prove his worth as yet.

'Well, either way, I need you to spread the tale of what really happened here. The people must know the truth,' Merren told Romon, before turning to Martil.

'Is everything ready? Thanks to Archbishop Nott, I slept until the dawn, and never had the chance to go through the final preparations with everyone.'

'We are ready,' Martil said shortly.

'I have a dozen priests, as well as every wizard, healer, bonesetter and apothecary in the three towns, also a number of men, like Romon, who will help drag the wounded back to us,' Nott answered, having dropped to one knee to cuddle Karia, and inspect the heavily sugared remains of her porridge.

'Captain Martil, I think the Queen will need some protection during the battle. How about Sergeant Kesbury and a squad of men?' Milly suggested. She had never seen a battle before, and was dreading what might happen that day, even without the fear of losing the battle.

Martil nodded. 'I'll send him over. Although I'm hoping it won't come to that.'

'I'll speak to them myself,' Merren corrected. 'I want the Rallorans to know how much I trust them.'

'Perhaps you had better talk to them now. It seems Gello is getting ready also. His men are forming up.' Quiller pointed down the hill, to where Gello's camp was a hive of activity.

Martil glanced down with a professional eye.

'It will take them a full turn of the hourglass to form up, and most of another turn to be in range,' he stated.

Merren took a deep breath. She was trying to keep her mind on the mundane. The prospect of losing this battle, and the thought of seeing men die for her, was making her stomach churn and her head swim. She had barely been able to keep down a cup of tea. What if she was making a terrible mistake? Should she have just run?

'Don't worry, my Queen. You will have a victory today,' Martil said softly.

She looked up and locked eyes with him. At that moment he wanted to take her into his arms. He wanted one last kiss before he went to his death. But he could not; not in front of everyone.

Merren wanted to hold Martil then. Wanted to feel his arms around her, wanted to feel his muscled back under her hands, wanted to smell that mixture of sweat and steel that seemed to cling to him. But she could not; not in front of everyone.

Instead, she held out a hand.

'Thank you, Captain. Thank you for everything. I could not have asked for a better Champion.'

He took her hand, feeling the warmth of her fingers, and brushed his lips over them, the way he had seen nobles do, while still keeping his eyes on hers. They had not stopped looking at each other all that time and he did not want to let go, of either her hand or her gaze. He wanted to tell her what she meant to him, how he was happy to give his life for her cause, about so much. But all he could do was look at her.

Merren felt his lips on the back of her hand and almost shivered, remembering how they had felt elsewhere. She wanted to tell him so many things, her growing love for him, what he had done for her since becoming her Champion and how he made her feel. But all she could do was look at him.

How long they stood there, neither could tell.

It was probably only a few heartbeats but felt like forever.

Martil would have been happy for it never to end.

'My Queen! I am here!' Barrett's booming voice broke the spell.

'Sorry I am late, I was just talking to the other wizards. We've found three oak trees, and, if it all goes wrong, we should be able to get all the important people away,' he announced.

'Everyone here is important,' Merren told him.

Barrett flushed a little. 'I know that. I just meant that we cannot let Gello win. Anyway, the other wizards are all ready to help the Archbishop.'

'Are you ready?' Martil asked him.

'Of course. Just tell me when and we shall go.' Barrett nodded.

'What you are both doing is incredibly brave. Make sure you return,' Merren said, rather stiffly. 'Now, I want to speak to the Rallorans, then the Norstalines, before Gello begins without us.'

'Do you think he will offer terms, or the chance to surrender?' Romon asked. 'I would like to be there for the formal declaration of battle.'

Martil laughed shortly. 'Don't expect something out of the sagas,' he warned.

They followed Merren down the hillside to where the Rallorans were slowly stamping out fires, drinking the last of their tea and moving into line.

'Silence for the Queen!' Nerrin bellowed, when he saw her approaching, and they immediately snapped to attention.

'What we face today is simple. This has become a battle between good and evil. Gello has the support of the Berellians and, worse, Zorva — while we have Aroaril and the Dragon Sword on our side. But we also have you, the finest warriors on the continent. The Berellians could not beat you and I know Gello's dogs will not trouble you either!'

She paused there, which prompted a cheer from the ranks.

'I know you have all had to sit back while our enemies spread lies about you. But, after today, the whole country will see you for the good men you are. And, as a symbol of my trust in you, my honour guard today shall be led by Sergeant Kesbury!'

This provoked more cheers, and Kesbury was pushed out of the ranks to be applauded.

'I thank you all for being here and I know that together we shall emerge victorious!'

She clapped them, and they cheered her back; Merren acknowledged the cheers until Kesbury and his squad had joined her, then she waved once more and began to walk around to where the Norstaline companies were hidden.

'To your places, lads!' Nerrin roared, and they sprang into action.

'The men are ready, sire,' Feld reported.

Even though he had been ordered to stay with his regiment, the heavy cavalry was not expected to see any action that day. Instead, he was acting as the liaison between Gello and the troops. He had a squadron of his men to guard Gello, and a further squadron to act as runners during the battle.

'Do you want to address them before the battle?'

Gello looked across the field to where the regiments were drawn up in tight blocks, flags fluttering. It was a glorious sight, almost too good for the rabble they were about to destroy.

'Is there any point? All they have to do is march

up a hill and destroy a pack of Rallorans. Surely you can handle that, Feld?'

'Yes, sire. But the men would appreciate some stirring words.'

Gello ground his teeth. Could these men do nothing without him?

'Have all the captains tell the regiments that I am watching them, that they will write a glorious chapter into Norstalos's history, that the enemy is outnumbered and scared and will probably run as soon as they get a taste of Norstaline steel. Got that?'

Feld saluted. 'Yes, sire.'

'Very wise, sire. Save the speeches for when you really need them — this is just a meaningless massacre. When we face a real enemy, like the full Ralloran army, then the men will need inspiration. Here, they should win without half of them even bothering to draw swords,' Ezok announced.

'Very true, Ambassador.' Gello nodded. 'Well, Feld, you have your orders. Have the captains speak to the men, then get going! I want those Rallorans dead by noon!'

'You all know what is at stake. Every man here is a hero, worthy of a place alongside King Riel himself! Many of you will not have fought in a battle like this before. But neither has our enemy! Norstalos has not fought a battle for centuries! Our enemy will not be expecting you. Your charges today will send them reeling back down the slope! Hold your ranks and listen to your officers. Aroaril is with us, the Dragon Sword leads us! And we have men such as yourselves! How can we fail?'

It was a variation of the speech they had already heard back at Sendric, but Merren knew it was important to stiffen backbones before the battle. After all, the only time any men of Gerrin and Berry had fought, they had seen their leader die and many of their number slain.

'Already we have many heroes. Men such as Wime, Tarik and Forde, who gave their lives for this cause. They are looking down on you now. Think of them, and fight harder! Aroaril bless you all!'

They cheered her then, and she waved at them, moving down the lines, speaking to men she remembered from the forest, asking names of those she did not know. Behind her came Nott, Milly and Quiller, as they had also done for the Rallorans, offering blessings to any who wanted them — and many did.

'Your majesty. We need to get into position,' Martil said finally.

He had been sitting down with Karia, just reading a saga and trying not to think. But he could feel time slipping away, and knew Gello's men would be marching soon.

Almost as soon as he had spoken, a runner rushed over.

'Captain Nerrin's compliments, and Gello is advancing!' he gasped.

Merren's face paled, but her back was straight and her eyes defiant. 'Are we ready?'

Martil gave her the ghost of a smile. 'We shall find out,' he said simply.

18

Kay could feel the sweat trickling down his back, although there was still a chill in the air. The day promised to be fine and sunny but, in some ways, it made it worse. Kay and many of his men were having the same thought: Would this be their last day? The early morning sunshine was brilliant, the air redolent with the smells of grass and flowers, every hint of birdsong impossibly loud and sweet, every buzz of an insect clear as a bell. Kay had spent a sleepless night wondering what to do. He knew what his heart felt: he should not be fighting for Gello this day, or indeed ever. But he had no idea how he could possibly escape that fate, or the death that surely waited for him if he did not fight.

So he marched with his men, bow in hand and a pair of arrow sheaves, each with twenty arrows, slung over his shoulders. He would not fit the string to his bow until they were closer — leaving it strung weakened the weapon. Beq was leading both the archers and the rangers this day, while Grissum had taken command of the two conscript regiments, the militia and the criminals. Kay knew they were marching somewhere behind him and to his right. Kay had hardly listened to the speech Beq had yelled at them before they began to advance, and he guessed few of his men had taken it in, either. Most had been complaining about the lack of food. Half an oatcake per man was hardly enough to keep them fighting through a long day, although there had been rumours that supplies were coming.

Kay could sense the fear in the ranks — even though they had not eaten much, men kept breaking ranks to void their bowels, or to throw up their meagre rations. Others were talking much too loudly, laughing too hard. They had trained for years but this was the first time they would face an actual enemy. His own anxiety was not for himself — it was for what he was about to do.

He wished he could have talked more to that Sergeant Hutter and the criminal, Kettering. The time was coming when he would have to draw his bow in the service of the King and, once he did that, there was no going back.

'What's the word again, Sarge?' Turen asked nervously.

'There are several words,' Hutter said patiently. 'When we decide to kill the officers, the call is "Sword". If we decide to run, the call is "Hill". Now, don't worry about that. Just keep your ears open. We're behind Kettering's men, so he'll be the one to make the call.'

'Should we trust a mad bastard like that, Sarge?'

Hutter grinned and slapped the young man on the shoulder. 'Finally, you are thinking! But you're forgetting one thing — we're about to go into battle. That's the perfect place for mad bastards.'

He was trying to project a bluff confidence he did not really have. He had spoken to many of the other sergeants after talking to Kettering. Some were not sure if they should trust a pack of murderers. And he had to admit, they had a point. And there was the whole issue of running away from Gello. After this battle, he would be the undisputed ruler of Norstalos. Where would they go then?

Kettering had made sure he was in the middle of the regiment. Not because he was afraid, but because he wanted to be right behind this Captain Grissum, who was supposedly leading them. He could almost smell the terror of the other men; he was sure several had already pissed themselves in fright, Menner included. The small dressmaker was sobbing softly, partly in embarrassment because he had ruined a fine pair of trews.

'I'm going to die!' Menner had wailed.

'We're all going to die one day,' Kettering replied. 'But you can choose how you die. Gello did this to you. He is the one to blame. Think about every humiliation, every blow, every piece of abuse you have suffered. You have to take your anger, and let it swamp your fear.'

Menner had tried to nod, and smile, although Kettering did not know if the dressmaker could truly understand what he was trying to say.

Kettering had made sure the men he most trusted were clustered around Grissum and the rest of the officers. He just had to give the order, and they would die. That would happen. He just hoped afterwards he would have the chance to kill the Berellian who had started it all. He did not care about anything else.

* * *

The slope of Pilleth made the rangers and archers, who wore only thick leather tunics, sweat and mutter. For the bulk of Gello's infantry, who all carried heavy shields and wore heavier hauberks, it turned the advance into a crawl, their legs and backs protesting. From the expressions on their faces, many of the men were happy to delay the advance for as long as possible.

'Take the archers ahead, the infantry'll catch you up,' Feld ordered Beq.

Beq saluted and waved the archers on, so they kept going, while the heavy infantry took a break, then followed at a much slower pace. They would only speed up when they came into arrow range. Feld knew it was no good pushing them too hard up the slope so they were exhausted when it came to fighting. He also waved to Grissum, who took the lightly armoured conscript regiments off to the right, forming them on the outside of the main body, so they would, unbeknownst to them, take the brunt of the expected cavalry charge.

In the midst of the rangers, Kay stumbled as he walked across a shallow trench dug into the turf. Why anyone had bothered to dig a trench barely a hand deep, but a good yard across, seemed a mystery to him until he looked up — and it became clear.

'They've reached the first marker! Loose the ballistae!' Martil ordered.

He was relieved this was finally starting. He had become used to the tension before battle. But knowing he was going to die in it seemed to have taken the edge off. He felt relaxed, at peace. He could see his men were struggling. They were all veterans of a score of battles, some nearly as big as this. But they had never faced odds this bad before. He could see the sweat on faces, hear the over-loud laughter. Others refused to let it affect them, earnestly debating the best inns in Norstalos City, or the worth of a spear over an axe — anything to help them pretend there were not thousands of men advancing to kill them. He was grateful the Queen's Norstaline companies could not see this. They would have found the sight of so many of Gello's men terrifying. But the enemy would be just as frightened — and they would also be the first to suffer in this battle.

Making the ballistae had been a long, infuriating process, but they would prove their worth now. Because it took so long to shape a spear for them, there were only a few for each machine — and they took ages to reload. Nevertheless they could be a fearsome weapon. Normally they worked like a giant crossbow, spears flying high in the air before dropping down on their target. But Martil had ordered the back to be raised because of Pilleth's slope. This meant they would fly straight down the hill.

Rallorans used heavy hammers to release the ballistae's restraining levers, and the machines bucked and kicked, flinging their heavy missiles down the slope. One or two missiles dug into the ground, then cartwheeled uselessly down the hill before coming to a stop. A few more flew high, arcing up to land in the space between Gello's archers and the rest of his infantry. But the rest punched holes in the tight ranks, impaling two or three men at a time and flinging them back down the slope in a spray of blood and a tangle of limbs.

'Reload! Faster!' Nerrin bellowed. 'Show them what you can do!'

* * *

Kay watched in horror as the next volley of ballistae spears was loosed. They made a strange hissing sound and seemed to move slowly through the air at first, then leaped down the slope to crash into the ranks on either side of him. One struck with a hideous noise just four men to his right, picking up the man in the first rank, slamming him back into the man behind, and flinging them both ten feet through the air, impaled on the heavy wood.

Men cowered from the noise, the blood and the fear of the missiles; those in the path of the ballistae were trying to edge sideways, squeezing the line together.

'Spread out! Speed up! As soon as we get close enough, they'll fall back!' Beq was screaming, hauling men to their feet, kicking them into line, shoving them up the hill.

Kay knew he should be saying something similar, but he was more concerned about the ballistae that was almost in front of him — and its crew, which was reloading it as fast as they could, using levers to wind back the thick arm.

'Aroaril save us!' someone cried, down the line.

Up the hill, to his right, a ballistae being reloaded suddenly broke under the strain, throwing chunks of wood high into their air. Kay saw at least one Ralloran flung away, as well.

Elsewhere, wounded men behind the nervously advancing line were screaming for help, for their mothers, for someone to take away the pain.

'Keep going!' Beq's call went down the line. They were almost within bow range.

Kay saw the crew leader on a ballistae pick up a

hammer, glance down the slope, then swing the hammer down. The missile seemed to be coming straight for him and he watched it, mesmerised, sure it was the last thing he was going to see. Then, at the last moment, it flew up and over him, the force of its passing making him stumble back. A hand pushed him forwards.

'Don't die yet, sir!' Sergeant Ryder called.

Kay did not have time to reply, as he stepped into another shallow trench.

'String your bows! Give them a taste of what Norstalines can do!' Beq screamed.

Kay fumbled his string from his belt pouch and strung his bow, missing the first time in nervousness. All along the line, archers and rangers were doing the same. Then someone glanced up.

'Watch out!'

Martil watched with approval as the ballistae crews, less the one that had been killed, ran back to their place in the main battleline, leaving the way clear for the Ralloran archers, reinforced with Tarik's former hunters and every other bowman they had found in the three northern towns. It was a pitiful force compared to the near two thousand bowmen facing them. But they had the advantage of the high ground — and on Pilleth it was a massive advantage indeed.

'Loose!' Nerrin ordered. 'As fast as you can!'

The white-tipped arrows hissed down and slammed into the front rank. Dozens of men went down instantly, either dead or screaming for help, which Kay thought was worse.

'Loose!' Beq bellowed.

Kay did not bend his bow, but just about every other archer did, and the resultant arrow cloud looked far more impressive than the shower of Ralloran arrows that had come in. But it did nothing. Kay saw the entire volley waste itself in the turf, a good forty yards short of the Ralloran archers.

'We're falling short! March forwards!' Beq roared, trying to urge men on.

But it was not an easy thing, to get men to walk into the teeth of an arrow storm. The Rallorans were not loosing in one big volley, but as fast as they could, which meant that arrows were falling all the time. Every step forwards brought another arrow, as well as the fear that it would strike you.

The rangers and archers had been unnerved by the ballistae that had torn holes in their lines, and many were looking back over their shoulders, to where the rest of the infantry laboriously advanced. It was easy to feel isolated, abandoned — and their instinct was to stay where they were, not risk themselves further.

Kay felt he was still safely out of range, so he stopped and loosed a couple of arrows before walking any further.

'Hurry! Hurry!' Beq was now out front, trying to lead by example. 'The King is watching! Every man who wants his favour, follow me now!'

The officers, sergeants and men that Kay thought of as Beq's favourites followed his example, both from the rangers and from the archers. The rest, like Kay, hung at the back and loosed arrows uselessly, which wasted themselves on the turf. Kay had no more interest in winning favour from the King. Gello had sent his men up here to be slaughtered. His strategy cared nothing for the men who had to carry it out. Kay did not want to lead his men into death — especially when it was for no good reason. But they were being drawn slowly up the hill, led by Beq's group, perhaps three hundred strong. Although this group was suffering badly — every step they made, another fell, as the Ralloran archers nocked and loosed like madmen on the hill above.

'We're almost in range!' Beq screeched.

But Kay could see the Rallorans were starting to take a step back, after loosing a couple of arrows. They were keeping safely out of range, while their arrows were taking a wicked toll of Beq's men. Eventually, however, they would be hard up against their own battleline. What would happen then?

Martil watched as Nerrin slowly retreated up the hill, all the time his archers taking a heavy toll of the men below. And it was working — more than three-quarters of Gello's archers were hanging back, obviously unwilling to march into death. But Martil's Rallorans only had about thirty paces to go before they would be forced to stop — and then they would start taking casualties. He glanced over his shoulder to where Barrett stood. It was almost time. He could not let his men die. He gripped Karia's hand, and his other instinctively touched the hilt of the Sword.

'For Aroaril's sake, someone kill that bloody officer!' Nerrin bellowed, pointing to where Beq was running up and down the enemy line, encouraging his men forwards.

Arrows had been falling all around him, as archers sought to kill him. Any man who came near him was pierced, but the officer seemed to be leading a charmed life.

Men were running down from the top of the hill, bringing replacement arrow sheaves for those who had run out. Only a handful of Rallorans had been wounded, mostly in the leg, and only three had had to leave the line for treatment.

'And kill some more bloody archers!' Nerrin shouted. He could sense they would soon be up against the shield wall, and then it was a case of stand and take it for as long as you could, before an arrow killed you.

Rocus and Conal exchanged glances, as they heard the roar of orders, the screams of the injured and the sound both of bowstrings and falling arrows. They had heard the ballistae loosed on the enemy and now they wondered what was happening on the hill. A glance behind, at the pale, sweaty faces of the men, told them they were not the only ones.

'We hold. We wait until we hear from Martil or Barrett,' Rocus said loudly.

Conal nodded. He had thought the fight in the gate tunnel had been terrifying but this waiting, not being able to watch, was somehow worse. Your imagination had too much time to work.

'Kay! Get your men up here! We've almost got them pinned!' Beq screamed.

His men had been whittled down — of his most trusted companies, two-thirds were dead or wounded, struck by the never-ending stream of arrows the Rallorans were sending down. But he could see success was just ahead. The Rallorans had nowhere to go now. Another few paces and his arrows would start to kill them. All he had to do was bring up Kay and the rest of these laggards, and the slaughter could begin.

'Kay! Are you listening! Get up here now or I'll have you arrested!'

But Kay's doubts had suddenly cleared and his head felt calm. He could see that he could advance his men, and both sides would suffer terribly. The Ralloran shield wall would hardly be touched; the Ralloran archers would eventually all be slain, although they would be able to kill many of his men. And for what? So Gello's favourites could advance in safety.

'We will not do this. Sergeant Ryder, I want the men marshalled to the left, at the Ralloran marker trench,' Kay ordered.

Beq stopped and stared in shock and horror as the men who would achieve his victory turned around and started walking away.

'Kay! Where are you going! Kay!' he bellowed down at the officer, forgetting for a moment where he was and why he had been trying to keep moving.

The air was thick with the hiss of arrows. His ears only registered a slightly different sound at the last moment. He had time to turn, but no more. Three arrows slammed into him, picked him up and threw him to the turf.

Less than one hundred of Beq's men remained, and more were dying every moment. Without Beq's influence, they just broke and ran, throwing away their arrow bags, their bows, everything that slowed them down. They ran past where Kay had drawn up his men, off to the side and away from the path of the advance, where they would not be seen as a threat. The running men went around the solid block of advancing infantry and kept going, heading for Gello's camp.

Gello watched in mingled shock and fury as the bulk of his archers moved off to the flank, almost removing themselves from the battle, while the remnants ran past his phalanx of infantry towards the camp.

He signalled to Feld.

'I want those cowards ridden down! Every one of them is to die, understand?'

Feld opened his mouth, then closed it and saluted instead.

'At once, sire!'

Gello watched, feeling a little happier, as a company of light cavalry formed up and rode to intercept the archers who had fled all the way down the hill. These men, seeing the drawn swords, slowed to a walk, or even turned around — but it was too late. The order was given and the horses spurred to the gallop. This was no harder than the training field, and the cavalry troopers rode over the scattered archers, hacking them down with swords.

Some of the smarter archers fell to the ground, rolling into a ball to avoid the merciless swords. Others tried to run back up the hill. But the troopers split up and hemmed them in and the swords did their deadly work until all were either dead, pretending to be dead, or wishing they were dead.

'That will show those dogs what happens if you run away!' Gello applauded.

'And the rest of the archers, the ones on the hill, sire?' Ezok asked carefully.

'They can stay there. We shall deal with the cowards after the battle. In truth, it is not a great setback. The few archers the Rallorans have will never be able to stop us. See?'

Gello gestured to where his infantry was advancing again, shields held high. 'It will cost me another fifty dead, but they are easily replaced,' he told Ezok confidently.

'Your majesty is wise indeed,' Ezok agreed.

Martil stared down the hill in amazement. The archers had broken! They had actually driven them off!

'We won!' Merren exclaimed, stepping forwards to be close to him. 'We won that, didn't we?'

'We did!' Martil declared, hardly able to believe it himself. He let go of Karia's hand. 'I'll be right back, I just have to see Nerrin.'

Karia had been trying not to look at what was going on down the hill, but she was not about to let go of his hand that easily.

'He'll be right back. Here, hold my hand,' Merren offered.

Reluctantly, Karia swapped hands, and Martil hurried down to where the exhausted archers were cheering each other.

'We're going to do the same again!' Nerrin was roaring at them.

Martil joined Nerrin in clapping men on the back, and congratulating them. All were nursing sore arms and backs, as to draw back a longbow was the equivalent of lifting a woman into the air. They were frantically replenishing their arrow bags, and drinking water.

'This time it'll be the infantry. They'll have shields high, but they'll be much slower, and they can't do anything back to you. Pick your targets and take your time,' Martil ordered. 'Every one we merely hurt is one less we have to fight! You can't walk up a hill with an arrow in the leg!'

'What about the rest of the archers?' Nerrin gestured to where they sat or stood, a solid mass, to the Rallorans' right, on the side of the hill.

'I don't know what they are thinking, whether they even have any officers left. But we leave them alone, unless they start to advance again.' Martil shrugged. 'I don't think they'll play any further part in this battle.'

'What now, sir?' Sergeant Ryder asked.

Kay was silent. The truth was, he had no idea. He had decided he was not going to throw away his men's lives for no good reason but had not thought beyond that. The way Gello had ridden down the archers most loyal to him had shown them all what fate awaited those who tried to run.

'We shall just wait here, Sergeant,' he said finally. 'If the Rallorans break, the cavalry will be more interested in riding after them. I will tell the King that Beq ordered us back, just before his death. If that does not work, then I shall take responsibility. You will not die for me, I promise. Are there any men left who might cause trouble?'

Ryder laughed. 'All those who were the big supporters of Beq and the King are either dead at the top of the hill, or dead at the bottom of the hill. Don't worry about them, sir. Likewise the archers. Most of their officers are dead, the others are happy to follow you. They won't be no trouble.'

'Bring them over, anyway,' Kay ordered.

'Sir! I'll walk slow, give you a chance to think of what to say to them.'

Kay smiled thinly. He had plenty to think about. Like what had come over him to order such a thing?

The senior infantry captain was a mustachioed swordsman called Heath, who had actually shared a room with a young Lieutenant Gello, when the then ruler-in-waiting arrived to spend a few months learning how the infantry trained and fought. He summoned the other officers to pass on Gello's orders.

'We'll advance slowly until we get within arrow range, then we advance at the quick. Shields high, pass the word for the ranks behind to keep shields over their heads, because the Rallorans will be dropping arrows on them,' he ordered. 'We can do this job without the bloody archers. Now move! The King is watching!'

The six thousand infantry stood in a tight column, each regiment in six lines, the whole formation thirty-six ranks deep. Against them was a thin line of Rallorans, just as wide but only six ranks deep. Once the infantry was close enough, the front lines would move into wedge shapes, and aim to pierce the Ralloran line in half-a-dozen places. Once that happened, the Rallorans would break and be killed. Heath was under no illusions that the advance up a hill, under constant arrow attack, would be easy. But he knew it would bring victory.

'Should we order Rocus to charge?' Merren asked as soon as Martil returned, and even before Karia had a chance to grab his hand yet again.

Martil hesitated for a moment, then pointed towards a small block of infantry that had swung out to the flank and then stopped, taking position close to where the valley entrance opened onto the hill.

'It looks as if they are expecting us,' he said grimly. 'So we must delay; wait until they do not expect us and move that reserve of men.'

Merren nodded agreement, although she felt sick. So far everything was going well — the archers had managed to defeat a force more than ten times their size, something that should have been impossible. Now the Rallorans only had to defeat a force six times their size. It seemed possible — barely. But she was trying not to hope too much.

'We'd better send a runner to Rocus, to tell him what is happening,' Martil suggested, and waved one over.

'What about the ballistae? Can we use them again?'

Martil sighed. 'I wish we could. But we have no more missiles for them.' He looked down the hill, to where Gello's infantry was making its slow, implacable progress up the hill. Should he go now? But he wanted Gello's attention to be completely on the battle before he attacked. And at least the infantry would not do any damage until they arrived.

'How long before we charge, do you think?' Jaret asked.

The former militiaman from Gerrin was sitting on his horse beside the former guardsman, Wilsen. Since being forced together by Merren, they had become friends.

'Don't know. Talk about something else,' Wilsen grunted.

Jaret nodded. He had already been behind a tree, and felt like he needed to relieve his bladder once more.

'I wish we could see what was going on. This waiting is driving me mad,' Jaret groaned.

'Trust me, you don't want to know what's going on. And the longer you stay out of the battle, the happier you'll be.'

'What was Sendric like?'

'Brutal. Now, will you talk about something else? My guts are churning enough as it is!'

'I didn't do much the last time we fought. I'm scared of letting everyone down again,' Jaret said softly.

Wilsen punched him lightly on the shoulder. 'Stick with me, and you'll be fine. Just talk about something else, for Aroaril's sake!'

'What are we doing here, Sarge?' Turen asked plaintively.

'Don't know. But I don't like it. What does that cutting over there look like to you, lad?'

Turen followed Hutter's pointing finger. He looked at his sergeant carefully, to see if this was a trick question. 'A bit like a small valley, Sarge?' he ventured.

'Like a good place to hide some of your men. And who's now protecting Gello's flank in case of a surprise attack? Us!' Hutter felt he should do something more than just wait there. He could not explain it — it was just a feeling.

'Hutter! Hutter!'

He looked across to where the call was coming from, and saw Kettering waving at him from the adjoining ranks of the criminal regiment.

'What?' he bawled back, hoping the man did not yell out anything incriminating.

Kettering waved again, but said nothing. Hutter cursed, then ducked down and hurried along the ranks of men, hoping he would not be noticed. When he reached the end of the file, he was only a few yards from where Kettering stood, at the end of the criminal regiment's corresponding file of men.

'What do you make of that?' Kettering gestured to where the archers and rangers had formed up, across the other side of the hill, out of the way of the battle. 'Do you reckon it was that ranger officer?'

'Could be,' Hutter said guardedly. 'What do you think?'

'I think the time is coming when we need to do something,' Kettering admitted. 'Something crazy.'

'Hutter! Back to your place!' a voice roared.

Hutter glanced over his shoulder to see an officer waving at him furiously. He glanced around to ask Kettering exactly what he meant but the man had already vanished back into the ranks of criminals.

Nerrin watched the slow approach of the infantry and wished he was back in the ranks, fighting as a sergeant and responsible for just a dozen men, rather than hundreds. He was trying not to think too much about what would happen once the enemy made it to the top. Instead, he was wondering why he had taken that commission from the fat merchant to protect a caravan heading to Sendric, instead of the smaller offer for a caravan across to Cessor. If he had taken the Cessor trip, he would probably be sitting in an inn around now, eating a hot meal and lining up some drinks, and possibly a woman, for the evening. Yet here he was, standing on a hill. Despite Martil's words, Nerrin thought he was probably going to die — but he had never considered running. After Bellic, there had been nothing to run towards. His life was not so wonderful that he would regret leaving it, so he could watch the advance quite dispassionately.

Gello's men were showing plenty of discipline, keeping their lines straight, their shields tight. There would be few spaces to hit with an arrow. Between the helm, shield, mail hauberk and their tall boots, no doubt reinforced with metal, they were well protected. But it was not impossible. He saw the first men stumble across the shallow ditch that was their marker and drew a deep breath.

'Draw! Pick your targets and loose!'

Heath heard the whistle of the arrows before he saw them. 'Shields up! Protect the ranks in front of you!'

The front rank crouched behind their shields, while the men in the ranks behind held their shields high. Arrows began to thud home — a couple of men screamed as arrows slipped between shields to strike shoulders and heads; others cursed as arrows struck legs and feet. The lines adjusted and kept going, flowing around the wounded.

'Keep together!' Heath bellowed.

The arrows were falling regularly now, striking in unexpected places. Some archers were obviously aiming at the rear ranks, dropping arrows from high; others were snapping the arrows in on a flat trajectory, aiming at the front rank. The men shuffled forwards, slowed by their natural fear of closing with their foes, as well as the many bodies of archers on the ground, and their own wounded. The wounded archers screamed or begged for help as the heavily armoured infantry marched over the top of them.

'Leave them! On! On!' Heath was frustrated by the slowness of the advance but at least they were making progress. He risked a glimpse out from under his shield, to see the Ralloran archers had fallen back almost to their shield wall. Not long now, and Gello's men would have their revenge.

Nerrin was calling out targets to the nearest archers to make himself feel useful. In truth, by the time he had drawn something to the attention of an archer, the shields were back in place and an arrow was pointless. Many of the arrows were being wasted on shields, although some were still finding the gaps whenever any showed themselves. A man just had to stumble and drop his shield for a moment, and two or three arrows would flash into the gap; that man would fall, creating more of a gap, and more arrows would pour in. But the line would quickly close, then slowly begin to advance again.

What they needed was something heavier, to punch a hole in the line. At Mount Shadar, the Berellians had used smaller round shields, which offered far less protection. And the Rallorans had used cavalry to rip their ordered lines apart. He glanced over his shoulder, to where Martil stood under the giant dragon banner. Nerrin had done about all he could, but he had only stung Gello's infantry. The only other thing he could do was draw his sword and stand in the line.

'Archers to the rear! Front rank! Brace!' he shouted, stepping between two men in the front row, his sword sliding into his hand.

'Let's show these pretty boys how real men can fight!'

'Do we send in the cavalry now?' Merren asked, as the phalanx inched ever closer, leaving a trail of dead and wounded men behind.

Martil sighed. The time had come.

'I'm afraid they have foreseen the use of cavalry, my Queen.' He pointed down the hill. 'What I need to do now is go with Barrett, and kill Gello. I shall give you the victory you deserve.'

Their eyes locked for a long moment, but he had no time to say any more.

'Aroaril be with you,' she told him softly.

He drew the Dragon Sword, saluted her with it, then bent down to Karia.

She had been holding tightly to his hand, but looking away from the fighting. Now she clutched tightly to his leg.

'Karia, I have to go now.' He tried to gently disentangle himself, speaking softly so Merren would not hear what he planned to do.

'I won't let you go!' she turned a slightly tear-stained face around to him, which was set in the stubborn expression he had come to know so well.

'Karia, people's lives depend on me. I have to do this, for everyone.'

'But what about me?'

He hugged her then, feeling his resolve waver. But she deserved a happy life and the only way she could get it was for him to sacrifice himself.

'I am sorry but it has to be this way.' He looked into her eyes and tried to find the words to explain to her. 'It is a parent's job to look after their child. Your mother gave her life so that you would live. I have to do the same. This is the only way I can be sure you will be safe. I can't let other people die, just so that I can be happy. I can save everyone. And my life is a small price to pay. I cannot use the Dragon Sword to win this battle, so I must do this, instead.'

She could hear what he was saying, but it made no sense. All she was getting was the message that he was going, and was not going to come back. 'But I just found you! I don't want to lose you! Who will take care of me?'

'Father Nott, Conal, Barrett, Merren — they will all look after you. And I will be there, although you cannot see me. I will always love you.'

He hugged her again, for the last time, although she did not want to let go. He did not want to let her go either. He knew as soon as he went through that tree he was a dead man.

'Martil!' Barrett said urgently.

With great difficulty, and with tears in his own eyes, Martil managed to step away from Karia, who then flung herself onto the ground, sobbing.

'Martil!' Merren exclaimed.

Martil stroked her hair with his free hand, then wiped his eyes before turning to face them, drawing a deep breath to bring himself back under control.

'I am sorry. But I am ready now, wizard,' he said thickly.

He became aware that everyone was ignoring him, instead staring down the hill. He had only been listening to Karia, the sum total of his awareness had shrunk to the pair of them. But now the sounds of the battle began to intrude again — and they were all wrong.

'Look!' Merren cried.

Martil stared.

Kay had greeted the remaining ranger and archer officers, none of whom had the slightest idea what they should do now.

The one archer who suggested explaining things

to King Gello was greeted with silence, before Ryder said, 'You want to end up like the men the King ordered killed?'

'Well, we are going to have to decide soon, because Heath's men are not going to be stopped by little more than a company of archers,' someone muttered up the back.

'Perhaps we should join Heath again; the Rallorans must be short of arrows, and we could thin out their line just before Heath hits home,' the first archer suggested again, half-heartedly. 'We would be back in the King's favour again.'

'No!' Kay suddenly spun around. 'I will not fight for Gello! He has tricked and lied to us, he has been happy to waste our lives, and he has allied himself with Berellians! I was the captain of the Royal Guard! I should have stopped him before this, and it is to my eternal shame that I did not. But I can make up for that now — we can all make up for that now!'

Kay started pacing, getting the words out as they came to him. He had been so confused, for so long, but now it was all becoming clear, as if by magic.

'It was not the Queen who led us to this — it was Gello. Already he is sacrificing our nobles and dumping their bodies at night. How long before he moves on to our families?'

'What? Sacrificing the nobles?' a ranger officer called. 'Why did you not tell us before?'

'Gello has sold himself to Berellia, and they have sold themselves to Zorva. But we can stop them,' Kay insisted.

'How?'

Kay pointed at the slow-moving phalanx of infantry, just fifty paces away.

'We turn our bows on them.'

The men stared at him.

Sergeant Ryder stepped forwards.

'He is right, lads. If we are going to stop Gello, then this is the time.'

'But we'll all be killed!'

'We'll all be killed anyway! And even if we survive Gello's wrath, how long do you think it will be before he sends us out to be killed by the Tetrans, the Avish and the Rallorans?' Kay challenged them. 'How will we live our lives? In fear and regret, wishing we had seized this chance? Will we go screaming to our deaths, having seen our wives and families sacrificed to Gello's black ambition? Or do we die like men?'

For a long moment he thought they were going to turn on him. But then he felt a sudden certainty, almost a wave of confidence. He was doing the right thing. He had wanted to regain his honour, and this was the only way.

'You are right,' someone said.

Kay looked over to see the archer officer, the one who had suggested rejoining the attack, step forwards.

'I don't know why, but I feel this is the right thing to do. And even though my head tells me we will all die, that this is the act of a fool, I cannot ignore what my heart is telling me,' he said.

'Your name?'

'Lieutenant Cropper, sir.'

'Welcome, Cropper.'

They shook hands, then turned to the others.

'Who else will stand with me? For, if not, you should start running now,' Kay challenged.

'We will all be there!' Ryder roared, his words echoed by the other men. 'Damned if I know why — it's as if someone's cast a spell on us,' he continued.

'Or broken one we've been under,' Cropper agreed.

'Form line! Get your men ready!' Kay cried.

The archers and rangers moved swiftly into position. With every passing moment, Kay became more and more sure that this was the right decision. And none of his rangers or the archers showed even the slightest hesitation as he ordered them to turn their bows on their erstwhile comrades. Kay stepped out the front, where all could see him. He knew this meant the infantry would probably turn on them, and that light armour and swords were no match for a shield wall. But he did not care. He now knew, if he had the chance again, he would have fought Gello when he came to arrest the Queen. But this was the next best thing.

He glanced to his left and right, and saw the massed archers were ready. Taking out an arrow, he waved it above his head, signalling to them all. 'Draw!' he roared.

Taking the strain, feeling the tension in his arm, shoulder, chest and back, he pulled the string back to touch his ear. From there, you could not aim by eye, but by instinct. He looked at the massed infantry marching in front of him, and felt a moment's pity for what he was about to unleash. His order had made some turn, and these were frantically trying to warn their fellows and bring shields around.

Too late.

'For honour!' Kay bellowed, and released the string.

His arrow leaped away, followed an instant later by hundreds of others.

The first Heath knew of the attack was when his entire left flank collapsed, screaming and crying, to the tune of arrows slamming into shields, helms and armour. In an instant, his careful, ordered advance was thrown into chaos, as scores of men crumpled. For perhaps ten heartbeats, he just stared in horror at the sight of hundreds of archers he thought were on his side, not only attacking his column, but preparing to loose a second volley.

'Shields!' he screamed. 'Take cover!'

Another hail of arrows poured in, and this time many of the men had their shields up, but the sheer volume meant anyone not completely covered was peppered. He guessed he had two hundred men dead or wounded already.

'Get those shields up, re-form the ranks!' he snapped, then left it to the junior officers and sergeants to organise.

'Get a message to the King! I can't attack the Rallorans with the archers on my flank — does he want me to kill the archers first?' he ordered one of his mounted officers, then watched the man gallop madly down back towards the camp.

'What in Aroaril's name is going on?' Merren demanded. 'Why have those archers turned on their own side?'

Nobody seemed to have an answer for her. Most were just staring, open-mouthed, at this extraordinary turn of events.

'Didn't we think the rangers were secretly on our side?' Barrett offered.

'I think there is a more logical explanation. Martil, show us the Dragon Sword,' Nott said briskly.

Martil, who had the Sword in his hand, reversed it to display the hilt to Merren.

'The eyes! The eyes are alight!' Merren exclaimed.

Martil turned the blade around and saw the ruby eyes glowing at him.

'The hilt's warm, as well,' he said stupidly, realising it for the first time.

'Well, you know what this means!' Merren said excitedly. 'You don't need to risk your life in a mad attack on Gello — you need to stay here now! The Dragon Sword has worked on those archers and rangers, just as we hoped and prayed it would! Now we just have to wait and Gello's army will collapse around itself!'

'He has to stay!' Karia pushed her way through the crowd to leap up at Martil, who managed to catch her in his free hand.

'This doesn't mean we are going to be victorious,' Martil warned. 'There are still enough men down there to defeat us. We have to see what Gello tries next. Going for him might still be the best way of winning this battle. We don't know if any of the others down there will turn to us.'

'Then we should attack now! Attack while he is not expecting it!' Barrett declared.

'Those infantry may be pinned down, but there's still too many for us to handle,' Martil argued. 'We have all the advantages now. To throw them away would be foolish. We have to see what Gello's next move is …'

'I think we can already see that,' Nott said, pointing.

Gello had been watching Heath's slow advance up the hill with a rising frustration. He wanted them to get to grips with the Rallorans, smash through their lines and set them to flight. He wanted his cousin captured, and her tame Ralloran dead. And he was sick of waiting for it to happen. But his frustration was replaced by horror when his archers turned their bows on Heath's men and the advance stopped as the infantry cowered under the arrow storm.

'They can't advance through that, sire!' Feld warned.

'I know that! But those archers will run out of arrows soon — and then we can slaughter them like the dogs they are!'

Feld cleared his throat. 'If I may, sire? The conscript regiments. Have them move across and attack the archers — even if they fail, the archers will use their arrows up on them, leaving our infantry free to either finish them off or attack the Rallorans.'

'But what of the cavalry attack?'

'Sire, if they had cavalry, they would have used them by now. They certainly did so at Mount Shadar. The risk of that is less than the risk of losing our best men for no reason!'

Ezok was tempted to remind them that was not true — but thought having Gello's best troops take the brunt of a cavalry charge was a better option.

Gello hesitated for a moment, but only a moment. The battle was still his, he had more than enough men. But he did not want to waste his best troops on the archers. Far better to use the conscripts. They were unimportant.

'Use the conscripts to clear the archers away. And send a few companies of light cavalry around to the left flank, in case the archers break. I want every last one punished!'

Riders were sent galloping up the hill, even as a rider from Captain Heath tore into the camp, asking for orders.

'Tell Heath to hold; the conscripts will come

around beneath him and charge the archers. Once they are occupied, he is to resume his advance on the Rallorans,' Gello instructed, and the man, his horse sweating heavily, raced away.

'What would make those men turn on their own side?' Ezok mused. It was an interesting development. Did it mean Gello did not have quite the grip on the men that he imagined?

'Who knows how the brains of peasants work? Perhaps my slut of a cousin promised each man a free ride,' Gello joked.

Ezok joined in the laughter, but noticed the likes of Feld really had to force themselves to laugh.

'Move!' Captain Grissum bawled. 'We're going around the back of the infantry, then we're going to charge the archers. They're a bunch of traitors, so the King wants them dead! They've only got swords, like you, so they'll be easy meat! Quickly now!'

It was simple enough to run across the hill, rather than down, although there was some confusion in the ranks as these men, new to soldiering, struggled to turn around and re-form in neat lines. Hutter took advantage of this to slip out of his line, to where he could see Kettering jogging along.

'What should we do?' Hutter cried.

Kettering grinned. 'Simple. We stand with Kay.'

'What?'

Kettering shook his head. 'We have to take sides, and take sides now. It must be Kay! He has made a choice, and so must we. My men are going to fight Gello. You do what you must.'

Hutter stared at him. Everything he had learned on the streets told him this was not a fight he wanted to get involved in. He had spent his whole life looking for the comfortable life, the path of least resistance. But, in that moment, he realised it had led him away from everything he had once believed in. He could either be a fat, foolish militia sergeant in a backwater village or something more. He felt an unstoppable surge of certainty — this was the time to act.

'We will stand with you! Let's do this!' he bellowed.

Kettering saluted him, a fierce look on his face. He could not explain why he had to do this either; it just felt right.

'Sword! Sword!' he roared at the top of his voice, a cry he could hear being taken up by his men, as well as Hutter's men.

Kay sighted on a gap between two shields and released — only to see it close in that instant and his arrow sink deep into a shield, not the flesh behind it.

'Sir! 'Ware right!' Sergeant Ryder screamed.

Kay turned to see a ragged attack forming downhill, to his right. The two conscript regiments were running across the hill, and seemed to be massing for an attack on his right flank. He almost laughed. So this was Gello's response? His men would slaughter them.

He was wondering if he should try and make a run for the top of the hill, where he could at least stand with the Queen. But it would mean forcing his men to run the gauntlet of Gello's infantry. Few would survive that. In the short term, they were far safer where they were.

'Follow me, Sergeant,' he ordered, striding down to take command personally. He would need several companies to keep the pressure on Heath's infantry, so they would not be tempted to attack him. He glanced over his shoulder to where the Rallorans waited at the top of the hill. What were they thinking about all this, he wondered idly. Would the Queen ever find out he had returned to her service?

'I think we should go and help them,' Merren declared.

'But, my Queen, if we go down there, we will have to take on more than five times our number of infantry,' Martil pointed out. He was trying to work out what this turn of events might mean. He had never seen anything like this before. Part of him was suggesting he should immediately attack, attack with everything he had — but another part was afraid for the men he was going to send into the attack. 'And by us going down there, we will force the archers to stop aiming at Gello's men, for fear of hitting us. What they need to do is come up here. Only they can't get past Gello's men without being cut to pieces. We are stuck.'

'And what about them?' Merren pointed to where the conscripts were running across the hill.

'It looks like Gello wants them to attack the archers, to allow his infantry to move on us,' Martil guessed.

'But that means we can use our cavalry to attack now!' Merren exclaimed.

Martil reflected that she had perhaps proved too quick a learner when it came to strategy. 'We still need to wait,' he insisted, the memory of how few men he had left after Mount Shadar strong in his mind.

*   *   *

'Let them get close, then we'll make every arrow count,' Kay instructed his men. 'We'll pile them up, and the survivors won't want to go past the wall of bodies we'll make.'

He had no doubt his men could create slaughter. These were not heavily armoured infantry; the conscripts did not carry shields and were wearing leather jerkins. His arrows would pierce those as if they were paper.

'Sir! Look!' Ryder cried.

The conscript regiments were slowing down now, while two men broke away at the front and raced towards the archers, waving.

'What in Aroaril's name is going on, sir?' Ryder asked.

Kay peered at them. Why would just two men attack ahead of the others? And they seemed vaguely familiar; one was a big man, carrying some extra fat around his waist, while the other was lean.

'Kay! Kay! We're here to help!' the big one was bellowing.

'Sir! Your orders?' Ryder snapped.

'Wait here, Sergeant. If they kill me, make sure you turn them into pincushions,' Kay said, and jogged out to meet the two running figures. As he drew closer, he recognised them — Hutter and Kettering, the pair from last night.

'What do you want?' he demanded, as they slowed to a walk, puffing a little.

'We're here to help you,' Kettering growled. 'The King is a liar and a traitor and a friend of Berellians. We will fight with you.'

Kay gaped at them.

'We'll keep running across, but instead of attacking you, we'll form up in front of you. Then, when Gello's men attack the Rallorans, we can hit them from behind and drive them off,' Hutter panted.

Kay was momentarily too stunned to say anything.

'Well, speak up, man! We don't have all day before Gello wakes up to what we are doing!' Hutter puffed.

'But your officers — what do they say?' Kay gasped.

'Not much. We killed them,' Kettering said laconically. 'Now, tell your men to leave their arrows off their strings while we form up.'

For a heartbeat, Kay wondered if this was all some elaborate trap, but dismissed that. What would be the point?

'Welcome!' he said simply, holding out his hand.

The three of them shook hands, suddenly grinning like idiots, then Kettering and Hutter waved to their men and Kay sprinted back to where Ryder and his rangers waited.

'They're going to help us. They'll form up in front of us,' Kay panted, as soon as he got back. 'No one is to loose an arrow at them.'

'This may be my first battle, but I'm sure they're not supposed to go like this,' Ryder muttered, then began shouting orders.

19

'What!' Gello leaped out of his seat, where he had been enjoying a shoulder massage from Lahra.

Nobody spoke. They just stared up the hill, to where the conscript regiments had run around, as they were supposed to, but instead of attacking the archers, they had formed up in front of them, facing Gello's infantry. Far from being locked in a death struggle, they seemed to be shaking hands and slapping the backs of the archers.

Gello watched wordlessly, almost apoplectic with rage. How could these fools do this to him? He had given them simple instructions and they had bungled it again! Instead of facing one thousand Rallorans, he now had thirty-five hundred hostile Norstalines on his left flank, while the Rallorans were just standing there, laughing at his incompetence!

'All is not lost, sire,' a voice said.

Gello turned, fingers working convulsively, ready to rip the throat out of the officer who had spoken, only to see Ezok had stepped forwards.

'You have been given bad advice by little men,' Ezok continued. 'Your officers told you those men were loyal, that they were ready. That was a lie.'

Gello agreed. If he was not sure that Beq and

Grissum were dead, he would have had them skinned alive.

'But you still have more than enough men on the field to win this battle. This is a time for courage, for boldness. Send your infantry in to wipe out the traitors first. They are lightly armed, and hardly trained. Your best men will make short work of them, and you will still have more than enough men left to shred the Ralloran scum.'

The words began to penetrate the red mist inside Gello's head. It made sense. He still had the best part of six regiments on that hill, facing one good regiment and four bad ones. Those were still very good odds.

'That is what we shall do. Order Captain Heath to wipe out the traitors, but keep two regiments back, in case the Rallorans or cavalry decide to attack at the same time,' Gello decided.

Ezok bowed, his heart singing. By the end of this battle, Gello would be in no position to betray his ally; he would be dependent on Berellia if they were to conquer the rest of the continent.

'Feld!' Gello roared. 'Take those orders to Heath, and tell him not to bother coming back down unless he has my cousin in chains!'

'This day will truly show the world your greatness,' Ezok added, signalling to Lahra.

Under her coaxing, Gello was persuaded to sit back down; wine was poured for him and, as she began to rub his shoulders, he even smiled again.

'What counts is the final victory, not how it was achieved, eh, Ambassador?'

'As always, your majesty is right,' Ezok agreed.

* * *

'What is happening?' Merren demanded.

'Merren, if I knew, I would tell you,' Martil admitted.

They were all staring at the strange battlefield below. Now there were four of Gello's erstwhile regiments facing his infantry, although the losses the archers and rangers had suffered made them somewhat smaller than the usual size.

'Why?' Merren asked.

'It has to be the Dragon Sword,' Kesbury declared, then flushed, as he remembered he was only supposed to be guarding the Queen, not speaking to her, a flogging offence under Rallora's King Tolbert. 'Sorry, your majesty.'

'No need to apologise. I am happy to take advice from anyone. Especially if that person has any idea what is going on!' Merren said exasperatedly.

'It is the Dragon Sword, in part, but more than that. Aroaril has brought this together, so that everyone can do their part,' Nott declared. 'He has done all He can; now it is up to you. Up to swords, courage and a little magic to win the day.'

Merren looked at the old priest suspiciously. Was it Aroaril's doing, or Nott's doing? He certainly seemed to have been pulling the strings of many people. What else had he been up to?

Nott turned to her and smiled, as if reading her thoughts.

'All is ready, now you must seize the opportunity you have been given,' he announced.

Martil looked down at the Ralloran battle line, then at the thickly packed Norstaline infantry.

'They will be able to outflank us, and there's still so many of them,' he stated.

'Look! They're moving!' Barrett pointed.

The thick column was adjusting, re-forming before their eyes.

'They're going to attack the archers and conscripts first, wipe them out and then come for us,' Martil realised. 'They must fear an attack from the rear if they leave the archers alone.'

'We have to help them!' Merren declared.

Martil nodded. He had a duty to the men on this hilltop, the men he had led into the horror of Bellic. But he also had a duty to those men down there, men he had put in this position because of the Dragon Sword. Sacrificing himself was not an option now. If he died, the Dragon Sword would be useless, and where would that leave all those men? He knelt down beside Karia.

'I am going to fight now, but I will be back,' he told her. 'I promise.'

She gave him her biggest hug, then a kiss on the cheek.

'I know. I'll be watching you and protecting you,' she said seriously.

He grinned. He was suddenly filled with the conviction that he was safe that day. He knew it was foolish but, after being forced to say goodbye to Karia — and then have the Dragon Sword come alive — he could not stop the sudden happiness bubbling through him, wiping away everything that had happened that morning. He changed the Dragon Sword into the left hand, drawing his old sword in the right hand. 'And see, I'm taking your advice.'

He saluted Merren.

'Your majesty, when we have Gello's infantry fully committed, I shall signal for the cavalry to attack —' Martil began.

'Then we shall send Rocus, Sendric and Conal in to finish them off,' Merren declared. 'Go now!'

Gello's infantry were almost ready to advance, and Martil, distracted by this change in plans, did not explain that Barrett had to give the order. He hurried to where Nerrin and the confused Rallorans waited.

'This is where things change from Mount Shadar!' Martil cried. 'This time we come to the rescue, and win it! Those men down there are risking their lives to fight for us. We will not let them die in vain! Follow me!'

They let out a huge roar as he led them downhill.

'Nerrin, take command of the left flank — don't let them get around us! We'll march in line, then change to wedge formation just as we reach them, push through and link with the archers.'

'Yes, sir! Are we really going to win?'

'Better than that, we're going to destroy Gello!' Martil laughed. He felt as if he could do anything now.

Heading downhill, the tendency was to speed up, but Martil tried to make sure the men did not become ragged — they had to hit Gello's men together, or they would break upon the bigger, deeper shield wall.

'They love Berellians — so let's show them what we do with Berellians!' he bellowed.

Heath received the orders from Gello with some relief. He had been afraid the King would want him to still attack the Rallorans first, and expose his back to the conscripts and archers. But he was confident he had more than enough men to smash the fools to his left, then destroy the Rallorans. Finally, he would not have to worry about anyone but his own men. And he would show the King just why he should be the senior captain, not Feld.

'Wheel left! Shields up! We'll push them off the hill, onto our waiting cavalry below,' Heath ordered.

It was not a particularly tricky manoeuvre, but was made more difficult by the steady rain of arrows, meaning they had to do everything with shields held high. Just when the ranks had aligned and dressed themselves, changing around so they could march left, Heath glanced up to where the Rallorans waited — only to see they were not waiting, but marching downhill!

Health reacted again, transforming what had been a square of men into a right angle, forming one shield wall with two regiments to hold off the Rallorans, while a second shield wall would crush the archers and conscripts.

'We will outflank the Rallorans on our right, so wrap around their flank and start rolling it up,' he declared.

This promised to be a hard fight, but he had most of the advantages — the biggest being sheer weight of numbers.

'Attack!' he bawled.

'I think they're going to attack us first,' Kay declared, as the red-clad infantry began to shift positions.

Kay had introduced Hutter and Kettering to his officers, while the archers, criminals and militia furiously ripped off their red surcoats, partly because they didn't want to be mistaken for Gello's men, partly because they wanted to show that they no longer fought for him. They all wore the sleeveless boiled leather jerkin, giving them a uniform look, although many of the men had bare arms, or just a grimy undershirt, under the jerkin. Kay was surprised to see one plump little man wearing an orange shirt with puffed sleeves. If he had had the time, he would have asked about it.

'What about the Rallorans? Will they come and help us?' Cropper asked.

'Doesn't matter if they do — Gello's got enough men to hold off the Rallorans until we're dead, then he can turn on them,' Kay shrugged.

'Then we should attack!' Kettering declared.

'But they've got armour and shields — we've just got swords,' Hutter pointed out. 'We'll break on their shield wall.'

'We can open up their shield wall for you but unless those Rallorans have some other plan in mind, we're going to lose,' Cropper warned. 'We don't have many arrows left.'

'You break that shield wall and we'll do the rest,' Kettering said confidently.

'We will?' Hutter muttered.

'Did you really expect to come out of this alive?'

Hutter grimaced, then admitted, 'I had hoped.'

'If we can link with the Rallorans, anything is possible,' Cropper pointed out.

Kay found himself grinning. 'I think we're all mad.'

'Aye, well, seems it's catching,' Hutter murmured.

Kay clapped him on the shoulder. 'Run at the shield wall. Just before you get there, we'll punch holes in it — you have to get inside those holes before they can close, or you're all dead.'

'We will.' Kettering nodded.

'Tell me, what crime were you arrested for and

what did you do before, to inspire a regiment of criminals?' Cropper asked.

'They're not all criminals. Many are like me: accused of a murder I did not commit, and plucked from my quiet life.' Kettering hesitated, then shrugged. 'If you must know, I was the under-manager for a big inn at Wollin, in charge of looking after guests and hiring bards.'

'Really?' Kay could not help but ask.

'Really,' Kettering growled.

'Aroaril knows what you would have achieved if you were the full manager then.' Cropper smiled, offering his hand.

After a moment, Kettering took it.

'If you had told me I would be trusting my life to a pack of chocolate soldiers and criminals before today, I would have said you were mad,' Kay offered.

'You still are,' Hutter declared. He and Kay shook hands.

'Do you think they will be able to hold the open flank?' Merren asked, worried.

Kesbury looked around, then realised she must be talking to him.

'It will be difficult, my Queen. They have a great advantage of numbers ...'

'That is what I thought.' Merren nodded. 'I am safe here. Take your squad and Barrett to help them.'

'But, my Queen—'

'Sergeant, you and ten men could mean the difference between victory and defeat down there. But if Gello's men break through, do you think your squad can protect me from regiments of infantry and cavalry?'

Kesbury shook his head wordlessly.

'Then go! Barrett, you too! Your magic could prove the difference!'

Barrett, who had been talking with Tiera, half turned to tell Merren how only he could get Rocus to charge, but Tiera leaned forwards and kissed him.

'Be safe,' she told him, barely able to meet his eyes.

Barrett flushed, and all thought beyond wanting to impress her fled from him. Hefting his wizard's staff, which had seemingly grown of its own volition to a massive size, he raced downhill to catch up with Kesbury.

'Stay close to me,' Kettering told Leigh, Hawke and a visibly shaking Menner.

'We're not going anywhere — we know you're the deadliest man on the battlefield.' Leigh smiled, although his eyes were darting left and right.

'We don't stop until we reach the other side, or we're dead! Everyone understand!' Kettering ordered, and received grim nods from almost all the men in reply.

Interspersed with his men were Cropper's archers, who would loose arrows at the last moment to disrupt the advancing shield wall. Kettering did not even bother looking at them. He just drew his sword. The part of him that had once struggled to deal with even mild customer complaints looked at the wall of steel and wood marching towards him and quailed — but that was a tiny part now.

'Charge!' he screamed, and broke into a run.

On edge already, the massed criminals roared and raced after him.

Kettering fixed his gaze on a tall infantryman

directly in front of him. The man wore a shining steel helm with a thick nose guard, a long mail shirt that stretched to his knees, and polished leather boots with strips of metal riveted to every side. His heavy wooden shield, with a thick metal boss in the middle, was painted with Gello's crossed-swords badge and had an arrow sticking out of the top. He had a short, wide stabbing sword in his hand and a longer one at his waist.

In contrast, Kettering wore simple leather boots, woollen trews, a thick leather jerkin with a dirty cotton vest beneath and he carried just the one sword. But he had spent an hour working on it with a whetstone and he was ready to let his anger free.

He seemed to fly across the grass separating him from the infantryman, who, along with his fellows, had stopped his advance and braced himself, adding his shield to an unbroken wall.

'Bastards!' Kettering screamed, drawing out the word until it was almost a battle cry.

He could hear men shouting, screaming, yelling to either side of him, trying to work up the guts to charge into that wall of metal and death.

Kettering saw the shield wall seem to dip down, as the men behind it braced for the impact, and he lengthened his strides, so he would be able to leap the last yard into the attack.

'Hold! Hold hard!'

He could see the colour of their eyes now, peeking over the shields. Time seemed to slow, and he saw the sharp sword in the infantryman's hand, saw it draw back, ready for the thrust that would try to impale him.

Then arrows whipped past him, one stirring his hair it passed so close.

Spaces suddenly appeared in the line, as skilled archers put arrows into eye sockets and tiny gaps between shields. Men on either side of Kettering's target fell, the one on the right dragging down the infantryman's shield as he went, and causing him to stagger slightly.

Howling with triumph, Kettering leaped high and slammed his sword down, driving it over the shield and into the man's throat. Blood fountained and Kettering dragged his blade clear of the dying man.

Beside him, Hawke used the body of a fallen infantryman as a springboard, propelling himself into the air to slam down on the second rank, his weight and momentum sending men in all directions. A red-clad infantryman raised his sword to kill Hawke but Kettering was quicker, thrusting his sword into the back of the infantryman's neck.

'Killer!' Leigh brought his sword down, deflecting a blow meant for Kettering's back.

Snarling his hatred at the men who had ruined his life, Kettering slashed at the soldier's face, feeling the shock as his blade ripped out the man's eye before it rammed into his nose guard.

More of Kettering's men arrived. Hawke surged to his feet, picked up a fallen infantryman and hurled the body into the other ranks, opening the hole wider.

Kettering wiped blood from his face with his free hand and slashed furiously at an infantryman, keeping him occupied while Leigh stepped around the shield and hacked him down.

All the momentum was with the criminals. The first line of Gello's infantry had been pierced and the lightly armoured criminals poured in, making up in ferocity what they lacked in skill.

'Kill them all!' Kettering screamed.

But while they were savaging the first rank and attacking the second rank, the third rank was untouched, and holding firm. Although archers were dropping arrows on them, those behind had their shields up. Criminals who tried to attack found their blows blocked by one or more shields, then the short, stabbing swords licked out and claimed another life.

'Come on!' Kettering hurled himself into the attack, using his sword to try and haul down a shield and expose the man behind it.

Hutter and Turen fought back to back. Hutter had led the charge, ruthlessly crushing the fear he had felt and refusing to think of his family as he raced towards the imposing defensive line. Then the arrows had whipped in, gouging holes in the infantry. Hutter sidestepped a lone infantryman's lunge and rammed his sword through the man's mail and into the flesh beyond, feeling the steel grate on bone. The man shook like a fish on a line, mouth open in a silent scream until Hutter twisted his wrist to break the suction of flesh around the blade and hauled it out of the man's body. He bent and picked up a fallen shield, using it to deflect an attack, then slammed the heavy metal boss into an infantryman's head, hearing it ring on the metal nose guard over the sickening sound of breaking bones.

He spared a glance over his shoulder to see Turen had picked up a shield as well. 'Stay with me!'

Together they isolated an infantryman; Turen's sword bit into his leg, then Hutter finished him off with a cut to the neck.

'Get their shields! Hold them off! Wait for the Rallorans!' he yelled at the surrounding men.

He knew he could not win this battle by himself; all he had to do was keep the infantry back. But the infantry were not content to sit back and wait — more were pushing into the attack by the moment. Even with the help of borrowed shields, the militia was hard-pressed to stop the advance.

'Hold them!' Hutter said again, more in hope than anything else.

'Wedge formation!' Martil bellowed, waving to his right and his left, when the Rallorans were just twenty paces from the infantry line. He had deliberately shortened his line, risking being outflanked, so he could add weight to his charge. He was trying to push his way through a shield line twice as thick as his own, and Gello's men were braced, shields locked tight — but Martil knew how to break them.

With his best men as the points all along the front of the Ralloran line, little wedges of men were formed. Rather than the two shield walls meeting directly, where each man would be fighting against two or three opponents, both sides working together to hold their line, the Rallorans could now put their best men against his opposite in Gello's line. Martil knew, with the two men just behind him holding off the ones to either side of his target, he could isolate the man he faced. And, once through the first line, the wedge shape of each point would widen and hold the break. They had used this method countless times, and the men at the tip of each wedge were his best fighters, every one of them big and skilled, several even carrying long-handled axes for just this task.

Martil was not carrying a shield, which could have been a disadvantage in close-quarter fighting.

But he trusted the men behind him to protect his sides — and he had the Dragon Sword, which was better than any shield. He focused on the man in front of him. He could not see much of him, except that he was a tall warrior.

'Come and die!'

'Barbarian bastards!'

'Let's see how you fight against real men, not women and children!'

'Death to the Butchers of Bellic!'

Martil could hear the insults that Gello's men were screaming, but he ignored them — they were nothing compared to what the Berellians had screamed. The Rallorans did not answer back; they had found a silent, implacable approach was more effective in throwing fear into the enemy. Unlike Gello's men, they had fought in enough battles not to need to inspire themselves by shouting insults at the enemy.

Closer and closer they marched, and Martil could see, by the way the men in front of him kept touching and retouching shields, that they were scared. After being so sure he was going to die that day, he felt invincible. He knew he was going to be able to cut through this line and throw Gello's infantry into confusion, force them to commit all their reserves to stopping him — and he knew that a cavalry attack then would finish them off.

'Now!' he roared, and ran the last few paces.

He just had time to see the frightened blue eyes of the man he faced, before he brought the Dragon Sword around in a massive blow that sheared not just through the top of his target's shield, but the shields to either side. The infantryman had time to register that he had no shield left before Martil's other sword lanced into his throat.

Martil hurdled his body, shoulder-charging the man on his right, while the Dragon Sword cut through another shield, as well as the arm holding it, in front of him. An instant later, the Rallorans behind him slammed into the hole he had created; the men without shields died a moment later, then the Rallorans stepped close to Martil, protecting him as the second line of Gello's infantry tried to close the gap.

But even though Gello's men had the numbers, this was the type of fighting that could not be taught on the training field; you learned it the hard way, or you died. You were close enough to smell the breath of the man you killed, see the fear in his eyes, hear his desperate breathing as you beat him down with your sword.

More than that, Martil could smell that the man he faced had pissed himself in fright. But he did not let pity stop him. The Dragon Sword sliced his opponent's shield in half from top to bottom, lopping off the man's left hand at the wrist as it did so. Screaming, the man dropped his sword and clutched at the stump. Martil slammed the pommel of his other sword into his helmet, then stepped over the writhing body to face the next man.

All along the line it was a similar story, although Martil had cut further into the line than anyone else. The men with the axes had used them to haul down shields, then cut down the men behind. Others had used the opposite method: instead of pulling down the shield, they had used their superior strength and skills to knock the shield up, then cut underneath with a sword. Either way, the result was the same. The first line of the infantry had been cut in a dozen places; the gaps were being widened all the time as the wedges pushed deeper into the line. Gello's men were facing attacks from two directions, from the front and side, and they did not stand a chance.

Martil knew the only point of danger was his line's open flank. He stepped back, allowing other men to take the lead. He had done his job, now he needed to see what was going on.

Nerrin had held back Dunner and a score of men to help seal the open flank, but was relieved to see Kesbury, his squad and Barrett arrive to help.

'We'll form up at a right angle to the end of the line, so there's no open side. But we'll be glad of any help you can give us, sir,' Nerrin explained.

'I think I can show you — and Gello's dogs — just how a wizard can fight,' Barrett promised. The thought that Martil had now unlocked the true power of the Dragon Sword was a disquieting one. It looked like Martil was going to be the hero of this battle. Well, Barrett was determined to show them — especially Tiera — just how valuable he was.

He was surprised to see the men on the far end of the line stagger as the two shield walls came together with a massive crash. But the Rallorans kept going forwards, while Gello's men shuddered as their line was pierced.

However, that only helped the men at the open end of the line. As the Rallorans pushed forwards, Gello's men, who outflanked them, naturally wrapped around the end, and in an instant Nerrin and his men were fighting hard, and even more of Gello's infantry were threatening to get around the open end.

Then Barrett struck.

His staff, enlarged and propelled by arms magically strengthened, swept through the air. With each stroke, two or three men were sent flying, screaming through the air, to land among their fellows and cause even more disruption and damage. Behind each blow was Barrett's anger and frustration, and he wielded that staff with speed and precision. Not one of the infantry got close enough to even try to land a blow on him. With a final swing, he sent two men soaring ten feet into the air, where they thumped into a squad of others, sending them all rolling back down the hill.

That was enough for Gello's men. The pressure on the open flank was gone, as Barrett only had to poke his staff in their direction and men scrambled over each other to get away.

'We needed a few wizards like you in the Ralloran Wars,' Nerrin said admiringly. Blood had splashed his mail, while a pair of his men were lying behind the line, being helped by their friends.

Barrett let his staff reduce in size with a final flourish and wiped sweat off his brow.

'It was nothing.'

'Here they come again!' someone shouted.

Kay sent another arrow arcing through the sky, and cursed. It was no good. He could not direct his arrows where the fighting was, for fear of hitting one of Kettering's or Hutter's men. And, everywhere else, Gello's men knew to keep their shields up. Worse, he could see the criminals and militiamen being pushed back everywhere, leaving dead and wounded behind. The archers were not helping them. Worse, they were almost all out of arrows.

'Sir, what are your orders?' Ryder asked, seeing Kay's bow hanging loosely from his hand.

Kay dropped his bow.

'Draw swords! Attack!' he roared, charging forwards.

Heath was desperately trying to gauge where his men were best needed. The Rallorans were proving formidable opponents, as he had feared. They had cut their way through the best part of a regiment and were starting on another. On the other fronts, things were much better — his men had repelled the criminals, while the militia were not going anywhere. No, the Rallorans were the only concern. He had half a regiment in reserve, held back just in case of cavalry attack from the right. He had heard the Berellian, Ezok, explain how the Rallorans had used that tactic with such success and he was scared of what even a small cavalry force could do to him. But he was also worried about what the Rallorans could do. He had hoped to be able to outflank them, and take the pressure off that way. But, apparently, the Rallorans had the Queen's Magician working for them. There was no easy way around them.

'Sir! We have to stop the Rallorans! They're cutting the men to pieces!' one of his senior lieutenants screamed.

Heath nodded. The decision had been made for him. He could not delay any longer.

'Lieutenant Pointer, take our reserve companies and attack the Rallorans's open flank. I don't care if we have to choke the magician with the bodies of an entire company, I want those bastards forced back!'

Heath watched the reserves swing out to the right and march swiftly into position. Surely even a wizard like Barrett could not stop that many men.

* * *

Martil saw the new force swinging out to attack his open flank and nodded acknowledgement to himself. The pressure his Rallorans were applying to Gello's infantry had to force his opponent into a different approach — and this was the obvious solution. By attacking Martil's open flank, he would force the Rallorans to pull back. But Martil had the perfect counter to this — Rocus and his cavalry companies. In truth they were not real cavalry, but they were men with swords mounted on cavalry horses, and several hundred of them smashing into the back of the infantry phalanx would end this battle. Or so he hoped.

He signalled to his standard-bearer, who began to wave his flag furiously. Up on the hill, Merren's standard bearer dipped her flag to show they had received the message.

Still, he had to hold off those infantry until Rocus could come and save him. He grabbed a lieutenant, who was catching his breath in the rear rank after coming out of the front rank.

'Lieutenant Baker, isn't it?' he asked.

'Yes, sir!' The officer, whose shield was dented and his mail spattered with blood, straightened.

'Baker, get every second man in your company and follow me,' Martil ordered.

Merren saw Martil lead half a company of men across the field to reinforce where Barrett, helped by Dunner and Kesbury, held off Gello's infantry — and were about to be swamped by hundreds more.

She grabbed Romon, who was still waiting his chance to go and help the wounded.

'Find Lieutenant Rocus and Count Sendric. Tell them the Queen orders them to charge,' she told him.

'Yes, my Queen.' Romon nodded, then dashed away.

Merren turned back to the battle, and tried to control her nerves. Once the cavalry was attacking, she would feel better. Or perhaps worse. It was hard not to think of the men she knew down there, as well as the ones who had changed to her side, and what was happening to them.

Kettering bellowed with rage, daring the infantry to come closer. Leigh, who had taken a sword thrust to the leg, lay on the ground screaming, while Hawke was bleeding from several cuts, although his sword was bloodied to the hilt. Kettering knew too many of his men were either dead or wounded, that courage and hatred had kept them in the fight long after they should have run. But their swords had become blunted by smashing into mail and shields — and a dull sword just bounced off a mail coat. Now he, Hawke and Leigh were surrounded and surely moments from death. Even as he thought that, he saw the spears reaching to claim Hawke and he felt a moment's regret that he would not gain revenge on the Berellians.

Then an unearthly scream made everyone turn their heads.

A small figure, wearing a ridiculously puffed orange shirt under his leather jerkin, burst through the infantry ranks. It was Menner. A massive swing of his sword killed one man; the backswing chopped down another. Two others tried to stop him but, in a blur of movement, he drove them backwards, hacking and slashing like a madman.

Before Kettering and Hawke could reach him, an infantryman rammed a spear through his chest.

Part horrified, part astonished, Kettering watched as Menner merely reached out to grab the haft and trap it inside his body. Time seemed to slow, and everyone, including the infantry in red, watched as the little dressmaker hauled himself along the shaft, spending his lifeblood as he did so, until he was close enough to ram his sword into his attacker's neck.

In that moment Kettering heard a roar from behind but dared not turn his head. He saw the surrounding infantry back away and brace themselves, as a flood of men in leather jerkins, waving swords, rushed past him to crash into the shield wall.

'It's Kay!' Hawke cried.

Kettering saw the ranger captain snatch up a fallen shield, slam into an infantryman, then hack down at the man's leg, bringing him down.

'Get Leigh away from the fight and strap up his leg so he doesn't bleed to death,' he told Hawke.

'What about Menner?' Hawke looked up from where the dressmaker, his trousers still stained by fear, his bright orange shirt now red, lay entwined in death with the three huge infantrymen he had killed. 'He saved my life!' The bearded criminal sounded as though he could not believe such a thing was possible. 'He was pissing himself with fright, but he saved us!'

Kettering sighed. He was covered in blood, of which only a small amount was his. Months ago, in another life, he might have debated what this meant, how a man could be driven to do mad, impossible things in war. But he did not have the words, just a roaring anger. He bent down and picked up a fresh sword, a sharp sword.

'We can't do anything for him now. But neither will we forget him,' he merely said.

Hawke reached down to help Leigh, and Kettering was surprised to see tears running down the face of the brutal killer.

'I wish I could tell him ...' he grunted, but could say no more.

'He already knows,' Kettering told him, then returned to the fight.

The addition of the archers held the infantry's advance, and even pushed them back slightly, but the shield wall was holding firm against an increasingly weary attack. Kettering was too angry to feel tired, but not so angry that he could not hope the Rallorans and the Queen had some better plan than this.

Hutter was not sure at what point he had given up trying to win this battle and instead decided just to stay alive. He thanked the nameless sergeant who had made it a personal mission to get him fit again. Without his cruelty, there was no way Hutter would still be on his feet. As it was, the breath was sawing harshly in his throat, his right arm and shoulder were on fire and his shield arm was bruised and battered. But he had managed to keep Turen alive as well, so he counted that as a victory.

The militia had formed a rudimentary shield wall, but too few of the front rank had shields, and the second rank had none. So the men in the front row faced an ugly choice: keep their shield high and risk the thrust underneath, the one that ripped into the groin or disembowelled, or keep the shield lower and expose their heads to an overhead cut. The best Hutter could say was that they were pretty much holding their ground — although it was costing them many good men.

Thoughts of seeing his family again, or victory, were long gone. Hutter was just concentrating on surviving the next blow aimed at him.

Romon found the cavalry waiting, out of sight, although formed up ready for the charge. Out the front waited Count Sendric, Lieutenant Rocus and Conal.

'The Queen orders you to charge!' he puffed, as soon as he ran up to them.

He saw Conal and Rocus exchange a look, but thought nothing of it.

'Thank you. You may leave it with us and return to the Queen now,' Conal told him.

Romon nodded and ran away, eager to get back.

'What do we do now?' Rocus asked, as soon as he had gone.

'Do? We attack!' Sendric snorted.

'It's not that easy. Martil swore both Rocus and myself to ignore the Queen's orders to charge. He told us to wait for an order from Barrett. Barrett would know when Martil had completed his mission, and when — and if — we should charge,' Conal explained.

'If this is one of your jests …' Sendric threatened. 'It is not the time!'

'It is no jest. Martil told me he planned to sacrifice himself to save the lives of these men. If we go out there, we will betray what he died for,' Conal said sadly.

Sendric just stared at him. 'So his plan to kill Gello — he doesn't intend to return? The Queen would never have agreed to that!'

'Exactly. So we must give him the time he needs. We cannot let his sacrifice be in vain. We have to trust Barrett,' Conal told him. 'He will let us know. Martil made me swear on my life not to lead these men out to their deaths. I cannot break that oath.'

Sendric sighed. 'I hope you are right,' he said finally.

'Just trust in Barrett. We have to do that,' Rocus repeated.

Barrett sent a pair of men flying. They crashed into others following them, knocking more down. He wiped sweat away from his brow in between blows, while Martil darted forwards on his left, the Dragon Sword slicing away swords and shields — and sometimes the flesh beyond it. The pair of them were on the far end of the Ralloran line; on their inside, Nerrin, Dunner and Kesbury were rallying the shield wall against the fierce attack of Gello's infantry. Lieutenant Baker was lying behind the line, dying from a sword blow to the head.

Martil had been furious to see Kesbury at first, demanding to know why he was not guarding the Queen. But when Kesbury had explained why he was there, he had grudgingly agreed to let him stay. Now he was glad of it. Kesbury had always been a good man with a spear, and he had found one from somewhere. Not only was the spearhead red, but half the shaft was soaked in blood. Standing at the end of the line next to Barrett, Kesbury had built up a small mound of bodies in front of him to further block the advance of the infantry. But the enemy was threatening to go further up the hill, right around the line.

Barrett gestured with his free hand, and the grass at the weak end of the line, the open end, sprang into the air, growing twice the height of a man, forming an impenetrable barrier. Some of the infantry hacked at it then, frustrated, backed away. The only way forwards was through the Rallorans.

'Where in Aroaril's name is that cavalry! Surely Rocus got the order from the Queen by now! What is he playing at?' Barrett gasped, leaning on his massive staff as he sucked in air.

Martil sliced off the sword hand of an infantryman with the Dragon Sword and then opened the throat of the man next to him with his ordinary blade. Momentarily free of attackers, he stepped back a pace — and turned as the import of Barrett's words registered.

'He won't attack! I ordered both Rocus and Conal not to charge, on their lives, until you told them to!' he cried in horror.

Barrett gaped at him. 'I forgot!' he gasped.

'Go!' Martil cried, furious at himself for not remembering either. He had spoken to Kesbury but hadn't given Barrett a second thought! The joy, the certainty that had filled him until now just leaked away.

But the attackers flooded forwards, refusing to stop, perhaps sensing the wizard was tiring.

Desperate now, Martil changed hands, and instead of disarming and wounding men, the Dragon Sword began tearing the life from them. He did not want to do it, but men's lives were at stake.

'Get back! Tell Rocus to charge!' Martil commanded Barrett, then turned back to the fight.

The mage turned away and began to stumble uphill, but the exertion of fighting non-stop had drained him, and the hill seemed to get both higher and steeper. He sank to his knees and toppled over.

*　*　*

434

Gello surveyed the battle with satisfaction. He had been concerned at the progress of the Rallorans, but their advance now seemed to have stopped, while their open flank was under extreme pressure. Soon they would break, and Heath's men could begin rolling up the Ralloran line. As to the other side of the battle, the conscripts were no more than a nuisance. Once the Rallorans were destroyed, they could be outflanked and snapped up. It was only a matter of time now.

'May I congratulate your majesty?' Ezok said smoothly. 'It seems you will shortly have a famous victory!'

Ezok was pleased to see it had not been an easily won fight. Gello's infantry, ever the backbone of an army, was being gutted up there. Exactly what he had hoped.

'You may congratulate me,' Gello agreed. 'I only wish I could see my dirty little cousin's terror as her foul trick has failed!'

Merren listened to Romon's report with a smile, then sent him down to help the priests, who were administering to the wounded. She was all alone on the hill now, sitting on her horse, Martil's Tomon, with just her standard bearer for company. Karia had been sent back, where she could not see the bloody battle. Any moment now, she told herself. Rocus will lead the cavalry out and then my cousin will watch his foul plans crushed!

But no cavalry was appearing from her left. Surely by now they should be riding out! How long did it take to organise a cavalry charge?

She waited and waited, expecting that at any moment, the first riders would appear. But with every passing heartbeat, her fear and concern grew. What was going on?

She glanced down to where Gello's infantry seemed to be pushing her forces back in every direction. As she watched, Barrett staggered away from the battleline, fell to his knees, then hauled himself up, trying — and mostly failing — to walk up the hill.

Merren felt an icy fist close around her heart. Something was terribly wrong here. She turned her horse's head and galloped across the hill, her standard-bearer following.

Heath could not restrain a smile as he watched his men's progress. True, he had suffered heavy casualties, but he could feel the mood of the battle now. The men he was facing, even the Rallorans, were worried, and perhaps a little desperate. His superior numbers, armour and weapons were beginning to tell. He could almost taste the rewards Gello would shower upon him.

'We have them!' he told his sergeants. 'When they break, there is to be no mercy! Kill every man, and especially every wounded traitor we find!'

Kay wished he had spent more time training with the sword. Working with the bow had always been his priority — and a natural one, at that. An archer needed to practise for ten years to become skilled and even then you had to use your bow every day if you were to survive a battle. But all that left little time for swordplay. Kay had mastered the basics, of course, but hacking straw dummies was a far cry from this.

He slashed furiously at the head of an infantryman, who blocked the blow on his shield, forcing Kay to bring his sword around frantically so the next infantryman along did not stab him.

'Stay back!'

Kettering hauled Kay away, saving him from a disembowelling blow.

'They won't follow us here, not yet,' Kettering explained.

'Here' was the charnel house of bodies where they stood. Infantry, criminals and archers lay thick on the ground, moaning, screaming, sobbing, begging and wailing. If the infantry tried to pursue them, their careful ranks would break apart on the uncertain footing and the criminals would be on them like wolves onto a pack of sheep. It had happened three times already but it seemed the infantry had learned their lesson and were keeping their ranks.

'They're just holding us here — why?' Kay panted, massaging his right shoulder.

'They just want to keep us back while they destroy the Rallorans — then they can clear us away,' Kettering growled.

'We have to help them!'

'We've done all we can,' Kettering told him.

Martil stood, Dragon Sword in hand, daring men to attack him. All those who tried were met with the Dragon Sword, which cut through their shields, sword, metal and flesh as if it were nothing. Those who could not face him were driven in, where Dunner and Kesbury stood shoulder to shoulder, spear and sword flashing.

Martil tore into the men in front of him. He had brought his Rallorans to this; worse, his orders to Rocus and Conal were now causing deaths, not saving lives. His anguish gave strength to his skills.

Enemies seemed to move as if they were wading through thick mud, while his next move seemed laughably obvious. The bodies that were piling up before him were forming their own barrier now.

The noise was almost indescribable. Men screamed insults at each other, hacked and slashed at heads and groins, thumped shields and clawed at their opponents, most of whom were only inches away. They stumbled over corpses, slipped in entrails, brains, blood and shit and trod on screaming wounded as they sought to stay upright and alive. Without Barrett's grass wall to their left, they would be dead by now. But even with it, their time was limited. For every infantryman who fell, there were two to take his place. For every Ralloran who fell, there was just a gap.

Romon vomited. He straightened, wiping his mouth, then took hold of the screaming Ralloran and began to drag him over to where Bishop Milly, bloodied to her elbows, was healing men as fast as they could be brought to her. The Ralloran had taken a sword blow under the shield that had torn through his mail and ripped into his groin. Blood spurted as he writhed and screamed, intestines poking through the gash in his armour.

Romon had tears in his eyes as he hauled the man across the bloodied grass. Bishop Milly could heal anything, but would this man even want such a wound healed? Would it not be a greater kindness to let him die? Romon had read — and performed — just about every saga written. None of them talked of this. He had never thought to see men soiling themselves in terror, weeping with fear, begging for mercy, for their mothers, for an end to their pain.

He had only performed verses about men wielding swords and singing as they died. Not slipping on entrails and having a blade rip into their vitals, leaving them screaming and bleeding, and begging for death. He had always wanted to find the truth but now he held it in his hands, he wished he had never seen it. Grunting with the effort, he gripped the man under the shoulders and pulled him to the pile of heaving, moaning men waiting to be helped by the priests.

Merren could barely speak when she saw Rocus, Conal and the other men just sitting on their horses, waiting patiently but doing nothing.

'What are you doing?' she bellowed, as she rode up to them.

Rocus and Conal exchanged guilty looks, while Sendric just opened and closed his mouth.

'There are men dying out there, and if you do not charge, we shall lose the battle!' she shouted, reining in Tomon in a spray of dirt, right by them.

'Is Martil … back yet, your majesty?' Conal asked carefully.

'What has that to do with anything?' Merren almost screamed at them. 'You need to charge! Now!'

'But has Barrett returned …?' Conal began.

Merren controlled herself with only the greatest of difficulty.

'What are you blathering about? I tell you men are dying out there and you want to ask about Martil and Barrett! Why in Aroaril's name are you refusing to follow my order?'

Rocus groaned. 'I'm sorry, your majesty, but Martil made me swear …'

'I am sorry.' Conal bowed his head, speaking at the same time. 'But Martil …'

Merren stared at them for a moment in stunned silence. In a flash, she saw she could take them out to the lip of the valley, show them the battle below and explain what was going on. Obviously Martil had planned something noble and stupid, and the Dragon Sword working had thrown all that into confusion. But she also knew there was no time. Too many men were dying out there and she could not have that.

Rocus wore two swords, a short one for fighting on foot, and a longer one, for horseback. She leaned across and drew his shorter sword before he even reacted.

She stood up in the stirrups, waving the sword so that every man in the column was looking at her.

'There are men out there dying for me. I am going to save them, even if I go alone!' she roared, then turned Tomon and thumped her heels into his ribs.

Tomon burst into a gallop and she tore up the valley, sword held high, her fine mail coat shining silver in the sun, her standard-bearer desperately trying to keep up.

Conal and Rocus exchanged horrified glances.

'What are we waiting for!' Sendric bellowed.

'The Queen!' they yelled, and frantically rowelled spurs in their horses' flanks.

In an instant the entire column was at gallop, men racing each other to reach the Queen, to get in front of her, protect her and prove they were worthy.

Gello stood and stretched luxuriously. The Rallorans were providing dogged resistance but he could see their lines starting to bend backwards. Any time now, one man would break and then they would all follow. Success was here at last. The victory would be his, and never again would the memory of the Dragon Sword rise to humiliate him.

'I want the cavalry ready,' he ordered. 'Not one man of theirs is to leave this battlefield alive. And I want a few companies ready to take the town of Sendric. I want to sleep there tonight, ready to be entertained by my cousin's death on the morrow.'

'Sire!' Feld shouted.

Gello turned swiftly, thinking the Rallorans had finally broken, only to see a pair of riders appear out of the valley to the right of the hill. He stared, then laughed. One was his cousin, waving a sword, the other her standard-bearer.

'Who does she think she is?' he sneered. 'A battlefield is no place for a woman — although it'll be useful to have one like her available after the battle, eh?'

Everyone laughed loudly as Gello threw back his head and roared out his triumph.

Then the laughter died away.

Boiling out from the valley, riding as if they were fleeing from Zorva himself, came cavalry. Hundreds of them, screaming and waving swords

'The Queen!'

Their battle cry seemed to shake the very hill and silence the desperate battle as they charged onwards.

Gello's mouth sagged open in horror and he stared desperately at the men around him. None could meet his eyes.

Rocus and Conal realised at once that things had changed dramatically from what Martil had told them. The battle in front of them was right across the hill. The men in red were stretched out fighting men in blue and others just in brown leather.

They also saw Merren was galloping straight for the heart of the red army. Unspoken between them was the thought they had to get in front of her. But she was showing no signs of slowing down.

'You take the right, I'll take the Queen!' Rocus roared.

Conal knew there was no time to argue, so just waved his arm and swung out to the right, to where he could see Martil hacking and slashing furiously, and a thin line of Rallorans in blue holding against a mass of Gello's red.

Rocus leaned low over his horse's head, trying to urge the last bit of speed from the beast. But Merren was lighter and on Tomon, who seemed eager to get into battle. Rocus glanced left and right, to see a pair of men catching up to him; he recognised one of his guardsmen, Wilsen, as well as a man from the debacle at the ranger barracks, Jaret.

'The Queen!' Jaret was howling.

The three of them lashed their horses, urging them forward.

Ahead, a red-clad officer was trying to turn some of his men, trying to form a shield wall. But the speed of the attack was too much, he would not have time to block them.

Merren concentrated on screaming orders and shoving soldiers into a rudimentary line. She was not thinking about what she was doing, or whether she should be doing it. She just knew everything was at stake here — and she was not going to sit back, like some simpering saga heroine, and let men save the day.

Three men in blue managed to get past Tomon and form up in front of her. She recognised Rocus, Jaret and Wilsen but did not check Tomon's charge.

She was conscious of the rest of her men right behind her; she was conscious of every tiny detail in that moment before they struck the line. There was no time for fear — and yet time itself seemed to slow.

The wind was whipping her hair, mud from the horse's hoofs was being flung high, men were screaming, brandishing swords or spears, trying to give themselves courage by the sheer volume of noise they were making. To the right, Merren could see Conal about to lead a company into the men threatening Martil. To her left, down the hill, she fancied she could see Gello, and hoped he was filled with fear. The red lines in front of her were already trying to run, to escape from their doom, and she knew, in that moment, they had won.

With a noise like a hundred blacksmiths striking their anvil at the same time, the cavalry crashed into Gello's infantry.

Rocus, shouting some wordless cry, kicked his horse into a jump that went through a pair of crouching infantrymen. As he soared over their heads, he hacked down with his sword and Merren saw blood spurt high in the air.

The closest infantry were gone in a moment, cut by swords, pierced by spears, ridden over by the big warhorses. These were doing the job they had been trained for: kicking out at any man that came near, and biting at others.

Merren squeezed Tomon's flanks and the big horse gathered himself and jumped, his shoulder smashing an infantryman out of the way. She did not need her sword — her men were all around her, hacking and cutting at anyone who dared to come close.

Strung out, their lines stretched, Heath's men did not stand a chance. The cavalry had unstoppable momentum; they tore into the helpless rear of the red lines and rode them into red ruin.

Merren reined in Tomon and looked for her standard bearer, while Rocus and the others unleashed their anger, fear and frustration. She watched Sendric, sword reddened, slash down again and again at cowering men, his eyes wild.

'Link up with the archers and Rallorans!' she cried, directing men to the attack with her sword.

Martil had almost stopped fighting when he saw Merren gallop out alone, then breathed a sigh of relief when the desperate charge of Rocus and the rest of his men had caught her before she struck the line of infantry.

The pressure on the Ralloran line vanished when Conal's company struck home; the cavalry drove deep into the massed red ranks, hacking and cutting furiously.

Instantly the Rallorans went on the attack, and the men facing them broke, running in all directions.

But there was no escape. The mounted Norstalines were in a grim mood, having thought they had lost the battle for the Queen, and they rode down the running men.

Martil did not join in the pursuit. Instead he began running across the hill, to where he could see the Queen and her standard.

If waking up to see a dead stableboy in front of him and a bloodied knife in his hand was the worst sight of Kettering's life, he decided the cavalry charge across the hill had to be the best.

Even better, the infantry who had killed and wounded so many of his men instantly turned to face the bigger threat.

'For Menner!' Kettering was not even aware he had screamed the words as he led the attack, slamming his sword into the back of an infantryman.

Moments later, the surviving criminals joined him, ripping into their tormentors, cutting them down from behind without mercy.

No troops could stand that, and the red-clad ranks simply dissolved, turning from an unbreakable wall into a rabble in a heartbeat.

Hutter just stayed where he was when the infantry dissolved in front of him. Some of his men, as well as scores of blue-clad Rallorans, were cutting down the slower runners, as well as any who tried to defend themselves. But Hutter did not have the energy. He dropped the shield from his bruised arm, and patted Turen on the shoulder

'You did well, my lad,' he told him.

Turen did not answer. He had taken a spear meant for Hutter in the chest just before the Queen's charge.

Hutter gazed across the closest part of the battlefield at the carpet of bodies, many still writhing and screaming.

'So, this is a victory,' he told Turen numbly.

'We need to recall and re-form!' Martil roared as he raced up to Merren. 'Gello's still got two regiments of cavalry down there!'

Merren, who had been watching with rising jubilation as the red ranks fled downhill pursued by men in blue, waved in acknowledgement. She signalled to her standard-bearer, who fumbled out a horn from his belt and began breathlessly blowing the recall signal.

By now Martil was beside her, reaching up to grab her hand. 'You did it, Merren! You won! You have your throne, you have your country!'

At that moment, he felt his heart would burst when he looked at her. She had saved him, she had won the battle — he wanted nothing more than to take her in his arms.

Merren slid down from Tomon's back, her legs trembling. It was almost too much to take in. She had spent much of her whole life — and certainly the last few years — fighting Gello. Now she had actually defeated him. Everything she had dreamed about, the promises she had made, not just to herself but to the men and women who had suffered and died to bring her to this point, they could come true. All because of this bloodied hillside. It was almost impossible to believe, and certainly overwhelming.

Martil was a grim, but welcome, sight. The Dragon Sword was spotlessly clean, but he was covered in blood — his surcoat was a rusty red, it was in his hair and all over his face and hands. Wordlessly he dropped his swords and held out his arms, and she clung to him, the smell of blood, sweat and leather thick in her nostrils. But it was still a comfort. For a long moment they embraced, hidden from the battlefield by Tomon.

'Merren …' he murmured.

'Do not say anything,' she whispered. 'I need this moment — but I do not know what else we can have.'

He could smell her hair, see a fleck of mud clinging to the top. Carefully, he eased it away and restrained the urge to run his hand through her hair, covered as it was in blood, and worse.

'You won the battle for me. You managed to unlock the Dragon Sword. It saved us all,' she told him.

Martil smiled. 'This was your victory. Not mine. I made so many mistakes! Without you, I would never have been able to use the Dragon Sword. And without your cavalry charge, we would all be dead. You rose above everything to bring us victory. You are the risen Queen.'

She looked at him.

'What next?' she asked.

'We'll go and offer Gello's men their lives in exchange for his. His captains will hand him over when they know we have won.'

'I mean, what next for us. I know those things you said to me — you only said them because you thought you were going to die.'

Martil grinned. 'My apologies, my Queen, for living.'

She slapped his mailed chest with the heel of her hand.

'I am serious!' She softened her voice 'You will be my Champion. If you can be anything else … I cannot say that yet.'

Martil nodded. 'I can wait,' he agreed, hoping that was true.

Merren smiled, and touched his cheek. 'But now I must go. The real work begins.'

'Yes, my Queen.' Martil opened his arms and bowed, retrieving his swords at the same time.

By the time he looked up, she had stalked off, to where Sendric, Rocus, Conal and a score of problems waited for her.

Martil looked downhill. What was Gello doing?

Gello watched with mounting shock, fear and horror as his seemingly victorious army was shattered and sent running for its life. It was the throne room all over again. Six regiments had marched up that hill; little more than one was running down, casting aside shields, weapons, anything that might slow them down and see them killed by the vengeful blue-clad ranks.

He stopped himself from throwing up only with the greatest effort. He had lost an unlosable battle. The last time he had run from the scene of his shame in tears he had been protected by his mother. But she was gone now. He missed her suddenly, and desperately. He wanted someone to tell him what to do, make everything all right again. He was conscious of the deathly silence from those around him, and the feeling of every eye on him. He had to do something! He was Gello the Great!

'Cav—' he tried to speak, felt his throat close up and had to cough before speaking. 'Cavalry! We still have two cavalry regiments! Feld, I think a charge is in order.'

Feld had turned white. 'Sire, the Queen has more than one thousand archers up there. Not one in ten of our men would survive to reach the top trying to gallop up such a hill, over the bodies that would obstruct us.'

'What?' Gello roared, turning on him, glad to find an outlet for his anger and fear. 'Do you dare contradict me?'

Feld straightened. 'I will lead the attack myself. But I tell you now, sire, you will throw away the last of your men on such an attack.'

'He is right!' Ezok declared, and Gello spun again.

The Berellian stalked forwards, until he was close to Gello.

'You have lost this battle, your majesty. But you do not need to lose the war. Berellia stands as your ally in your time of need. If we leave now, we will escape before your cousin can think about pursuing. With the men you have left, along with Berellia's finest, we can return and take back your throne.'

'Leave Norstalos?' Gello said stupidly.

'That is right, your majesty,' Ezok said. 'We shall leave now, but we can return with an army even the Dragon Sword cannot stop!'

Gello looked around desperately, hoping someone else would have a better suggestion. He couldn't lose! He couldn't! He couldn't run away in tears again!

'All is not lost, your majesty,' Prent said suddenly, stepping forwards from the back of the crowd of hangers-on. 'All that has happened is your eyes have been opened to the truth. You did not embrace Zorva, you thought you did not need His help. But Aroaril has helped your enemies and now look at what has happened. In Berellia we can regain our strength, and return in triumph!'

Gello looked around. Nobody else would meet his eye.

'We are outmatched,' Feld said stolidly. 'Cavalry is all we have left, and they cannot beat massed archers. Soon they will stop pursuing our infantry, and think about a bigger prize.'

Almost as soon as he had spoken, the recall signal sounded from up on the hillside.

'They will be marching down here. But we can get back to Norstalos City, secure the treasury, and be on our way to Berellia before they catch us,' Ezok explained.

'The treasury?' Gello was still trying to come to terms with the sudden reversal of his dreams. 'Leave the country? But I can't leave!'

'You have no choice. But we take everything with us. Your cousin will get a country that is broke, its nobility gone, its people fearful of the men who put her back on the throne. When we return, how do you think she is going to stop us?' Ezok demanded.

'And this time we will be ready, really ready, to face the powers working against you,' Prent promised. 'You can still regain your reputation, and your throne. Zorva can save you.'

Gello clutched at that thought the way a drowning man clutches at a rope. He could not lose again! He would not be forever known as a failure. Whatever it would take, whatever it needed to wipe this out, he would do it. Nothing, and no one, mattered.

'Then let us go! The infantry can keep up with us as best they can, if they want to live,' he decided. 'We shall return, and let the world tremble then!'

Ezok and Prent exchanged a look of satisfaction.

Martil watched Gello's men begin to ride away, the surviving infantry clutching on to the stirrups of the cavalry. The Queen had too few cavalry to pursue Gello but, at least with the few men he had left, Gello was almost helpless. Rocus would follow him at a distance, and report back. Wherever he tried to hide, they would catch him.

He left Nerrin in charge of collecting arms and armour; Conal in charge of helping the wounded; Merren to speak to the survivors, especially the conscripts, rangers and archers. He had had enough. He hoped with all his heart this was his last battlefield. Saying goodbye to Karia like that, thinking he was going to live, then thinking he had lost the battle, killed his own men — he could not bear going through that again. Pausing only to pull off his bloodied mail and wash the gore from his face and hands, he hurried up the hill. He was tired, but the thought of seeing her gave new strength to his legs.

'Karia!' he bellowed.

A small figure leaped up and sprinted down the hill, hair flying out behind her, arms held wide.

'Daddy!'

20

Merren almost did not know where to begin.

Gello had arrived back in Norstalos City at dusk four days after the Battle of Pilleth, and stayed just long enough to ransack the palace, strip the treasury and either take or burn every report, tally scroll and account in the place. For good measure, he had had many of his men use her old bedroom as a toilet. Then he had left. Rocus, with two hundred men, had followed at a safe distance, tracking him all the way south to the Berellian border. There, apparently, he had been greeted with open arms. Rocus had reported seeing a grand welcome, with flags, trumpets and speeches.

Merren was torn between anger he had escaped and relief she did not have to lose more men to finish him off. Having him in Berellia was a concern but, for the moment, he could not hope to hurt them. That made it a problem for another day.

And she had more than enough problems.

The entire noble class had gone, for one.

Captain Kay told her Gello was killing many of the nobles, sacrificing them to Zorva. And certainly they had found many bodies. But any that were left had fled with Gello. While there were few that she trusted, they were still the administrators of the country. And, as Gello had disbanded every town and village council, as well as dismissing the entire militia, to say the country was in chaos was almost an understatement.

Kay was restored to commander of the rangers, now down to about six hundred men. Lieutenant Cropper, now Captain Cropper, led the archer regiment, which was a little less.

Conal, with Hutter as his deputy, had been put in charge of the militia, and had begun to bring the country back under the rule of law. More than one hundred and fifty militia had died in the Battle of Pilleth — it was only thanks to the priests that so many others lived. The survivors were all made into officers or sergeants, so at least Merren knew the men in charge of the militia could be trusted.

But it was not just a matter of re-forming the militia.

Nott and Milly were in charge of the church, of course, and were trying to rebuild its numbers and weed out those who had lost Aroaril's favour.

Kettering and his men had all received pardons, and given the option of either returning to their families and former lives, or joining the army. A third of that regiment had died in the battle, and many just wanted to return to their old lives. But most of the remaining real criminals — not just the men arrested for defying Gello — had joined the army, led by Kettering, Hawke and a healed Leigh. For Kettering, it had not been a hard choice.

'I cannot go back to my old life, for I am not that man any more,' he told the Queen. 'But I will serve you still, and faithfully.'

Above all, the greatest problem was the legacy of Gello's short rule. Many people had taken the opportunity of a complete absence of authority to enrich themselves, while others now wanted to gain revenge on those who had supported Gello's reign. And Gello had done his best to persuade the entire country that she was some sort of evil witch who had brought thousands of murdering Rallorans into the country to kill their children.

If she stayed in Norstalos City, and tried to deal with the problems there, she knew they would multiply beyond her control. But her experience in Sendric had shown her that people responded if you went out to speak to them.

She wanted to speak to every person, which was simply impossible. Instead, she hired several of the guilds, asking their members to speak to as many people as possible and send back reports for Sendric and Conal to compile into an accurate picture of what opinion was across the country. She did not have the money for this of course, having instead to promise tax credits to the guilds. But the information she was getting back was priceless.

Naturally there was no better way than hearing it for yourself, which was why Merren also went on a tour of the country, using Barrett's powers to whisk her from town to town, village to village. With her went Father Quiller, to speak about how the church had been betrayed and was being rebuilt; Romon to explain how the bards had been forced to lie, and offer his new saga, called The Risen Queen; and Sendric and Gratt to explain how the people would be able to choose their own town council, rather than have one hand-picked by the local lord. This took a fair bit of explaining, as the concept of having a say in the running of each village or town — and that each district would choose an ordinary person to sit on a new, expanded Royal Council — was a concept most of the people found hard to grasp.

Last to speak was Martil — and he was usually only needed to show the Dragon Sword.

It was slow, but Merren felt she was making progress. The main sticking point was still the people's fear of the Rallorans.

Despite the best efforts of Romon, several other bards, Nott and the priesthood, the people seemed obsessed with the thought they were the Butchers of Bellic. It came up, time and again, in the reports Merren was getting. Wherever the Rallorans went, disquiet followed. Finally, she decided to solve two problems in one by posting them down on the border where, under Nerrin, they patrolled watchfully. They were out of sight, out of mind for the country. Meanwhile her southern border was now secure. Gello might have been thrown out but she was under no illusions that he was completely defeated.

'The Berellians might like to try something — but they have few enough men,' Martil had assured her. 'They might be able to scrape together five thousand. With Gello's three thousand, that would look a strong force, but it would be nowhere near enough to invade a country as big as Norstalos. After all, the people might still be scared of Rallorans, but they would soon rally if there was a Berellian invasion. They've been worried about that for centuries.'

Merren had accepted his assurances, but wanted Rocus to start recruiting more men to rebuild her army. Hutter and Conal were also recruiting militia who, in an emergency, had shown they could fight.

With just three under-strength Norstaline regiments — two of those archers — and one of Rallorans, she felt vulnerable.

Several hundred of Gello's infantry had survived their wounds from the Battle of Pilleth, thanks to the healing powers of Nott, Milly and the priesthood. Some of them — not enough to even make a company — had come forward and asked to join her. Many of these were relatively new recruits, deceived into joining Gello's army and then forced to fight. But Gello's veterans just wanted to return to their homes where, she had no doubt, they would foment trouble. Nerrin had even reported catching a handful of them trying to slip across the border into Berellia.

It was now autumn, and winter was approaching. Thanks to Gello stealing the royal treasury, there was little money to buy food from countries such as Tetril until they could rebuild with gold from the mines. Merren had had to ask Barrett to persuade wizards all around the country to use their powers to help boost the harvest. And all she could do was promise the people less tax, which was only putting the problem off for another day.

So she had many problems that kept her working from dawn until past dusk, when Louise and Gia usually forced her to stop working, eat something and rest.

And now Bishop Milly was presenting her with this.

'Say that again,' Merren insisted.

'You are pregnant,' Milly said calmly.

'But that's impossible! How can you tell?'

Milly sighed. 'It is at a very early stage. But I have been given the power to sense such things.'

Merren leaned back in her chair, her tired mind rebelling as she tried to absorb this.

456

'You do know what this means?' she accused Milly.

'Of course. The next King of Norstalos will be half-Ralloran,' Milly continued softly. 'Both I and the Archbishop—'

'Nott!' Merren surged to her feet. 'He was the one who suggested this! He knew what was going to happen! He's to blame for this!'

Milly restrained her. 'He gave you a choice. But if you had not seduced Martil, Gello would have won at Pilleth.'

Merren wrenched her arm free of Milly's grip. But she also sat down, breathing heavily, trying to think. 'Do you realise how much trouble this will cause?' she almost moaned.

'I know. Most of the country is still terrified the Butchers of Bellic are on the loose and looking for blood. They believed the bards, as they have always done. Then there is the whole issue of being the first Queen of Norstalos. Many people are suspicious of a ruler who cannot take up the Dragon Sword. Even without anything else, it would take time to win those over. At this stage, with the country in chaos, to tell the people you are pregnant to the last Butcher of Bellic, and his son will be their next King—'

'His son!'

Milly spread her hands. 'I am sorry. I should have asked you if you wanted to know first. He is a healthy child, and you will have no problems through your pregnancy. If that is any comfort.'

'Not really.' Merren touched her belly absently.

There was certainly no sign there that anything was happening — and she had not felt different. Or had she? She had certainly been thinking more about

Martil — but had been far too tired to think of doing anything about that.

'This could undo all the work I have done so far, and make it almost impossible to win them over. They will no longer trust me, and it is doubtful they would ever accept Martil's son as King,' Merren said slowly.

'All true,' Milly admitted.

Merren bit her lip. 'It might be easier for all of us if I visited an apothecary,' she said carefully.

Milly almost recoiled in horror. While she knew that there were apothecaries who would mix up a special herbal potion for women, it went against everything the Church taught.

'Your majesty, I am not saying this because what you suggest is repugnant to me — I understand why you say it. But I have to tell you that, if you end this child, there will be no more for you.'

'Is that you saying it, or Aroaril?' Merren snarled at her.

Milly held her gaze. 'That is what Archbishop Nott told me, and I believe it.'

Merren sat there for a while, trying to come to terms with it all. The thought of harming the child growing inside her made her feel sick. Going to an apothecary would have been the hardest thing she had done — although she knew she would have done it for her country. But not to ever have another child — that was even worse. And to top it all, it would allow any child of Gello's to step up to the throne.

How could this have happened? She was pregnant, with Martil's son? She had not even thought about the possibility of getting pregnant. Stupid to think of it now, but then, surviving the battle with Gello had taken priority. So how did she

458

feel about it? She was being forced to make a choice here, between what was good for herself and what was good for the country. Only that was not really a choice — she had to put the country first. She tried to search her feelings, but swamping everything was the fear of what this news could do to her country. She was working so hard to win it back, she could not throw that away now. Not just for her, but for all those who had suffered and died to put her back on the throne. But she could not end the pregnancy, and could not let it be known it was Martil's son. There had to be a way through this. Think!

'Sendric,' she said thickly.

'Your majesty?' Milly looked up.

'I have to marry Sendric. He is the last remaining noble loyal to me and the only man the country will accept as my Prince Consort in the short time before my pregnancy becomes obvious. I can tell him the truth. He will do this because he swore an oath never to disobey me again. It will be a marriage in name only but only he, I and you can know that.' Merren bit her lip. 'This is going to rip Martil apart again, but, if I tell him the truth, he might do something stupid.'

Milly reached out to hold Merren's hand. 'My Queen, what you do now is braver than charging into Gello's army.'

Merren shook off her hand.

'I have to talk to Sendric now, before I change my mind. All I can say is, if this is Aroaril's idea of rewarding us in our fight …'

'Don't think like that, my Queen,' Milly warned. 'Be assured, this is part of something larger.'

'Part of something larger? Do you know how little comfort that is?' Merren said through gritted teeth.

Milly bowed her head. 'I wish I could offer you more. You deserve far more, my Queen. All I can give you now is a little time to yourself. I shall be back with Count Sendric in half a turn of an hourglass.'

Merren nodded, not trusting herself to speak. She knew she had to put her country first. It was the right thing to do. Why, then, did it feel so wrong?

Gello — he still thought of himself as King Gello, and insisted that all Berellians both call him 'sire' and bow when they spoke to him — waited impatiently by the dock.

'What are we waiting for?' he growled at Ezok. 'Why don't you ask Markuz what he wants and why we aren't marching across the border even now?'

Ezok bowed. He was tired of dealing with Gello, who seemed to become more unstable by the day. Before, he had been easily controlled — now he was simply obsessed with marching back into Norstalos and destroying everything in his way. Ezok had also caught him muttering conversations with his 'Mother' more than once. Ezok's ability to manipulate Gello was also his ticket to power and riches but he was already worrying that, as his influence over Gello waned, so did his worth to Onzalez. The Fearpriest was the real power here. And once Gello's usefulness was over, Ezok wondered if the two of them would be discarded, like a pair of emptied wineskins. But that day was some time away and Gello still needed to be humoured.

'Sire, we are here because we are expecting a ship from over the seas, bringing with it the way in which we shall restore you to your throne,' Ezok explained patiently.

Gello just grunted.

He had found the last few weeks intensely frustrating. True, the Berellians were generous with both food and wine, and he had Lahra to provide amusement and diversion. But otherwise he had nothing to do except wait for the Berellians. Without them, he was helpless to seize back the throne that should have been his — and had been his for too short a time. Meanwhile, he fretted that the country was laughing at him behind his back. After the way he had manipulated the bards, having them tell the country about the Witch Queen and her Ralloran Butchers, would Merren be doing the same? Would everyone be laughing at the tale of how he had run crying from the throne room after being refused by the Dragon Sword?

He wished Mother was here. She would know what to do. He had brought a small portrait of her with him, one he had stolen from the palace. He talked to her every night, told her how sorry he was for hurting her. So far she had not said anything back, but he was used to that. She had often refused to speak to him when he had been a bad boy. But, eventually, he was sure she would forgive him, and speak to him again.

And he sorely needed her advice.

When he had crossed the river, bringing three thousand men with him, he had expected to stay just long enough to collect the Berellian army, then sweep back across the border and into the capital.

But while he had been greeted warmly by King Markuz and his adviser, the hooded Brother Onzalez, there had been no word of him being given an army to lead back into Norstalos.

And that, apart from flowery speeches, endless bottles of wine and performances by bards, had been the last conversation he had had. He had almost been ignored.

Meanwhile, Prent had been embraced, particularly by the hooded adviser with King Markuz.

'Welcome, Brother!' The man had taken Prent off to one side, although Gello had been careful to listen to what was being said.

'Now you are here, I can help train you — and the first lesson is, never show your face,' Brother Onzalez had declared.

'Show my face?' Prent had replied, confused.

'Your face. Wear your hood up always. For there may come a time when you are glad that others do not know what you look like.'

Prent had nodded and lifted his hood, although obviously not really understanding Onzalez's words.

Prent had been summoned daily to work with Onzalez. He had only been able to report that he was undergoing secret training in the arcane arts of Zorva — and knew nothing about the plans for retaking Norstalos.

Gello's horses and men were given comfortable quarters at a town near the border, as were the remaining nobles; now just Cessor and Worick, whose loyalty was unquestioned but whose value was doubtful. Meanwhile Gello, Prent, his officers and a small honour guard were given luxurious rooms in the capital and treated with great honour. He had been asked to choose only those wounded men who had been saved by Prent — and converted to Zorva — for honour guard duty.

Gello had wanted to rage at the Berellians, demand they tell him what was going on — only he knew full well that he was helpless without them. So he had swallowed his temper and waited.

And now he had been summoned to the docks of the capital, along with Prent and his remaining officers, Feld, Livett and Heath — who had only survived the debacle at Pilleth by running for his life and leaving his men to die. Now the five of them stood quietly, surrounded by a squad of his red-clad guards.

'Do you think it is some new weapon?' Livett asked nervously, as the five Norstalines stood a little way apart from King Markuz, Gonzalez and Markuz's many black-garbed guards, watching a ship sail towards the docks.

'Like what?' Feld grunted.

Gello let them talk. He was thinking the same thing but did not want to show weakness — or rather, any more weakness — in front of his host.

The ship in question was of a strange design. Ships of Norstalos, and indeed the other countries on the continent, tended to be one- or two-masted, slim in shape, with long, pointed bows. But this one was bigger, wider and taller than the usual ship — and propelled by oars. Twin banks of oars on either side of the boat saw it move smoothly into the harbour, even against the wind. The rowers on one side lifted their oars and the ship pivoted smoothly; both sides drew the oars and it came to rest gently by the dock, where ropes were thrown down from its decks and made fast to the jetty.

Again there was a wait, and, as a company of men marched down the gangplank and towards where the royal parties stood, Gello could not restrain a gasp of surprise.

Half wore what looked like the skins of an animal, a fanged creature with black spots on a yellow hide. The pelt had been tailored to fit over them: the creature's forelegs stretched down the men's arms, the back legs down their legs, while the head, complete with sharp fangs, had been drawn over the men's heads, like a strange helmet.

The rest wore cloaks made from bird feathers over their brightly coloured armour, which looked something like padded leather. The bird whose feathers had supplied the cloaks was some type of eagle, for its head, sharp beak open forever in a silent cry, was stuck on the helmets the second company wore.

And their weapons! Both companies carried what looked like a cross between a club and an axe, with the head not of bright metal but a strange black rock.

'Where are they from?' Feld wondered.

From their ranks strode two men, who marched over to where Onzalez stood behind King Markuz. Gello watched them carefully. Each was obviously a warrior — both showed scars on their arms and legs. The pair prostrated themselves on the ground, hands outstretched.

'Welcome, warriors of Tenoch! Your arrival is timely indeed! Rise!' Markuz boomed.

'Where is Tenoch? I have never heard of such a place!' Livett muttered.

'Prent, go and ask them,' Gello ordered.

'I think we are going to find out,' Prent whispered back, 'sire.'

The two men stood slowly and came to attention. The one with an eagle's head attached to his helmet took a half-pace forwards.

'High one, we have travelled far across the sea to serve you. A day behind us are the rest of our ships. We have Tenoch's foremost fighters with us — eagle warriors, leopard warriors, as well as spearmen and slingers. Every man has fought in a score of battles, every man has taken at least one prisoner and seen him sacrificed to Zorva!'

Gello heard the words but it took him a few moments to understand them — the man had a strange accent. Then the import sank in and he had to grind his teeth to stop himself from shouting out. The Berellians must have sent for these men long ago! Certainly before he had been defeated at Pilleth! All this time he had been planning to turn on the Berellians, and they had seen it, prepared for it and would have met his treachery with their own! Only the fact he had nowhere else to go stopped him from walking away. He dearly wanted to talk this over with Mother. But he already knew what she would suggest were she to actually reply. He should nod and bow and pretend to be their friend, then, when he had the throne of Norstalos again, they would learn the folly of trying to trick him!

'Warriors of Tenoch, I thank you for your help, as does my friend and ally, King Gello of Norstalos. Together, we shall win both victory for ourselves, and triumph for Zorva!' Markuz stepped forwards and embraced both men.

As if on cue, the assembled crowd burst into cheers.

An immaculately dressed courtier hurried over to where a seething Gello waited.

'His majesty would consider it an honour if you joined him and the warriors of Tenoch for a war council.' The man bowed.

Gello forced a smile.

'It would be a pleasure,' he murmured.

Sendric tapped on the door. 'My Queen, you sent for me?'

Merren had her back to him, and seemed to be deep in thought.

'Count, come in, sit down — and close the door please.'

Sendric did so, settling himself into a chair.

'What is it, your majesty?' he asked.

Merren sighed. 'Sendric, you have been a great help to me these past few weeks. You and Gratt have been able to show the people a way forward; how commoners could hope to take the place of our absent nobility. And your reports, your surveys of the people, have been of immense use.'

'It has been a pleasure. And it gives me a target to aim for — I am the last noble, and when my job is complete, I shall retire my title. I have no children to inherit a worthless name. And no desire to do anything other than see Gello held to account for his crimes. Seeing you these past few weeks — my Queen, you are everything that Norstalos needs. I can retire to my estate and know the country is in the best possible hands.'

Merren nodded dutifully at the compliments, then looked over to where a carafe of wine and a pair of goblets stood. She would have dearly liked a drink but, given Bishop Milly's news, that was not a good idea. She shook herself. She had to do this, for her country, no matter what it meant for her.

She looked Sendric squarely in the eye. 'I want you to marry me,' she declared.

Sendric smiled broadly and leaned back in his chair, waiting the punch line of this amusing joke. After an uncomfortable silence, he leaned forwards again.

'My Queen, surely you are not serious?'

'No jest. You are the last remaining noble. Sworn

to my service. I need you to swear on your oath and your honour to do this.'

Sendric's face paled. 'But, your majesty! I watched you and Rana grow up together! I could not—'

Merren cut him off. 'Sendric, I am pregnant.'

His face whitened even further and he sagged back in his chair.

'But who is the father …' He trailed off then looked up at her with horror in his eyes. 'It is Martil!'

Merren sighed. 'It is.'

Sendric stood abruptly. 'So you want me to play the surrogate — give the appearance of respectability to this — for the people will not accept a Ralloran mongrel on their throne!'

Merren surged to her feet. 'Have a care, Sendric — that is my son and your future King you talk about!'

Sendric managed to control himself only through an effort, and years of practice.

'And I am to play the dutiful Prince Consort, publicly supporting you, but sleeping in another bedroom while you and that Ralloran romp in another?'

'All correct except for the last,' Merren told him coldly.

'How long has it been going on? How long before I am the laughing stock of the country?'

'It happened the once — and it will not happen again,' Merren snapped. 'It only happened because Archbishop Nott told me it was the only way to secure victory.' *And if I tell myself that enough, it might even become true*, she thought.

Sendric slumped back into his chair.

'I know why it has to be me, your majesty. But why did this have to happen now? I thought our problems were over!'

Merren smiled grimly. 'I don't know why you are complaining, Sendric. I would have thought the problem was much bigger from my side — and only going to get bigger with time!'

Sendric groaned. 'I will be despised, ridiculed! All my life I have tried to preserve my dignity and my final act of public office will be to trample that dignity into the dirt! The baby will not look like me — everyone will know I was cuckolded by a Ralloran … Is there not someone else? Is there not something you can do …?'

'No!' Merren surprised herself with the force of her anger. 'Sendric, don't you think I have considered all this? I am not giving you a choice. You will do this. I am sorry. Believe me, I wish I did not have to do this. But I did what was necessary to save this country, and I will do so again. The people will not accept a Ralloran Prince Consort, much less a half-Ralloran Crown Prince. I will not let this country destroy itself. You must put your personal feelings aside for the good of the country. We will announce the engagement tomorrow — and the wedding will be the week after.'

Sendric's eyes glittered as he looked up. 'I will hold to my oaths,' he said sullenly. 'I remember what I said. Naturally I shall not speak a word of this to anyone. But do not expect me to like it.'

'Then that makes two of us,' Merren told him coolly.

Inside, her heart was ice. If it had gone so badly with Sendric, how would Martil take it?

One thing about the Berellians — they certainly knew how to treat their guests, Gello reflected. Stunning serving girls, all in Markuz's colours of gold and black, ensured every man had wine and food. You only had to raise your hand and your glass would be refilled. The food was superb — exotic dishes that Gello had never thought of trying before. Roast boar, an entire cooked bear, strange cheeses and pickled cabbage — it was all delicious. He was even able to forget, at least for a while, that the Berellians obviously had plans of their own.

He had brought Count Cessor and Earl Worick along to join him, feeling that the Norstalines were sadly outnumbered by Berellian nobles and officers. He was already at enough of a disadvantage. He talked to them but he could not bring himself to talk to Ezok — he pointedly ignored him, until it was obvious to all at the table. The Berellian had been lying to him.

This dining room was also clearly a touch of Berellian luxury. The wooden table was massive — another thirty guests could have sat around it in comfort — while beautiful tapestries covered almost every inch of the pale stone walls and an enormous rug covered the wooden floor. The cost of any of these would feed a family of peasants for a year, Gello judged. But, of course, it would have been wasted on them.

Finally the plates were cleared and the servants vanished, leaving only Markuz, Onzalez, Ezok, the Berellian war captains, the two Tenoch warriors and the seven Norstalines.

'Bring your wine with you,' Markuz invited warmly, as he ushered them over to a separate table, where a huge map of southern Norstalos and northern Berellia almost covered the polished surface.

Gello, who had been forced to leave his precious maps behind when he fled the capital, almost gasped in awe. It was incredibly detailed, drawn in colour, and had numerous wooden carvings, depicting regiments, lined neatly along one side.

'Our friend and ally, King Gello, has been forced to flee his country, thanks to the foul plotting of Aroaril and His agents — and because he was betrayed by men he thought loyal. But with our help, and the aid of glorious Zorva, we shall give him back his throne,' Markuz intoned.

'Because he and his men did not believe! They have learned the folly of not embracing Zorva. If only He had been there, Aroaril would not have been able to save the Witch Queen of Norstalos! But, with my loyal fighters from Tenoch, we will crush her! And once we have Norstalos, the rest of this continent will be at our mercy!' Onzalez declared.

Gello realised with a shock that Onzalez was the true power in this room, if the Tenoch warriors were loyal to him.

'High One, what will we face in this Norstalos?' the eagle warrior asked.

'The council recognises Itlan of Tenoch,' Markuz announced.

Onzalez turned to where Gello and his men stood, almost on the outside.

'King Gello. What forces does the Witch Queen possess?'

Gello stepped forwards. 'She has one regiment of infantry, two under-strength regiments of archers and one of Rallorans — all Butchers of Bellic.'

The Berellians in the room all hissed.

'They will also form another regiment from the militia, and even then will have less than five thousand. But they have the Dragon Sword. It appears it is working. They will try to form an army

470

of peasants and shopkeepers to stop us. But they will not be trained and few will be armed. They will not have the time. Or the money,' Gello added, unable to stop his smile at the thought.

'The Dragon Sword? What is this?' Itlan asked sharply.

'A magic sword, the symbol of kingship in my country. It was stolen from me by the Witch Queen and her foul Rallorans.'

'Noble Yertlaan and myself will lead fifteen thousand onto the field,' Itlan announced and his companion, the leopard warrior, nodded fiercely.

'Berellia has eight thousand men armed and ready to march,' Markuz added.

Gello could see where this might end. He could almost hear his mother's carping voice telling him of the dangers ahead. He was clearly the junior partner — and there was every chance the Berellians and their mysterious allies, the Tenochs, would turn on him once his cousin was destroyed. But this was the only way he was going to get his throne back; they would need him, even if he was just a puppet, to hold Norstalos for them. Well, just let him get his backside on the throne and they would learn their mistake!

'I have three thousand loyal men, including the only heavy cavalry. We faced the Witch Queen on a ground of her choosing, where I could not use my cavalry. This time we shall fight her where we want, where my heavy cavalry could win the battle all by themselves,' Gello told them, looking hard at the men from Tenoch. They might dress prettily, but fancy feathers and furry coats would not stop a lance.

'So the Witch Queen's trained men will face an army five times their size. Any peasants they raise will be like chaff — easily swept away. And there is no possibility any of these men will desert us, despite the best efforts of Aroaril and His foul magic and loathsome minions,' Onzalez proclaimed exultantly.

'So when do we march? Every day we linger, we give my cousin more time to strengthen her hold on the country.'

'The border is guarded by the Rallorans,' one of Markuz's captains pointed out. 'They will not be easy to brush aside. As we know, they are experts at slowing an advance.'

'But the pleasure of crushing them will be sweet indeed,' Markuz said gleefully.

Gello suddenly saw an opportunity. If, while defeating his cousin, the Berellians and Tenochs were to take almost all of the losses, it would only help him. And if they massacred a few villages of peasants along the way, it would make the others more amenable to Gello's calls for them to rise up and throw the invaders out …

'Your majesty, I would like to suggest a way we can bring the Witch Queen to battle — and give you the Rallorans,' Gello said slyly.

Markuz gestured to the map. 'Show me, my friend.'

Gello moved the carved wooden tokens representing his cavalry regiments and solitary infantry regiment around the map, until they were poised in Tetril.

'If we all attack from the south, they will keep retreating, trying to wear us down and leave our men hungry and tired. They have used such tactics against me, and against you as well, during the Ralloran Wars,' Gello reminded those around the table.

'That is true,' Markuz agreed.

'If we all attack from the same direction, we will be unable to forage, we will compete with each other for space and they can retreat to wherever they want. But if you attack from the south, and we drive in from the east, they will be forced to split their forces and we can bring them to battle at the capital. The land around there is flat — perfect for cavalry — and there are no hills or passes for them to use. They will be caught in the open, with no escape.' Gello manoeuvred the counters into position, until he had his cousin's forces surrounded and outnumbered.

Everyone looked at the map.

'How do we know they will not try to defeat you first, then us?' Itlan asked.

'If you advance through southern Norstalos as you advanced through Rallora, you will be able to keep their focus on you.'

Several Berellian officers grinned at that.

'You understand what you are saying? That you have no objection to us driving out the people with fire and sword, and sacrificing our captives to Zorva?' Onzalez said sharply.

Gello kept his smile fixed. 'They are just peasants. It is their fault for not siding with me when they had the chance. It will be a good lesson for the rest of the country to learn. Obey me or pay the price.'

Yertlaan pointed to the map.

'It is a good plan — but we can make it better. King Gello advances from the east, King Markuz from the south and we land our men on the west coast. We all meet at the capital.'

'The west is the area most loyal to me,' Gello said mildly, struggling to keep his emotions hidden.

'It is our land!' Earl Worrick declared hotly.

'Then we shall not destroy it. If the people welcome us with open arms, as you suggest, then we shall march on. If they try to stop us …'

'But if they see an invading army, they will react …' Cessor, now perspiring heavily, said nervously.

'Then you shall accompany us. Flying your recognised banners, the people will know we are there to set them free from the Witch Queen and the foul Aroaril,' Yertlaan stated.

'Brilliant, noble one!' Markuz exulted. 'They will not know where to go, which threat to counter. And wherever they try to run, we will already be there. We can trap them, hold them and destroy them!'

Gello caught the eye of Worrick and Cessor and, with a look, told them not to argue. This was a time to seem supine. Once Merren was destroyed, then they could wrest back control.

'And what of the north? Should we not try to attack from there as well?' Yertlaan added.

Gello chuckled. 'There is nothing up there — just mountains and a race of primitive men. We call them goblins. Once they lived in Norstalos's northern forests but now they cling to caves and valleys in the colder north, too stupid to know their time has ended and they should just die out.'

'Who do they worship?' Onzalez asked sharply.

'Not Aroaril. They have their own, false, gods,' Prent added helpfully.

'It might be amusing to offer them our help. To set them loose in the north, to take back what is theirs.'

'The north is traitorous and must be utterly destroyed,' Gello agreed. 'But it is also the source of almost all our gold and silver mines.'

'I did not say they could keep the north, just that they could sweep it clean. Then we can destroy them once we have finished with the Witch Queen,' Onzalez suggested. 'If they do not believe in Zorva, they do not deserve to live anyway.'

Gello grinned. At last, an idea he agreed with! 'It would be symbolic.' He smiled. 'The men fighting for my cousin all come from the north — I want them to face us on the battlefield, knowing their deaths are but moments away — and knowing that their families and homes have been destroyed already. It will make my revenge all the sweeter.'

'Will these goblins listen to an emissary from you?' Onzalez asked.

Gello smiled apologetically. 'Unfortunately there is little trust between Norstalines and goblins — or Derthals, as they call themselves. We need someone who can trick them, fool them into thinking we are there to help. Someone like Ambassador Ezok, perhaps?'

All eyes swung to Ezok, who had gone white at the thought.

Markuz looked from Gello to Ezok, then glanced at Onzalez, who nodded abruptly.

'Then we shall send Ezok,' Markuz announced. 'But, in recognition of the service he has done us, I will send Cezar along, to keep him safe. And to get them there, we shall send Khiraz, the Royal Magician. It will be a difficult task, but no doubt these primitives will be easily impressed by magic. And, if they succeed, you will be richly rewarded.'

Ezok looked to Onzalez in mute appeal, but the Fearpriest was facing away from him. Nothing for it but to agree. Besides, with Cezar and Khiraz by his side, surely he would return?

'You had best go prepare, Ezok.' Markuz dismissed him.

With a deep bow, Ezok left the room. Gello watched him go with satisfaction.

'If we succeed in taking back Norstalos, you will all be richly rewarded for your help,' Gello added, knowing it had to be said but hating it nonetheless.

'For Berellia, we shall discuss anew our southern border. For the men of Tenoch …'

'Sacrifices. We have all the gold we need,' Itlan announced.

'Then so shall it be.' Gello inclined his head. 'One for every man who lives through the battle. And for Brother Onzalez, the pleasure and privilege of working with our own Archbishop Prent to convert the country to Zorva.'

He had no intention of keeping those promises, just as he knew they would have no intention of restricting themselves to just those rewards. But the gesture had to be made.

Markuz nodded in pleasure. 'How soon do we march?'

'My men will need at least two weeks to recover from the long voyage. They will then be ready to fight,' Itlan said immediately.

'I would not want to wait any longer,' Gello said. 'But I will need time to obtain permission from Tetril to move my men through their borders.'

'Then it shall be so,' Onzalez agreed. 'And we will have some duties before then. King Gello and his men will all need to convert to Zorva, if we are to ensure success.'

Gello inclined his head, although he could sense Cessor shifting nervously behind him. There was no choice, as far as he was concerned. He would do whatever it took to win back his throne. His legacy was at stake here — and Ezok had been right about one thing: Aroaril had done nothing for him. Zorva could only be better.

'Of course. And I would like to suggest an auspicious sacrifice,' he said loudly.

'Please, tell us,' Onzalez invited.

'I have a whore who looks just like Queen Merren. Seeing her sacrificed would surely be an omen of success?' Gello had the sense that, could Onzalez's face be seen, he would be smiling.

'It would be a fine omen. And excellent practice!'

'Then let us drink to that!' Markuz roared.

21

Martil was playing catch with Karia when the summons came.

The Queen's grand tour of the country had taken them to the country's east and they were staying at Darry's Inn on the border, where he had met Nerrin what seemed like a lifetime ago — before he had even taken up the Dragon Sword. Darry had been a proud host and they had spoken to not just the villagers but many of the surrounding farmers, who had walked or ridden to the village to hear what the Queen had to say. It had gone reasonably well, although these people were just happy with the knowledge that the bandit Danir wasn't terrorising them any more. The next day they would move further west, visiting other villages and eventually the town of Wollin. Already riders had gone ahead, to tell the people of the Queen's imminent arrival.

The few weeks had been rather mixed. The joy at surviving, and winning, the battle had been tempered with the knowledge of how many of his men had died that day. If it had not been for the work of Nott, Milly, Quiller and the other priests, even more would have died. Even so, those who had lost hands, arms or legs would not be able to fight again. But, despite their sacrifices, the people still feared them. The first questions at these meetings were always: 'Where are the Rallorans? What are they doing? Will they be sent to punish us if we do not obey?'

In private, Martil shook his head at it. Merren told him it would change, and they were all working towards that. Her surveys showed the country was slowly warming to the Rallorans. But acceptance was still a long way away.

Of course, he had Karia to cheer him up. What they had gone through had brought them much closer together. Sometimes he had to force himself to think hard to remember the name of her real father, Edil. As far as he was concerned, if she never remembered those days, it would be best for her. Every morning they had breakfast together, then he took her to whichever room, or house, or tavern Barrett was staying in, so she could have her magic lessons. That was also the time he usually joined Merren to speak to the people of the particular town or village they were visiting. Then he would collect Karia, they would eat lunch together and he would help her with her reading and writing, as well as playing catch, or chase, or tops, or dice or — if he could not escape — dolls. They would all eat dinner together, then it was usually time to move on to the next town or village, thanks to Barrett's magic, and he and Karia would share a cup of hot milk and a quick saga before bed.

It was almost normal, and he was happy each day and slept well at night — although he would have felt happier had he been able to talk to Merren. One night together had been fine when he had expected to die. But now he wanted to live, and he wanted more of her. Perhaps sensing this, she had been careful to only see him when there had been plenty of people around.

And now this summons had come from her. His first thought was of rising excitement, tempered by the thought he had to do something with Karia. Desperately he cast around for a way to give himself a free afternoon. A couple of turns of the hourglass, at least!

'What is it?' Karia asked, wandering over with the ball in her hands.

'I've got to go and see the Queen,' Martil said absently, knowing that Barrett would never help him out, and wondering if Conal could be the answer.

'Great! I'll come too!' Karia said brightly.

Martil managed to keep the horror from his face at the thought. 'No, it says only me — probably some talk about forming a new army. And you know how bored you get by that …'

'Oh, it's all you adults do!' Karia agreed. 'Talk and talk and talk! It's boring! You should just play with each other, instead.'

Martil silently agreed. 'Why don't we go and see if Conal is free?'

Conal was, fortunately enough, talking with Louise, while her children played, and Martil was able to leave Karia with them with considerable relief. He almost ran to the room where Merren was staying, though he did take a moment to go to his room and rinse out his mouth, as well as change his somewhat sweaty tunic for a clean one and quickly brush his hair.

He knocked on her door — coincidentally the one he and Karia had shared when they stayed at the inn.

'Come in!'

He opened the door, wondering what he might find

inside. After all, she had hardly been backwards in being forward with him on that night back in Sendric.

But she was sitting down behind a table when he walked in.

Still, his heart was beating a little faster as he sat down across from her.

Merren could feel her own heart beat a little faster. Looking at him now, thinking of the child she carried, she nearly changed her plans. After all, they had nearly nine months to persuade the people that the Rallorans could be trusted. But it was a slow process — and would be derailed if the people thought this was all a Ralloran plot to seize the throne. She was under no illusions. There were some people who thought having a queen was an affront to the Dragon Sword and Aroaril. They did not remember her rule with any fondness and some, particularly those who had been affected by some of the Royal Council's stranger rulings, were still bitter. No, this was the only way to secure the country.

'Martil, I wanted to talk to you privately, before I make this announcement at the next Royal Council — and then have Romon and his bards start spreading the word publicly,' she said solemnly.

Martil nodded cautiously. This was not exactly what he had in mind when he had walked in.

Merren looked at him and took a deep breath. There was no way but to say it straight.

'I am to marry Count Sendric,' she said firmly.

Martil thought he had misheard. 'Merren, did you just say you will be marrying Count Sendric?' he asked carefully.

'Yes, I said I will be marrying Count Sendric. Of course nothing will change as far as you being the Queen's Champion, until I have a child who will take the Sword,' Merren ground on remorselessly, determined to get it all out.

Martil could barely hear her for the pounding in his ears.

'Sendric?' he croaked finally. 'Why?'

Merren took another deep breath. 'He is the last noble. Martil, you know what the reaction of the people has been. They mistrust all Rallorans, and will view me with suspicion for some time to come. I have to secure the country. Now I have a Champion, I can make a politically approved marriage. Sendric is the only noble left.'

'But why now? Can't you wait, to see if the people's attitudes are going to change? Give them time!' Martil almost pleaded.

'I cannot.' Merren shook her head. 'I have to put the country first! My feelings are irrelevant. This is what the country needs.'

Martil stared at her. She had told him she loved him! His hopes, his daydreams — and night dreams — of Merren were being destroyed. He wanted to get out of there, drown himself in drink again. He wanted to leave with his dignity intact, beyond all else, but his stubborn pride — that had served him both so well and so badly before — made him ask one more question.

'So, that night back at Sendric. Was that real or was that for the country?'

Merren looked into his eyes and longed to tell him the truth. Tell him it was his child she was carrying, that the marriage to Sendric was a union in name only. But for Sendric's sake, as well as Martil's, she knew she could not.

'It was for the country,' she said evenly, feeling a wrench deep inside her as the words left her.

Martil nodded once, jerkily, then pushed back his chair.

'Excuse me, your majesty,' he managed to say, then stalked out of the room, only just stopping himself from slamming the door.

Merren watched him go and bit her lip to stop herself from calling after him. *It had to be done*, the spirit of her dead father told her. *Your first duty is to your country, not yourself.*

'It was decisions like this that saw the Dragon Sword kill you,' she hissed aloud at his memory.

Martil staggered down the corridor, not thinking where he was going. Since Pilleth, he had nursed a dream that one day they could be together. And now she was marrying Sendric, of all people! He liked the old noble well enough but to imagine her with him ... He shook his head. He could not think about it. He recognised the anger rising within him — months ago he would have gone looking for a fight to take it out on someone. He knew he should go and see Karia instead, let her silliness and games soothe some of the raw pain inside him. Yet he found himself at the bar instead.

'What'll it be?' Darry invited warmly.

Martil was about to order whisky but decided one goblet of wine might be a better idea.

'Your best wine. But only one goblet, mind. Don't serve me any more,' he said heavily.

Darry tapped a small cask expertly and drew out a goblet of rich, red wine.

'Something the matter?' he asked, in his best innkeeper tone.

Martil looked down the bar but there was hardly anyone else there. Just some of the Queen's guardsmen enjoying a meal at a table up the back and a couple of farmers talking down the far end over pots of foaming ale.

'Tell me, do you hate the Rallorans?' he asked.

Darry chuckled. 'Hate them? Why, they've been some of my best customers for years! I never believed any of those stupid sagas about you lot, either!'

'And your customers?'

Darry's smile faded a little. 'I grant you, there has been some talk of late. But after you and the Queen showed up, folks think different!'

'Do they?'

Darry leaned on the bar. 'Most of them. There's still some who think you're about to drink the blood of every Norstaline child, but then there's always a village idiot or two.'

'And if you heard the Queen was going to marry a Ralloran? What would the people think then?'

Darry's eyebrows almost disappeared into his hair. 'Marry a Ralloran? King Tolbert's son?'

'Could be.' Martil swallowed half his wine in one gulp.

Darry rubbed his chin. 'That would concern folk. After all, that would make him almost as good as our king — and mean our next king would be half-Ralloran. Why, it'd almost be like being part of Rallora! Nothing good would come of that!'

Martil drank the rest of his wine. 'Well, you can sleep easy. It won't happen. She's marrying Count Sendric instead.'

Darry beamed. 'Really? Well, that'd be good news!'

Martil pushed the empty goblet towards him, then fumbled into his belt pouch and dug out a silver coin.

'For some people,' he said coldly, then walked

away, knowing he had to — or he would stay there until he fell, or knocked someone down.

Merren had tried not to confront Archbishop Nott. But after what she had been forced to do to Martil, she knew she had to get it out of her system.

'Archbishop!' She stormed into his room, where he was quietly working through a pile of reports.

Nott looked up slowly. 'Yes, my Queen? What can I do for you?'

Merren waited until he could see what she was doing, then deliberately slammed the door.

'I see what you are here for then,' Nott said mildly. 'I am a little surprised it took you this long.'

'Did you know?' she demanded.

Nott rubbed his face and offered her a seat.

'No,' he said simply. 'But if I had, I would still have told you the same thing.'

Merren glared at him. 'Explain yourself!'

Nott shook his head. 'I am afraid I cannot, at least not to your satisfaction. I told you I am not skilled in divination. Bishop Gamelon was the last priest I knew who was really able to discern a pattern in the future — and yet look what happened to him. I am being guided, towards a destination I do not know, by a course I do not understand. All I can do is pass on what I have been permitted to know. If you had not slept with Martil, we would not have won Pilleth. We both know that is true. We both did what we had to, to ensure victory. In doing so, we helped save Martil's life, for the Dragon Sword was growing impatient with him. Soon, it would have begun to draw the life from him. Given that Martil is now the guardian of my granddaughter, that is also something I am grateful for. I did not know you would fall pregnant. But you do need an heir to take up the Dragon Sword. And who better than the son of the latest wielder?'

'So you're happy about it?' Merren growled. 'Don't you understand what I had to do? What I must do, now I am carrying this child? I've got to marry Sendric, put aside everything I want for the country, hurt two good men — and all because—'

'And don't you understand what I have to do?' Nott leaped to his feet and was in front of her in an instant. Shocked by his transformation from quiet, gentle grandfather to a figure of strength, power blazing from his blue eyes, surprised by the firmness in his grip as he seized her hands, she fell silent.

'I thought I would be dead by now! I thought I would have found peace! But no, I must give up my granddaughter, I must take on duties I never wanted, that I turned down when I was younger, and stronger. I have been shown a frightening future, where pyramids to Zorva infest the land, where screaming crowds cheer as blood-splattered Fearpriests cut out the hearts of children to glorify their foul god! I don't want to have to fight, I don't want to have to tell people to do things that are against their wishes, against their nature! I don't want to have the responsibility! But it has been given to me and I cannot shirk it! Just like you! I will do whatever my God wants, as you do what you have to for your country. But don't you ever think that I enjoy it, or take it lightly, or, God forbid, I am happy about it! I understand what you did. I grieve for the position you are in, for what you are forced to do. But we are talking about ensuring a life not just for the child you carry but for every child on this continent, on this world!'

Merren stood there, too shocked to say or do anything, as Nott slowly walked back to his seat, and pulled his pile of papers back towards him.

'There may be another purpose for that child. Do not seek answers before you are ready,' Nott said tiredly.

'What else have you seen?' Merren whispered.

'Nothing I can tell you, for fear of having exactly the opposite effect. Zorva tells his agents what to do, when to do it and why. Aroaril gives His people the power to choose. If you want to go and work for the Dark God, all you need to do is follow orders. But here, you can follow your heart. That is something I would not change. Now, if there is nothing further?'

Merren took a deep breath. Part of her still wanted to rage at him, get rid of her frustration, her fear, her self-loathing at what she had done to Martil. But the part of her that had been raised to royal duty saw that Nott was just as trapped as she was. Screaming at him would make her feel better, perhaps, for a moment — but then she would just feel worse afterwards.

'No, there is nothing more,' she replied.

Now that preparations were finally under way to return to Norstalos, Gello felt much happier about being in Berellia. Part of that, he supposed, was due to his conversion to Zorva.

Along with his officers, and Cessor and Worick, he had gone to an underground cavern, where an altar to Zorva waited.

'We are building a traditional pyramid to Zorva, so all can see as the sacrifices are made,' Onzalez told them. 'But such things take time. The site we chose had a church to Aroaril. It was demolished, and then the area had to be cleansed of the stink of Aroaril before we could begin. There is still lingering support for Aroaril here, but we are stamping it out. Apparently there is an underground society of priests somewhere. When we find one, we flay them alive and impale them, which is reducing their numbers.'

Prent officiated over the conversions, while Onzalez merely watched his protégé. Although Gello was to sacrifice Lahra, his officers and Cessor and Worick had been told to sacrifice one of their family.

'The first-born son is traditional, although it can be any child,' Onzalez said.

The rest of the families were not permitted to witness the rites. Only men could witness the sacred rites of Zorva — women and children were only allowed on top of the bloody altar.

Gello's officers had agreed readily enough. The power and wealth he had offered them over the years was enough to secure their support for almost anything. Worick seemed willing, as well. But Cessor was blubbering as his youngest daughter wailed in fear.

'Can't someone shut the little bitch up?' Gello muttered to Onzalez. 'I can't hear what is going on!'

'Zorva loves to hear screams,' Onzalez assured him.

The children had been first; Cessor wept uncontrollably and Prent had to grip the ceremonial dagger with him to strike the fatal blow. Lahra was last and she had screeched and begged for mercy, offered to do anything that any man in the packed cavern wanted in exchange for her life.

Gello had hesitated, strangely reminded of his mother's last moments: He had stood above her prone body and had stilled her annoying voice forever. He had been almost lost in the memory, and Prent had had to nudge him, while Lahra screamed and begged. Then Gello brought the knife down, ending her cries forever, as well as any remaining shred of guilt.

The feeling that surged through him when he offered Lahra's heart and his soul to Zorva, had left him shaken. His memories of running from the throne room in tears, of fleeing Pilleth and his victorious cousin, which had seemed so vivid, now seemed remote. For years he had been able to conjure up every moment, every emotion from his throne room humiliation. Now it seemed as if it had happened to another man. Which, of course, it had.

Once Gello and his men were all converted, they found themselves invited more and more into the King's confidence — and especially into the confidence of Onzalez, who was clearly the real power here. Well, not all of them. Fat Cessor kept pleading sickness, and refusing to turn up. Gello was beginning to think the fool would be better off dead. He was certainly useless.

After all, the conversion meant they were even permitted to watch the warriors of Tenoch exercising on the plains outside the city. That was exceedingly interesting. Rather than fighting in tight ranks, they fought man to man, using speed and agility to counter their lack of shields and light armour.

Gello had been fascinated with their slingers, men capable of sending a fist-sized stone crashing into a target seventy paces away with unerring accuracy. They had none of the range of the longbow or crossbow but they could be devastating at close range. As to the rest of the Tenoch armoury, he had been amazed to discover how sharp the black rock, which Itlan called obsidian, seemed to be — either as a spear head or embedded into a wooden club to make their strange club-axes. These had all the fearsome impact of an axe, with the speed of a sword. Despite himself, he was impressed.

But, most of all, he could feel a new power inside himself. Aroaril had thwarted him at Pilleth but now he would crush his cousin once and for all. After that, he would help the Berellians and their Tenoch allies crush every other country on the continent. And after that, he would ensure he was the supreme ruler of them all. The Dragon Sword and his shame would be wiped away in a wave of blood, while screaming crowds chanted his name.

As Bishop Milly inspected the group of prospective priests and priestesses, she was hard-pressed to keep a smile from her face when she saw the large one at the end, whose robe appeared to be too short in both the arm and leg.

'Unusual uniform you are wearing there, Sergeant Kesbury,' she said softly.

'I have had my fill of fighting. I have seen too much and I want to change my life,' he replied quietly.

Milly considered him for a long moment. 'You can begin the process. Who am I to say if Aroaril has not called you up into His service? But I can foresee problems. You have talents that may be required elsewhere. What if Captain Martil needs you, or the Queen?'

'I have spoken to Captain Martil. He will not call on me unless he has no choice,' Kesbury said confidently.

'You are Ralloran. Would you not be happier ministering to your own people? Particularly given what has happened here, the way in which Gello has tried to paint you as monsters?'

Kesbury stared down at her defiantly. 'There is nothing for me in Rallora. And if I cannot win over a Norstaline village, then I do not deserve to be a priest.'

Milly smiled at his answer.

'An excellent reply. Well, let's see if you can be a warrior for Aroaril.'

Father Saltek had been ministering to an ever-decreasing flock for months now. His worst fears, and the predictions of Earl Byrez, had come true. The Fearpriests ruled in Berellia now and the number of people who would admit to worshipping Aroaril was being whittled away every day — both through fear and the efforts of the Fearpriests.

Many Berellian towns and villages were beautiful to look at. Stone houses overlooking cobbled streets and small squares, ornate churches and impressive castles. Civic pride meant the streets were clean, the fields rich and well tended. But behind the gorgeous façade, behind the smiles of the men and women, evil was festering.

He was still holding services, being smuggled from house to house by loyal worshippers, men and women determined not to fall under the sway of the darkness pervading their country. Although it was getting harder. Luckily he was still being blessed by Aroaril, which had allowed him to escape his pursuers three times now. But they had powers of their own, and it could not be long until they caught up with him. While he had breath, he was prepared to worship, which was why he agreed to go to a small house in the rich quarter of the city — against his better judgement — after a desperate plea from a woman he had known for years, a stallholder from the city's markets.

As he walked through the door, he almost ran back out again — the smell of fear was ripe in the small lounge room. A middle-aged woman and her two teenage daughters greeted him by falling to their knees and grabbing his hands. But strangest of all was the fat man in the big chair by the fireplace, who sat silently weeping and toying with a long dagger.

'What is going on here?' Saltek demanded, preparing to call on Aroaril to hold these people while he ran for safety.

'Father, I am the Countess Cessor, these are my daughters Ladria and Yvonne. My husband is the Count Cessor; we are all fugitives from Norstalos. But we all love Aroaril. You must help us!'

'What about your husband?' Saltek said harshly.

The man named as Count Cessor raised his tear-streaked face. 'They made me kill my daughter! They made me worship Zorva! I have to atone!' he wailed.

Saltek waved at him furiously. 'Keep your voice down! Do you want us all to die?'

'I want to die,' Cessor confirmed, 'but I want you to save my family — and I have an important message for you in return.'

Saltek sighed. He might have wished he had never come but he could sense there was a desperate need here. 'There can be no bargaining. Tell me all, so I can judge how I may best help your family.'

'But—' Countess Cessor began.

'But nothing! It is highly likely I am the last priest of Aroaril left in Berellia! I have a responsibility not just to you but to all those who still wish to keep His light flickering in this pit of darkness!' They fell silent and he sighed.

'Start at the beginning,' Saltek suggested gently. 'Why don't we sit down?'

It was a long tale, and one that made Saltek shudder. But the part where Cessor described how an army of Zorva was preparing to march on Norstalos, then see that country converted to worship of the Dark God, the first step in a campaign to take over the entire continent, made his skin crawl.

'The Fearpriest, Onzalez, has summoned men from a country called Tenoch, thousands of them. Norstalos does not stand a chance. King Gello does not care what happens to the people, he just wants his throne back. He has offered a chunk of southern Norstalos to Markuz, and is happy to set these monsters from Tenoch loose in the west — his old Dukedom! And once Norstalos has fallen, no other country could hope to stand against them,' Cessor explained. 'I want you to contact Norstalos, to smuggle my family back across the border, so they can take a warning to Queen Merren. That information might just save their lives.'

'And you?'

Cessor offered him the ghost of a smile and twirled the dagger in his hands. 'I shall open my veins and beg forgiveness of my daughter when I meet her,' he sighed.

Saltek controlled the urge to offer him a comforting hand. 'You do know that will not save your soul? That is pledged to Zorva, for now and ever,' he said quietly.

Cessor looked at him with liquid eyes. 'I do not care. I deserve any punishment I receive.'

'Would it not be better then, to take another with you? The Fearpriest, Onzalez? You have access to him, he trusts you now. Kill him and you will do more for Aroaril than simply ending your life.'

Cessor sighed gustily. 'I am old, fat and weak. I am also a coward. I would fail, they would take me and I would tell them all about my family, about my warning — and about you. I cannot let that happen. Better that I die now.'

Saltek looked at him carefully. 'Then Aroaril have mercy on you.'

Cessor embraced his weeping wife and daughters, then watched as Saltek led them out the door and into the night. It was strange, but all his fear was gone now. He rolled his sleeves back, then slit each arm from wrist to elbow. He let the dagger fall to the floor where his lifeblood was pooling and leaned back in the chair. He had been a fool, and worse than a fool, he knew. And even this action was not going to guarantee the survival of Norstalos or his family. But it was the only thing he could do. He hoped his torment would be immense — if that meant his daughter would find peace.

Saltek led the three women deeper into the night. He would split them up, hide them with several different families that he trusted. That part was easy enough. But contacting Norstalos — that would be difficult indeed. Using Aroaril's power would alert the Fearpriests. They would close down the capital, possibly impose a curfew, certainly redouble their efforts to seize him. But it had to be done. The survival of more than one country depended on it.

'What is the matter?' Conal asked, as Martil arrived to collect Karia.

Martil thought about brushing him off, but the Militia Commander was too canny a man to fool. Sometimes Martil almost preferred him as a drunken old fool. But he needed to talk to someone, and Conal was the only one who knew how he felt about Merren and who might offer some sympathy and advice. He certainly wasn't going to get that from Barrett.

'Merren is to marry Count Sendric,' he muttered.

'What?'

'What I said. Merren is marrying Count Sendric,' Martil repeated.

Conal shook his head. 'But why?'

'Says he's the only noble left in the country, and the people want to know there is going to be a succession. She says the people are still frightened, and want reassurance.'

'Aye, well, she has a point there. But Sendric! Aroaril's beard, the man's old enough to be her father!'

'Well, it's not like she has much of a choice, is it?' Louise bustled over, from where she had been watching the younger children. Karia and Louise's eldest daughter, a girl called Sarah, were playing with dolls in another room. 'Besides,' she continued, 'you'll still be the Queen's Champion. And you know what the sagas all say about that!'

'I don't care what the bloody sagas say!' Martil growled.

'You might, if they were coming true around you,' Louise pointed out.

'The last thing I need is for my life to resemble a saga!' Martil snorted. 'Anyway, she told me she doesn't have any feelings for me. Now, where's Karia?'

'Through there,' Louise said, and pointed.

She and Conal exchanged glances as Martil stomped off, picked up Karia and stalked away.

'You think there is more to this than Martil was saying?' Conal asked.

'You know there is!' Louise scoffed. 'The Queen is too clever a woman to do something like this without a good reason. And she has to be careful of gossip. Most of Norstalos has also read those sagas about queens and their champions.'

'Do we tell Martil that?'

'Leave him be,' Louise advised. 'It will work out over time. I don't know if they are even right for each other.'

'And of course you would be the one to know, eh?' Conal grinned.

'Get away with you! I mean it! The Queen isn't the only one who has to worry about gossip!'

Conal, still smiling, allowed himself to be pushed out the door.

Barrett and Tiera sat outside the village, watching a patch of flowers that grew, sprouted glorious blossoms, then shrank back to seedlings again.

'Your control is improving greatly! Are you finding your stamina is growing, as well?' Barrett asked.

Tiera nodded. 'It is! Even a week ago, that would have left me exhausted, even though we are only borrowing the magic, and returning the plants to their natural state.'

Barrett smiled at her. She was certainly maximising her limited talents. But then, working every day with the greatest mage in Norstalos was something most apprentices could only dream about.

Having a fellow pupil as talented as Karia was also a spur to her improvement. Barrett told himself it was merely his concern for her that led him to spend so much of his other, supposedly free, time with Tiera. The way her hair hung artlessly over one eye, the way a shapely lower leg showed from underneath her demure skirt, that had nothing to do with it.

'What will happen when this tour of the country is over?' Tiera asked.

'Well, the Queen will return to the capital, as will I. You could go to the capital but I would suggest setting yourself up in a small town, where the competition is less … fierce. All the best mages are in the big cities — and often leave only slim pickings for new mages.'

'A small town?'

'Somewhere close, perhaps. I would like to visit you — and of course, as long as there is an oak tree nearby, such a journey would take but a heartbeat.'

'I would like that. My friends were all left behind in the kitchens or servants' quarters. Sitting at the tables of the rich and powerful is a strange experience. I am more used to cleaning them!'

Barrett laughed with her. 'Just remember, we are no different. Underneath our clothes, we are exactly the same.' Then he blushed a little as he realised what he had said. Although she seemed not to have heard it.

'Tell me again about grand balls at court. Will the Queen have them again? And would you take me to one?'

Barrett smiled. 'Of course! I would be delighted to have you as my guest! I didn't go to many balls myself — I'm not much of a dancer, but I'll tell you what I remember …'

'Cessor is dead. He killed himself, and his family's gone,' Worick reported nervously.

'What?' Gello roared. 'I bring the fat fool here, give him everything, and this is how he repays me!'

'What should we do, sire? Do we alert the Berellians, ask their militia to search for his family?'

Gello thought for a moment. 'No. We shall show no sign of weakness. We shall tell them that he died of a weak heart. They may not even ask about him. Give them no hint that we are less than their equals.'

'As you wish, sire.'

22

Hutter walked in the door and collapsed into a chair with a groan.

'Let me get you a drink.' His wife hurried over, a pot of ale in her hand.

He took it with a wan smile. His family certainly liked their new house — the second-in-charge of the country's militia lived in an imposing stone building in the capital, which came with a pair of servants and a large garden. But the amount of time he was working was certainly more than what had been expected back in Chell, where it was a rare day indeed when he was not home by midafternoon. Now, he was leaving home before dawn and returning well after dark.

'You're working too hard,' his wife told him.

Hutter tried a broader smile this time. 'Has to be done. We have to get the militia back into the towns and villages, get some control back over the country. There's still places where there's more unsolved crimes than militiamen to look into them. Then there's all the criminals that we had to give pardons to — the word about that didn't get out to all the militia branches — and then there's all those men who were arrested for no reason by Gello and need to have their names cleared.'

'Well, it's no good you working yourself into the ground,' she scolded him fondly.

She had never expected to hear that her husband was a hero. There was even talk he might get his own saga — or at least a verse in one! And in her wildest dreams she had not thought of meeting the Queen and hearing Hutter named as a full captain of militia!

Hutter downed half his ale in one gulp. 'Let me tell you, after surviving Pilleth, this is not hard work. There was nothing harder than that,' he said solemnly.

'So we decide who represents us?' a farmer asked in confusion.

'That's right,' Gratt said patiently. 'I was a servant, now I am head of the town council for Sendric, and entitled to a seat on the new Royal Assembly. The Assembly will then decide which of its members goes to represent it at the Royal Council.'

'But that's the job of the nobles!' someone else protested.

'There are no more nobles,' Gratt pointed out. 'And, anyway, did they do such a good job? Not one of them had worked a hard day in their life! What did they know about your problems?'

'And everyone gets to choose — even women?' one grizzled old man snorted.

'We have a queen who will be the greatest ruler Norstalos has seen! And do you want to be the one who tells their wife they don't think they are clever enough, or important enough, to choose?'

'I don't want to tell her, but I don't think this is right, neither!' the old man growled. 'Women rulers! People deciding what to do! No nobles! 'Tain't right, I say! No good will come of it!'

Gratt sighed. He had lost count of the number of times he had given this talk, and he had heard the same complaints time after time. Most of the people were starting to get the idea, even sounding excited about the prospect of having someone they actually knew and trusted to represent them. But many others, especially the older ones, were suspicious and distrustful and it was showing up even more in the Queen's weekly surveys. It would take time for them to accept these dramatic changes.

The trip west to a village twenty miles from Darry's Inn was accomplished in a matter of moments. Forewarned by riders, the villagers, as well as many people from surrounding villages and farms, were there to welcome their arrival.

'The Queen!' The cry went up as Merren rode through the village to the inn, which had been emptied specially for the occasion.

Merren made sure she stopped to talk to some of the people; accepted a bunch of flowers from a child; praised the owners of nearby houses; and tried to make sure all felt she cared about them, that she was not just another royal, riding past a pack of peasants.

It was a slow procession through the village, and she was determined to take her time. This would be the first time a ruler had visited this village in its history, and she knew this day would be told and retold through the generations. Naturally she wanted them to talk about how much they had enjoyed it.

'They love you, my Queen.' Barrett smiled as they dismounted outside the inn.

'For now. We must never take that for granted,' Merren warned him. She stretched.

'Louise?'

'Here, my Queen.' Louise, who had ridden straight to the inn, bustled forwards.

'We need to find water for these flowers. We shall have a full council meeting in half a turn of the hourglass — for now, I feel the need for a bath.'

'One is all ready for you.'

Merren smiled. 'I could get to like this — sometimes I almost wish it would not end!'

Father Saltek settled himself in a chair and tried to get his thoughts in order. He would have to make the contact as brief as possible — the longer he maintained it, the greater the chance a Fearpriest would detect the use of Aroaril's power. But there was so much to say!

He took a deep breath. Cessor's family was safe — or as safe as they could expect in Berellia. The way the people had fallen under the spell of evil horrified him. Certainly there were those who held themselves back, even tried to help others. But still … The most evil, the most horrendous deeds were now seen as merely commonplace. Once he had wondered why the followers of Zorva were called Fearpriests. Now he knew — the stench of fear was thick on every street. Every person feared they would be the next sacrifice. Not a day went by without some poor soul publicly tortured and killed in front of cheering crowds.

But none seemed to have the strength or courage to speak out. Through fear, the people were cowed, willing to do anything they were told in exchange for another day of life. For a man who believed in the essential goodness of people, it was hard to watch. But he had his duty, and would continue while he had breath in his body. He would contact the Norstaline Archbishop, then get as far from this house as possible. A saddled horse, fast and fresh, stood waiting for him. He had received word that Earl Byrez's son wanted to see him — and out of respect for the memory of his dead lord, he would do what he could to meet the man. After this. He closed his eyes and began to pray.

On the whole, Merren felt her announcement went reasonably well.

Sendric had sat there with a face like thunder, while Martil refused to look at her. Barrett dropped the glass he was holding and the general gasp around the table would have blown out every candle in the chandelier, had it been lit.

'Sendric? But he's so old!' Karia whispered in a voice that carried the length of the table.

'The ceremony will be in a week's time and will be rather low-key, given that we are struggling to find enough money to keep the country running — and won't get any decent tax revenues until next spring,' she continued, trying to ignore their reaction. 'We shall take a break from this tour around the country for the wedding but, the next day, shall continue. That is more important. We shall be too busy to take an official honeymoon. This is probably a surprise, but it is what is best for the country. Norstalos is in a dire state, and we are slowly raising her up. Seeing a royal wedding, presided over by the new Archbishop; this will give the people hope again!'

Father Quiller was the first one to his feet. 'May I congratulate your majesty, and the Count, and wish you both a long and happy life together!'

There was a horribly long pause, before everyone except Martil raised their glasses or goblets. Conal, sitting next to Martil, nudged him, and Martil reluctantly also joined the toast.

'Well, now let us move on,' Merren said briskly, trying to gloss over the awkward moment. 'What new business?'

She looked around the table and realised Archbishop Nott was absent.

'Father Quiller, where is the Archbishop?'

Quiller looked a little troubled. 'He was receiving a message from a priest when I left. But I would have thought he should have finished by now.'

'How goes the struggle to rebuild the priesthood?' Merren asked.

'Slowly, your majesty. We have many novices under training, but it will be six months at least before they are ready to go out to the people. In the meantime, priests are travelling from church to church, holding services whenever they can.'

'Perhaps, Romon, you could get your bards to proclaim that news?' Merren suggested.

The newly appointed Royal Bard bowed his head. 'Of course, your majesty.'

Even Martil had to admit Romon had been extremely useful in the days and weeks since Pilleth. The Norstalines had lost trust in the bards — it seemed they no longer believed everything they were told — but to have the real story being spread around the countryside was still a help. Then there was the way Romon had helped drag the wounded over to the priests during Pilleth. There were at least six Rallorans alive and walking today because Romon had got them to the priests in time. And the experience seemed to have affected the bard; certainly his new saga, The Risen Queen, was actually a realistic depiction of the battle.

'Your majesty! Terrible news!' Nott raced into the room, his face agitated.

'He's just heard about the wedding to Sendric then, eh?' Conal murmured to Martil.

But Martil was not in the mood to appreciate the joke. He had never seen the old priest look so upset.

'Archbishop! What is it?' Merren leaped up instinctively.

Nott clutched her shoulder, his mouth opening and closing soundlessly.

'Your majesty, I have just heard from Berellia,' he finally managed to say.

'Archbishop, sit down! Someone get him some water!' Merren snapped.

Barrett jumped out of his chair, allowing Nott to sink down. Quiller bustled over with a goblet of water and Nott drank deeply before looking up at the ring of concerned faces.

'I have been contacted by one Father Saltek, who claims to be the last practising priest of Aroaril in Berellia.'

'It could be a trap. The Berellians are notorious for such things,' Martil said immediately.

Nott shook his head. 'This was no trap. No priest can use Aroaril's powers and lie at the same time. Besides, I remember Archbishop Declan speaking of such a one — Declan had been in touch with a Berellian priest. This man. He told me he had been ministering to the family of Count Cessor.'

'I did not think that fat fool would still have the hide to try and pretend to be a churchgoer still,' Merren sniffed.

'He's dead. He slit his own wrists, because he was forced to convert to Zorva — and sacrifice one of his daughters as an example of his loyalty to the Dark One,' Nott said bleakly. 'His last wish was that his surviving children and wife be given safe haven in Norstalos.'

Barrett laughed harshly. 'Why should we care what happens to them? It was the work of Cessor, and others, who brought us to this state. His family can reap the crop he has sown.'

'There must be more to it than this,' Merren said coolly.

'Indeed there is,' Nott agreed. 'As a symbol of his good faith — and knowing it gives his family no guarantees — he wanted to let us know what Gello is plotting.'

'Go ahead,' Merren said calmly, although her stomach was suddenly churning.

'It is worse than we feared. Not only are the Berellians ready to go to war to put Gello back on the throne, but Gello's conversion to Zorva has meant the Fearpriests have summoned help from their homeland.'

'What sort of help?' Martil interrupted.

'Warriors. From the land of Tenoch. Cessor saw them in action. He says there are fifteen thousand of them, everything from spearmen to slingers. With Berellia's eight thousand and Gello's three regiments, they have amassed an army big enough to take not just Norstalos but the entire continent — they intend to convert us all to Zorva, by fire and spear. And they are coming soon. Within weeks.'

506

'And their plan of attack?' Martil asked in the horrified silence that followed.

'Three-pronged. The Berellians will come straight over the border; Gello and his pack of traitors will travel up through Tetril and attack from the east; the Tenochs will land their boats on the west coast and attack from there; all three prongs to meet at Norstalos City.'

There was silence around the table. All knew what the victory at Pilleth had cost. Now they were facing three such armies …

'The Dragon Sword,' Merren said through lips that had suddenly gone dry. 'We must use the Dragon Sword to raise an army big enough to match Gello's plan.'

'I don't think it is Gello's plan any more, my Queen,' Nott said apologetically. 'It is now the Fearpriests who are in charge. Gello will be their puppet, no more.'

'I know Gello, and he will be no puppet. He will be seeking to turn this to his advantage,' Merren disagreed. 'Although it does not matter whose plan it is. Three armies!'

'Forgive me, my Queen. But they are actually planning four armies,' Nott interrupted. 'They want to attack from the north as well.'

'With what?' Conal cried.

'Goblins. Or rather, to give them their proper name — the Derthals. The Fearpriests are sending a mission to convince the Derthal High Chief that they can keep any land they seize.'

Merren seemed to slump at this, but rallied determinedly.

'We have the Dragon Sword. As we proved at Pilleth, we also have a Champion who can wield it. We shall rally the people—'

'My Queen, we cannot,' Martil called, hating himself for having to say it.

Everyone looked at him. 'And why not?' Merren demanded.

'I cannot just raise the Dragon Sword and gather people together. Even if it worked …'

'What do you mean, even if it worked? I thought you had unlocked its power?' Merren exclaimed.

'It will surely know that I do not want to use it to raise an army,' Martil said strongly, to gasps around the table. He looked at them carefully. 'Not like this. Because those men would be slaughtered. We have arms and armour to outfit a few thousand, but the rest would be fighting with what they bring. It would be a massacre. I have said it before — I hope not to say it again. Life is not like a saga. You don't wave a magic sword and have an army appear to defeat your foes! It does not work like that. I saw what happened when Rallora marched conscripts against the Berellians. And you all saw what happened at Pilleth to the conscript regiments. We would murder thousands of men — *and still lose*. My Queen, I am sorry, but even if you commanded me to, I could not use the Dragon Sword to call men to their deaths.'

'But this is their country they are fighting for! Surely the people will fight harder, knowing it is for their families! We could inspire them, use the Dragon Sword—' Merren cried.

'Bravery is no match for a wall of shields and years of training! Let us call in Kettering and Hutter, ask them how their regiments fared at Pilleth! Ask Kay! His rangers took on a shield wall and were cut to pieces! We would have a mob; at Sendric the mob managed to win, because there was no room for the soldiers to use their numbers and training. On a battlefield, the mob will be destroyed. I have seen it happen.' He stopped then, overcome with memories. 'I cannot use this Sword to call up thousands of men, just to lead them to their deaths.'

Merren gritted her teeth. 'So what do you suggest? That we give up?'

'Get everybody into the north. Let the Berellians strike at nothing. We must try and hold the passes long enough to train an army to defeat them,' Martil said immediately.

Barrett gasped. 'Evacuate the whole country? Are you mad? Have you any idea what that would entail?'

'Better than leaving them to Gello and his Fearpriests,' Martil growled.

'Tens of thousands of people, across a massive country — dear Aroaril, it would take months for the south to walk all the way to the north, carrying their possessions — and that's assuming they are even willing to go!'

'Leave the possessions. You can always build a new house,' Martil said simply. 'It's more difficult to give life to the dead.'

'It could not be done! Half the people still don't trust us — they might think that Gello was here to save them from the Butchers of Bellic!' Barrett pointed out.

'Then that'll be the last mistake they make,' Martil snarled. 'I've seen what the Berellians do when they invade a country.'

'We need help from somewhere! The Rallorans, the Tetrans, the Avish. Surely they would see what is happening and come to our aid?' Merren suggested.

'The Tetrans would be useless. Their army is a joke. And anyway, isn't Gello coming through their border? Sounds like they've done a deal with him. As for the Rallorans, how would they get here? Neither the Berellians nor the Avish would let a Ralloran army march over its borders. Just one regiment of Berellians would be able to hold the Rallorans back for a few weeks. By then we would be finished.' Martil paused, then went on. 'Also, Rallora is tired of war. They will not begin a new one for Norstalos. Not when King Croft refused to come to our aid. King Tolbert is still bitter about that. Norstalos stood apart, proclaiming the southern wars to be none of their business, when you could have stopped them.'

'Nonsense!' Barrett snorted.

Martil glared at him. 'Ask for help — and see how much you get. Arrogant Norstalos is feared and envied by the southern countries — they will not rush to your aid. If we want to save Norstalos, we have to do it ourselves. So, we should head north. Don't forget, it is already autumn. Winter will make it impossible for them to maintain so many men in the field. We won't need to hold for long before they'll retreat.'

'If we can hold those passes — you showed yourself how easily they can be taken,' Barrett scoffed. 'We could be marching ourselves into a death trap! And, don't forget, there'll be an army of goblins attacking the north!'

'It's a better chance than taking them on in battle! As for the goblins, we must give them a better deal than the one the Berellians can offer. Surely there is something they want!' Martil argued.

'What would the goblins want?' Merren asked. 'Sendric, what do you think?'

Sendric shrugged. 'Your majesty, they are simple hunter–gatherers. They have no use for gold or silver,

510

pottery, clothes, art, wine or anything else we would consider of value. Of course we could offer them food, but we would be hard-pressed to feed and shelter our own people as it is.'

Merren looked down at the table, trying not to feel sick. She had begun to hope again — and now this. Suddenly the problems she was having with Martil and Sendric seemed insignificant

'If we tried to evacuate the country — say we were able to rescue most, if not all the people, get them to the north. Could we really hold those passes long enough to train an army?'

Martil looked at her carefully. 'It will be hard. But it is our only chance. We cannot beat them in battle,' he answered honestly.

'Your majesty, I can't believe we are talking about this! This is no hope at all!' Sendric cried. 'And even if, by some miracle, we were able to hold the passes, train an army and win, the country would face ruin, as well as starvation! The south is where our iron mines are, as well as the ironworking industry. It is also home to our best quarries, and stoneworkers. The west is home to the tanners, the potters, the spinners and the weavers. The east is our bread basket, our farming heart. We would lose all those industries; we would be reduced to the level of goblins!'

'Count Sendric, that is the last time I want to hear the Derthals referred to as goblins. If we are to stop them becoming allies of the Berellians, and win their aid ourselves, we need to treat them with respect,' Merren snapped.

'Win their aid?' Sendric repeated.

Merren stopped, almost surprised at herself. She had meant merely to deliver a rebuke to Sendric but, the more she thought about it, the more the idea appealed.

'You said yourself the Derthals are hunter–gatherers. Could they fight?'

Sendric gazed blankly at her. 'Well, yes, your majesty. They use spear and club every day to hunt down their prey, as well as to fight rival clans that are encroaching on their territory. Back in the days when they would attack our towns and villages, they were said to be a dangerous enemy. They are smaller than a man, but are strong for their size — they are deadly up close. But against cavalry they are helpless.'

'Your majesty, what are you thinking?' Quiller asked.

Merren smiled. 'I am thinking we would offer a deal to the Derthals. Perhaps we could bring them to our side. We could hold the passes if we had thousands of extra spearmen.'

'My Queen! Surely you do not mean to talk to the gob— to the Derthals! They are godless abominations of nature!' Sendric gasped.

'They are Aroaril's creatures, as are we. And they are able to think and converse,' Quiller interjected. 'I spent six months with them, trying to show them the path to the light, with some success.'

'Captain Martil, could you hold the passes with an extra five or ten thousand spearmen?'

Martil smiled. 'Of course, my Queen.'

'This is madness!' Sendric exclaimed.

Merren cut him off with a wave of her hand.

'We have no choice,' she said simply. 'We need all the help we can get. We shall ask the Rallorans, Tetrans and Avish. And we need to send an embassy to the Derthals. If nothing else, we must stop them from joining the Berellians. Meanwhile, we need to get people moving, get them out of the path of the invading armies. And we shall need to slow the various invasions down, to give our people time to get away.

'Conal, Sendric, I want to see plans for evacuating every town south of the three passes. Martil, I want to see how you can use our trained men to slow down three invasions at once. Archbishop Nott, I want ideas on how we can shelter and feed these refugees, as well as how the priests can prepare the people to move north. And, Father Quiller, I want a list of ideas as to how we can win over the Derthals. Romon, I want an emergency proclamation announcing the evacuation. You have until tomorrow midday.'

She stood then, determined to show them none of the fear that was raging inside her.

'Hope is not lost yet,' she told them.

Nerrin had received some strange orders in his career but this one was a real concern. It had been delivered by a magically enchanted bird, but he had become used to that by now.

'Do you think the people will obey us, sir?' Dunner asked.

'That, Sergeant, is what we need to find out,' Nerrin sighed.

The orders were clear enough. Thousands of Berellians were massing over the border and would smash through the south, driving up to Norstalos City, where they would meet with Gello's traitorous Norstalines and strange warriors from a country called Tenoch. Nerrin and his men knew all too well what a Berellian invasion would mean. They had seen it first-hand. The Berellians had perfected the art of sacking a village. Two companies would work their way around the back of the village, while a third would make a sudden charge, roaring and blowing trumpets. The frightened villagers would naturally run — right into the trap, where they could be killed far easier and quicker than if the Berellians had to fight house to house. Then they would go through the empty village at their leisure, making sure every hiding place was found, every person killed, everything of value stolen. There were ways to stop this. The best way, of course, was to defeat them on the battlefield. But Nerrin was not ordered to fight. He was ordered to judge the reaction of the nearest village when given the order to leave everything but food, warm clothes and livestock, use anything with wheels or hoofs to begin the long trek to Sendric, more than five hundred miles to the north.

It was staggering. Such a journey would take weeks, if not months — and the Berellians could attack in days. But, if it was to be made, it had to begin now. Nerrin had to give the order, then report to the Queen on its success. He would have liked to make a stand on the River Brack, the first natural defence, fifty miles to the north, try and stop the Berellians there. But it looked more like he would have to conduct a fighting retreat all the way to the passes, using his men to buy the refugees time.

'Well, sir, ready when you are.' Dunner saluted.

Nerrin nodded, and waved to the men. Not wanting to overwhelm the village with armed men, he had brought just two squads with him, wearing just their blue surcoats over tunic and trousers. They had left their mail shirts back at the camp.

'We'll ride to the church, dismount, then ring the bell. That should bring them running,' Nerrin predicted.

This village was barely ten miles from the border, sitting astride the main road south, and was obviously peaceful and prosperous. The houses were all of wood or stone, neatly thatched, the fields were well tended, there was plenty of livestock penned nearby and even the manure heaps were tidy. The inn was particularly large, as was the old priest's house. Children waved to them as they rode in and assembled by the church.

'You never know, their replacement priest could even be Kesbury,' Dunner joked, after he had sent a pair of men inside the church to ring the bell.

The village had been without a priest since Archbishop Nott took over, as this particular priest had lost Aroaril's favour years ago and, under Nott's new church, had been ordered to stand down from his post. Replacements for these villages were still months away. The church was empty, although the villagers had kept it clean.

'A priest who was a former guard on a brothel. I can't get over that.' Nerrin smiled, watching the surrounding houses for the reaction.

'Let me tell you, sir, we saw plenty of priests visiting the brothel — they all said they were there to make sure the girls were healthy — but they had a funny way of checking, if you know what I mean!' Dunner chuckled, as the bell began to peal.

'Quiet now,' Nerrin advised, as villagers flooded out of houses and the inn, and began to hurry over.

'What is going on?' The innkeeper was the first man there. 'I am Loft, the head of the village council and I demand to know what you are doing!'

'Loft, good people of the village. I am Captain Nerrin, commander of Queen Merren's forces in the south. We have received word the Berellians are planning to invade. Within weeks, possibly even days, thousands of Berellians will be coming through here, to kill and steal and burn. We cannot stop them. To save yourselves, and your families, you need to pack any food and warm clothing you have, then leave now. Make for the north, put as much distance between yourselves and the border as you can.'

Cries of shock and alarm came from the villagers, but Loft waved for quiet.

'How far north? The River Brack?' he demanded.

'Further,' Nerrin had to admit.

'Where?' Loft pressed.

Nerrin gritted his teeth. 'Sendric.'

Stunned silence greeted his reply, as well as a few laughs.

'You cannot expect us to go to Sendric!' Loft gasped, stunned. 'Where would we sleep, what would we eat?'

'You will sleep wherever you can. As for eating — as the innkeeper, these people will need you to hand over your stocks, to help feed them on the way north,' Nerrin told him.

'And you will pay me for this?' Loft asked, quietly.

'We cannot,' Nerrin admitted. 'But you will have the gratitude of your country and your neighbours.'

'Gratitude! Do you think that pays the bills! This is an outrage! What about the army? Why isn't it here?' Loft snarled.

'The Queen's victory over the usurper Gello has seen the army decimated. We have too few soldiers to stand. That is why we must escape to the north, where we can hold them off while we train a new army,' Nerrin declared.

'This is unacceptable! I pay taxes, I expect

protection!' Loft roared, and many in the crowd, which was still growing, agreed with him. 'My inn, everything I've worked for — I mean, everything the people here have worked for, you can't expect us to just hand it out for free, then walk away from it! I'll be ruined!'

'But we cannot stop eight thousand Berellians! I tell you, I have seen a Berellian invasion. They do not take prisoners and they do not know the meaning of mercy—' Nerrin tried to explain.

'You have seen a Berellian invasion? So you and your men are Rallorans?' Loft snapped.

Nerrin had to admit they were.

'the Butchers of Bellic! Why have you been posted on the border? No wonder the Berellians are invading! After what you did, I would cross a border to punish bastards like you!' Loft spat.

'It's not like that!' Nerrin said hotly.

'Well, it sounds like it to me! The Berellians are after a little revenge, and who can blame them! They probably want nothing to do with us! As long as we stay out of their way, and don't try to hide you, we'll be fine!' Loft looked around the crowd, trying to rally them to his point of view.

'I am telling you this for your own safety,' Nerrin warned.

'You probably just want us out of here so you can rob the place! Leave here with just our food and clothes and animals? In other words, give you everything else!'

Nerrin realised that while he was trying to have a quiet, calm conversation with the man, most of the crowd was not hearing his words, just Loft's bellows.

'The Berellians are coming! They will kill and destroy everything in their path! If you want to save yourselves and your children, pack your things and get moving!' Nerrin roared.

'Don't listen to him! Don't trust these bastards! They're the Butchers of Bellic and want us to get involved in their war with the Berellians! We're safe here! Stay!' Loft bawled at the crowd, and actually started moving people away, chivvying them back to their homes.

'Don't do this! I don't have enough men to protect you!' Nerrin could not believe what he was seeing. Back in Rallora, all you had to do was mention the name 'Berellia' and people would have their things packed and be halfway out of the village on anything that could move before you finished speaking. But these Norstalines …

'Think of your children!' Nerrin implored. 'Do you want them to live?'

'Don't trust them! You know what the bards said, you know what the priest said about these men! They're killers and thieves! It's a private war between them and Berellia! Go home! Off with you! Any that leave here, I'll have your fields, I'll have your homes, you'll never live here again!'

At this, many people began heading home; the ones who stayed were the drinkers from the inn, most of whom still carried their pots of ale, and who seemed to think this was some sort of entertainment.

'What are we going to do, sir?' Dunner asked quietly.

Nerrin stared at the vanishing villagers. A handful of families seemed to be moving with some purpose, as though they actually planned to pack up and leave, but more than three-quarters of the village appeared to be heading either home for dinner or back to the inn.

'People! Listen to me!' Nerrin started forwards, thinking if he spoke to the people individually, he might have more luck — but Loft barred his way.

'Stay away from us! We don't need your type here! If it wasn't for you, Norstalos wouldn't have had any of this trouble! Duke Gello wouldn't have tried anything if the Queen hadn't hired you bastards!' Loft declared.

'That's a lie!' Nerrin growled, trying to keep the anger from his voice. 'My men have fought and died for your country! We are going to fight and die to keep the Berellians away from you again!'

'As far as I am concerned, you are scum, and I wouldn't believe you if you told me the sun was going to rise tomorrow,' Loft snarled, turned on his heel and walked away, receiving some drunken cheers from his customers as he did so.

'Let me take him, sir,' Dunner hissed. 'I'll sit the idiot on his arse and then maybe they'll listen to us.'

'No, Sergeant. We can't start a fight with these people. We'll try another village. If they hear everyone else is running away, they might change their minds,' Nerrin decided.

The next village was just as bad. The opposition here was not led by an innkeeper, but an ex-priest who had stayed on in the village after being dismissed from his post — and was obviously less than happy with the new regime. Like Loft, he was also less than impressed at the idea of sharing out stored food and drink among the villagers. Nerrin suspected the size of the ex-priest's house — twice as big as anything else in the village — had everything to do with that.

'This doesn't involve you!' the ex-priest, Chanlon, roared at his former flock. 'We can trust King Gello!

He is just returning to take back the crown that was stolen from him by these Ralloran mercenaries! And we know the Berellians — Berellians come through here with goods to sell! They're not the monsters this murderer would have you believe!'

'Did you not hear of what happened during the Ralloran Wars?' Nerrin tried. 'The Berellians will sweep through here with fire and sword!'

'They would not dare! This is not some mongrel country like Rallora, this is Norstalos! Blessed by Aroaril, honoured by the dragons themselves! Nobody would dare attack us! No, the fight here is between the King and the usurping queen! The dragons did not want us to have a queen, such a thing is against the natural order of life! We should welcome these Berellians, for they will restore King Gello to the throne and Norstalos to its rightful place at the head of the world! Leave here? Share out all we have earned, give it to those who do not deserve it! I never heard the like! *This is against the natural order of things!*'

Trained by years of speaking in the pulpit, Chanlon's voice whipped into the villagers, drowning out Nerrin's rational argument and turning all but a handful against the Rallorans.

'Come on, Sergeant. We can do no good here,' Nerrin said sadly.

'Ride away! We don't want to see your like again!' Chanlon screamed at them.

'So what do we tell the Queen, sir?' Dunner wondered.

'That getting everyone to flee to the north is not as easy as it sounds,' Nerrin said lightly, although he felt sick inside. He was almost happy to see the likes of Chanlon and Loft impaled on Berellian spears but, for most of the villagers, their only crime was to believe what they had been told by barcs and priests. Worse, he was going to have to risk his men to save villagers who hated him.

'I hope she has some more ideas for persuading the people.'

The farewell from Berellia was full of the pomp and circumstance that country did so well. Gello had found himself mightily impressed by the way the Berellians had managed to devote their whole country to the pursuit, and celebration, of war.

Cheering crowds lined the streets as immaculately uniformed men marched past in perfect step, banners held high. The crowds then packed into a massive open square where King Markuz, his voice helped magically by the Royal Magician, whipped them into a frenzy. The fatherland was threatened by the vile Witch Queen over the border. Berellia's ancestral lands had been stolen and its people needed more living room. It was time to secure the people's safety by invading and taking back this land. After this war, Berellia would take its rightful place as leader of the world.

If he had not been talking about Norstaline land, Gello might actually have believed him.

'One people, one state, one leader!' Markuz's voice bounced from the stone walls that lined the square. The crowd chanted the words back at him. Atop the walls was an entire regiment, every man carrying either a torch or a banner. As one, they cheered and stamped their feet on the battlements. It was amazing; Gello could feel the hair on the back of his neck rise with the power and the passion Markuz was inspiring in the huge crowd.

This was how to prepare a population for war! They would do anything for Markuz now, he saw. His own people were too passive. He needed to inflame them like this, if Norstalos were to truly rule the world. It was a valuable lesson, he decided.

He was distracted by a huge cheer, marking the end of the rally. Then, the crowd was given a sacred duty.

'We may lose our gallant men in this war, so it is every Berellian woman's duty to start a new generation to fight for the fatherland!' Markuz roared at them. 'And every soldier's duty to father his replacement!'

Gello liked that touch. Every woman's duty to get herself pregnant that night, for the sake of Berellia. And the perfect way to get men fired up for a battle. He tucked that thought away for another day.

'Sire, do we let our men join the fun?' Feld asked.

Gello grinned. 'Of course! But let them know that tomorrow we march. We have further to go, and must be in position by the next full moon. But, for now, we should honour the country that shelters us by sampling their customs.'

Feld laughed. 'Aye, sire!'

522

23

Merren looked down at the table for a long moment after hearing Nerrin's report.

'Your majesty, we can expect some of the people to begin moving — and we can also expect others to start fleeing once they see the neighbouring villages going up in flames. We can provide some protection to the fleeing people,' Martil concluded. He had earlier explained how his Rallorans would slow down the Berellian advance, while the rangers would delay Gello, and the archers and Rocus's Norstaline companies tackled the Tenoch warriors.

'We have to get the people to the north! There is no alternative!' Merren looked around the table, but none could meet her gaze. 'Well, Conal, I want every militiaman you have knocking on doors, telling people to go. Use the soldiers as well. Get every bard out spreading the word, every priest telling their parish that servants of the Dark One are coming. We will keep telling them until they believe us!'

'Of course, but there are not enough of them, your majesty,' Father Quiller said. 'And not everyone will be convinced. After all, the people have discovered that both the priests and the bards have been lying to them.'

Merren sighed, her heart faltering at the thought of what was going to happen to her people.

'Perhaps I should make contact with Gello directly. If I agreed to go, to let him return …'

'My Queen, you cannot even consider that,' Nott said firmly. 'Not only would it betray the sacrifices already made, it would do no good. Gello is not in charge any more, the Fearpriests are. There can be no peace, no arrangement made with them. We fight or we die.'

Merren inclined her head. 'Then we must have more time. Martil, I know what you said about Rallora, but an attack on Berellia's south would at least keep most of the Berellians at home …'

Martil sighed. 'For King Tolbert to declare war on Berellia again … It might be possible but it would be a long and complicated negotiation. Then he would have to concentrate the army on the northern border — by the time he was able to do that, I fear the Berellians would have already invaded.'

'Nevertheless, we must try. The Ralloran ambassador will be here later. We shall speak to him and, if necessary, Barrett and I will travel to Rallora to speak to King Tolbert,' Merren ordered.

'The Avish?'

'They have refused to help — all the ambassador would say was how much he hated Captain Martil.' Sendric sighed.

'Well, what about Tetril? I know they are a small country, with a small army, but if they could at least stop Gello's men …'

'I have been trying to contact the Tetran ambassador but he seems to have disappeared,'

Sendric reported. 'I suspect he may have left deliberately, to avoid speaking to us. I will keep trying but I fear we shall have no joy there.'

'We must get the people moving!' Merren insisted. 'We need more ideas! Anything to get them moving! Meanwhile, we must have a safe haven for the people in the north. The Derthals. We must not only prevent them from joining our enemies but convince them to help us. Father Quiller, what can we offer them?'

Quiller looked across at Sendric before answering. 'I think there is only one thing that they would want. The return of their ancestral forest.'

'What!' Sendric raged.

'Hear me out.' Quiller held up his hand. 'The forest where the Queen was able to hide from Gello's men so successfully is hardly used by our people. Meanwhile, its cave systems would provide shelter, its streams both water and fish, and its abundant game would be far richer for the Derthals than the mountain deer and goats they struggle to hunt and subsist upon now. Life in those mountains is harsh. Derthals are considered old at thirty, ancient at forty. Cold, disease, hunting accidents and lack of food claim both young and old alike. But if they were given the forest back, I do believe they would be willing to help us.'

'Have you lost your wits, man? Aroaril above, they cannot be trusted! Bring ten thousand of those screaming savages down below the mountains and no farmer or villager would be safe!' Sendric barked. 'My forebears risked life and fortune so that Norstalos's northern border could be safe, the gold and silver mines secure, the rich farmland accessible—'

'Wrong, Sendric,' Merren interrupted. 'It was their land and we were the invaders. They only tried to defend what was theirs. There is no reason Derthal and Norstaline cannot live side by side, in peace. And you forget one important thing — without them, we will not have a Norstalos. Quiller, I want deeds of ownership drawn up immediately. Once I have seen the Ralloran and, hopefully, Tetran ambassadors, I will decide where to go first. But I will make the trip north. The Derthals must meet me, not some emissary.'

'My Queen, that would be even more foolish than giving land to them! Once you go north, you would not return!' Sendric protested. 'You may think them harmless, and I grant you there has not been a serious goblin incident for fifty years, but I was raised on tales of their screaming attacks! There was a reason Sendric was built with a secret escape route! They are a deadly enemy!'

'All the better to have them on our side then,' Merren said coldly.

King Markuz was in full armour, which was not unusual, but he was also on horseback, which was.

'I will meet you at Norstalos City! I am personally leading my men into battle, so there can be no mistakes,' Markuz announced, offering Gello his hand.

'We shall meet you there,' Gello acknowledged, as his men prepared to leave.

The Berellians had not only replaced his men's weapons — although some of those were the strange club-axes the warriors of Tenoch used — they had given Gello enough supplies to get his men through Tetril and eastern Norstalos. Plenty of the cured sausage the Berellians seemed to love, along with their raw cabbage dish, cheese and black bread. Some of the Norstalines, more used to hardened oatcakes, had muttered about the 'foreign food' but most had been happy to pack the food for what they saw as a triumphal march back into Norstalos.

'And the Tetrans will give us no trouble?' Gello asked cautiously.

'Correct, my friend! We have signed an extensive treaty with them, one which they have been agitating about for years now. Of course we are going to break it, but the fools don't know that — and, by the time they realise it, it will be too late. Same with the Rallorans. Tolbert thinks this is purely a matter between you and the Witch Queen. And his suspicions have been allayed by the large payment we promised. His country is still poor as a peasant after the Ralloran Wars; he won't jeopardise that much gold by doing something foolish, like helping the Witch Queen. And he doesn't like making a decision. If she asks for help, he'll dither, and we'll seize Norstalos — then we can go south to finish what we started in Rallora sixteen years ago!'

Gello smiled. That sounded perfect. Let the Berellians go and refight the Ralloran Wars, while he rebuilt Norstalos.

'And noble Itlan and Yertlaan? Are they ready?'

'Ready and eager. They will leave a day after you, with your Earl Worick to guide them to safe harbours. A shame your other noble could not help also,' Markuz said blandly, but Gello saw there was steel underneath the voice.

He kept his own voice light, uninterested. 'He was always a fool for food. And your rich food proved too much for him. We are better off without him: he would have eaten enough of your sausage to feed an entire squad. He might have even sunk one of the Tenoch ships!'

Markuz roared with laughter and offered his hand again.

'To victory, and the return of your throne!'

'Victory and my throne!' Gello echoed with a smile.

Merren stormed out of the audience chamber, leaving Martil to hurriedly follow.

'How on earth did the Rallorans win their wars, when they are not able to see past the ends of their own noses?' she raged, as she stormed back to the throne room. They had returned to the capital to see the ambassadors. The Tetran ambassador had turned up, but her relief at that had been short-lived. He had made it quite clear the Tetrans would not be using their small army to try and stop Gello's forces, having recently signed a treaty of 'mutual defence' with Berellia. He had then announced he was leaving, his term of duty having finished — although he had been there barely a year.

Merren was annoyed, but it had not been unexpected. After all, Tetril could be snapped up by anyone, if they so wished. The only thing stopping its bigger neighbours from crushing it was knowing the prize was hardly worth the effort.

But the Rallorans! Despite Martil's warning, she had expected more from them than this!

Martil tried to catch up with her. 'My Queen, I did warn you that Rallora was tired of war. They cannot see the danger. The border with Berellia is well fortified, after what happened at Bellic ...' he coughed and then went on. 'They think they are safe, the Berellians broken. And Tolbert will not take risks. If he had agreed to finish the job of invading Berellia in the first place, we would not be in this mess. He thought our losses would be too high. He would always rather take the easy course, than the difficult but necessary decision.'

Merren shook her head. 'Of all the stupid, selfish, short-sighted …!'

Martil merely nodded agreement.

'If I go to Rallora, can I change his mind?'

Martil's face showed his struggle to come up with an answer. 'It is possible. But I have never seen him change his mind,' he warned. 'And the ambassador was only passing on the message he had been given by Rallora. Peace and goodwill between nations, a new start, Berellia has made a gesture of trust … I would guess they are offering back-payment of the tribute they try to reduce each year. King Tolbert needs money — lots of it. The pension bill of men who fought to free the country is huge, and he was forced to waive taxes on large amounts of rich farmland so people would resettle close to the border.'

Merren slowed to a stop. 'So I must decide on my priority. Trying to win over Rallora, or win over the Derthals. I must judge who might help me more than the other.'

'Merren, you would have to better Berellia's offer before Tolbert would consider helping you. Even then, there are no guarantees the Berellians could be diverted from us.'

'So we must see the Derthals. We cannot have them on Berellia's side. If nothing else, we must make sure they do not invade the north.' She sighed.

'Good sense says we should devote every effort to win over the Rallorans. After all, the Rallorans hate the Berellians and have a veteran army. With ten thousand Rallorans attacking southern Berellia, Markuz would have to take his army back to stop them. Forcing the Berellians to fight us both, at opposite ends of the continent, would give us a strong chance of victory. But only if Markuz cares about his people. The Rallorans could attack and he could ignore them to finish us off. I fear that is exactly what he would do. So good sense is actually foolish. Why waste our time and effort on the Rallorans, when they cannot give us what we need? And I confess I feel somehow drawn to the Derthals. Could they really secure those passes?'

Martil smiled. She had absorbed everything he had tried to teach her about strategy — and more. 'Thousands of their warriors at the passes … Of course it would help! Those passes are exactly the sort of territory they should fight well in.'

'As long as we can get everyone safely there first,' Merren said. 'I will see Conal, Sendric and the others again before we leave. They have to find a way to get the people moving.'

'One step at a time. Get the Derthals on our side first,' he suggested.

Merren smiled at him, almost said something warm, then remembered that she could not give him even a hint of her feelings.

'Captain, as my Champion, I will expect you to come with me when we travel north, to win over the Derthals.'

'Merren, I know you need to impress them, but surely it would be better to send Sendric. You are too valuable—'

'No, I am not,' she told him. 'I am no more valuable than any of you. Besides, if you, Barrett, Karia and Quiller cannot protect me, who can?'

Martil opened his mouth to argue further but she silenced him with a look.

'Get the others together. We shall leave at first light. We cannot delay any longer.'

'Your majesty.' Martil bowed.

'I need to tell you about the Derthals,' Quiller instructed carefully.

'What are they like?' Karia asked, bouncing up and down.

Against Martil's better judgement, she was coming along. But he had to admit, she could be useful. Apparently none of the Derthals could use magic — and were impressed by those who were able to demonstrate the power. And, as they could not bring along many guards, anything that could offer protection would be welcome. It was going to be a close-run thing. To get the Derthals on their side, and persuade them to march enough of their warriors south, they had to swiftly win over their High Chief. And that was going to be no easy thing. Quiller had made contact with a priest called Alban, who had been living and working with the Derthals for more than a year. Through him, he had arranged a meeting with the Derthal High Chief, who had agreed to meet with the Queen of the Norstalines. But meeting with him was one thing. Overcoming centuries of hatred, persecution and mistrust was another. Merren had thought it best Sendric not come along; not only was he unable to stop calling the Derthals 'goblins' but he was also the symbol of Norstaline betrayal and invasion.

Meanwhile, Sendric and Conal would try to get the people moving. The evacuation of the country was going slowly. Too slowly. The east was moving; people heading inland, towards the capital. But in the west and south, where the invasion would be led by Tenoch warriors and Berellians, there was much less progress.

The west had always been Gello's land, and many of the people there were highly suspicious of the Queen. Most of them, especially the richer ones, were looking forward to Gello returning, thinking they would be treated far better. Hutter and Kettering were hard at work there, trying to get people to move away from the coast, and away from the roads leading to the capital. But even in the most co-operative villages, more than half of the inhabitants just refused to move.

The south was a little friendlier, but equally reluctant. A trickle of refugees was heading north on the roads but too many people were just staying put. That would change, but the cost would be high. Merren was trying not to think about it.

'The people have become complacent and arrogant. They are not ready for this trial of blood and fire. But, if we survive, we will become a stronger country,' Nott had predicted.

Merren did not take much comfort from that.

'You have to find a way to get the people moving! You have to! Don't let me down!' she told Conal and Sendric. 'Try anything you want — you have my full authority to do whatever it takes. Have the militia carry people out of their homes, if you must!'

'And the ones closest to the border? Time is already running out for them,' Conal warned.

'Then we must decide if they are worth sacrificing

our soldiers to protect. It will be judged on how many there are, the roads they must use and whether they have skills we can use or supplies we need. A village of ironworkers is vital — farmers, we have plenty of. I shall leave you detailed instructions. Carry them out as best as you can. I trust you.'

She felt bad about giving them this responsibility but there was no point in getting the people to leave their homes unless they had somewhere safe to go to — and for that she needed the Derthals.

Now she, Barrett, Quiller, Martil and Karia were preparing to head north, using one of Barrett's magical gateways to jump to the most northern oak tree he could find. They would ride the rest of the way, to where an honour guard of Derthals would meet them. As for guards, all they were bringing were Jaret and Wilsen.

They sat around the table in Barrett's kitchen. Wilsen and Jaret were packing food for the journey and Barrett was devouring a plate of fruit, then they would leave through the tree in Barrett's garden.

Quiller was lecturing them carefully. 'The first thing you need to remember about the Derthals is they are not monsters. They look like men, but are different in many ways. They care for their families and are capable of complex emotions. Concepts such as good and evil do not necessarily apply to them. They consider what is good for them, what is good for their family and what is good for their tribe. Family disputes are settled by the chief, tribal disputes by the High Chief. But, if necessary, disputes can be settled by combat. The winner is judged to have been the one telling the truth. Their loyalty to their tribal chief is absolute but while those tribal chiefs obey the High Chief, they are not necessarily loyal to him — particularly if they think they should be High Chief.

'What we are asking the High Chief to do will test the bonds of his tribal chiefs — if they support him, we will have an army. But if they refuse, at best we will only have the Derthals from the High Chief's own tribe. Many of the tribal chiefs, as well as the more important warriors, will speak our language, having learned it from generations of priests. So we must tread carefully. They will be suspicious of us, and it will be easy to give offence. If we lose this chance …'

'We lose everything,' Merren finished. 'So we give them respect, do whatever they ask to prove ourselves worthy of trust. Understand?'

'When can we see one?' Karia asked.

Merren ignored her; she was thinking her father would be apoplectic at the thought of handing over part of Norstalos to anyone, let alone 'goblins'. There would be many other Norstalines who would be outraged, as well. As with the Rallorans, she just had to hope that the people would accept the Derthals when they came to save them. She was afraid she could save the country, only to have it reject her, for using Rallorans and Derthals to achieve victory.

But there was no other choice. The Ralloran King was too blind to see his best chance of long-term survival was to attack the Berellians. Although she had had no reply when the Ralloran ambassador had pointed out: 'You could have saved Rallora, your majesty, by invading Berellia's north, when the Ralloran Wars started. But I believe the reply your father, King Croft, offered our desperate pleas for help was along the lines of: "This is a matter between Rallora and Berellia. It is none of our business."' She was reaping what her father had sown.

The only bright spot in all this was nobody had mentioned her marriage to Sendric. He had been given the task of organising a simple ceremony while she was north. It was not much of an incentive to hurry back.

'When we get there, the honour guard will lead us to the High Chief. After we greet him, we should be given the chance to wash and eat. We must use this to talk to Father Alban. There, we may find out the latest situation among the Derthals, whether there is a strong chance of success and if any of the tribal chiefs will oppose us. Any other questions?' Quiller finished.

'Can they understand us?' Merren asked. 'Can we talk among ourselves without fear of being understood?'

The indecision on Quiller's face spoke louder than words. 'There will be some who can understand our language — but, more than that, there are many among the Derthals who are able to read your body language. The Derthal language is simple but words can be given emphasis by how loudly they are said, and the accompanying gestures. So if you say one thing, but mean another, they are often able to pick up the hidden meaning before the verbal one. It is something that priests have learned, to their cost.'

'How fluent are you in their language?' Merren asked sharply.

Quiller shrugged. 'I know a few words. That is all. I would not try to interpret. The chance of making a mistake, possibly a fatal mistake, is too high.'

Merren took a deep breath. 'We should leave now. Quiller, let Father Alban know we shall be there soon. Barrett — are you ready?'

'As always, my Queen.' Barrett looked up from his plate.

Merren had noticed he had not taken the news about her marriage to Sendric too badly. She did wonder about that. She had expected him to sulk, at least — and quite possibly fall into fits of petulant anger. But there had been nothing. She was not sure if this was because of the attractive young student he was devoting so much time to — or because the marriage was not to Martil. Either way, she was relieved not to have to worry about it.

'Do you think I can play with some of the young Derthals?' Karia asked. 'Da used to say he would send me away to play with the goblins. I want to meet them!'

Martil shuddered at the thought. 'Perhaps.' Then he smiled at her. 'But how will we know which one is you? I mean, you probably already look like a goblin!'

'Dad!' she said, outraged. 'They're ugly!'

Martil laughed at the expression on her face. He had grown accustomed to only using humour to try and keep his sanity among the madness of war. Now he was enjoying using it with Karia, watching her jest back at him.

'Well, you smell like a goblin!' she told him and he laughed again.

'Anyway, we have to make sure they are our friends first before we play with them.'

She nodded and he turned to where Jaret and Wilsen were hefting large packs onto their shoulders.

'Stay close to the Queen, both of you,' he ordered.

'The Derthals might seek to test us, might even challenge us to see what we are made of. Do nothing unless I tell you, but do not let the Queen come to any harm, for anything.'

'Yes, sir!'

Martil would have liked to bring along a pair of his Rallorans — Dunner and Kesbury for preference — but Kesbury was trying to become a priest and Dunner was needed down on the border. Besides, after they had led the charge to get in front of Merren at Pilleth, the Queen had asked for Wilsen and Jaret to come along — and he could not ignore that.

'When you are finished, I am now ready,' Barrett announced, swallowing a last mouthful of apple.

Martil reflected that, just a few months ago, he would have shuddered at the thought of trusting himself to a wizard. But now he took it for granted. And, although he and Barrett were no longer likely to be friends, at least they were not trying to attack each other at every opportunity. Barrett must be teaching Tiera more than magic, or she might be teaching him, Martil thought to himself. He had already endured Karia complaining about how Barrett's attention was not entirely focused on her now that Tiera was around. Not that Martil was likely to ask Barrett about it. Especially as his better relationship with Barrett was more than compensated for by the problems he was having with Merren. Even now he could not look at her without feeling a pang. He stared out the window to avoid watching her.

'Come on, Daddy! They'll go without us!' Karia grabbed his hand and broke his reverie.

'I'll be there.' Martil smiled at her. At least he still had Karia.

*   *   *

Hutter had always suspected that the west of Norstalos, being near the coast, believed itself to be far superior to the rest of the country. It even held itself up as being the 'true' Norstalos. Westerners were known for looking down their noses at the 'easties', who they often termed country bumpkins, or worse. As a born-and-bred eastie, and a former sergeant in an insignificant village, his words were unlikely to impress the genteel westerners. And having a one-armed ex-bandit and pardoned criminal as his boss was hardly a recommendation, either.

But he had his orders. Cessor, with its wide, natural harbour and large fishing and trading fleet, was an obvious place to land. Worick, with its large river mouth and straight, paved road to the capital, was the other. If he was invading by sea, he would have landed at either, or both, of these places. What he would have loved to have was a fleet of warships to unleash on the Tenoch boats. But there had never been problems with piracy; the Norstaline navy consisted of two small ships. Trying to attack a fleet of warships with fat trading ships did not seem like a good idea to Hutter — and the Queen had forbidden it, fearing she could lose her men far at sea.

So now he was reduced to persuading suspicious town councils that they should flee. They had been less than co-operative, so he had just sent his militiamen into the streets to tell the people to get out. But this was not working particularly well. He strongly suspected there were plenty of people here who would be happy to see Gello back.

'We would have nothing to fear,' one councillor had even told him.

538

As far as Hutter was concerned, they could suffer and die when the Tenochs arrived. As long as they didn't take too many ordinary people with them.

They had emerged from an oak tree at the edge of a wood far to the north of Sendric, and climbed onto the horses they had brought with them.

'The only thing further north of here are a few mines, and of course the Derthals,' Quiller had announced as soon as they stepped out of the tree.

'How come the Derthals don't attack the mines?'

'Two reasons — firstly because they have no use for gold or silver. They used to attack farms to get food, or attacked towns in an attempt to drive us off their land, but they are afraid of holes in the ground. The second reason is the mines are well defended and hard to get into. They have learned to leave the mines alone, because they end up with dead warriors, to no purpose,' Quiller explained.

'I wonder how the prisoners we sent to the mines are getting on. Perhaps we could get them to fight for us, now we have the Dragon Sword working ...' Merren mused.

Martil knew he should not seize every opportunity to argue with her, but it just seemed to work out that way.

'Apart from the fact they hate us and want you dead, Pilleth told us what happens when you go into battle not being able to trust part of your army. If they defected back to Gello at a critical point of the fight ...' Martil grunted.

Merren sniffed.

They rode on in silence — well, almost in silence, because Karia was always full of questions. Then Quiller told them they were in Derthal territory.

'How can you tell?' Barrett asked.

'He's right — don't everybody look now, but there's three of them over to the right, watching us,' Martil said quietly.

Too late. As it was pointless to hide their curiosity, Martil joined the others in staring at what looked like three short men standing quietly under a small tree. Being watched did not seem to make them run, or attack, so Martil looked closely.

They were shorter than a man; Martil was average height and he guessed the tallest would only come up to his shoulder. But they seemed solidly built, with heavy shoulders, barrel chests and powerful arms. All three carried spears, but not the long, iron-tipped version taller than a man that Martil knew and had used. The Derthals' were no longer than a sword, about the length of a man's arm, with a thick shaft and a huge stone head, easily the width of a man's hand at the base, tapering slowly to what looked like a fine point. This was a spear for close, thrusting work, Martil saw at once. With those massive arms, shoulders and chest, the Derthals would be able to deliver a powerful blow. Even though the spearheads were stone, he guessed a Derthal could probably drive it through a mail shirt. And it would deliver a terrible wound.

Their faces seemed unusual, but Martil could not see them clearly. All three wore what looked like deerskin tunics.

'What are they doing?' Merren asked.

'I would say they are waiting for us,' Quiller suggested quietly. 'I told Father Alban our route. By the look of them, these three could well be personal guards to the High Chief.'

'So what do we do?' Merren demanded.

540

'We go over to them, slowly, and greet them,' Quiller decided. 'Better let me lead the way.'

'As long as you are ready to call upon Aroaril's protection at a moment's notice,' Martil snapped. 'One of those spearheads would drive a big enough hole through you for us to see daylight on the other side.'

'Really! How?' Karia wanted to know, but Martil managed to quieten her.

'Stay close to the Queen,' he told her. 'Jaret, Wilsen, watch the Queen in case there's any more around. Father, let's go and say hello to your Derthals.'

Together, Quiller and Martil rode across to the three figures, who watched them approach calmly, making no move to either run or attack.

Martil looked even closer at them. Their arms and legs were hairy, but no more than he had seen on a normal man. Their faces were also without beards, although their hair was long and wild. Up close, their large noses dominated their faces, while a low, overhanging receding brow and chin made them look somewhat like a man, yet strange enough to be something set apart.

'Greetings! We come in peace!' Quiller called loudly, and slowly, then repeated his words in a guttural language.

'I thought you didn't speak their language,' Martil muttered.

'I don't. I just know that phrase,' Quiller whispered back, neither of them taking their eyes off the three Derthals.

Then one, the biggest, bowed his head slightly.

'Welcome to Queen Merren. Follow us,' he said, his voice low and harsh, as though unused to speaking the human tongue. Also, he seemed to struggle with the pronunciation of Merren.

'You speak our language? You are from the High Chief?' Quiller said with a smile.

The three Derthals exchanged a look, then the first one spoke again.

'Khoniz,' it sounded like, with a guttural inflection. Then he cleared his throat and tried again. 'Welcome to Queen Merren. Follow us,' he grunted.

'I think they only know that phrase. Probably been taught to say that, and no more,' Quiller sighed with frustration.

'So what do we do?'

'Follow us!' the Derthals all said together, then turned and began trudging away, up a grassy slope.

'I suppose we follow them. Should we take the horses ...' Quiller said.

The Derthals turned and waved.

'Rella!' one called, then the leader waved again. 'Follow. Us!'

Merren rode across, Barrett, Karia and the two guards following her closely.

'Well, that seems obvious. They're here to guide us,' she declared.

'Should we leave the horses here?' Barrett asked.

'Take them. They make us look more impressive,' Martil said immediately. 'I go first — Jaret, Wilsen, you watch the rear.'

They rode after the three Derthals, who were not setting a fast pace but, when they saw they were being followed, seemed to stride out a little more, over the top of a small hill and onto what looked like a game path. This seemed to wind into the hills, which themselves soon turned into mountains. Patches of trees clung onto the ground in between the hills, but the way the mountains loomed over all told Martil that this was not a hospitable place. Logically it should be warmer the further north you came, but the height they were at made it colder. Even though the sun was out, and it was mid-autumn, there was a chill in the air, and the odd gust of wind told him it would be a brutal place to survive in winter. He spotted a circling bird, high up and many miles away. It looked to be a fearsome size. No doubt there were other, unfriendly creatures here, too.

24

The Derthals led them along the game trail at a steady pace. Martil was examining the three of them trying to see whether or not they would be good warriors. He wondered how far into the mountains they were going. And he was not the only one.

'How much longer are we going to ride for? I'm hungry!' Karia grumbled. 'And the Derthals don't talk to us. That's boring!'

'Well, they probably can't get a word in with you talking all the time,' Martil suggested.

'Ha ha, Dad. Very funny. One of your jests.'

'Be patient — we are their guests,' Martil said.

'Why can't we ask them to stop, so we can have something to eat?'

'Because we don't know their language,' Martil pointed out.

'Could we try to talk to them, the way we can talk to animals or birds?' Karia asked Barrett.

'But they are not animals or birds — they are men, they just have a different language. Using the magic to communicate with them could be a dreadful insult.'

'What?'

'You'd make them angry,' Martil explained.

'Oh.' Karia rode on in silence for a little further. 'Can't we just stop anyway? I'm really hungry!'

Perhaps the Derthals heard her, and understood the tone of voice, if not the words themselves — or perhaps they had always planned to rest at this point of the journey. The trail led up around a huge boulder, and they stopped here and waved to Martil and the others.

'Kacha!' the leader boomed — or at least that was what it sounded like to Martil. Then he burrowed in a pouch and produced what looked like a package of meat, wrapped in a skin. 'Kacha! Har?'

'I think they're hungry as well,' Martil concluded. 'We can rest here.'

In the shelter of the huge boulder sat a circle of small, blackened stones, suggesting this was a regular stop for Derthals. A pile of firewood had been set beside the circle, both thin, small sticks, and several larger chunks of wood. The leader opened a small bag, which looked like it had been made from the skin of a rabbit, and produced a handful of fine wood shavings and leaves, which he placed in the centre of the stones with due ceremony. Then the other Derthals produced a thick stick with a hole inside, and a slimmer stick. The slim stick was placed inside the hole, then one Derthal held the base steady while the other whirled the slim stick in his palms, spinning it, faster and faster. The muscles in his thick forearms bulged and writhed as he worked.

'Geya! Geya! Geya!' the Derthals chanted as they worked. A wisp of smoke was soon drifting out of the larger stick, while the thinner was slowly growing smaller.

Then the smaller stick was removed and the Derthal tipped glowing ash from the hole in the larger stick onto the shavings and leaves. It began to smoulder, and the leader kneeled over it, blowing gently, until suddenly the tinder flared into life. Small sticks, then larger ones, were added to the blaze until a fire was ready.

Quiller applauded and, seeing that, Merren joined in, nudging the others to follow. The Derthals grinned at them.

'Geya! Yodum!' the leader nodded, while his two companions speared chunks of what Martil suspected was deer meat onto long sticks, and began to roast it over the fire.

'Fascinating!' Quiller murmured. 'Steel and flint would work twice as fast, but their skills are obviously advanced.'

Karia had looked outraged when she saw their lunch was being carried in the skin of a small deer, but Martil had kept her quiet with the help of an oatcake, and the smell of roasting venison soon had her ignoring her fury, and focusing on the charring meat instead.

'Kacha?' The leader held up several blackened sticks with their cargo of cooked meat, and offered them out.

'I think we should take them,' Merren said determinedly.

Following her lead, they accepted the chunks of meat, blackened on the outside but still pink inside.

'Careful, it's hot,' Martil warned Karia, as she accepted a heavily laden stick enthusiastically.

After much blowing and other theatrics, Karia sat down and began ripping pieces off with her teeth. The others were already doing the same; Martil ate slowly. The venison was fresh, the meat surprisingly tender. He knew that, in order for the meat to be so tender, the prey had to be killed quickly, not chased so its muscles hardened into toughness. With no sign of bows or arrows, that meant the Derthals had killed the deer with a spear, probably from ambush. That was impressive.

He was thinking about that, and its possibilities, when he realised that Karia had wandered over to the fire, her meat already eaten, and was looking for more.

'Can I have another one, please?' she asked.

The Derthals, who were eating their own pieces of meat by now, looked up at her.

'Please?' Karia pointed to where the fire was already dying out and waving her blackened, greasy stick, on which only a fragment of deer meat remained.

The Derthals looked helplessly at their leader, who shrugged. The fire was going out, and was obviously not hot enough to cook any more.

'Geya!' the leader said, and one of his companions added two large handfuls of sticks to the embers and prodded hopefully. But they did not seem to catch.

Resignedly, he turned away, to where the firesticks waited, but Karia was not about to wait. She pointed at the sticks, and they burst into flame.

'Ooo-wa!' The closest Derthal jumped backwards in shock, and all three leaped to their feet in alarm. The expressions on their faces would have been comical, had this been a different situation.

They all started forwards at the same time and Martil was on his feet in an instant, hand on his sword hilt, but Merren held up her hand to stop him.

The leader was inspecting Karia's fire, holding out a cautious finger, then jerking it away when it was clear this was indeed just as hot as a normal fire.

'Yodum! Yodum!' he gestured, pointing from the small girl to the blaze, then the three of them burst out laughing.

Martil walked over, although he kept his hand away from his sword, as the leader speared more meat on a stick and began cooking it, grinning up at Karia all the time.

'Well done. But perhaps next time, ask me to get it for you?' Martil said softly, keeping a smile on his face.

'But they're nice! They're friendly!'

'So far,' Martil agreed. 'But next time, ask!'

The grinning Derthal handed the cooked meat to Karia, then smiled at Martil. He picked up his firestick and pointed from it to himself, then pointed from Karia to Martil and back again. Then all three Derthals laughed.

'I think he is suggesting that you bring Karia along as your firestarter.' Quiller smiled. 'They seem to think the notion is amusing.'

'Very funny,' Martil grunted, face aching with the effort of keeping a smile on his face.

Further around the boulder a drip of water formed a small pool that trickled away in a stream down the hillside. The Derthals scooped water from the pool, while Jaret refilled waterskins for the humans to drink. The water was both chilly and refreshing. Martil had grown so used to the leathery taste of water stored in a skin, or in a barrel, that this fresh water almost took his breath away.

'Yodum, har?' The leader nodded at Martil's expression.

'It is good,' Martil agreed.

The food and drink had improved everybody's mood considerably, as well as eased Martil's tension. The atmosphere had definitely relaxed; even the Derthals seemed happier as they walked along. They still kept up a good pace but the terrain was getting harder and Martil was beginning to wonder if they should leave the horses.

The trail dipped a little, going through a small valley, at the centre of which was a thick wood. The Derthals pushed on ahead, although the humans had to dismount, as there were too many low branches.

'Wait!' Martil called.

The Derthals had got a good twenty yards ahead of them by now, but turned at Martil's cry. The leader waved, to acknowledge he heard. Martil turned to help Karia down, then a scream made him whip around again.

The ambush had been planned perfectly. A score of Derthals hidden in the trees and undergrowth pounced on the unsuspecting guides. Martil had wondered how they would fight with the spears and he was about to receive the perfect lesson. He had to admire their skill, not only with the spears but in springing the ambush. He had been spotting ambushes for years — was only alive because of this talent — and he had not noticed anything unusual.

The attacking Derthals, these ones wearing a different type of skin, used their spears in an underhand grip, thrusting upwards, rather than down. It was horribly effective. The broad spearheads smashed through skin and bone, and when they were ripped out they sent blood spurting high into the air.

Two of the three guides were dead in a heartbeat but the leader dodged the blow aimed at him and slammed his own spear into the chest of his attacker.

Before he could even draw it clear, two more Derthals had plunged their spears into him.

Then Martil had the Dragon Sword in his hand.

'Barrett! We're going to need you!' he called. 'Jaret, Wilsen, with me, we'll cover your retreat!'

But before they could do anything, a Derthal with a headband made of what looked like wolf fur ran forwards, waving his arms. Unlike his fellows, he did not hold a spear.

'Do not fear! We come in peace! We are friends!' he roared.

'Let's get out of here.' Martil ignored what was being said. Actions spoke louder than words and, anyway, the vicious ambush was all he needed to see.

'Wait!' Merren commanded. 'We cannot just leave. Let us hear what he has to say.'

None of the other Derthals was moving forwards; they stood patiently, except for the ones dragging the four bodies off the narrow track.

Martil hesitated. His instincts were screaming for them to get out of there, although there was no obvious threat.

'I am Chief Rath, adviser to High Chief Sacrax,' the Derthal continued, still holding out his hands to show he had no weapon. He was now closer to Martil than he was his warriors. 'Those three we killed were leading you to death. When I saw what they were doing, I had to stop them.'

'You speak our language well,' Merren called. The situation was certainly strange, but hearing words she could understand was reassuring.

'I learned your words from your priests, like the one you have there,' Rath called, pointing towards Quiller.

'Why did you kill them? Why not just stop them and talk to us?' Merren asked.

Rath smiled. 'They all had spears. As soon as they saw us, I knew they would attack. I could not risk it. We are a people who fight better than we talk. You must have fear but please, listen.'

'Go ahead, Rath,' Merren instructed.

'Word of your arrival has created much talking, much anger among my people. There are those who say you are not to be trusted — you drove us out of our land before; your deeds drip with the blood of Derthals. Others say that was many, many moons ago. That we should listen to you, it could be a new dawn for the Derthals. High Chief Sacrax wants to listen to you, but there are many who would like you dead. I found out those three traitors were meeting you. They were taking you in the wrong direction. So I brought my picked warriors to ambush them. Now I can take you to High Chief Sacrax.'

'What of Father Alban?' Quiller asked sharply. 'Does he know you are here?'

Rath stared at him. 'Father Alban is with High Chief Sacrax. He says we should listen to you, that you will bring great benefit to Derthals. But how can he see where I am now?'

'It seems he speaks our language relatively well, but does not grasp all the complexities,' Quiller said quietly to Merren. 'Nevertheless, I cannot detect him telling a lie.'

'Come with me. I will take you to High Chief Sacrax and Father Alban,' Rath repeated. 'We won't let any more traitors get near you.'

'I don't trust him,' Martil glowered. 'Those three Derthals could have attacked us at any time, but didn't.'

'You don't trust anyone,' Barrett sniffed. 'And how could three of them defeat us all? No doubt they were leading us into an ambush. But this Rath and his warriors — they could attack us, and are not doing so. They mean us no harm.'

'They might want us in those trees, where we can't escape or use magic,' Martil hissed.

'We have to keep going. We cannot give up. The Derthals are our last hope,' Merren told them coldly. 'We must see where this goes.' She raised her voice so Rath, who was standing patiently a few yards away, could hear. 'Which way are we walking?'

'You were going in the wrong direction. We need to go over there.' Rath pointed to the west, away from the trees.

'Could you not just give us directions to the High Chief?'

'I could,' Rath admitted. 'But then you would probably meet more traitors. There are no roads here. I cannot take the risk. High Chief Sacrax would not want me to do this.'

'Quiller? Is he lying?' Merren murmured. 'Can you tell?'

Quiller kept his head very still. 'Aroaril allows me to detect when someone is telling a lie. And what he just said was no lie.'

'We have to keep going,' Merren told the others quietly. 'Failure is not an option here. And if he gets us to High Chief Sacrax, it does not matter if he has the blood of others on his hands.'

'This feels wrong,' Martil insisted.

'There is no other way,' Merren said bleakly. 'You told me so yourself.' Again she raised her voice, to include Rath. 'Lead on, and we will follow.'

Rath grinned and then waved to his warriors. 'This is the right choice for both our people.'

His warriors had used bunches of leaves to clean

their spears and faces of blood, but some still had blood spattered on their skins. Unlike the three deer-clad guides, these warriors looked to have plenty of wolf fur decorating their crude tunics.

'I will walk with you so you know we are not going into another ambush. I am unarmed,' Rath offered. 'Also, we can speak about our people.'

Even Martil grudgingly admitted that they were unlikely to be heading into a trap if Rath was offering to stay with them.

The Derthals led them off in a different direction, creating their own path until, after a few miles, they struck another, running more west than north. Like their previous guides, the warriors marched in silence, most of them not even bothering to look over their shoulders at the curious humans riding behind.

Rath, however, was eager to talk. He was fascinated by Karia and charmed her; he smiled often and was obviously friendly. Martil disliked him immediately.

'When I learned to speak your words, I told my father it was useless, that I would never use them.' Rath smiled. 'I did not dream that one day I would need all these words, and more, to speak to you!'

'Was your father a chief, also?' Quiller asked.

'My father was a mighty chief; he could have been High Chief, except Chief Sacrax was the stronger of the two.' Rath shrugged. 'So now I work for my people.'

'So do most Derthals hate us?' Merren asked.

Rath seemed to think about that for a moment. 'Do you hate the snow? The wind? You do not like them, for life would be sweeter without them, but Derthals do not hate others. We do what we must to survive up here, to keep our people alive.'

'How bad is it in winter?' Martil asked.

'Snow covers the ground; prey is hard to find, the old and the young die easily,' Rath said coolly. 'But we live.'

'Tell me,' Barrett said, 'what is the meaning of the word "kacha"?' He stumbled over the guttural sounds.

'Hunger, a desire to eat,' Rath replied casually.

'And "yodum"?'

'Something yodum is good.'

'"Geya" would be fire?'

'Har — yes,' Rath agreed.

'It is a fascinating language,' Barrett marvelled.

'It is words for hunting, for fighting and for survival,' Rath dismissed. 'Your words are so much more, words that do not always mean the same thing. It allows the speaker to say one thing and mean something else. It is good to have these words but is also why many Derthals do not trust you.'

'But will those Derthals obey the High Chief, if he orders them to help us?' Barrett asked.

Merren tried to silence him with a glare but it was too late, the words were out.

'So you seek our help?' Rath said wonderingly. 'I thought as much. I could not believe you were here to right old wrongs.'

'Will they obey the High Chief?' Merren pressed, hoping to at least get that answer.

'Of course. We do not disobey the High Chief. But he has not said we are to help you yet. He has only said you must be brought to him, so he can speak to you. That is why you are in danger.'

Barrett opened his mouth to ask another question but this time Merren's glare struck him before he could speak, and he subsided. They rode on in silence, rounding a bend in the trail to see another patch of thick wood below.

'How much further is it?' Martil asked. He had been watching their progress against the mountains. Unlike their previous guides, who had taken them towards the high peaks, Rath was leading them no closer. He spotted another of those giant birds, swooping away in the distance. Or perhaps it was the same one. He thought of asking Rath about it, but decided not to.

'Not far,' Rath said casually. 'There is a test you must pass before you can go and see the High Chief.'

Now they were riding down through the wood; it was not large, perhaps the size of three fields, but Martil was comparing it to the forest where Rath and his warriors had prepared a brutal ambush.

'Test, what test?' Merren demanded.

'I will show you.' Rath gestured to his warriors, who loped off through the wood.

Martil noticed they moved almost silently through the undergrowth. But the hair on the back of his neck was up, and the Dragon Sword was in his hand before he thought about it.

'If you plan another ambush, you will not live to see the result,' he growled.

'I plan an ambush, but not on you. I need you to help me do something before we see High Chief Sacrax,' Rath said simply.

'Tell us what you want,' Merren commanded.

Rath pointed through the wood, to where a trickle of smoke could be seen.

'There is a small village of traitors in there. I am going to attack it, and you will help me.'

'What?' Merren exclaimed.

'After killing and burning my people out of their homes, making us live here, you come now, saying you want our help. That you will give us back what you stole from us in the first place, if only we will do something for you. Forgive us if we do not trust those words, or rush to help you. We know you can say pretty words. We want to see if your actions meet your words before the High Chief decides if we will help you.'

Martil felt they were seeing the true Rath now. His eyes blazed and he seemed taller than his actual height.

'So help me destroy this settlement, then we shall travel to see the High Chief and he can judge for himself the value of your words against your actions.'

'Destroy a village?' Martil spat.

'Do you want our help? I tell you this village must be destroyed before you see the High Chief. He must know what you are prepared to do!'

Merren glanced towards Quiller who shrugged. 'Not a lie,' he mouthed. She glanced at Barrett, who closed his eyes. She hesitated, then the mage nodded.

'I cannot detect a lie either,' he admitted.

'Show us the village,' Merren said tiredly.

'But Merren—!' Martil began hotly.

'We cannot fail here. If these Derthals are marked for death anyway, then we must do as he says, if it is to win over the High Chief—'

'But—'

'Martil, you are my Champion, and you will fight when I order it,' she snapped.

Martil slammed the Dragon Sword into its sheath, seething. 'I will see this village,' he told Rath.

'We all will,' Merren said firmly.

Rath nodded. 'Leave the horses here. You will be seen otherwise.'

'Quiller, you and Barrett stay here with Karia,' Martil suggested. 'We're only going to look.'

So Merren, Martil, Jaret and Wilsen followed Rath along the trail, the four humans stumbling and tripping and showing their clumsiness with every pace, while the Derthals glided from cover to cover, moving silently and with grace.

'How do you want us to help? We only have three warriors and you have many,' Martil whispered.

'You will ride in along the trail, making as much noise as possible — even more than the noise you make now,' Rath said and gestured. 'As soon as you are in sight, attack any Derthal you see. The rest will run — and will run straight onto the spears of my warriors. None will escape that way.'

Martil gritted his teeth to stop himself from saying anything. It was a good plan. Too good. It reminded him of something the Berellians would do.

'Where is the village?' Merren whispered.

'Look here.' Rath led them off the trail, then used a short stick to part the leaves of a bush.

Martil peered through, to see a collection of about a dozen huts in a clearing. Derthals were in sight, although there were obviously more inside the rough huts. Huts was probably too good a word for them — they were low, crude shelters of sticks and leaves. Not even a Derthal could stand up in one. But Martil was not thinking so much about the huts. He was more concerned about the fact every single Derthal in sight was either a woman or a child. Not one warrior.

'I have seen enough, we need to go back,' Martil mouthed.

He stalked back up the trail, feeling a burning anger inside.

'You see the way to do it? The huts all face the trail — make as much noise as possible and the traitors will all run,' Rath said with relish. 'We shall kill them all — eventually.'

'We are leaving. We will not do this,' Martil told him coldly, his stomach roiling with disgust.

'What?' Rath spat. 'Do you not want our help?'

'Of course we do!' Merren blazed.

'Didn't you see that little village? It's full of women and children! I will fight to save your life, my Queen, but I will not murder for you!'

'But the High Chief wants to test us!' Barrett snarled. 'It is a test we cannot fail! I know you don't trust me when I say Rath is not lying but you cannot doubt Quiller! He also said it — Rath speaks the truth, so this is the only way to win the Derthals' help! Have you forgotten what waits for us back in Norstalos? There's a huge army — three huge armies — ready to kill our people! Without the Derthals we are lost!'

'I don't care! I won't do it! Finally my dreams are free of the horrors of Bellic! I won't replace them with fresh nightmares!'

Merren grabbed his arm and pulled him away from the others.

'Martil, I know what I am asking. The thought revolts me. If Barrett and Quiller were not telling me Rath speaks the truth, I would walk away. Aroaril knows I want to walk away as it is. But my country's survival, maybe even the world's survival, rests on this! Don't you understand? The forces of Zorva will not stop at Norstalos! All of those people, all of those deaths, will be on my conscience! Against them are a handful of Derthals, who are marked for death anyway! They are all traitors, probably their warriors are all out hunting for us! Martil, I cannot go back to Norstalos and tell all those men and women and children back there that I failed them, that they are going to die! Sometimes, a small evil has to be done for the greater good. If the end result is our victory, then their sacrifice will be worth it.'

She was almost pleading with him now. If she had not said she felt nothing for him, if she had told him the truth, would he do this for her now out of love, not obedience? But it was too late to take back her earlier words. She had been horrified to see the village herself; as soon as she understood what Rath wanted, she had almost thrown up. If Quiller and Barrett had not said the Derthal was speaking the truth … While her heart screamed that she could not do this, her head was saying something more powerful. A people, a world, depended on her. She could not let them down. And still the voice of her father came back at her. *A king would do anything to protect his kingdom. Do not be weak. Do not let your heart rule you. Sometimes you must grasp the nettle. The end justifies the means.*

'Martil, surely you see we have no choice here. To win over the Derthals I was prepared to offer them land, hope. They want to see we are willing to keep our bargain. We must seal this pact with blood. It is the only way to save the world.'

Martil shook his head. 'I don't care about the world,' he said simply. 'I know this is wrong. And I will not slaughter innocent victims to save others. If I learned one thing from Bellic, it is that there is no small evil — it is all the same. I will fight the Berellians, Gello and the Tenochs. I will defend

Norstalos to the last drop of my blood but I will not do this. Never.'

'Perhaps your other warriors are more loyal,' Rath said coldly. 'I only need two or three for the plan to work. Ignore this fool. Help me kill this village and I will take you straight to the High Chief! I will tell him myself what you did. If you want our help, you need to pass a test. And time is running out.'

Desperately Merren looked at Quiller, who merely nodded sadly. Merren turned away, trying to think. Despite all she had told Martil, she found his words more believable than her own. But even though everything within her told her to refuse Rath, her brain hammered at her the thought that she could not let her people down. She had to do whatever it took to save them. And if Quiller and Barrett said this Derthal spoke the truth, had been telling the truth since they met him, then she really had no choice.

'Jaret, Wilsen,' she began heavily.

'Don't do this, my Queen,' Martil almost begged. 'Because I cannot stand by and watch murder done. I will stand with those Derthals against you.'

'What?' Rath growled.

Martil drew the Dragon Sword. 'You heard me. The only way to that village is through me, goblin.'

Rath's face twisted in fury as Merren and the others gasped in shock and horror at Martil's words.

'Da-ad! You said the G-word!' Karia whispered.

'So you will not do this?' Rath spat.

'I will not kill those women and children for you, for anyone,' Martil declared. 'And I'll cut down every one of your goblins that tries to do so.'

Rath laughed harshly. 'You may try. What of you, Queen of the Friny? Will you do as I ask?'

Merren sighed. 'No. I am sorry. You will have to tell the High Chief that we failed his test. But I still believe he will want to hear us out. What we have to say to him is of vital importance to us both.'

Rath spat. 'You will not speak to the High Chief. He does not need to hear anything you say. I will not guide you to him.'

'Then we shall find him ourselves,' Barrett declared.

'No,' Rath disagreed, backing away. 'You will find only death.'

Before Martil could stop him, he darted into the trees.

'He's gone to get his warriors — Barrett, can you use any of these trees to get us out of here?' Merren demanded. Inside she had turned ice cold at the thought they had managed only to win the enmity of a senior Derthal chief, but her first instinct was to get away safely.

'There is no oak I can see — perhaps if we went further in …' Barrett suggested.

'Go further in and you'll end up with a spear in your gullet,' Martil snapped. 'We can outrun them. They won't be able to keep pace with the horses.'

'Too late!' Quiller pointed behind them, to where a dozen Derthal warriors had appeared to block their retreat. From the wood the rest of them slowly appeared, led by Rath, who now carried a wickedly sharp spear.

'The Dragon Sword will open us a path through the ones behind — Barrett, can you hold the ones in the wood — do your thing with the plants?' Martil cried.

Barrett closed his eyes for a moment, then opened them again, eyes wide in panic.

'There is something wrong with the magic! I cannot reach for it …'

'Never mind! Just stay close to me!' Martil growled, swinging onto his horse. He guessed the Derthals would try to sink their spears into Tomon first, bring the riders down to their level. But Tomon, and he, knew how to fight that. He was just disappointed he did not have time to kill that Rath.

'Death!' he roared, pointing the Dragon Sword at the Derthals blocking their escape, then prepared to kick Tomon into a gallop.

But before he could do anything, a huge shape dropped from the sky.

'Dragon!' Karia screamed with a mixture of delight and fear.

Martil felt his jaw sag open as the massive creature flared enormous wings, stopping an impossible dive in a ridiculously short space. A long tail sent half the Derthals flying, then its bellow of challenge sent the rest running.

A dragon!

Martil had never thought he would see one. Thanks to Karia, he had read more sagas about them than he cared to remember, but the stories did not do them justice.

This dragon was golden in colour, but not the muddy yellow of gold coins. Instead, its scales rippled and shimmered, seemingly changing colour every heartbeat, a dazzling array of shades of gold. Its neck was long, its head regal, its wings wide, its legs graceful and strong, its tail powerful. Astride its back sat a strange-looking man.

Martil could not tear his eyes from the sight.

If as many as one in one hundred people saw a dragon in their lifetime, that was unusual. It seemed to be looking at him and, as it did so, the hilt of the Dragon Sword burned cold, then pleasantly warm and the dragon on it flashed. Almost of its own volition, it swung around to Martil's right.

Automatically, his head followed — just in time. Taking advantage of his distraction, Rath had crept closer and now leaped at him, that wicked spear drawn back, ready for the killing thrust. If the Sword had not moved, Martil might have died — but as it was, he had time to slice the head off Rath's spear, then reverse the blade and behead the Derthal.

Rath's corpse, fountaining blood, collapsed on itself and, with that, the last of Rath's warriors ran, throwing down their spears.

'What in Aroaril's name is going on?' Quiller spoke for them all as they stared at the dragon.

'I think we are going to find out,' Merren said, as the rider stepped onto the dragon's foreleg and was lowered to the ground, where he walked over to the bewildered party, and bowed.

'I am Havell. And I seek the wielder of the Dragon Sword,' he called.

'You're an elf!' Karia exclaimed.

Havell shook his head. 'I am of a race of men called Elfarans, who serve the dragons. I do not know this word, "elf". Where is the wielder of the Dragon Sword?'

Martil urged Tomon forwards. 'I am the wielder of the Dragon Sword,' he replied. 'We thank you for your help.'

Havell bowed again. 'You must come with me now. The dragons are dying. It is the time of the Dragon Sword, and we have need of it on Dragonara Isle. Without it, all the magic will be gone and all life with it.'

Martil turned to Merren and saw his own shock and confusion mirrored on her face.

'Does this mean I'm going to get a ride on a dragon?' Karia asked excitedly.

25

Martil had heard stories about the elves, or Elfarans, or whatever they wanted to call themselves, how they were not a different race at all, but a nation of men who had been permanently changed by the magic, until they resembled something other than men. Seeing Havell now, he could believe it. Havell was average height, although with a slimmer build than Martil, but it was on his face that the greatest changes had been wrought. It looked as though his face had been stretched out like that of the dragon behind him — his chin was long, his cheekbones high, his eyes almond-shaped, his ears swept back and elongated.

'He cannot go to Dragonara Isle! He is needed here!' Merren gasped. 'What are you talking about?'

'It is the destiny of the Dragon Sword wielder. The Sword was given to the Norstaline people in the full knowledge that one day the dragons would require a service in return. Surely your legends tell you of this?'

Martil looked at Merren, who looked at Barrett, who looked blank.

'No matter,' Havell said impatiently. 'The dragons need the Sword, and its wielder, now.'

'What for? And for how long?' Martil demanded, a moment before Merren.

Havell stared at him. 'Isn't it obvious? The dragons are dying. In order to secure their rebirth, and the rebirth of the magic, the Dragon Sword must be used to pierce the Dragon Egg, before sunrise of the day after the last dragon dies. As soon as this solemn duty has been performed, the wielder can return, with the eternal thanks of the dragons, and the safety of the world ensured.'

There was a horrible silence while everyone looked at each other disbelievingly before realising Havell had actually said those words.

'The rebirth of the magic? The end of the world? What are you talking about? How can this be possible?' Merren demanded, her head whirling. Could nothing ever be simple?

'Do we have the time to go through this now?' Havell asked impatiently.

'You want to take away the Dragon Sword, and its wielder, at a time when our need for them is at its greatest! You talk of the end of the world and the rebirth of magic! I think we deserve an explanation!'

'It is simple. Our need is greater,' Havell said. 'All things must die, and be reborn. The power of magic comes from the circle of life, therefore it, and the dragons, must be part of this circle of life. They are dying and must be reborn, in order for the magic to continue.'

'Simple for you, perhaps!' Merren protested. This was all too much. First they had lost their chance to gain the support of the Derthals, then they had been nearly killed — and now a dragon wanted to take Martil and the Dragon Sword! She already felt sick inside, for thinking what she had nearly done at

Rath's behest. It was a shame that would burn inside her for as long as she lived, but she had to put it aside and try to find some sense in this. 'Start at the beginning. How can there be an end to the magic?'

Havell's face showed a flicker of irritation. 'Ask your wizard there. Magic is subject to exactly the same strictures as all life. You cannot have anything, even something as wise and powerful as a dragon, living outside the laws of nature. It could destroy the very fabric of this world!'

'But why now?'

Havell threw up his hands. 'It is not for me to determine when the magic must die, and be reborn. All I can do is tell you it is happening! Believe me, I would not choose this moment for the magic to die. If I had my way, everything would go on as before. But it is not my choice and we have to follow the path the dragons have laid out — or see the world end.'

'Barrett, is he telling the truth? Could this really happen?' Merren asked. She was clutching on to the faint hope that this Elfaran, or whatever, was mistaken, or lying, although everything in Norstalos's history and lore said that elves were never wrong, and never lied.

Barrett felt every eye turn to him and licked his lips nervously. 'My Queen, he could be right. There are some things that wizards learn—'

'For Aroaril's sake, stop being so bloody mysterious and just tell us!' Merren roared.

Barrett opened his mouth in surprise, caught sight of the look on Merren's face and decided now was not the time to have a debate about the arcane secrets of his order.

'Every young apprentice, upon gaining the First Circle, is told how the dragons guard and protect the magic. But those of us who have attained the higher Circles are told the full story, how the magic flows through the dragons. If the dragons were to die, then … well, I could not see how the magic could continue. And Havell is right. Nothing can exist outside the laws of this world, which say that everything is born, uses magic as it lives and grows, then dies, to release the magic back into the world. It follows that even dragons must die.'

'But why now? Isn't there enough happening?' she cried. 'Now you're saying we must choose between saving a country and saving the world? What does Martil have to do now?'

Havell coughed a little. 'Well, I make it sound dramatic, that all life on the world will end, but that is only so you understand the gravity of the situation. I do not ask for the Dragon Sword wielder lightly. For the Dragon Sword wielder, it will be a simple, short duty; no one will feel anything, no one will know anything, but the rebirth of the dragons, and through them the magic, will have been achieved. All for the work of but a few moments. Then the wielder and his companions can return and life can go on as before.'

'So when will it be? How long before he can return?' Merren asked, aghast.

Havell shrugged. 'It is hard to say. This is not something that has happened before. The dragons knew it was coming, of course, because they planned for it with the Sword and Egg. The first dragon has died, which has triggered my coming here. It could be months, or even a year before the last one dies. But we are talking about the survival of the world. It is not something you want to leave until the last moment. The wielder, and as many of his friends as a dragon can carry, will dwell on Dragonara Isle until he is needed to perform this vital duty. If it is not done by sunrise on the day after the last dragon dies, the sun will never rise again.'

'A year?' Merren gasped. 'You don't understand, we are about to be invaded by Berellians and Tenochs! In a year's time, there won't be a country for Martil to return to — and while he might have saved the world, it will only be so Zorva can rule it!'

'That is not my concern. Surely you have other warriors who can help you?' Havell pointed at Jaret and Wilsen.

'Can we go? Can we go please?' Karia begged.

'Help us!' Merren cried. 'Bring the rest of the dragons to fight for us, then you can have the Dragon Sword for as long as you need!'

'Impossible! The dragons protect the magic, not the people! If we interfered in this petty little fight, then we would have an endless stream of people at our door, wanting us to save them, or fight for them! Besides, the cost in magic alone would be catastrophic! Nothing — not child nor calf nor chick — would be born around the world for a year. Would you sacrifice a generation to save yourselves?'

Merren, the guilt of almost ordering the death of Derthal women and children still thick in her throat, wordlessly shook her head. Besides, there was another life, one inside her, that would pay the price …

Martil had been trying to make some sense of all this. The situation was spinning out of control. One moment he had been prepared to fight and die against the Derthals, then he had been saved by a dragon, and now that dragon's rider was demanding he leave Merren, leave Norstalos to the Berellians, while he sat around with a bunch of elves and dragons, waiting to shove the Sword into an egg and restore the world's magic? It was too much. It was madness!

'It's madness!' he said aloud.

'I beg your pardon?' Havell stared at him.

'You want my help, then you have to do what I say,' Martil growled. 'I have had enough of being pushed around by queens, gods, dragons, destiny or whatever! I'm not at the world's beck and call, ready to pick up a sword and save everyone! I wanted some peace, and this is what I've got — I have to save Norstalos from the bastards I thought I'd beaten in the Ralloran Wars, then I have to save the world's magic because your stupid lizards can't go and f— breed like everything else! Well, I'm not a bloody hero for hire! This is not a bloody saga, and if you don't like it, then you can take your pointy ears and your flying lizard and piss off back to wherever you came from!'

'Daaa-ad!' Karia was outraged. 'This isn't funny!'

Havell whitened with anger at Martil's tirade but, seeing as Martil was spattered with Rath's blood, and carrying what the Elfaran knew to be an invincible sword, he did not make a move.

'I could indeed piss off, as you crudely suggest, but I could also have this dragon seize you, and take you to Dragonara Isle as its prisoner. Perhaps that would teach you some manners!'

'And when I got there, I'd cut through anything that tried to stop me, including dragons, with this same Dragon Sword — the only thing that would be safe from me would be your stupid egg!'

Havell looked as though he was about to explode but, instead, he offered a stiff bow.

'Obviously I have given you a great deal of

information, too quickly. Let us start again. What is it you need from us, in order that you may fulfil your duties as the Dragon Sword wielder?'

Martil glanced at Merren. 'I need to make sure Norstalos is safe.'

Havell's face tightened. 'I already told you, the dragons will not join your fight—'

'Your stupid lizards don't have to get their paws dirty,' Martil snapped. 'But at least get the Derthals to help us instead. Nothing impresses more than a dragon; with you we should be able to get the help Norstalos needs. Once Norstalos is safe, I will come with you to Dragonara Isle. If, as you say, it could be a year, we have plenty of time. The Berellians will invade within weeks — either way, it will be over in a month.'

'Firstly, dragons are not lizards. And they are not stupid! They are the most wonderful, intelligent creatures that could ever exist …'

'Whatever. If you want to kiss its scaly arse, then go ahead. Don't bother me with your talk of how pretty it is. Do we have a deal?'

'What if you are killed in battle? What then?'

'I haven't met the Berellian who could kill me. Besides, your magic Sword should be able to keep me safe. If you're really worried, some of your pointy-eared friends could come and fight with us.'

'My people do not fight. It is not in our nature. And our ears are not pointy, as you describe it, they are just narrower at the top than the bottom,' Havell said stiffly.

Martil grinned humourlessly. He was enjoying taking his frustration out on this elf. 'Why don't you just take the Sword, and you, or one of your pointy-eared mates, can stick it into the egg?'

Havell looked, if possible, even more stricken. 'Because my people, the Elfarans, have been part of the dragons' magic for centuries. Once, we were men like you. But serving the dragons has changed our appearance, as well as expanded our life far beyond the span of a man's dreams. When the last dragon dies, we will follow in the next breath.'

'Really? Not much of a reward for centuries of cleaning up dragon dung,' Martil said callously.

'Is he always like this?' Havell appealed to Barrett.

'I am afraid so. I'd like to say he grows on you, but it does not get any better,' Barrett sniffed.

Martil ignored this byplay. 'Do we have a deal?'

'You do not make deals with dragons, sir! Have you forgotten your oaths, the sacred duties you took on when you picked up the Sword! The legends taught to every Norstaline child! You must put those ahead of tawdry duties to kings and queens!'

'I took no oaths,' Martil declared.

Havell spun to face Queen Merren. 'Is this true?'

Merren sighed. 'He is a Ralloran. And he drew the Sword after it was stolen. Not in the traditional ceremony in the palace.'

'Well, where were you?'

'In a flea-bitten inn in Tetril, accompanied by a stinking one-armed bandit, who was covered in his own piss,' Martil said with great relish.

Karia rolled her eyes at him, so he winked at her.

Havell shuddered. 'I can only hope you are making sport of me. Queen Merren, I really must protest! This is utterly without precedent! The Dragon Sword wielder swears those oaths for precisely this situation! Nothing is more important than the survival of the magic …'

'To you, maybe,' Martil grunted.

Havell continued, ignoring him, 'Nevertheless, I must insist that you return with me now. If necessary, I can call on Argurium to bring you. Once on Dragonara Isle, you will learn the wisdom of this decision.'

Merren stared imploringly at Martil. But he was already speaking.

'You forget one thing,' Martil said harshly; the time for jesting was over. 'The restriction that calls on the wielder to be a good man. If I came with you, abandoned my oaths to Queen Merren and Norstalos, abandoned men who trusted in me, left them to die at the hands of Berellians, I would not be a good man. I would have left friends to die, when I could have saved them. If your dragons do not die quickly, the Sword might drain the life from me and you would be left without a Sword wielder to perform your precious duty.'

Martil could see that argument hit home by the way Havell stood there opening and closing his mouth like a fish.

'This wasn't supposed to happen! Norstalos was blessed with the Sword because it was so big, so potentially powerful! United, it would never be under threat, so its greatest warrior would always be at our service!' he wailed.

'I thought Norstalos got the Sword because some old king saved the life of a dragon?' Martil said suspiciously. 'A captured dragon that was about to be killed by the goblins? Thus making Norstalines think they had been blessed, and that goblins were foul creatures who deserved to have their land stolen and be driven into the mountains?'

'What do they teach you in Rallora? A dragon, killed by Derthals? That's ridiculous! Not even a starving Derthal would attack a dragon — and there is no way a dragon would be captured.'

'Well, that's the story the Norstalines brag about in their sagas,' Martil replied defiantly.

'He is right. That is the legend we are taught,' Merren agreed.

'Well, I have never heard such nonsense! King Riel was approached by the dragons and presented with the Sword, with the express warning that the dragons would, one day, need this favour in return!'

Everyone stopped at that. Martil was the first to break the silence, throwing back his head and laughing bitterly.

'So he did what most kings do: he changed the story to make himself look good, give him an excuse to seize land from the Derthals and unite the country, all in one! And the whole foundation of Norstalos thinking it is better than everyone else is based on a lie?'

Havell glanced at an ashen Merren. 'It would seem so,' the rider agreed.

'Can we stop talking and go for a flight on a dragon?' Karia demanded.

Martil sighed. 'Here is my deal, elf.'

'Elfaran!'

'Whatever. You and your dragon, Argot or whatever its name is, help us convince the Derthals to join our fight against the Berellians and Tenochs. Then you follow me down to Norstalos. If, at any time, it looks like I am about to be killed, you can swoop down and save me. Once we have saved Norstalos, I will fly with you to Dragonara Isle and save the world. And after that, every bloody royal, dragon, God or country who wants a hand can leave me alone!'

'Ahem!' Karia said loudly.

'Oh, and Karia gets a ride on the dragon,' he added hastily.

Havell stared at him carefully. 'I am not authorised to make deals. I will put your terms to Argurium, and then relay her answer to you.'

Martil's eyebrows rose. 'So the dragon's in charge, and you're just the messenger boy?'

Havell's lips tightened. 'I serve the dragons. Now, if you will excuse me.'

They watched as he walked back to the dragon.

'Could this day get any stranger?' Martil asked.

'You could have been more polite to him! He's an elf, and that's a dragon!' Barrett snarled.

'He's an Elfaran. You're a wizard and you annoy me. So what?' Martil was in no mood to be polite or think of others. Everyone wanted something from him, and he was just about sick of it. All he had wanted was peace, but coming to Norstalos had brought him nothing but trouble. Well, almost nothing.

Karia leaped from her horse and raced over to him, grabbing him around the middle in a huge hug.

'I think it's great! I can't wait to have a ride on a dragon and see Dragonara Isle! This is the best present ever!'

'It's not quite a present for Martil,' Merren said, more softly.

He looked up from Karia to see Merren was looking at him with sympathy and more than that, he could swear, in her eyes.

For her part, Merren was feeling a wave of affection for him. He had defied her, and she had feared he had doomed them all by his actions — but, with the arrival of the dragon, it seemed he had in fact helped them. Events were moving fast, almost too quickly to keep up with. But she recognised her confusion was as nothing compared to what Martil was facing.

'What you are being asked to do is almost too much for one man,' she told him. 'But you are not alone.'

'Really? I thought wielding the Dragon Sword left me that way — and I thought you made it clear that was the way it would stay?' Martil couldn't resist saying.

'Perhaps not,' was all she said.

Martil wanted to grab her, demand she tell him what she meant, but she would not look at him.

'Here comes the dragon!' Karia squealed, jumping up and down.

Even Martil had to be impressed by Argurium's approach. In the air she was poetry, on the ground she was sheer grace. Her walk seemed more regal than the most noble king or queen. She lowered her huge head with her wide, beautiful eyes and gentle snout, and he felt ashamed of calling her a 'bloody lizard' to Havell. By his side, Karia was jiggling around in a mixture of excitement and fear, peering around his leg to see her better.

'Captain Martil, I understand the dilemma you are in,' the dragon said, her voice high and musical — within its rich tones was wisdom, kindness and compassion. Martil had to restrain himself from falling to his knees.

'You are a man of honour. You have been asked to fight for a land that is not your own, for a people who do not love you, and you refuse to leave them, even if it means risking all life in this world. I apologise for putting you through this, and for asking more of you than is right, or fair. But we had to test you; the Dragon Sword had only just accepted you. Your actions now, and at the Derthal village, show us the Dragon Sword chose correctly. We will accompany you to see the Derthal High Chief. We shall not involve ourselves but no doubt our presence will have some effect. If successful, we shall watch over you in any ensuing battles. When your duties here are over, you may accompany us to Dragonara Isle. There, I assure you, the task will not be difficult, only ceremonial. It sounds as if it is a mission of life or death — the survival of the world — but it is not like that. It will be the work of but a moment, a beautiful moment of rebirth and wonder.'

Martil gripped Karia's hand. The dragon's tone was so warm, so friendly, that it seemed the most natural thing in the world to instantly agree. This was why he was determined not to.

'So the business with your elf or whatever he is was all just a test? And if I had agreed with his idea to run off with you right now?'

'You were correct — the Dragon Sword would not have approved. And we would have had to conduct a more extensive search for a new wielder.'

'You would have killed me,' Martil said flatly.

'No, your own actions would have doomed you. We had to be sure, you understand. The task you have is simple, but it is vital. Without it, the magic cannot be reborn, and the circle of life will end. We have to be sure the person entrusted with that task is going to be worthy.'

'Is this all connected with what Father Nott was telling me about, that I was chosen for this task?' Martil asked suspiciously.

He could have sworn Argurium smiled at that. 'We do not serve either of the Gods. We are independent, servant only to the world's magic. If you are fulfilling destiny, it is not by our design.'

Martil nodded, feeling not the slightest bit happier about the whole situation. But what choice did he have? They had to get the Derthals on their side, and after the disaster with Rath, the dragons were the perfect way to persuade the Derthals to help. And sticking the Dragon Sword into some magical egg so a horde of baby dragons could fly out did not sound too hard.

'So we have a deal?' he said finally.

Argurium bowed her head. 'We have a deal,' she said gravely.

'So when can I have my ride?' Karia demanded instantly.

With a dragon to guide them, finding the cave of the Derthal High Chief was easy. Argurium led them straight there, along a path that, to Martil, looked suspiciously like the one they had been following with their initial three guides, the ones killed by Rath's warriors.

'When are we going to be there?' Karia complained.

'Just over the next ridge,' Havell offered, glancing up to where Argurium flew high above them.

The Elfaran had chatted happily to Barrett and Quiller, had even talked with Karia, but tried to stay away from Martil.

'It's funny, you would think the Derthals would have had some guard on the road, or something,' Martil muttered as they rode along.

'Perhaps they have and you haven't seen them,' Barrett suggested.

'Impossible!' Martil snorted.

But, as they rode over the ridge, a horde of Derthals appeared out of nowhere, from behind rocks, out of trees and tall bushes. Roaring with anger, brandishing their wicked spears, they rushed forwards.

Martil drew the Dragon Sword but it was obviously not going to be enough — he barely had time to open his mouth to shout for Barrett to do something when Argurium landed in front of the little party of humans.

With an enormous roar that echoed off the surrounding cliffs, she stopped the Derthals in their tracks. Throwing aside their spears, the warriors turned tail and ran.

Beyond them, Martil could see the valley housed scores of small huts, as well as a dozen cave entrances in the side of a mountain. Below them, hundreds of Derthals, females, warriors and young, were running in all directions, looking like an ant's nest disturbed by a child's stick. All were hurrying for the safety of the caves. Derthals tripped over each other, pushed and shoved as Argurium gave them another warning roar. Martil had to admit he couldn't blame them for running. Karia was hunched over, hands covering her ears, and if he had not known the dragon was on their side, he would have been terrified as well. All the warmth and compassion was gone — the roar was nothing more than the hungry call of a monstrous creature.

By the time its echoes had died away, every last Derthal was inside the caves. A few penned goats bleated nervously, while a litter of discarded spears, skins, bowls and other items marked the villagers' desperate flight for safety.

'What now?' Merren asked.

'Now we wait,' Havell said simply. 'They will send someone out to talk to us.'

It took a while, but finally a small group of Derthals appeared out of the largest entrance and, spears pointed nervously at the dragon, inched towards them, followed by what was unmistakably a priest. He had short dark hair and a close-cropped beard and appeared to be in his mid-forties. He did not even look at the dragon, just at Merren.

'Queen Merren, it is you!' he said warmly, walking towards her.

'Yes. And you are?' Merren asked coolly.

'I am Father Alban. Thank Aroaril you have arrived safely. There have been strange developments, which explains the reception waiting for you. But luckily you were more than equal to the task. High Chief Sacrax has sent me out to find out who you are and what you want.'

'Who we are you now know — as to what we want, I must meet the High Chief and talk to him! We have been led in circles, first by three Derthals who met us, then Chief Rath and his warriors.'

'Chief Rath? How did you meet him?' Alban gasped, his composure vanishing.

'He ambushed our original guides, killed them and told us they were traitors. Then he wanted us to help him wipe out a Derthal village, to pass the High Chief's test — and when we refused, he tried to kill us. Only Argurium's intervention saved us,' Merren explained, feeling a surge of shame that she had insisted they join in Rath's attack.

'What? Rath was the one who sent a message saying a group of Friny — enemies — were loose in the north and killing every Derthal they could see. That was why there were so many guards waiting for you. If you had had your guides with you, you would have been safe. But without them ... Luckily the dragon was with you. So Rath wanted you to kill a village of Derthals?' Alban was trying to make sense of it all.

Merren wanted to understand what was going on, as well.

'He wanted us to attack a village, then he and his warriors would kill the inhabitants,' she explained.

'It's becoming clear now. I am afraid you have walked into the middle of a bitter dispute among the Derthals over who to support. Rath hates all humans, or Friny as he calls us — enemies.'

'He called me Queen of the Friny,' Merren confirmed.

'He is cunning,' Alban said, almost admiringly. 'He decided to stop talking and take action. It must have been a trap for you. I expect the village would have belonged to High Chief Sacrax. How many warriors were there? Where was it?'

'It was hidden in a small forest but there were no warriors, it was a small group of just women and children,' Martil said.

Alban gasped in horror. 'That was no village, that was the High Chief's household! Those were his wives and children! To touch them is to bring a sentence of death not only on your head but on your entire clan!' The priest shook his head. 'Rath is one of the smartest Derthals I have met. He could have killed you all, but that would have been disobeying the High Chief and probably resulted in the order for his death. Instead, he tried to trick you. If you had obeyed Rath, he would have dragged you before the High Chief. He would have won over many minor chiefs to his side and everything he wanted would have come to pass.

The High Chief would have killed you and tried to destroy your entire clan — Norstalos.'

Merren shuddered to think how close they had come to falling into the Derthal's trap, and looked at Martil, wanting to say she was sorry, wanting to say something, but he was carefully avoiding her gaze.

'He was very clever. He made it sound like he was from the High Chief, and sent to test us. Every word he spoke was not a lie, but was also obviously not the whole truth. He must have learned of the power of the priests to detect falsehoods.' Quiller sighed.

'Oh, Rath believes in knowing his enemy,' Alban agreed. 'Where is he now?'

'Dead,' Martil said shortly.

Alban smiled. 'That is the first good news I have heard today. We might be able to use this to our advantage. I shall go and explain to the High Chief what happened. But things might be difficult. If you had arrived with your guides, he would have accepted you. But Derthals died as soon as you came north. It will complicate matters further. There have been more developments here, apart from Rath's deception.'

'We must speak to the High Chief! Tell him that the only way the dragon will leave is if he will speak to us — and any treachery will see the dragon destroy every last Derthal,' Merren instructed.

'But—' Havell began, only to have Merren silence him with a look.

Alban nodded. 'An excellent gambit. I am sure he will speak to you, under those conditions. Although how the dragon can take part ...'

'I shall wait outside. But Havell can speak on my behalf,' Argurium said musically.

'Wait here. I shall return.'

They watched Alban hurry down the path.

'Your majesty—' Havell began, but she cut him off.

'I know Argurium will not do that — but they do not need to know it. Agreed? Anyway, this Alban, can we trust him?' Merren asked.

'He is a priest of Aroaril. He also has Aroaril's favour,' Quiller said stiffly. 'The only caution I have is his position is very delicate. He has to have the trust of the High Chief in order to stay, and survive. He must tread a careful path of helping us, without offending the High Chief.'

'Do you think the High Chief will listen to us?' Merren worried.

'With a bloody great dragon sitting outside his front door, I think he has to,' Martil grunted.

'At least we avoided Rath's trap! When I think of how close we came to disaster …' Quiller grimaced. 'Your majesty, I am so sorry …'

'My Queen, I also made that mistake,' Barrett said.

Merren waved away their apologies — she did not wish to speak of it again. They had provided her with bad advice but the decision was ultimately hers, and she had to take responsibility for it, not blame others.

They waited impatiently in silence, except for Karia, who wanted to touch the dragon's scales. She pestered Martil until he asked Argurium for the favour. Smiling, the dragon extended a foreleg for Karia to lightly touch with her fingers.

'They're so warm!' she told Martil. 'Warm and soft and smooth!'

Martil smiled back, although it was a struggle when he thought about all the tasks that seemingly waited for him.

'I suppose you'll want one as a pet, next?' he suggested.

'I want two!' She laughed with him.

'Here comes Father Alban!' Quiller called.

'The High Chief will see you, and guarantees your safety,' Alban announced as soon as he arrived. 'Thank Aroaril you had a dragon with you — I haven't seen him this angry ever and doubt he would have agreed otherwise.'

'Why not? I thought you said he had agreed to a meeting, that was why we came here,' Merren asked sharply.

Alban looked uncomfortable. 'Things have changed since then. Look, we must hurry. I don't want to leave High Chief Sacrax alone with them for too long.'

'With who? What is going on?' Merren asked, but Alban had already started walking.

'Come on!' he waved impatiently.

Merren shrugged, then signalled for them all to follow, although Argurium stayed where she was.

The Derthal camp was crude, but it showed evidence of organisation and tool-making: skins were stretched on wooden frames, being scraped; meat was being smoked; spears were being made. Martil was reminded of the camp where he had found Karia. It had that same bedraggled, grim look to it.

Even though they were on horses, they only caught up to Alban when he paused at the main entrance to the caves.

'Now, when we get in there, do nothing rash, no matter what you see,' Alban warned.

'What will we see? Father, you are being unnecessarily mysterious!' Merren snapped.

Alban wiped a sweating brow. 'I am not allowed to say. The High Chief wants to see your reaction. It must be natural or he will suspect something, and I will lose his trust. This business with Rath was troubling enough but this … Look, I warn you not to underestimate Sacrax. He is very intelligent, a cunning fighter and a strong warrior. He, too, has studied us, and is no friend of the Norstalines. But he will do what is best for his people, not for himself.'

'But …'

'No more time! We cannot delay. Follow me!'

Alban strode into the caves and they had no choice but to follow.

The first thing that struck Martil was the smell. The cave opened up into a wide passage, with many side tunnels. A few torches lit the area and the smell of smoke was thick in the air, along with the smell of unwashed bodies and untanned animal skins. Eyes peered out from the shadows, and Martil had the impression there were scores of Derthals packed down the side tunnels, watching nervously.

Alban strode ahead, looking neither left nor right, leading them into a much larger cave, which was better lit.

The first impression was there were two groups of Derthals in the cave — although that was not quite right, Martil saw. In fact, it was two types of Derthals, in three groups.

The first type was older, although obviously powerful, wearing some sort of animal-skin headband, similar to the one Rath had worn. These were likely to be chiefs. Many of them bore evidence of wounds. Scars from talons, broken arms or legs that had been set crudely and never healed properly, or even missing limbs — almost every chief in this cave showed some sort of wound. The second type was younger; unmistakably warriors.

Along one side of the cave was a large group of mixed chiefs and warriors; along the other side was a smaller group of chiefs and warriors, while the final group were the only armed Derthals, a double line of about twenty young warriors, all carrying the spears that Martil had seen used with such effect. They stood near a crude wooden throne at the far end of the cave. In it sat a powerful-looking Derthal. He wore no headband like the other chiefs but he carried what looked like a huge mace, carved from the bone of some creature. It was his only sign of office, but there was an air of authority about him that proclaimed here was the High Chief of the Derthals.

The three figures standing beside the throne captured Martil's attention almost immediately after his eyes left the High Chief.

The first was obviously a wizard, judging by his bright orange robes and long wooden staff decorated with bones and feathers, while the other two wore armour — and the black-and-gold surcoat of Berellia.

Then he heard Merren cry out.

Merren had tried to focus on High Chief Sacrax; she knew she needed to make a strong impression after the way their mission here had got off to such a bad start. But the three figures to the side of the throne had drawn her eye.

The wizard she did not recognise — but the other two ... It was Ezok, the former Berellian ambassador to Norstalos, and with him the assassin who had killed Wime, Forde and so many of her men — and almost herself.

'It's him!' she cried.

'Murderer!' Jaret roared, drawing his sword.

Martil heard Merren call and that only hardened his first instinct, which was that the Berellians were here for the same reason they were: to win over the Derthals. As far as he was concerned, the best Berellian was a dead Berellian, so he drew his swords as well and advanced on them. If the third Berellian was indeed the Champion who had killed Wime and Forde, as Merren's cry indicated, then he would take no chances.

'Hold!' High Chief Sacrax's voice echoed through the cave, and instantly his score of warriors stepped out, blocking the way between them.

Martil stopped, but did not lower his swords; the Berellians appeared to be smiling.

'I will not have fighting in my audience hall,' Sacrax boomed, his accent thick but his words understandable. 'Put up your weapons or leave, never to return.'

Martil reluctantly sheathed his swords but noticed the Derthal warriors did not relax or move back to their original positions.

'Welcome to my hall, Queen Merren of the Norstalines. You arrive strangely. I sent you guides, three trusted warriors, instead you come with a dragon.'

'Our guides were killed by a Derthal called Rath. He tried to tell us that, in order to gain an audience with you, we would have to destroy a village of your wives and children,' Merren said strongly. She decided that the best way to proceed was to confront this straightaway, and prove that the Norstalines were too noble to fall for such a trick — even though she almost had.

'What?' Sacrax said, and even though not all of the Derthals in the chamber knew what was being said, they recognised the alarm and anger in his voice. Instantly there was tension in the room and Merren could see the Derthals who did understand the words hurriedly translating for the others.

The smaller group of chiefs and warriors began muttering, and Merren could hear the word 'Friny!' being repeated. That seemed to indicate they were the ones who had supported Rath, and she was pleased to see they were the smaller group.

Father Alban stepped forwards.

'High Chief, as I warned you, Rath had his own plans. I believe he has been making secret deals with the Berellians. He wanted to use this Queen's noble mission to destroy you. He wanted them to kill your wives and children, knowing you would be weakened, knowing you would have to go to war with Norstalos in response. His dream was not just war, but to take your throne. As well as refusing, the Queen and just three warriors were prepared to fight Rath and a warband of his finest warriors to save your wives and children.'

'How do they survive then?' another chief, his shattered left arm strapped to his body, shouted out.

'We were saved by a dragon. The same dragon that brought us here and waits outside these caves,' Merren replied.

That set the muttering off again, until Sacrax tapped the butt of his mace on the floor, the dull thud an effective call for silence.

'And why does a dragon want to help you?' Sacrax rumbled.

Havell, hearing his cue, walked forwards from where he had been standing at the back.

Instantly the Derthals in the chamber began talking among themselves, and there was much gesturing and pointing.

'I am here because the dragons have created a powerful magical object, the Dragon Egg. To make this work, we need the Dragon Sword wielder. But his help has a price. He wants me to help convince you to fight for his queen, Merren.' Havell turned and gestured to her. 'On behalf of the dragons, and the respect you bear for them, I ask that you help Queen Merren.' He turned to the Derthals and repeated his words in their language.

The effect was dramatic. The Derthals began shouting at each other, shouting across the room, and the small group of chiefs and warriors began chanting.

'N'ga! N'ga! N'ga!'

Merren could sense the meaning: they were working themselves up for a fight.

'I think you could have been a little more convincing,' she muttered.

'I cannot lie,' Havell replied loftily.

The High Chief leaped to his feet and let out a roar of anger. He slammed the base of his massive club into the ground, and the combination of the cry and the booming strike of the club silenced the chamber.

The High Chief signalled to what looked like the captain of his guards, and spoke softly to the man, who grabbed a pair of warriors and hurried out of the chamber.

'Tell us why you are here, Queen Merren of the Norstalines,' the High Chief said heavily, sinking back into his chair.

'I offer you friendship, a new start. I have learned that the enmity between our peoples was based on a lie. I would make up for centuries of hatred and hurt. I offer you your ancestral home, the northern forest, to live undisturbed, at peace with my people. Further, we will give you clothes and food, help you through the winter,' Merren declared. 'I offer a lasting peace, and the chance for Norstaline and Derthal to make a new beginning.'

'And what do you want in return?' Sacrax said immediately.

'Your help in defeating an invasion of those who would kill both Norstaline and Derthal; we need your warriors so that the land may be preserved for both our peoples. Without them, there will be no peace, for those who stand by your throne will not share land — they will lie, they will steal and they will betray. They follow the Dark One, and will not rest until you are enslaved, or dead.'

That got the rest of the Derthals muttering again, as the words were translated. Sacrax glanced over at the Berellians; Merren was already staring at them. Ezok was smiling and had placed a restraining hand on Cezar.

'It is interesting. For years your people never wanted to talk to us. All you wanted to do was kill us. Now, in one day, I have been visited by Norstaline and Berellian. And you both want my help. You both promise much — and you both say the other is lying. You have given me much to think about. And I will not decide until I know all,' Sacrax said heavily. 'I must know the truth of what you say about Rath. I will send for you when we need to speak again.'

Merren inclined her head. She did not want to appear to be too arrogant by pushing him to make a decision now. She also did not want to talk too much in front of the Berellians.

'Father Alban, take them to your home. I will send for you again when I am ready,' Sacrax instructed.

Alban bowed.

'Follow me,' he said quietly, eyes averted.

Martil did not want to leave straightaway. Instead, he stared coldly at the Berellian trio, who were being escorted out through another tunnel by a squad of guards.

The assassin stared back at him and Martil saw the hatred in his gaze. But there was no fear there. In fact the Berellian seemed almost happy to see him.

26

'Why did you not tell us about the Berellians?' Merren demanded.

The Norstalines and Martil — and the dragon — had been escorted to Father Alban's home, a large hut that also doubled as a crude church. Martil noted that while it was old, it did not seem to have seen much use. As well as the usual altar and a collection of crude benches, it had a curtained-off area for Alban to sleep in, and a small kitchen area. Alban had hurried around finding food and drink, which only Karia seemed eager to eat, while the others sat on the church pews.

'I could not tell you about the Berellians. High Chief Sacrax is confused. He knows little about disputes between southern countries. To him, there are the Norstalines and that is all. The thought that other countries, such as Berellia, lie below Norstalos and want to take its land, is causing an enormous stir in Derthal society. The Berellians have been talking of revenge, of winning back lands, and there are many chiefs who like that idea. But, to Sacrax, it is a concept that is both dangerous and worrying. He seeks more information before he will commit the Derthals to a course of action that could see one or more armies of men seeking revenge on his people. And where will he get that information about the different countries far to the south? From someone he trusts. Me. But he only trusts me as long as I am seen to be impartial. If I had told you about the Berellians, you would not have reacted like that — and Sacrax would have known I had betrayed his trust. He would no longer talk to me. Then we would have an even bigger problem than we have now.'

'Bigger how?' Merren asked.

'You saw how there were two groups in the chamber?'

'I assumed the larger one was for us, the smaller for the Berellians.'

Alban shook his head grimly. 'The larger group is for joining the Berellians and taking back their ancestral lands, while gaining revenge for centuries of persecution. The smaller group is for killing both groups and refusing to have anything to do with the wars of the Friny.'

Stunned silence greeted his words.

'So none of the chiefs are interested in what we have to say?' Merren asked finally.

Alban shrugged. 'You have to see it from their point of view. They have been massacred and driven from their lands, called goblins and made to live in this bleak place. Now we want their warriors to die for us. Would you want to help?'

'Then why is the High Chief not trying to have us killed? Why did he agree to meet me?' Merren asked.

'He is the one person who does want to hear what you say. The safety of his people rests with him. He will not make a rash decision. And the death of Rath, as well as his clever attempt to trick you, will work in our favour. As does the presence of the dragon.' Alban gestured out of the window, where a crowd of excited Derthals was keeping a careful distance from Argurium.

'So what are we going to do about the Berellians? That is the man who killed Wime, and Forde — and others!' Merren hissed.

'I'll challenge him,' Martil promised. 'No doubt he's the Berellian King's Champion — but I've already killed one of those. With the Dragon Sword, he won't be around long.'

'Be careful,' Merren warned him gently. 'He seemed fond of using throwing knives and darts.'

Martil just smiled grimly. 'If he was the one who killed Wime, I'll look forward to it,' he growled.

Martil found himself reading to Karia to make the time pass. The church was devoid of anything much, and Alban suggested they stay inside, just in case some of the Derthals ostensibly looking at Argurium happened to be agents of the Berellians, or followers of Rath, looking for revenge.

Merren wanted to get a chance to talk to Martil, to try and explain what she had been thinking back at the Derthal village, but Karia showed no inclination to leave him alone. Merren told herself she had to learn from that mistake; she knew she would. But it still burned. She had thought she had put aside her father's teaching, but it had been his philosophy of the end justifying the means that saw her place the lives of Derthal families above Norstaline families. Yes, she had an enormous responsibility on her shoulders, yes, she was under incredible pressure — and yes, she was also pregnant. But she could not use those as excuses.

Curiously it made her understand Martil better, see how Bellic could have occurred. The only consolation she had was thinking how she could turn it to their advantage, to win over the Derthals. She would have liked a chance to speak to Havell, about how the Elfaran could help them, but he was waiting outside with Argurium, keeping the curious at a safe distance.

She breathed deeply, trying to calm her mind. She tried to think about what she could say to High Chief Sacrax, to persuade him to help her people, but all that came to mind was how the Derthals had been killed and driven out, all for a lie. The Norstalines had discovered the passes that gave access to the north, then found huge forests, rich farmland and both gold and silver in the northern mountains. It had seemed like a paradise, except for the strange tribe of creatures already living in the area. Then King Riel had announced these 'goblins' had tried to kill a dragon, making them fair game for anyone who wanted land, gold and silver. History said that the Dragon Sword had united the people — and certainly it could have that effect — but how much was also down to all the gold and silver that flowed to the Crown? In one stroke, King Riel had new lands to promise to his faithful supporters, as well as money aplenty to buy soldiers and swords.

She forced that out of her mind and talked to Barrett about getting themselves more time. Creating a storm out to sea should slow down the Tenoch advance — and thus everyone else, as well. Barrett agreed with alacrity and began work immediately, which was what she wanted, but it just left her free to think. She wondered how Sendric and Conal were coping in her absence. Looming large was the knowledge Martil had to travel to Dragonara Isle and help the dragons in their rebirth. No matter how often Havell told them it was a simple, easy duty, she could not help but wonder why *now*. What else was in store for them?

More waiting, it seemed. The afternoon dragged on and on, and night was falling with still no sign of anything happening. Even the crowd of Derthals looking at Argurium had dwindled to a few hardy souls. Alban, who had spent the day talking with Quiller and Havell, served them a thin stew of venison, washed down with water.

'There is little fresh food here. The Derthals are gatherers rather than growers. Obviously I have a little vegetable patch but the growing season is short,' Alban said apologetically.

After the dinner, Jaret and Wilsen were instructed to keep watch, while Alban helped everyone make up crude beds on the pews; his own bed was given up for Merren. The pews were wide enough and long enough to sleep on, although they were hardly comfortable.

Conal looked at the scroll in his hand and managed to restrain a smile — but only just.

'I think we have finally found the key to getting the people moving,' Sendric agreed. 'It was a brilliant idea, my friend.'

'It wasn't bad, even if I say so myself,' Conal grinned.

With so many of the people disbelieving the threat now massing over the borders, and not wanting to leave their homes and possessions behind, Conal tried a different approach. His solution had come from one problem of the evacuation: People could carry only so much food. Food was going to be critical, both in ensuring the evacuation and that the people could survive a winter in the north of the country. Getting enough food into the north to feed the entire country was a massive task in itself. But Conal had decided one problem could solve the other.

Shopkeepers were ordered to close their doors and head north; all available food was to be loaded onto wagons and brought to the capital. Those villages and towns that refused to leave would find that their food was running short anyway — and if they wanted to feed themselves and their children, they needed to follow the food north.

'But is it going to be enough? There are many who remain,' Sendric said, throwing a serious note back into their conversation. 'Those in the west with the money have laid in supplies enough for a siege, while some of the farming villages have stores enough to last longer.'

'I agree. Two of the worst are villages closest to the Berellian border.' Conal sighed. 'But we cannot do any more. We will collect as much food as we can. Now comes the time for hard decisions — who we can save, who is worth saving. But we have done what the Queen asked.'

Sendric nodded. 'Indeed. Now it is up to her to save those who do make it north,' he said simply.

Martil, then Barrett, took over watches through the night — but nothing happened.

'But who would attack a dragon?' Karia pointed out the next morning to a yawning Martil. 'Can I go out and speak to her?'

But, predictably, Karia's confidence fled and she wanted to hide behind Martil's leg once they were up close.

'It is all right, child. Come out. I feel your magic. I know you have questions.'

'What is it like on Dragonara Isle?' Karia asked eagerly.

'It is a beautiful island, with plants and animals living in harmony. I love to soak in its warm sea and lie on its golden sands. But I rarely have time for that. We just sleep and eat on the island; usually we are out, travelling the world, making sure the magic is flowing and is always protected.'

'So what is your house like?'

Argurium laughed — a gentle, almost musical sound. 'It is not a house; it is a hall, a huge hall, made from rock and living trees. Inside, both we and the Elfarans can rest, so it is almost like two halls in one. There are passages and rooms for dragons, and passages and rooms for Elfarans. They intertwine and cross over, so that one creature may visit all other parts of the hall.'

'I would love to see that!' Karia cried.

'And you will, one day. When the Dragon Sword wielder comes to us, you may come with him.'

'So can you tell us any more about the duty I have?' Martil thought he might as well ask.

Argurium smiled and stretched. 'Only what you have heard. It is not a hard task, or a dangerous task. Compared with what you have faced, and what you will face, it is easy. The only requirement is that you have to be there at the right moment — and that will not be a concern.'

'And what of the Dragon Sword? Can you tell me more of that?'

'Yes. But we do not have time to talk of it now.'

Karia, bored with talk of duties and tasks, took over the conversation, steering it back to topics she was far more interested in, such as whether there were any fairies on the island.

Martil tried to stifle a yawn as Karia interrogated the dragon on every magical creature that had ever featured in a saga and which, according to Argurium, did not exist.

When Wilsen told them breakfast was ready, Martil struggled to control the urge to hug the man.

'She was very nice, but I don't think she's very clever, for a dragon,' Karia said critically, as they walked back.

'Why do you say that?' Martil asked.

'She's never seen a fairy! Or a gnome, or a dryad, or a sprite, or a talking rabbit! She mustn't get out much. Everyone knows they all live on Dragonara Isle, come out at night and dance around together, have exciting adventures … And Argurium said she'd never even been to a fairy tea party!' Karia shook her head, overcome with the thought of how deprived that poor dragon was.

'Imagine that. A dragon who doesn't know what a fairy is,' Martil said with a straight face.

They walked back into Alban's church to find the priest's supplies were not up to breakfast, and they were to eat the dried fruit and oatcakes they'd brought with them. After eating, Jaret and Wilsen went out to feed the horses.

'Well, what should we do now? Do we just wait for Sacrax to decide what to do with us?' Merren snapped, pacing up and down the church.

'He will want to speak to you again, before making any decision. But he will want no more surprises — he will only speak to you when he has discovered the truth of your claims about Rath. After he has spoken to you, then he might call for me, then he will think some more before making his final decision. It might all take some time. May I suggest your majesty lie down and take it easy, in your condition?'

'My condition? Being a woman? What nonsense is that?' Merren snorted.

'No, I meant with your majesty being pregnant,' Alban protested gently. 'Too much agitation and excitement is not good for a baby's development. May I suggest you sit down and I'll try to find you a glass of milk?' His jaw dropped as he caught sight of Merren's ashen stare, and the thunderstruck looks on everyone else's face.

'Was that a secret?' he asked, rather lamely.

Merren could feel every eye in the room on her and had to control the urge to hit the priest.

'I think you are mistaken, Father,' she said through gritted teeth. 'And you are also dangerously impertinent.'

Alban recovered slowly. 'Of course, your majesty. Please accept my humblest apologies. I have been among the Derthals too long. It must have clouded my vision.'

'Good. Let us say no more about it,' Merren said heavily.

But as she turned, she could see by the look on Martil's face this would not be an end to it.

'So that is why you are marrying Sendric,' he said slowly, looking at her in wonderment. The words seemed to have burned themselves into his brain, then sunk down into his chest, where they sat, like a lead weight. It made many things clear, but it also made them much worse.

'That was why you changed!' Barrett snarled at Martil. He had thought he had come to terms with

Merren's rejection, but to know she had rebuffed him for Martil ...

'This discussion is at an end!' Merren's voice cracked like a whip. 'This is not the time or the place! And there will be nothing more said! We are here to save a country, not to get involved in fights between ourselves! If any person here does not do everything in their power to help me, then by Aroaril I will kill you myself! Norstalos needs us all, and I will not allow us to fail! Do you understand?'

Silence greeted her words.

She stalked over to Barrett. 'Do I have your agreement?' she glared at him.

'Your majesty.' Barrett bowed stiffly, but she was already in Martil's face.

'And you? I will hear nothing more from you?'

'I need to talk to you, your majesty,' Martil said stiffly. 'Alone.'

'I thought I made it clear this discussion was at an end,' Merren hissed.

'Not to me,' Martil replied, then stared into her eyes. 'You owe me this much, at least,' he whispered. 'For the village, if not for Pilleth.'

Against her better judgement, Merren nodded jerkily, then stalked outside, Martil at her heels.

'This is why you are marrying Sendric. And the child is mine,' Martil stated flatly.

'Yes,' Merren admitted.

'But why? Why could you not tell me?' he implored.

Merren did not know whether to laugh or cry. 'Don't you understand? I had no choice. The people barely accept me. The thought of a base-born Ralloran Butcher of Bellic as their Prince Consort, his son as their future King ... You've seen the surveys, you know what people's attitude to the Rallorans is! We'd be lucky if they didn't rise up and demand Gello back again! They would never accept us, or him!'

'Him?' Martil seized upon that one word.

Merren felt like hitting herself or, better, hitting him. 'Yes, our son. The future King of Norstalos. But only if I do this my way.'

'I know the people don't like Rallorans, but marrying Sendric!' Martil protested. 'Haven't you talked endlessly about how a person should be judged by what they do, not how they were born? Doesn't this make that a lie? Can't we just give the people a chance to accept us? I mean, if we manage to save them from the Berellians …'

Merren held up her hand, and he trailed off.

She found herself close to tears, something she put down to her condition, for surely it was the only reason to feel so emotional. 'Don't you think I've considered all this? If we were ordinary, it would not matter. But there is too much at stake here. So many people have already died to put me back on the throne — more still will die before that throne is safe. How can I risk all of that, put my own happiness above my people? I had to choose between you and my country. You knew which one I had to pick!'

'But why did you have to lie to me?' Martil cried.

'You're a fine one to talk about lying! You were lying to me all through Pilleth! You wanted to sacrifice yourself and you refused to tell me!' Merren growled back.

'Well, maybe I should have died, then we wouldn't need to have this conversation!'

Merren turned away then, and Martil was

instantly sorry, reaching out a hand to touch her shoulder, but she jerked away from him.

'I don't want you dead. Surely even someone as wooden-headed as you can see that,' she said thickly.

'Then …'

'Then nothing. I must marry Sendric, give our son the chance to take up the Dragon Sword, and the throne. I have to put aside my personal feelings, I have a greater responsibility. Just as you did before Pilleth.'

'But, afterwards …'

She shook her head. 'It cannot happen. I promised Sendric this would never come out, that he would not go down in history as a laughing stock. Besides, if it ever became known, then we would still have the same problem with the people. No, for all our sakes, we cannot have a future. Any future. If you care anything for me, for this child, you will say nothing more.'

Martil groaned and turned away.

Merren stepped closer. 'We can never speak of this again,' she warned. 'Too much is at stake. I want you to swear on Karia's life that you will never mention it.'

Martil tried to look anywhere but at her. She reached up and grabbed his face in her hands.

'Swear it!'

Jerkily, Martil nodded his head. It was the last thing he wanted to do, but what choice did he have?

Merren took a moment to get herself back under control, then led the way back into the church — and into the middle of fresh arguments.

'How dare you! After all the warnings I gave you! I told you something bad would happen!' Barrett grabbed hold of Martil's tunic the moment he stepped through the door. 'I wish I had helped you die!'

'Let go of me, or there'll be someone else doing the dying here,' Martil warned, wrenching himself free.

'What's going on!' Karia screamed.

Martil stepped away from Barrett and went down on one knee to her.

'We're just having a discussion. It's nothing to worry about,' he reassured her.

'Is it true? Are you and Merren going to have a baby?' she demanded.

'Well …' Martil remembered how she had been raised on a farm, by a father who had no qualms about displaying naked women in front of a small girl. What to say?

'Are you going to leave me for the new baby?' Karia asked, almost in tears.

'No!' Martil protested. 'I would never do that!'

'But that's your real baby, I'm not yours really …'

'That's not right.' Martil grabbed her in his arms. 'There is no child I could want more than you! I swore I would look after you and I will never go back on that!'

'But …'

Martil kissed the top of her head. 'You have nothing to worry about,' he promised.

Merren would have joined in, but she could not escape from Barrett.

'How could you, Merren? After what you said to me back in the woods — you did the same thing with Martil, didn't you?' he accused.

'Don't you dare accuse me of anything!' Merren blazed back at him.

'But Martil! Look what is happening — I warned

you about this!' Barrett would normally have backed away long before now, but the thought of Merren and Martil together was eating him up inside.

'Wizard, you go too far! Have a care to what you say next!' Merren said furiously.

Quiller or Alban might have thought to intervene — only Quiller was ripping into the younger priest.

'Do you have any idea what you have done? This country is on a knife-edge as it is! If you had any suspicions, you should have raised them with me first!'

'Suspicions? The Queen is pregnant! Why should I think it was anything other than proper?' Alban growled.

'And show some respect for the Queen, for Aroaril's sake! Can you try and repair some of the damage?' Quiller hissed.

Alban held up his hand for silence; in that pause they all heard knocking on the door. Outside, Jaret called: 'There's a group of Derthals approaching.'

'Perfect timing,' Merren said fiercely in the sudden silence. She turned on them all. 'This did not happen. None of it. And if I hear of it in Norstalos, I know who to go looking for.'

Nobody spoke.

A moment later, Wilsen showed in a group of Derthal warriors, led by the one Martil recognised as the High Chief's guard captain.

'High Chief Sacrax will see you now,' he grunted. 'Follow.'

'Ask him where we are going,' Merren ordered Alban, and the priest, eager to make amends, hurried forwards, and barked out a question in Derthal.

The answer was brief, and Alban was able to turn with a smile.

'It is in his private audience chamber. Just us, and a few guards. It must be that he has found the truth of Rath's deception.'

Once more they collected Havell, left Argurium snoozing in the weak sunlight, and followed the Derthal guards back to the cave complex.

Unlike yesterday, there was plenty of activity in the Derthal camp. Out in the sun, young Derthal children played, chasing each other, while older male children were being taught how to use spears by a scarred Derthal warrior. Martil wondered why they did not try to throw the spears rather than thrust them, but supposed the balance was all wrong for throwing.

Derthal women were stretching and scraping animal skins, while others were heading off towards the distant forest, with baskets at their hips, still more were carrying waterskins back from a nearby brook, in a never-ending line.

They seemed happy enough, but it looked to be a hard, grim life up here, he reflected. He was trying to think about the Derthals so he did not think about Merren, and her marriage to Sendric. Because thinking of that made him want to draw the Dragon Sword and go hunting for the Berellians, to exorcise the massive anger, and hurt, and confusion inside him.

Then they plunged into the caves once more and were taken, not to the large cavern they had first seen, but to a smaller, more comfortable cave. Rushes made a crude carpet on the floor, while animal skins were hung over the walls and the horns from many deer decorated the edges.

Seated on a crude stool, not a throne this time, was the High Chief, who rose to greet them. Stools were brought for them, as was food: bowls of autumn berries and nuts.

When all were seated, and only a handful of guards remained stationed around the room, Sacrax bowed his head.

'My guards captured two of Rath's warriors, as well as finding Rath's body. They did not want to tell me the truth, but soon they were eager to say all. I owe you the lives of my wives and children. Rath wanted them dead. If you had helped him, they would be dead,' Sacrax said simply.

'Rath must have been working for the Berellians,' Martil said.

Sacrax turned his eyes on Martil, who met his gaze squarely.

'The Queen's warrior. You are smaller than I thought,' Sacrax said thoughtfully. 'I would like to see you fight.'

'Join us and I'll show you,' Martil said harshly. 'Turn on us and you might see more than you wished.'

Merren gave him a glare but Sacrax was laughing.

'I like that,' the Derthal admitted. 'But we are not here to fight, we are here to talk. Your deeds at my house have earned you much. The dragon you have with you adds weight to your words. But I must hear exactly what you offer.'

Merren took a handful of berries and made a point of eating a couple of them; both Alban and Quiller had said that was a gesture of trust among the Derthals.

'I am offering to correct a historic wrong. Your people were driven out of their lands, into these harsh mountains, because of one of my ancestors. Now I am offering your people the great northern forest, yours forever, written in our law, as well as recompense for the suffering you have gone through. There will be warm clothes for your people, as well

607

as seeds and help with farming, should you wish. And we will offer medicine, and healers. Your people and mine shall live side by side, as good neighbours, not as enemies.'

'That sounds good,' Sacrax admitted. 'But what is it you want?'

'For us to live in peace, we must have peace. My people are about to be invaded by three armies. We are outnumbered. We need your warriors to protect us while we train a bigger army. Hopefully your warriors would not even need to fight, just help block the northern passes. But, without your warriors, we are doomed. And if that were to happen, there would be no peace, no chance for your people to ever leave the mountains. For those we fight will promise you much — no doubt they are offering you all the land you can take from the Norstalines. But they will not let you keep it. Once they have finished with us, then they will turn on you. They want the shiny metals too much to let you keep what you could take. You can, of course, refuse us both. But then you will never leave these mountains. If you want to lead your people out of this misery, then we offer the only way. Yes, perhaps Derthals will be in danger. But they will just be there to scare our enemies, not to fight.'

Sacrax looked thoughtful. 'But what of the dragons? Will they help us?'

Havell shifted on his stool. 'The dragons do not fight. They act only to preserve the magic. But they will promise help to the Derthals. For the next year, no Derthal mother will lose their baby, and no Derthal mother will die in childbirth.'

Sacrax grunted. 'I have too many women and children already! Why do I want more?'

But Merren could see this offer intrigued him. She shuddered to think how many Derthal mothers and babies died up here. It made her think of the child inside her. She was not overly religious but she could not help but offer up a small prayer to Aroaril to preserve the child.

'In addition,' Havell continued, 'myself and the dragon Argurium will watch over any battle. While we will not take part, our presence will no doubt act as encouragement to your side, and cause fear in your enemies.'

Sacrax helped himself to some berries. 'Your offer is good, but it has one problem. What if we join you, and you are still defeated? Then your enemies will turn on us.'

'We shall not lose. With your warriors, I can hold the passes long enough to train an army to defeat our enemies,' Martil declared.

'He carries the Dragon Sword. It has never been defeated in battle,' Merren added.

Sacrax sighed.

'I have a problem,' he admitted. 'Rath's treachery makes me think the Berellians lie. But many of my chiefs like their words, like the idea of revenge on the Norstalines. Many, many deaths can be laid at your door. We lived in peace before you came, seeking the bright metals in the ground. Then you wanted more, wanted our grasslands. Then you wanted our forests, then you wanted everything. That is many memories. Yes, we want our home back. But if I agree to help you, then many of my chiefs may not want to follow me. They do not care that my family was saved. They worry about themselves. The dispute among my people is too strong.'

They sat in silence for a long moment, thinking about his words.

'Father Quiller told me how the Derthals decide a dispute the High Chief cannot solve,' Martil said suddenly. 'Trial by combat. The winner is seen to be speaking the truth.'

Sacrax nodded. 'That is right.'

'Then I shall fight the Berellian Champion. And your people will see that we speak the truth.'

'No!' Havell cried. 'The Dragon Sword wielder is too valuable to risk!'

'Good idea.' Sacrax smiled.

'Are you sure about this?' Merren turned to Martil nervously.

'What else can we do? We came here to win over the Derthals. This may be the only way to do it,' Martil pointed out.

Sacrax nodded. 'It is the only way. If you win, I shall be able to persuade my chiefs to march with you. If you lose, then I will let the others return to their fate in Norstalos, as thanks for saving my family.'

'I accept. It will be a pleasure to kill that Berellian,' Martil said immediately.

'No!' Havell protested again.

'It won't be a risk, elf,' Martil told him. 'No man can stop the Dragon Sword.'

Sacrax coughed. 'You must fight not with your own weapons, but with a spear, as two Derthals.'

'What?' Merren gasped.

Sacrax took another handful of berries. 'If you are to fight in the traditional manner, then it must be done properly. My chiefs must see which is the stronger side. For my people to believe it, you must fight as Derthals would, to prove you are worthy. If you will not fight, then the Derthals will stay in our mountains and let the men kill each other.'

Merren turned to Martil. 'Have you used such a thing before?'

Martil glanced over to where Karia was working her way through a bowl of berries on her own. He ignored her question, for she would not like the answer.

'We have no choice. I have to fight.'

'We can leave. You heard him, the Derthals will stay here. At least we will have headed off an invasion from the north.'

'But those passes! We can't stop the Berellians and Tenochs without the Derthals.'

Merren looked into his eyes. 'Perhaps there is another way ...'

Martil shook his head angrily. 'We both know there is no other way! Besides, you have all you need from me!' Before she could argue with him, or stop him, he rose to his feet. 'I accept your challenge. And when I have defeated the Berellian, you will join us.'

'If you win, I will fight with you,' Sacrax agreed, and surged to his feet. 'You must rest. Fight this evening, when all my chiefs can see you. Food will be sent to you.'

'And a Derthal spear?' Martil asked.

'You shall have your pick of spears at the fight. Not before,' Sacrax promised. 'I hope you win.'

With that he stood and stalked out of the room, followed by his guards.

'Well, I suppose that could have been worse,' Alban said thoughtfully.

'I don't want you to fight!' Karia protested. 'I don't like watching that!'

'Good, because you won't be watching. You'll be staying here with Father Quiller,' Martil said around his mouthful of food.

True to his word, Sacrax had sent food: cooked venison, as well as more nuts and berries.

'We should not eat too much,' Alban warned. 'A family will go hungry so you can stuff yourself.'

'I bet the Berellians aren't worrying about that,' Martil grumbled, but allowed Alban to give half the food back to the Derthal women who had brought it inside the church.

'I'm not happy!' Karia announced loudly.

Martil swept her up into his arms and tickled her until her scowl turned into a reluctant laugh.

'Go and find a saga you want me to read to you,' he suggested.

Dragging her feet, Karia slouched over to the bags.

'So what was this Berellian like?' Martil asked quickly.

'He was very fast,' Merren said soberly. 'He seemed to dance around our men. And he was deadly with the throwing knives.'

'Well, he won't have them,' Barrett pointed out. 'How does this trial by combat work?'

Alban cleared his throat. 'A traditional Derthal fight sees two warriors step into a square marked out by branches, wearing only a deerskin and carrying only a spear. Only one can step out again. No others can enter the square.'

'We can still just walk away,' Merren said anxiously. 'I don't want to lose you.'

'You mean you don't want to leave your child without a father,' Barrett muttered, then flushed as he realised what he had said out loud.

Merren had gone white. 'What did you say?' she asked, her voice dangerously quiet.

'My humblest apologies, your majesty, what I said was foolish and will never happen again,' Barrett said hurriedly.

'You are correct there. If I ever hear that again, you will be dismissed from my service. As it is, I don't want to look upon you again this afternoon. You shall stay with Karia. You can work on something useful. Continue preparing that storm out to sea, to slow down the Tenochs.'

Barrett opened his mouth to protest, thought better of it and closed it with a snap.

'So Barrett's staying with me? Great!' Karia said absently, as she walked through the adults to show a hefty saga to Martil. 'Time to read now!'

Reading to Karia at least took Martil's mind off the upcoming duel, although he kept missing words and Karia had to correct him. He had fought a Berellian Champion once before, a giant of a man called Hizek. Hizek had been massively built, with arms as thick as Martil's thighs. All that muscle made him slow, and even though he was able to use a war axe in each hand, Martil wore him down. But this new Champion was also fast. Speed was everything in a duel. And while Martil feared no man with a blade in his hand, he had never fought with just a spear before. His mind replayed Rath's brutal ambush of their guides.

'You're not concentrating!' Karia chided.

'Sorry.' Martil put aside thoughts of sharp spears and got back to reading about a princess who had been turned into a swan.

27

He was playing a game of catch with Karia when a group of Derthal warriors arrived, led by the guard captain, who carried a deerskin in his hands.

Father Alban was fetched, and after a short conversation, he turned to Martil.

'You must put this on and follow them. It is time for the fight,' Alban advised.

'I don't want you to go!' Karia wailed.

Martil kneeled down and hugged her close; she clutched him fiercely around the neck and would not let go.

'Why do you have to keep fighting? Why can't you just stay with me?' she demanded tearfully.

Martil had no words for her. He had said goodbye to her once before, before Pilleth. He could not do so again. So he just hugged her close.

'Come back,' she begged.

He looked into her big brown eyes. 'I promise to come back,' he said softly. 'Now you have to go with Barrett and Father Quiller.'

Reluctantly, she let go of him and allowed Father Quiller to take her inside the church.

Martil watched her go, saw her wave and blow him a kiss, and waved back. Then he took a deep breath.

'How do I wear this thing?' he asked.

With help from Alban, as well as some suggestions from the Derthal captain, the deerskin was wrapped around his waist, and tied in place. The Derthal captain grunted something and Alban chuckled.

'And what was that?' Martil growled.

'He said you have many battle scars. He thinks that is good,' Alban explained.

Merren and Havell were summoned, Havell protesting fiercely.

'What if he is killed? What are we to do then?' the Elfaran grumbled.

'You can fight on my behalf,' Martil offered.

Havell glanced at the wicked spears their Derthal escort carried and shuddered.

'I have to insist. You must not go through with this.' The Elfaran grabbed Martil's arm.

'We have no choice,' Martil hissed. 'Perhaps you should have been a little more persuasive when we talked to the High Chief!'

Havell whitened. 'That's it. I am going to call Argurium, get her to take you away from here.'

This time it was Martil's turn to grab the Elfaran's arm. 'You do that, and you are dooming a country, a continent, perhaps a world, to Zorva.'

'Do you have another suggestion?' Havell sniffed.

'How quickly can you call Argurium?'

'Usually I would call her name but it is likely to be noisy there. In that case,' Havell produced a small horn from a pouch at his side, 'I would use this.'

Martil nodded. 'Watch the duel. If it looks as though I am going to lose, I shall signal you, and you can call the dragon. Happy?'

Havell looked at him carefully. 'No. But your plan will be acceptable,' he said stiffly.

Martil gave him a half smile, then let the Elfaran get ahead of him. Then he grabbed Jaret's arm.

'Stay close to the elf. Don't let him blow that horn, whatever you do,' he ordered.

'But, sir …'

'The elf will give up in the first heartbeat. There hasn't been a Berellian born who can beat me. I'll wear the man down eventually. Give me the time I need. Don't fail me, Jaret! The Queen and I are depending on you!'

At this, Jaret straightened his back and nodded. 'You can rely on me, sir,' he promised.

Martil patted him on the back. That would fix the elf's plans.

The area outside the caves formed a natural bowl, and Martil gaped as they walked down into it: thousands of Derthals, mostly warriors but a number of women as well, lined the sides, while a space in the centre had been stamped out, fenced with branches and lit by flaming torches at each corner.

A massive roar greeted the Norstaline approach; an equally loud reaction greeted the Berellians as they entered the bowl from the other side.

'This is amazing!' Alban breathed.

'Half the nation must be here,' Merren gasped.

'It seems the High Chief wants to show his entire people which side they should be supporting,' Alban admitted.

'Good. Then they can see why they should join us,' Martil said defiantly, although his stomach was roiling at the thought of fighting in front of so many. This was not like battle. This was to be a careful, measured fight to the death, against a man who trained for this sort of duel. He shook himself. Everyone depended onhim. He knew he had to clear

616

his mind to fight properly, but he could not stop thinking about Karia and Merren — and his unborn son.

'It is not too late to walk away,' Merren said softly.

'I would advise walking away!' Havell declared, eyes wide at the roaring mass of Derthals that let them pass, then closed in again behind them.

'I don't think they'd let us!' Martil tried to smile. 'I have to do this, if we are to save Norstalos. Besides, I have never walked away from a challenge before. I am not about to start.'

He tried to think of Wime, of Forde, of Tarik and the other men he had befriended and trained — only for them to die in his opponent's trap at the ranger barracks.

The anger helped, but only a little.

They walked down to the marked-off area where Sacrax stood waiting, as did the three Berellians. The moment the two groups reached the square, Sacrax threw up his arms, and silence fell instantly across the bowl. It was an eerie feeling. One moment the assembled Derthals had been chanting, hooting and stamping their feet, the next, they were still.

Sacrax began to speak then, his voice booming out across the bowl as Alban hurriedly, and quietly, translated for them.

'The humans want our help. In return for the brave Derthal warriors fighting with them, both these humans want to give us land in the warm south. Fat land, full of game, where the leaves never fall and the bushes are never bare of fruit. But which side do we help? One side says they are the strongest. The other side has the dragons. Their champions will fight to see who tells the truth. They will fight like

Derthals. Whoever wins here will have the support of the Derthals.'

A thunderous cheer almost made the earth shake, while warriors and womenfolk alike thumped the ground with their feet.

Sacrax let the cheering go on for what seemed like ages before dramatically dropping his arms, and the silence was instantaneous.

He paced over to the square and pointed at the Berellian.

'Your name?' he asked.

The Berellian stepped forwards. 'I am Cezar, Champion to the Berellian King,' he declared.

Then Sacrax pointed at Martil.

'Martil, Champion to the Norstaline Queen.'

'Step inside the square; only one may step out.' Sacrax pointed to his guards, who moved into position, two to each side. 'Step out of the square and die.'

Martil nodded. His mouth was dry, his palms wet and he felt as though he needed to piss. But he would not give the Berellian the satisfaction of knowing any of that.

'Choose your spear.'

Six warriors offered their spears to Martil; another six to Cezar.

Martil took his time, checking the bindings on each spearhead, as well as making sure the shaft was straight. Finally he tested the edge of each spearhead. Here they were all the same — each one was sharp enough to shave with. He picked the one with the best binding, and a smooth, straight shaft, free of knots or bows. Glancing over, he could see Cezar watching him. The Berellian had chosen his spear and was now smiling. Martil noted Cezar's every muscle was shown in sharp definition. He felt like sucking his own stomach in; he was uncomfortably aware that afternoons spent eating cakes with Karia had left a little extra flesh around his middle.

'I know you can do this for me, for everyone waiting back at Norstalos,' Merren told him confidently, but her eyes betrayed her worry.

He tried to smile at her, and mostly succeeded.

'Don't get yourself killed,' Havell told him sharply.

'I'll do my best, elf,' Martil snorted.

'Begin!' Sacrax bellowed.

Martil nodded at Jaret; tried to find something to say to Merren but could not. A pair of Derthals escorted Martil to the edge of the square, while another pair did the same for Cezar. The noise from the watching crowd was building to a crescendo and Sacrax did not attempt to speak. Instead he nodded, and the Derthals pushed Martil into the square, before resuming their positions, spears at the ready, in case he tried to get out again.

The crowd fell silent.

Martil tested the ground with his bare feet — it had been smoothed and packed down, and would offer good footing. The square itself was about ten paces in each direction; it had looked small from the outside but now he was inside, it seemed huge, and Cezar seemed far away.

Martil hefted his spear. Its balance seemed all wrong, too heavy near the head. It would take a huge amount of strength to drive it home. He could appreciate why the Derthals had such massive forearms.

'I know you, Martil!' Cezar called, and Martil stared at him in surprise.

'Yes, you! The Butcher of Bellic! The last one!'

The Derthals did not understand the words, but they could sense a challenge when they heard it, and all seemed to lean forwards.

'I've dreamed of this, being able to kill the last Butcher!'

Martil circled cautiously towards him.

'Why is that, coward and killer of children?'

Cezar laughed at the feeble insults. 'I killed the rest! I cut the hearts out of your friends and gave them in a box to my King! Yours is the only one that has eluded me — until now! I shall take your heart back to my King and complete my set!'

Martil spat. 'I'd cut your heart out, Berellian, but your foul race doesn't have one!'

Cezar laughed again. 'How will you do that, Ralloran scum? Watch!'

He signalled to his companions, and Martil saw the Berellian wizard step forwards, wave his staff around in what Martil knew from seeing Barrett at work was a pointless display of showmanship, then point it at Cezar.

Instantly the Berellian's skin turned a deep brown colour.

Martil glanced over his shoulder to where Merren, Alban, Havell, Jaret and Wilsen waited, horror-stricken. They too had recognised the spell, which gave a warrior an almost invincible covering. It had saved Martil's life back at the battle of Sendric. But he needed a mage to cast it — and both Karia and Barrett were back at the church.

'I'll get Barrett!' Wilsen roared, and plunged into the crowd of Derthals. They resisted his progress, and he had to physically push his way past them, making slow progress. It was obvious it would be a long time before he could return with the wizard.

'Didn't think of that, did you, Ralloran? Forgot your mage, didn't you!'

Martil glanced across to where Sacrax stood, but the Derthal High Chief appeared unmoved. It seemed that once the challengers were inside the square, there were no rules.

Cezar saw the look and laughed. 'That's right! Now I'll cut out your heart for my King and take your ears for my own collection. I already took plenty of those from your men that I killed in Norstalos. They were hardly worth taking though, because they fought like little girls—'

Cezar never finished the sentence, because Martil was on him, anger burning in his chest. He used it to power a massive leap and stab, trying to drive his heavy spearhead through Cezar's magically protected skin.

The Berellian skipped away from the charge, spear held loosely in his hand.

Martil spun, almost on the edge of the square, and went after him. The fear was gone now, replaced by an icy anger. He was not thinking about Karia, or Merren, or trying to watch Wilsen's slow progress through the crowd. His eyes were on Cezar and his spear was at the ready.

He raced at the Berellian, lunging low. The special skin might stop a death blow but if Martil could cut him, he would weaken him — and a spear point in the groin would slow any man down. But Cezar skipped backwards, sideways, and danced lightly on his toes, using his spear not to strike but to deflect Martil's strokes.

Martil sensed he was the stronger, which was important with this sort of weapon, although they were well matched for speed. Cezar dodged his spear thrusts relatively easily and Martil felt a touch of frustration. It was such a crude weapon; you could not disguise or change its course the way you could a sword.

'Is that the best you can do?' Cezar asked scornfully.

The Derthals were howling, hammering, cheering and stamping at their every move but, for Martil, the world had shrunk to this square. The noise outside faded, and he could clearly hear what Cezar was saying. Not that he was taking much notice of it.

'I'll take your tongue when I've finished with you — Aroaril knows you use it too much,' he told the Berellian.

'You can try. But it's my turn now,' Cezar hissed, then darted forwards, spear at the ready.

Martil let him advance then leaped to close the distance, spear rising up viciously. Cezar swerved to his left, to give his right arm more room, and lunged at Martil's throat. Martil instinctively flicked his own spear up in a parry and swung his torso at the last moment; the razor-sharp spearhead slipped past his right shoulder.

Both men let their momentum carry them past, then swung again, spears at the ready. Martil circled to his left, feeling his right shoulder beginning to burn. For the last few months he had been using the Dragon Sword, which seemed to have no weight at all. Consequently, he had lost some conditioning and, besides, you needed different muscles for thrusting spears to the ones you used for a sword.

But Cezar did not give him a chance to relax. He stepped forwards swiftly, lunging thrust after thrust at Martil's chest and throat.

Rather than exhaust his arm and shoulder to deflect them, Martil stepped back and sideways, always making sure he did not get too near the edge of the square. Time and again he used his feet, a shift of his bodyweight or a swerve of the hips to avoid the deadly point. He was sweating now. His chest was starting to rasp and he spat out phlegm that was trying to clog his throat. But he knew he did not have to finish this bout; he just had to hold the Berellian off until Barrett returned.

Cezar seemed to sense that as well, because he adjusted his grip on the shaft of his spear.

'I'm going to give you a chance now, Ralloran dog,' the Berellian said conversationally. 'See if you are good enough, and strong enough, to break through this magical barrier. Because if you can't, I'll gut you.'

'Like all Berellians, you talk a good fight,' Martil panted.

This time Cezar approached more slowly, directly, spear held at the ready. Martil watched him come forwards warily. Surely the man could not really be planning to just walk onto his spear point? How good was this magical protection?

Cezar's slow approach turned into a leap, and Martil met him in midair.

Time seemed to slow; Martil saw Cezar's spear heading for his chest and swung his body away from it, while trying to drive his own spear into his enemy's chest. At the last moment Cezar also swung away but while Martil felt the tip of his spear gouge into Cezar, it did not strike cleanly; he felt it glance away. A moment later, Cezar's spear tore across his ribs.

They both landed and spun away from each other. Martil inspected his enemy first; Cezar's wound was just a thin scratch — it seemed his toughened skin had held well. But he could feel blood trickling down his right side and, glancing down, he saw a long cut had been opened across his side — deep enough so he could see the white of a rib there. Blood was pulsing out steadily.

'First blood to me,' Cezar told him smugly.

'It's the last blow that counts,' Martil replied.

Again Cezar charged in, and this time, instead of meeting him, Martil slid away.

'Run all you like. That wound won't stop bleeding,' Cezar snarled.

Martil ignored him. Sweat was dripping into his eyes, and his legs were beginning to ache now. Surely Barrett had to be getting here soon! He glanced over his shoulder but could see nothing, just a sea of cheering Derthals. As he looked back, he saw Cezar already attacking. There was no time to dodge away this time; instead he desperately parried and tried to spin away — Cezar's bloodied spear ripped a gash along the outside of his left thigh, while his own spear seemed to rebound from Cezar's hip, leaving only a pinprick of a wound.

He did not have time to check his leg; Cezar spun back to the attack, thrusting and then scything his spear as it came close to Martil. This was a new tactic and Martil could only partly block the blow. The side of the spear point was not as sharp as the tip but it was still enough to dig into the front of Martil's shoulder until it bounced off his left collarbone.

He ducked away and slashed his own spear in a wide arc, but Cezar blocked it easily.

Shifting his grip on the handle, Martil started to use the spear more as an axe, swinging it around and down. Back and forth across the square they moved, the shafts of the spears meeting with a loud crack as each blow was parried by one or the other. This sort of fighting was more to Martil's liking, and he felt his spear point slice thin cuts across Cezar's left pectoral and thigh, although the man's skin stubbornly resisted even the sharp spearhead. The Berellian also sensed he was having the worst of this exchange, for he changed tactics again, stepping inside Martil's swing and deliberately letting the flint point sear into his arm, so he could drive his own spear up at Martil's chest.

Too late Martil recognised the change and it was only his superb reflexes that stopped the spear from opening him up from ribs to throat. Somehow he flipped his torso back and away, nearly losing his spear in the process. Even so, he felt the wide spearhead rip another wound from his ribs up to his neck; his sternum helped deflect the blow, at the price of more blood.

His breath was coming harsh and fast now. His right shoulder was on fire from using the spear, his lungs felt as though they were like stone. His windpipe was raw, his legs beginning to tremble; his wounds stung as the salty sweat ran into them and burned as his blood seeped down to cover his torso and leg.

He realised, with surprise, that he could lose this if Barrett did not turn up soon.

'We have to get him out of there!' Havell roared, struggling to raise a small ivory horn to his lips.

'The captain's playing with him! Give him time!' Jaret yelled back.

Merren tried to relax her hands; her nails were digging into her palms. 'He needs Barrett!'

'Where is Barrett?' Alban agreed.

'Why wait? You're a priest, heal him!' Havell gave up his fruitless battle with Jaret; leaving the horn in Jaret's grasp, he shoved Alban towards the square.

'You fool! I have to touch him to heal him! And they're not going to let me in, or him out!' Alban shouted.

'Well, we have to do something! Where is the wizard?' Havell moaned.

Wilsen raced towards the church, heart pounding. It had been almost impossible to push his way through the Derthals — they might be a head smaller than him, but they were just as strong, and determined not to be moved out of the way.

'Barrett! The Berellians are using magic against Martil! We need you now!' he bellowed.

A moment later, the door flung open and Barrett tore towards him, then overtook him as he sped towards where thousands of Derthals cheered and chanted.

Wilsen followed, as fast as he could, praying the mage would be in time.

Martil gripped the shaft of his spear carefully and circled away from a grinning Cezar. He thought about signalling to Jaret but could not bring himself to give up. Once Barrett was here, he would be able to defeat this Berellian easily, he told himself.

'The great Captain Martil. Broken and bleeding. Do you know how many Berellians have prayed for this, how many would pay to see you like this?' Cezar taunted.

Martil could not be bothered to reply. He needed his breath. And he needed to win time for Barrett to arrive. He spat again, trying to clear his throat.

'After you're dead, I'm going to take that Queen of yours and see her screaming over an altar. And then I'll get that little girl—'

Martil did not let him finish the sentence, his anger got the better of his sense and he leaped again at the Berellian.

For a moment he thought he had won, that Cezar would be impaled on the spear point — then the Berellian managed to flip his body away, much as Martil had done just before. Instead of slamming home, it skidded off Cezar's protected chest. Cezar landed close to Martil and, as the tired Ralloran tried to bring his spear back from his massive thrust and regain his balance, Cezar slammed the butt end of his staff into Martil's head.

Martil's vision went dark for a moment, and he felt himself spin away and down to thump into the ground, losing his grip on his spear as he did so.

Barrett did not bother with trying to push past the Derthals — he used the magic to propel himself into the air in a huge leap, then actually ran over the Derthals, feet lightly touching their shoulders, floating down and across them.

He landed by Merren, just in time to see Cezar pick up Martil's spear and hurl it out of the square.

'Where have you been!' Havell cried, stricken. The Elfaran had been wrestling with Jaret but now the stunned man had let go of the horn. Havell sounded the horn — the noise was almost lost within the crowd, and he knew it would be too late, anyway.

Barrett ignored them and instead pointed at Cezar. Instantly his magical protection disappeared, his skin lightening to its normal colour and his wounds opening and beginning to bleed — although they were still nothing like the ones Martil had taken.

With a howl of anger, the Berellian mage stepped forwards, shaking his staff.

The Derthals switched their attention from the square to the two wizards facing off on either side of the square.

Cezar stopped his advance on Martil as his skin first darkened again, then lightened, then began to darken, then stopped.

The Berellian wizard chanted loudly and brandished his staff, waving it in complicated patterns, while his hand seemed to trace out arcane symbols in the air. Barrett, meanwhile, just stood there, his hand pointed at Cezar, his other clenched in a fist at his side.

For what seemed like an eternity they stood there, then Cezar's skin lightened completely. The Berellian mage stopped waving his staff and simply keeled over, falling face-first to the ground, where he lay, moving weakly.

The Derthal crowd went wild, hooting and cheering.

Inside the ring, Martil began to move.

'I came as soon as I could,' a puffing Barrett said, wiping sweat from his face.

'I knew you would,' Merren said, although her eyes were on Martil.

Martil decided it must be night, because he could see stars; then he moved his arm and the pain of his chest wound brought him back into focus. He looked around for his spear and saw it — lying outside the branch markers that it was death to cross. He glanced over to where Merren had fallen to her knees, tears in her eyes.

'I'm sorry,' he mouthed at her. 'Take care of Karia.'

She nodded jerkily, then turned away, burying her face in her hands.

'Your wizard was better than mine, but that does not matter. I am going to see your country destroyed,' Cezar gloated.

Martil looked back at the Berellian, to see him standing a few paces away, his magical protection gone but a wide grin on his face. He had no anger left; he did not have the energy for it. It was all going to end here. Part of him hoped it would be quick, hoped it would mean peace at last.

'My name shall be glorified above all others — the man who destroyed the great Captain Martil,' Cezar taunted.

But Martil was not listening to him. All he could hear was Merren saying she trusted him to save them all. He could not let them down. And over that he could hear Karia begging him to come back. He especially could not let her down.

Every part of him was burning, bleeding or throbbing. But, from somewhere, he found strength; he had never given up before. He could not give up now. He could not let Karia down.

'I'm coming, Karia,' he said out loud.

'What did you say?' the Berellian paused.

Martil was on his feet and on top of Cezar before the Berellian could do anything about it. Desperately, Cezar swung his spear around, and Martil let it sear across his upper back, not caring about another wound. He was inside the Berellian's reach, and slammed his fist into Cezar's throat. The Berellian gasped — and staggered back, but there was no escape, Martil slammed a head butt into Cezar's face, feeling the nose break and hearing Cezar's squeal of pain. He rammed his knee at the man's groin then, when Cezar instinctively tried to protect himself, switched his focus to the spear, ripping it out of Cezar's hands.

'No!' the Berellian begged, but Martil's thrust began at the legs, travelled through the hips and up his back, picked up everything he had left, sent it along his arm and down the spear, which slammed into Cezar's chest, slicing deep between two ribs and exploding out of the man's back in a spray of blood.

Martil felt the spear tremble as the dying man's heart still tried to beat against the wooden shaft. He made sure he stared into Cezar's shocked eyes for a long moment before he ripped the spear out, sending blood fountaining through the air.

The Berellian collapsed into a pool of gore and Martil turned away, covered in blood, arms wide to acknowledge the Derthal crowd, which was going wild: Derthals were jumping up and down, stamping and cheering, booming out their war cries.

Overhead, Argurium was circling; she had arrived in time to see she was not needed.

The Derthal High Chief raised his arms to his people. 'We fight for Norstalos!' he howled.

The Derthals' answering cheer rang from the skies.

Martil stayed where he was, because he was afraid he was going to fall if he took another step.

He was dimly aware of people running towards him, among them Father Alban, his hands reaching out; then Merren was there, her arms around him, holding him up.

'You did it!' she told him, her face wet. 'You stupid, bloody, pig-headed, foolish, wonderful man!'

'I love you too,' Martil told her, then his eyes rolled back and he knew no more.